America Takes the Stage

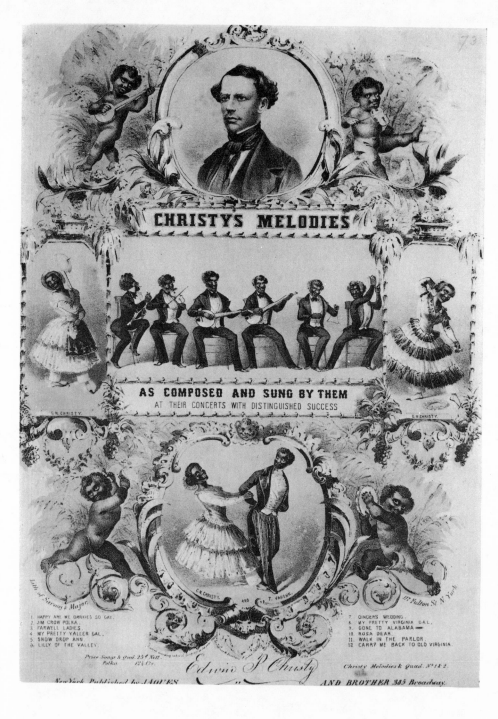

America Takes the Stage

ROMANTICISM IN AMERICAN DRAMA AND THEATRE, 1750–1900

BY Richard Moody

Bloomington   INDIANA UNIVERSITY PRESS

KRAUS REPRINT CO.
Millwood, N.Y.
1977

INDIANA UNIVERSITY PUBLICATIONS
HUMANITIES SERIES NO. 34
Indiana University, Bloomington, Indiana

PN
2226
M6

EDWARD D. SEEBER, Editor

DAVID H. DICKASON, Assistant Editor

AGAPITO REY, Assistant Editor

The Indiana University Publications, Humanities Series, was founded in 1939 for the publication of occasional papers and monographs by faculty members.

Reprinted with permission of the Indiana University Press

KRAUS REPRINT CO.
A U.S. Division of Kraus-Thomson Organization Limited

Printed in U.S.A.

TO

A. M. Drummond

Preface

THE GRAND panorama of American life and art up to the beginning of the present century has been rich in romantic details. The real-life adventures in the birth and growth of the new democracy, the causes, exploits, and individuals, were daring and extravagant. The American theatre of the nineteenth century, with its magic of make-believe and heightened reality, was a highly favored form of entertainment and a medium of representation in which the same causes, exploits, and individuals were illustrated and magnified. On the stage, in settings that were vivid, expansive, and sometimes gaudy, these heroes and events were larger and often greater than life.

In order that the full color of these remote performances and plays may be appreciated, they must be viewed in perspective, with a knowledge of the environment which nurtured them and the theatrical taste which accepted them. Without this perspective, and judged by present-day standards, many of them would seem feeble and imperfect. The present effort is to see them as they were, with all their natural and essential extravagances, against the vivid backdrop of their own time.

Any student of the American theatre is indebted to the explorations of William G. B. Carson, Barrett H. Clark, Oral Sumner Coad, A. M. Drummond, Allan G. Halline, Arthur Hornblow, Brander Matthews, Montrose Moses, George C. D. Odell, and Arthur Hobson Quinn. Their histories, annals, and anthologies not only have cleared the way for further investigations but have made many scarce documents available to the general student. I have tried, particularly in citing passages from plays, to refer the reader to the most readily accessible source.

My thanks are also extended to the authors and publishers who have permitted me to quote from their books. For the use of illustrations and passages from various manuscripts in their possession, I am indebted to: May Davenport Seymour, Curator of the Theatre Collection of the Museum of the City of New York; George Freedley, Curator of the Theatre Collection of the New York Public Library; William Van Lennep, Curator of the Theatre Collection of the Harvard College Library; R. N. Williams, 2nd, Director of the Historical Society of Pennsylvania; L. H. Kirkpatrick, Librarian of the University of Utah; and Mrs. Cecile S. Clark, widow of the late Barrett H. Clark.

The staff of the Indiana University Press has been most helpful at all times. My heaviest debt is to Walter Albee, whose skilled eye and ear have been overworked in my behalf. I am also grateful to the Graduate School of Indiana University and to Professor Edward Seeber for their assistance in the preparation of this volume.

Contents

Illustrations

CHAPTER I

The Romantic Spirit in America

FOR ABOUT two hundred and fifty years the political, economic, social, and art history of America was permeated with the spirit of romance. The period extended from the first settlement in the late spring of 1607, when the one hundred and sixty bold adventurers stepped on to the marshy edge of the continent, to the last years of the ante-bellum decade, when the ascending clamor of factory and mill and the fateful premonitions of the impending conflict turned men's minds to an increasingly realistic appraisal of themselves and society.

The romantic temper was not native born, nor was it entirely derivative. It was both. The Revolution of 1776 was the great romantic achievement in American history. But the spirit of the industrial revolution in Europe, of the French Revolution, and of the "Napoleonic legend" contributed more definitely to the cult of the middle class and the romanticism of the self-made, the characteristic romantic features of life in America from 1800 to 1850. The new land, the freedom from social or political restraint, the adventurous dream of unexplored frontiers were conducive to the rapid growth of a romantic spirit; but the theoretical foundations for romantic doctrine, which governed at least some aspects of romantic expression in America, were derived from abroad.

Before any attempt can be made to discover the manner in which foreign romantic doctrine filtered in and mixed itself with the roots of the indigenous gropings for romantic expression and before the demonstrations of romanticism in literature, painting, architecture, music, and the theatre can be surveyed, some working definition of the essential and peculiar characteristics of the romantic spirit must be fixed on.

When one observes the innumerable categorical grooves into which definitions of romanticism have been fitted, there is an inescapable wish to accept some single catch-phrase explanation. Mr. Lucas wrote in 1936 that he had discovered 11,396 books written on the subject of romanticism.[1] But in view of these many attempts to describe and analyze the romantic phenomenon, and in deference to the many genuinely searching investigations, one cannot casually accept a simple description of romanticism. At the same time, the futility of trying to reconcile the many conflicting opinions, leads one to accept Lovejoy's suggestion that one should not speak of romanticism but rather of romanticism*s*.[2] The varieties were, he found, so diverse that they could not be forced into a single pattern. If one adopts this view, the inevitable feeling of frustration at not being able to accommodate the various doctrines can be avoided. Specifically, the present endeavor attempts only to discover some characteristics of romanticism, however diversified, which will be helpful in describing the multifarious evidences of the romantic spirit in American drama and the theatre.

The clearest and most colorful traits of the romanticist are his loving and longing looks into the past and into the future, his delight in rosy recollections and fervid hopes, his easy and fanciful dreams of distant place and distant clime, and his preoccupation with the curious, the strange, and the mysterious. His revolutionary spirit prefers to act on faith, to trust the inner experiences of life, to follow the sentimental longings of his heart. He distrusts the strictures and painful rigidities of reasoned behavior. Inherited laws and customs, rules of conduct for life and art, and the barriers which would bind, encompass, and confine him to an earth-bound and prosaic existence fall before his insurgent protests. But vigorous as his insurgent rebellions may and do become, he remains a common man, tenderhearted and sentimental in his expansive love for his fellows and in his unshakable belief in a glorious future. When his dreams demand expression in painting, in literature, or in the theatre, he revolts against any calculated classical forms and delights in seemingly indissoluble mixtures, in the blends of contraries, in the irregularities of nature. He relies on each work to achieve its own form from its inherent association of ideas and the pervading atmosphere it creates, not from any traditional concepts. His art must be new, fresh, and persistently retentive of the illusion of the "first time."

Unlike the realist, who appears when the romanticist's dreams are beginning to lose color, he ignores the practical, steers clear of offensive details, and inclines toward an optimistic view of the world. The realist dwells on the homely, the humble, even the repulsive, and tends to take a pessimistic attitude. The manner of the romanticist is likely to be what Scott called "the big bow-wow style." He skips the vulgar details, sketching each scene and person with a few grand and general touches and with little regard for authenticity or consistency. The realist, on the other hand, specializes in minute details of character and, in general, prefers to view man and his environment at glaring noontide rather than at dawn or dusk.

Necessary as these hasty and fragmentary phrases of prefatory description may be to an understanding of the romantic temper, the romance of real-life events is more pertinent to a full background canvas for the study of American drama and theatre.

When the latent rebellious spirit of the colonists burst into the memorable, romantic Revolution of 1776, it kindled "a flame [which went] forth to astonish the world and enlighten mankind." [3] In 1789 the flame caught hold of the smouldering spirit of the French people and set the fire of freedom burning. No event in modern time so materially affected the status of common man in society as did the French Revolution. The economic and social status of the average colonist was not materially changed after the Revolution of 1776. The average Frenchman, on the other hand, was reborn after the Revolution of 1789; and the ideas for which the French had fought were soon filtering into America, arriving just at the moment when the citizens of the new United States were beginning to perceive social discrepancies which demanded adjustment.

The romanticism of youth, inexperienced and daring, was an essential ingredient of early American life. Wild and mysterious new worlds were always lying ahead waiting to be discovered. Life was felt to be continually fluctuating. Utopia was constantly being anticipated, and in this anticipation, long before the Revolution, there was an early expression of romanticism on the American scene.

The American settler had never experienced in this country the kind of constrictions and restraints against which the Frenchmen had rebelled. But there were evidences of other restrictions even in the "open air" of America, particularly in New England. Colonial America was, on the whole, fearful of innovation and inclined to abide by tradition, whereas the first great period of exploitation that followed fostered a spirit of adventure and a youthful and restless eagerness for a new and more bountiful life.

The years from the founding of the government to the second war for independence were years of a growing romanticism. Nothing was thought to be settled in the Union until the English had again been beaten. Only in 1817 were Americans beginning to see the possibility for a society of their own, independent of European models. The new and growing romanticism was invariably bound up with the glorification of the individual, but in various sections of the country it found expression in different ways. There were the growing, industrial and capitalistic East, the slave-exploiting South, and the moving frontier of the West. The need of the time everywhere was for men to do things.

And this faith in active progress, this buoyant spirit of hopefulness never ceased once it was accepted as the American romantic doctrine. It led to the two great romantic landmarks in American history: the election of Andrew Jackson to the Presidency, in 1829, and the Civil War, 1861–1865. Before Jackson, America had been struggling for complete romantic release in unequivocal freedom for the common man. From Jackson through Buchanan, Americans were riding the crest of the romantic wave as it swept west across the country; but after the Civil War they were becoming more critically aware of themselves and of their relation to the world of reality.

During these formative years of romantic expression the sectional divisions of the country were extremely important to the manner in which the romantic movement took hold. It was in Virginia that French theory—in this instance the doctrine of physiocratic agrarianism—was first applied. There was in Virginia, as a result, a strong romantic belief in the power of the land, but no equally strong belief in the romantic claim of equality for the common man. To be sure, Jefferson's political conception of a government modelled on Greek democracy, minimizing the importance and power of the political state, as the appropriate government for Virginia was to a degree romantic. But merely allowing that "no society can make a perpetual constitution, or even a perpetual law," gave small glorification to the individual. Another type of romanticism characterized the South of a somewhat later period, the romance of the easygoing plantation life, the chaste and sentimental vivaciousness of the Southern belle and the gallantry of the Southern gentleman.

Just as the South adopted its theory of physiocratic agrarianism from France, New England adopted its theories of idealism from France and Germany. The romantic movement in New England was, however, more vigorous and more tangible. It appeared a generation later than in Virginia, and its general tone was ethical and intellectual rather than political and economic. Puritanism was responsible for the predominantly ethical tone and theoretical temper which so long characterized romanticism in New England. The Puritans, on the whole, did not approve of the levelling movement which they had helped to stir up. To Boston of the time, democracy was merely a euphemism for "mob." Nevertheless, although the New Eng-

land romantics never allowed their romantic beliefs to have
any effect on the actual social status of the common man, they
did attempt to demonstrate the applicability of their theories
to practical living in the formation of such aristocratic utopias
as George Ripley's Brook Farm.

But the region that gave the vital spark to American romance
was that of the ever-enlarging frontier where men were equal
in their adventurous struggle for existence and where democracy inevitably became their common faith. The Ohio Valley
was, during the early years of the century, the specific repository
of the romance of the frontier. In the romanticism of this region two main concepts were discernible: "One localized itself
in Kentucky and took form in the poetic conception of the
Dark and Bloody ground; the other associated itself first with
the rivermen and quickly diffused its spirit through the backwoods and took form in the conception of western humor." [4]
Out of the latter was concocted one of the most stimulating
myths of our early history, the myth of Davy Crockett. Davy
typified the belief of the people in themselves. Under the rough
exterior of a daring bear-hunter and an outspoken congressman,
one perceived in Davy the sterling qualities with which men
endow their romantic heroes.

The first half of the century was a hardy and expansive age.
Americans were coming into their own. Each was able to stretch
himself out in search of his own individual rainbow. The Alger-
type hero could pursue his glorious and honorable career with
positive assurance of achieving his goal. America was a country
"where men start from humble origins . . . and where they
can attain to the most elevated position, or acquire a large
amount of wealth, according to the pursuits they elect for themselves. No exclusive privileges of birth, no entailment of estates,
no civil or political disqualifications, stand in their path; but
one has as good a chance as another, according to his talent,
prudence and personal exertions. This is a country of self-made
men, than which nothing better could be said of any state or
society." [5] These were the words of a contemporary observer.
It was not surprising, then, with this strong optimism ruling

the day, that foreigners from every land sought their utopia in America. And as they took up their work in the new country with the thumbprint of oppression still upon them and found a joyous release for their pent-up exuberance, they carried through the land a renewed urge to freedom and a strengthened belief in the just rights of the common man.

On the frontier there was no need, as there had been in New England, for the preaching of equality. Equality existed on every hand. It was there to be seen and not to be talked about, a perpetually rejuvenated spirit of willingness to discard the outmoded and to try the new. The touchstone of the age was "reform"; and to the frontiersman of the forties it held as much magic as the Chamber of Commerce "progress" holds for the "small businessman" of today.

Although after the Civil War the characteristic American outlook became more narrow and realistic, a large romantic frontier still retained the spirit of the ante-bellum days. Many local and regional attitudes did not conform to the capitalistic views of the fast-growing urban centers. The Pacific was still a long stretch from the Atlantic. Ideas did not move with any rapidity from one end of the continent to the other, and the romantic beliefs of father and grandfather were still accepted and admired well past the turn of the century.

A hasty glance at such a crowded hundred and fifty years can only touch some of the significant indications of the romantic temper in American life. The eighteenth and nineteenth centuries were filled with innumerable and multifarious manifestations of the romantic spirit.

LITERATURE

American literature could be nothing if it were not romantic. Classical literature "is the product of a nation and a generation which has consciously achieved a definite advance, moral, political, intellectual; and is filled with the belief that its view of life is more natural, human, universal and wise than that from which it has escaped. . . . A weakness, indeed, of classical art is that its work may be controlled by a spirit of etiquette rather than the requirements of essentially artistic form." [6] The fact that such an art could not exist, and had not existed, in the full-bodied, youthful, and experimenting American society is in a true measure the description of American romanticism in literature.

Eighteenth-century classicism had been transplanted in this country, but it never achieved the foothold it attained in its native habitat. There was in America none of the formal and highly refined living necessary to nurture such an artistic expression. Naturally then a revolt against such a feeble tradition in art, a tradition never really established, could not produce any revolutionary literary giants comparable to Rousseau, Goethe, or Hugo.

When the first attempts at romantic literary expression appeared, they were strictly individual efforts. There was no school of romantic poets, for example, as in England. Nor, until the transcendentalists, was there anything resembling a school of writers in America; and even the transcendentalists' individual expressions were of a highly diverse character.

In the early years of the nineteenth century "our literary history demonstrated a gradual change from poetry and didactic essay to romance and story of adventure; and by 1850, as in England and France, fiction had triumphed over all other forms of writing." [7] Similarly, there was a gradually increasing awareness of foreign literature and aesthetic theory. In 1835, for example, the *Western Messenger* was treating thoroughly all the English romantics. From 1840 to 1844 the *Dial* took full account of German literature and German philosophy. The novels of Scott and Bulwer-Lytton were widely read, particularly during the twenties and thirties. And during the same period American writers like American painters spent considerable time abroad absorbing the romantic atmosphere of England, France, Germany, Italy, and Spain.

It is difficult to find evidences of uniformity and contiguity in the expressions of romanticism in American literature. In fact, one of the prevailing aspects of romanticism is to be found in the emphasis on individuality. The nineteenth century was filled with a multitude of lesser literary artists; but the significant evidences of romanticism are to be found, I believe, in the thinking and writing of the few major romantic figures.

Charles Brockden Brown was the first noteworthy romantic novelist. During the last years of the eighteenth and the early years of the nineteenth century he gave expression to several aspects of the romantic temper that were to become prevalent in later literature. He frequently employed the medieval gothic themes of Godwin and Radcliffe, and in *Arthur Mervyn* (1800) he portrayed the name character contending for the intellectual rights of the individual, "Rousseau's natural man in America." [8]

Edgar Allan Poe carried the gothic quality into poetry. His "misty mid region of Weir" and his tales of horrible murder were touched with an artistry uncommon to the contemporary rendering of similar moods and actions. His life and art were filled with the romanticism of rebelliousness, of search for an ideal beauty, of delight in the mystic and obscure.

Like Poe, Washington Irving turned scornfully from the romance in the life around him to the picturesque atmosphere surrounding the life of an eighteenth-century English squire, or the exotic color of the old Moorish castle of the Alhambra. These represented Irving's earliest romantic inclination, but in a document such as *A Tour of the Prairies* (1836) Irving was one of the first to dwell on the romantic potentialities of the expanding American frontier. The native romance for which he is best remembered is, of course, his folk creation, *Rip Van Winkle*.

In many respects James Fenimore Cooper was the most significant, and at the same time the most confused, figure in American romantic literature. He gave a truthful representation of the admirable type of frontiersman; yet his aristocratic background and his critical regard for the vulgarity of Jacksonian democracy would never permit him to be completely in sympathy with the aspirations of the common man. Although he saw in the Jacksonian democrat "intelligence, kindness, and natural politeness," he also saw "coarseness and vulgarity." But regardless of Cooper's perpetual inner conflict over the just value to be placed on the Jacksonian democrat, the full-blooded romance of simple adventure pervaded his *Leather-Stocking Tales*.

William Gilmore Simms, the leading romantic writer of the South, adopted methods and materials similar to Cooper's, although thirty years later. Colonial and Indian life, the Revolution, and the frontier border country were the principal sources for his romances.

Ralph Waldo Emerson was the chief theoretical exponent of the belief in the "divine sufficiency of the individual." In 1837, in his Phi Beta Kappa address at Harvard, he said, "We will walk on our own feet; we will work with our own hands; we will speak our own minds." [9] He advised that man should trust to the prompting within him. The fruits of this belief would be good, for human nature was divinely good.

Transcendentalism was the label under which Emersonian philosophy appeared. It owed its fundamental belief, the importance of the ideal as contrasted to the real, to German philosophy; but its peculiarly humanitarian tone it owed to Emerson. Not until transcendentalism insisted on the transference of supernatural attributes to the natural constitution of mankind was the democratic ideal given a fullhearted philosophical recognition.

Emerson was a rebel and a nonconformist, but in this respect he was outdistanced by Thoreau. Admitting the danger of such generalizations, one may say nevertheless that Thoreau lived the gospel of transcendentalism which Emerson preached and which Whitman poetized. Emerson praised nonconformity. Thoreau demonstrated his nonconformity by refusing to pay his poll tax and by spending a night in the village jail. Emerson praised life close to nature. Thoreau secured from Emerson the use of a plot of land on Walden Pond, erected a rude shack, and for two years lived in intimate contact with nature. Like Emerson, Thoreau was a supreme egotist, but he did not wish to impose his views on others. He had a mystical love for the beauties of nature, and a fierce distrust of and antagonism toward political and social institutions.

Walt Whitman, in his supreme egotism, in his rebellion against any form of tyranny, in his faith in the aspirations of the common man, and in his poetic expression in native and homely terms, was the chief exponent of romanticism in America. His poetry carried Rousseau's view of the sanctity of natural man to its plain and inevitable conclusion. His optimism, his faith in divinely given self-sufficiency, his confidence in the future of America, and his unfaltering trust in the democratic ideal were apparent in all his writings. His ideas and his visions were set forth in simple, direct, and unequivocal language. He was the supreme lover of America, and one of the "giants" in American romantic literary history.

Herman Melville was the other "giant," but he was not a lover of America. Melville sought his romance and his utopia in the South Seas. He was melancholy, often morbid, perplexed by the problem of evil, and continually searching to fathom the mystery of the universe. The romanticism of his search was epitomized in his monumental *Moby Dick,* "the perennial story of man's struggle for spiritual victory in a world of harassing circumstance and in a world where fate opposes the individual in the form of his own thwarting self." [10]

These were the leading figures in American romantic literature. Except perhaps for Emerson, they represented no "schools" or "romantic movements." They were individual artists asserting their romantic ideals, sometimes in terms of contemporary society and sometimes totally removed from it.

PAINTING, ARCHITECTURE, AND MUSIC

Although the art historian finds it easier to point out the evidences of a growing realistic tendency, even a cursory examination of nineteenth-century art will reveal repeated instances of romantic spirit and practice in every decade. Generally, the romantic temper in American art up to 1900 was apparent in

(1) the imitations of English and Continental romantic practice, (2) the employment of the wild and picturesque natural
beauty of America as a romantic theme, (3) the representation
of the romance in American history, and (4) the representation
of the growing democratic and nationalistic spirit. Similar
phases of romanticism will be observed in the later sections
dealing with American drama and theatre.

Romantic art in America, as in Europe, was in its ascendancy
during the 1820's, reached its crest during the thirties and early
forties, dwindled away in the fifties, and from then till the close
of the century appeared only intermittently. Broadly speaking,
this chronological pattern was evident alike in painting, architecture, music, and drama.

To be sure, there were evidences of romantic art and the
romantic attitude before 1820. And even though the Colonial
limners and the pre-Revolutionary portrait painters, Feke,
Smibert, and Copley, following in the English tradition, were
occupied primarily with supplying their patrons with faithful
likenesses, the "versified catalogue" for Smibert's art exhibition
of 1730 indicated that romantic picturesque landscapes were
not entirely out of fashion:

> Roman ruins nod their awful heads . . .
>
> .   .   .   .   .
>
> Landscapes, how gay! arise in ev'ry light . . .
>
> .   .   .   .   .
>
> Thro' Fairy scenes the roving Fancy strays
> Lost in the endless visionary maze . . .
>
> .   .   .   .   .
>
> The same gay scene our beauteous works adorn
> The flaming Evening or the Rosy Morn.[11]

In the main, pre-Revolutionary painting and the greater
share of immediate post-Revolutionary painting adhered to the
accepted London fashions. The "studied rules" of English masters were difficult to evade. When Benjamin West proposed to
paint his "Death of General Wolfe" with the General shown
in the uniform of a Continental Army Officer, Sir Joshua Reyn-
olds advised him to abandon such a rash project. Dying gener-

als were, according to tradition, represented in the Roman toga. But the spirit of growing nationalism was stronger than the dictates of traditional art practice, and the huge, picturesque, patriotic studies—West's "Death of General Wolfe" and "William Penn's Treaty with the Indians" and his pupil, John Trumbull's, "Capture of the Hessians at Trenton," "The Battle of Bunker Hill," and "The Signing of the Declaration of Independence"—employed the full romantic color of the historical events themselves. Trumbull particularly—he had been an ardent Rebel soldier—glorified the heroics of these historical moments. He hoped, through his paintings, to inspire the patriots with even greater veneration for their country's heroes. Today, however, art critics generally agree that the historical paintings of West and Trumbull show little genuine fire or conviction.

The two leading portrait painters of the post-Revolutionary period were John Singleton Copley and Gilbert Stuart. Copley did most of his early work in Boston; but in 1774 his Tory sympathies compelled him to go to England, where he remained for the rest of his life. Stuart painted his early canvases in England, but in 1793 he returned to America. Stuart is important to a study of romanticism in America because of his three portraits of Washington, the most popular of which, the "Athenaeum Washington," provided the visual image around which has been woven the national heroic tradition of Washington. William Dunlap, another of West's pupils, although never a painter of the first rank, demands a brief mention. Although Dunlap devoted himself mainly to portraiture, he did paint several monumental works on religious subjects: "Christ Rejected," "The Bearing of the Cross," "Calvary," and "Death on the Pale Horse." [12] In the history of American art, however, Dunlap is remembered for his *History of the Rise and Progress of the Arts of Design in the United States* (New York, 1834) rather than for his paintings.

In the early years of the nineteenth century, historical events and personages continued to occupy the painters. Emanuel Leutze's "Washington Crossing the Delaware" and Chester

Harding's portrait of Daniel Boone were typical canvases of the period. But also during this period, one can perceive in the works of John Vanderlyn the first impulses to lush landscape painting. Vanderlyn's "Ariadne" was the first nude to be painted in America, but the romantic landscape in the background of "Ariadne" had a greater influence upon subsequent painting than did the nude figure.

The year 1828, the year of Stuart's death, is considered by most historians of American art to end the post-Revolutionary period and to mark the beginning of the romantic period. But evidences of the coming romanticism, more explicit than those already indicated, were apparent in the work of Thomas Doughty. Doughty was the forerunner of the Hudson River School. The reverential serenity of his paintings was not appreciated, however, until after his death. Allston, the most romantic painter of his time, following the conventional apprenticeship of a few years in France and a few years in England, settled in Boston in 1818, after which and until his death in 1843, his studio was the center of Boston's cultural life. In the darkened tones of his compositions and the "hinted notes of deepest tragedy" one perceives the first suggestion of the gothic influence in pictorial art. His frightful and appalling "The Bloody Hand," for example, was taken from Mrs. Radcliffe's Italian novel. In his taste for the gothic novel, the supernatural ghost story, and the inexplicable grandeur of the Old Testament, Allston was the model for later romantic artists. Like West and Trumbull, Allston painted his scenes on the grand scale. In fact, the impulse to paint on large surfaces can be marked as one of the distinguishing features of romantic painting in America.

The growing taste for the picturesque soon found its principal satisfaction in the magical natural beauty of the Hudson Valley. The Hudson was not a new romantic subject. Irving's *Sketch Book* (1820), Bryant's "Thanatopsis" (1821), Cooper's *The Spy* (1821), and *The Pioneers* (1826) had used the colorful background of the Hudson River country.

But neither novel nor poetry treated the Hudson as completely as did the Hudson River painters. It is important to keep in mind, however, that these painters, Cole, Durand, Kensett, and Church, were not mere journeymen copyists. They possessed a romantic aspiration for greatness, a passion for the sublime, a burning desire to penetrate the mystery of the supernatural, and a sincere love for the grandeur of untamed and unexplored nature. In the presence of the great mountains, the vast panoramas, the immense river, the ancient oaks, these painters found comfort.

Thomas Cole was the giant of the Hudson River School and unquestionably the leading American romantic painter of the nineteenth century. During his early years in America, he was poor, lonely, and frequently ill. This may explain his predilection for painting the dark sides of nature: hurricanes, thunderstorms, and deluges. Undoubtedly his early hardships were responsible for the gloomy mood and preoccupation with death in the series of canvases constituting his "Course of Empire" and "Voyage of Life." His early years in America were spent in Steubenville, Ohio, and in Philadelphia. (His family had immigrated to America in 1819.) Although he began painting early, it was not until his family moved to New York, and he attracted the attention of a buyer who arranged for his first trip to the Catskills, that he began his important landscape paintings. But as soon as his canvases of the Hudson began to appear in New York, they attracted the favorable notice of John Trumbull, Asher Durand, and William Dunlap.

Cole found solace from his troubled life in his solitary walks along the Hudson. He was continually searching for new vistas to record; and when a storm arose during his rambles, he was overjoyed. The magnificent phenomenon of rebellious nature had for him symbolic significance. He felt the "indescribable melancholy" of the wilderness, or in the lull during a storm, "the expectation [that] hung on every crag." And this symbolic significance was usually transferred to the canvas. For example, one feels an incomparable air of suspense, of solitude, and the mysterious silence of the woods in "The Catskills" (1826). Important ingredients of Cole's romantic landscapes are the sunlight (in "John the Baptist in the Wilderness"), the towering cliffs, the sharp-ridged mountains, and the cascades.

Although Cole turned toward allegorical painting even in the late twenties in such canvases as "John the Baptist" and "The Expulsion from Eden," his later and more mature works were devoted entirely to philosophical representations. The "Course of Empire" was a magnificent operatic conception showing man's life in morning, noon, full noon, evening, and night.[13] Cooper spoke of this work as a product "of the highest genius this country has ever produced." Cole's "Voyage of Life" showed the dark and vain struggle of man through "Childhood," "Youth," "Manhood," and "Old Age." In 1842 Cole became very devout, and the pessimism of "Voyage of Life" was forgotten in his zeal for religious painting. Of these later works the three-picture series, "Life, Death, and Immortality," and his final series, "The Cross and the World," were typical. He hoped they would provide a corrective for his earlier pessimism.[14]

Cole's doctrine contained the essence of romanticism. He believed the landscape painter should, by a process of selection, arrange his composition to represent a more beautiful view of nature than could ever be found in reality.

William Cullen Bryant was one of Cole's closest friends. When Cole died, in 1848, Bryant delivered his funeral oration. And in 1849, when A. B. Durand painted in Cole's honor a Hudson River landscape called "Kindred Spirits," he eulogized the friendship between Bryant and Cole. Nathan described the canvas as follows: "Through a framework of steep rocks and overhanging trees a wide view opens into a wooded valley extending in peaceful and unspoiled grandeur to the distant mountains gilded by the rays of the afternoon sun. The sound of water leaping over cascades fills the balmy air. Two middle-aged men stand on a rocky ledge at the left. One seems to enjoy the scene silently, while the other interprets its beauties to him." [15] The initials carved in the bark of a tree in the foreground clearly indicated the two figures were Bryant and Cole.

Durand and the other Hudson River painters never equalled

Cole's magnificent landscapes. Where Cole was sentimental, Durand was sympathetically literal. But in spite of his inclination toward literalness, Durand possessed a Cole-like regard for nature which the later followers of Cole lacked. The paintings of John Frederick Kensett and Sanford R. Gifford had lyrical grace and genteel atmospheric effects, but they exhibited none of the overpowering sublimity of Cole's canvases. None of the later painters had Cole's reverential affinity for nature. Kensett, for example, painted most of his White Mountain canvases from sketches, a practice which Cole would not have condoned.

Frederick Church, a pupil and disciple of Cole, chose the romantic glories of nature (rainbows over rivers, the smoke of a volcano, or the glow of the Acropolis) as subject matter for his panoramic paintings, but he was more intent on achieving topographical exactness than in creating a romantic atmosphere. His "Falls of Niagara," for example, was admired for its precise similarity. When looked at through a long tube, it is said to have been difficult to distinguish it from the real falls.

It is important to distinguish between the panoramic type of painting practiced by Church and others and the extensive panorama canvases usually painted by comparatively unknown artists and exhibited in specially designed halls. The panoramic paintings belong with the discussion of painting in general, whereas the panorama exhibitions are more properly related to the discussion of theatrical scenic displays. John Banvard was, however, one of the few painters of panoramas whose name as an artist was well known. Thus, he may justifiably be mentioned here. During the forties his panorama of the Mississippi was viewed, according to Saint-Gaudens, by some 4,000 Americans;[16] but because of its many showings in the metropolitan centers and throughout the country, 40,000 would seem a more plausible figure. In 1849 he took the gigantic canvas to England, where it met with equal success. For its repeated display in America and England, Banvard is said to have received $50,000. The idea for this canvas came to Banvard when he and another young artist piloted their floating art gallery from

New Harmony, Indiana, down the Wabash and the Mississippi to New Orleans. According to old-time gossip, the painting was said to have been three miles long. Old river men testified to its accuracy, and Longfellow found it sufficiently detailed to give him a clear notion of the natural background for the sections of *Evangeline* involving the Mississippi.

Other romantic aspects of the American scene were being recorded on canvas during the period 1830–1850. George Caleb Bingham painted the fur traders and Indians. George Catlin visited forty-eight tribes and painted four hundred and seventy-one full-length portraits of Indians. Many of Catlin's paintings were, however, as important for their landscape backgrounds and illustrative material on the life and customs of the Indians as for their portraiture.

Albert Bierstadt, in the early seventies, did for the Rocky Mountains what Cole and others had done for the Hudson. In the newly discovered, overwhelming grandeur of the West he found an abundance of material for his panoramic canvases. Thomas Moran was another who painted panoramic views of the Rockies. In 1871 he accompanied a Government expedition to the unexplored Yellowstone region; on this western trip he painted "Cliffs of Upper Colorado River, Wyoming Territory" and other pictures similar to it.

Many of the direct descendants of the Hudson River School continued to paint during the second half of the century. Church, Bierstadt, and Banvard did their most important work after 1850. There were, however, other painters of the second half of the century who were less in the Hudson River tradition but in some degree related to it. Among these were George Inness, Homer Dodge Martin, Albert Ryder, Albert Davies. On the whole, their landscapes were more intimate and lyrical and less monumental and sublime than those of Cole, Durand, and Church. Inness was the leading American exponent of the French Barbizon style of painting. The French painters in the Barbizon group were revolting against the rigid abstraction and devotion to form of the French Academy and were seeking for an ideal reality. Painting for them became a religious quest for truth in nature. This doctrine, in a measure, was certainly a reiteration of Cole's theory of the painter's art. Inness' landscapes were dreamy and mysterious. As Saint-Gaudens says: "He had augmented in a manner more elusive, and of greater poetic consequence to succeeding generations, the native tradition which had been established by the Hudson River School." [17] And Inness' statement of his purpose in painting contained the essence of romantic aspiration, "to reproduce in other minds the impression which a scene has made upon him . . . not to instruct, not to edify, but to awaken an emotion." [18]

Martin was a mood painter who followed the Hudson River tradition in rendering the White Mountains, the Adirondacks, and the Smokies. Ryder painted "landscapes of the unconscious mind." He was a visionary and mystic who found the moonlit sea his favorite subject. Frequently he has been called the American Blake, but he lacked Blake's ability in drawing and design. Davies' mood fantasies in water color were admired chiefly for their delicacy.

The genre painters of the second half of the century (George Bingham, William Mount, John George Brown, Eastman Johnson, and Thomas Eakins) were esteemed for their rendering of realistic detail with photographic accuracy. But frequent suggestions of romantic sentimentality were apparent in such paintings as Johnson's "The Drummer-Boy," and Brown's "Newsboys" and "The Music Lesson." Many of the vivid lithographs of Currier and Ives dwelt on the spectacular and sentimental aspects of life during the last forty years of the century. And although one would classify them ordinarily as realistic art, they were, in their sentimentality, romantic.

Although one can observe a gradually increasing attention to realistic detail in nineteenth-century American painting, the romantic urge to exalt the individual, to glory in the sublime and overpowering aspects of nature, to praise the deed and spirit of the growing democracy, and to delight in the unfamiliar, the obscure, the bizarre, and mysterious persisted to a degree through the entire century.

The main current of architecture until the middle of the nineteenth century followed the classical Greek and Roman patterns first adopted by Thomas Jefferson at Monticello and widely imitated in the rest of the country. This Palladian classicism, however, was opposed by a growing interest in medieval gothic. Even Jefferson, in the eclectic fashion so characteristic of American architecture through the nineteenth century, visualized a "Burying Place" adjacent to Monticello that would have "in the center of it . . . a gothic temple of antique appearance." Thus the gothic as well as the Greek revival of the second quarter of the century was anticipated by Jefferson.

Early in the century, the popularity of Mrs. Radcliffe's gothic romances encouraged many of the new American playwrights to adapt to the stage the gloomy atmosphere of medieval castles and the mysterious and bloodcurdling events of these stories. Scott's novels, during the second decade of the century, had assured Americans that the people of the Middle Ages were human; and his own mansion, Abbotsford, afforded proof that medieval dwellings were habitable.

Americans sought the authority of English architectural practice, and in England Turner had created a nostalgia for castles and ancient manor houses. Nevertheless, the strongest and most direct influence in popularizing the medieval romantic villa in America came from the writings of Andrew Jackson Downing. By his persuasive style, his blend of romance and democracy, and his numerous designs, he crystallized the romantic ideal of the house in the country. His words gave clear expression to the delights that were to be found in the shadowy dimness, the lancet windows, the latticed panes, and the pervading old-world atmosphere of gothic houses:

In this house there should be something to love. It must not look all new and sunny, but show secluded and shadowy corners. There must be nooks about it, where one would love to linger; windows, where one can enjoy the quiet landscape at his leisure; cosy rooms, where all fire-side joys are invited to dwell.[19]

.   .   .   .   .

The great beauty of this style, when properly treated, is the home-like expression which it is capable of. This arises mainly from the chaste and quiet colors of the dark wood-work, the grave though rich hue of the carpets and walls . . . and the quiet, domestic feeling of the library and the family circle. Those who love shadow, and the sentiment of antiquity and repose, will find in it the most pleasure.[20]

These gothic villas were not dream-creations of romantic antiquarian architects. Nathaniel Parker Willis, author of two of the leading romantic plays of this period, *Bianca Visconti,* and *Tortesa the Usurer,* wrote of his Idlewild on the Hudson: "The position is exactly such a one as a medieval knight would have selected for his strong-hold, and a little imagination may easily transmute the simple domestic cottage into the turreted and battlemented castle." [21] The subjective quality of the medieval mode, the old-world romance, the vastness, the freedom, and the endless variety of the gothic style suited the American romantic soul.

There were two periods of gothic design in America (excluding the modern collegiate adaptations). The first of these, from 1788 to 1840, delighted principally in the romantic atmosphere of the medieval architecture. The second, from 1840 to 1860, demonstrated a greater knowledge of medieval construction, an interest in archaeological detail, an allegiance to the aesthetic notions of Ruskin, and a tendency to copy directly the Continental patterns. Some of the earliest and most striking examples of gothic architecture in America were the Glen Ellen house, near Baltimore, designed by Alexander J. Davis in 1834; Trinity Church, in New York, designed by Richard Upjohn in 1839; Eastern Penitentiary, in Philadelphia, designed by John Haviland in 1825; and the New York State Prison, at Auburn.

In music, evidences of the romantic impulse were found as early as 1770. In that year Billings, one of the earliest of American composers, wrote a credo for musical composition that anticipated the nineteenth-century romanticism of Anthony

Heinrich. Billings believed there could be no rules for composition: "Nature is the best Dictator, for all the hard studied rules that ever were prescribed will not enable any person to form an Air any more than the bare knowledge of the four and twenty letters and strict Grammatical rules will qualify a scholar for composing a piece of Poetry. It must be Nature; Nature must lay the Foundation, Nature must give the thought!" [22]

During the first half of the nineteenth century the prevailing taste in music bore less relation to the theatre and drama than did architecture and painting, but a brief mention of some of the evidences of romanticism in music may not be misplaced. Very much as Cole was the leading exponent of romanticism in painting, Anthony Phillip Heinrich was the champion of romanticism in music. Heinrich began his professional career not as a musician but as director of the theatre at Pittsburgh in 1816. The following year, in Kentucky, he found that the romantic influence of the wild and newly discovered country inspired him to compose. And in the seclusion of his Kentucky log house, he wrote his first collection of songs, "The Western Minstrel, a Collection of original, moral, patriotic, and sentimental songs for the pianoforte, interspersed with airs, waltzes, etc." (1820).

A strong nationalism pervaded most of Heinrich's music. None of the native-born musicians[23]—Lowell Mason, William Bradbury, Thomas Hastings, Sylvanus Pond, and Isaac Woodbury—felt, as Heinrich did, a God-given mission to glorify America. He wrote a "Birthday to Washington," a "Hail Columbia," [24] and numerous versions of the "Yankee Doodle" refrain.

Heinrich, like the Hudson River painters, found his inspiration in the romantic American landscape. He sought out nature "in the workshops where she produces her mighty works. . . ." [25] Such a programme series as his "Bird as Prophet, the Ornithological Combat of Kings," with its four parts ("The Conflict in the Air," "The Repose," "The Battle on Land," and

"The Victory") was reminiscent of the pattern of Thomas Cole's "Voyage of Life."

Heinrich was the first composer to glorify the "noble savage" in music. In "The Indian Carnival," "Sioux Gaillard," and "Manitou Air Dance" he represented the Indian as the emblem of fairness, justice, breadth of vision, spirituality, ceaseless aspiration, and courage; but these shorter compositions were all eclipsed by the splendor of his full symphonic tone poem, "Pocahontas; or, Prize of the Wilderness." This appeared almost simultaneously with, and was probably inspired by, Forrest's first performances of Stone's *Metamora*. Heinrich was the precursor of the twentieth-century "cult of the Indian" adopted by MacDowell and Cadman.

Heinrich was not above adding to the collection of woeful ballads and merciless laments that were so popular during the 1840's, but his rivals far outdistanced him with such songs as "Where Can the Soul Find Rest," by J. C. Baker, "The Last Link Is Broken," by William Clifton, and "That Death Should Sever Two Hearts That Could Have Loved Forever," by Frederick William Crouch.

Just as the peculiar theatrical performance of the Negro minstrel show was one of the striking demonstrations of romanticism in American theatrical history, the equally curious musical exhibitions of the forties were similarly romantic manifestations. There were seances of "musical virtuoso-spitting" in Baltimore. A frightful Mephisto conducted an invisible orchestra with wild gesticulations and sardonic laughter. The pianist, Henry Christian Timm, played his concert with a full wine glass on the back of each hand.

Not all the musical exhibitionism in the forties was, however, absurdly exaggerated. On a higher level, but just as carefully tempered to meet the popular demand, were the concerts of Jullien, Russell, Ole Bull, Jenny Lind, and Louis Gottschalk. Ole Bull, "The Herculean Fiddler," could play all four strings on the violin at once;[26] and Jenny Lind, "the Swedish Nightingale," became, through the careful publicity arrangements of

P. T. Barnum, the idol of millions. A single ticket for her first concert in New York was auctioned off for as high as $225. Louis Gottschalk was the first of the matinee idols of the concert stage. The women of New York, the West Indies, and South America fought for a "scrap of the white gloves which he invariably wore on the platform, and took off with utmost deliberation, one finger at a time." [27] The exhibitionism of these musicians, it must be noted, was not unlike that of the leading actors, Edwin Forrest, Junius Brutus Booth, Edmund Kean, and William Charles Macready.

But at the same time that the populace found their musical sense tickled by these exhibitionists, the Transcendentalists of Brook Farm (1841–1847) found in music the "only idiom which has not yet exhausted itself. They discovered in great music, particularly in the music of Beethoven, a spiritual resuscitation similar to that which they found in their transcendentalism." [28] Like the Gothic cathedral, music is "never finished, forever yearning and striving upwards, the beginning only of a boundless plan, whose consummation is in another world." [28]

DRAMA AND THEATRE

American dramatic literature can boast no playwrights comparable to such writers as Cooper, Poe, Emerson, Whitman, or Melville. In dealing with the drama, one is compelled to consider, almost entirely, authors of smaller stature. The discussion in the chapters that follow is not directed, then, toward inspecting the clearest and most elevated perceptions of the romantic ideal. Rather it is directed toward demonstrating the persistence of the romantic temper in the theatre and drama, not only in the high-water years of the 1830's, but throughout the entire nineteenth century.

Before any attempt is made to survey in detail the manifestations of romanticism in American drama and the theatre, some general indications of tendency will be discussed in order that particular details may be placed in their proper relations.

As already noted, the classical tradition was never strong in

America. Rules for artistic expression had never been firmly established, and when the romantic theories filtered in from Germany, France, and England, they were applied directly to life, not to art. A vehement protest against nonexistent artistic principles was impossible, particularly in the theatre and drama. In France a large part of the romantic revolt in aesthetics was directed against the hidebound and outmoded conventions in the theatre and in drama. The rules and restraints presented a formidable object at which to strike. But in America there were no traditional practices. Except for a few odd pieces of dramatic literature, Godfrey's *The Prince of Parthia* (1767) and Mrs. Warren's *The Group* (1775) and *The Adulateur* (1773), there were practically no native dramas until after the Revolution. The popular plays were those of Shakespeare, Farquhar, Otway, Addison, and Rowe. A few scattered pieces of dramatic literature in the course of seventy years, that is, from the publication of *Androboros,* in 1714, to the *Battle of Bunkers Hill,* in 1776, could certainly not establish a tradition. There was in our national background no Racine or Corneille, no Congreve or Otway; nor was there any Comédie Française or Drury Lane. The American theatre partook only remotely and in a secondhand fashion of the established practices of the European theatre.

If there was any revolt within the theatre itself against past restrictions and inhibitions, it was against the moral restraints which the Puritans had placed on all public entertainments. The Puritans had levelled the first blow at the American theatre. In the act of driving symbolism out of the Anglican church —for symbolism smacked of "Popery"—they discovered that symbolism was at the base of theatrical entertainment. The theatre must be driven out. "When some English actors tried to put on a play in 1750, there was a small riot, and the Massachusetts General Court sternly reaffirmed its traditional ban on 'public stage-plays, interludes, and other theatrical entertainments, which not only occasion great and unnecessary expenses, and discourage industry and frugality, but likewise tend generally to increase immorality, impiety, and a contempt for religion.' " [29] This view, so firmly established early in our national life, was hard to eradicate. It seemed to tinge the thinking even of those who had no sympathy with Puritanical censorship. Our foremost literary men have always seemed to have a hidden contempt for the theatre.

The prevailing scorn of the theatre as iniquitous, the lack of theatrical tradition, the lack of faith in native playwrights, and the too close involvement with the actual business of living were the principal contributing factors in the shaping of the American drama and theatre. As Barzun has indicated, romantic drama, under these circumstances, appeared in life rather than on the stage: "Romantic work is first and foremost a display of contrasts, a dramatic view of life which does not take sides and is without hope of resolution. So defined, drama is the special mark of romanticism in art. The conclusion is not invalidated by the fact that the plays of the period are actually the weakest part of romanticist literature, for real drama often gets but a feeble footing on the conventional stage." [30]

Although we find no "giants" in our theatrical and dramatic history, we do find a continuous comment on the view of life held by each succeeding generation; and we do find an uninterrupted growth in dramatic and theatrical practice leading directly to the accepted standards in the twentieth-century theatre.

Prior to 1800 the evidences of romantic taste in American drama and theatre were scattered and diverse. Preference for faraway place and time and for heroic action was demonstrated in the public's taste for Shakespeare and the native playwright's preference for remote situations. *The Prince of Parthia,* for example, was laid in Parthia at the opening of the Christian era. Elaborate scenic spectacles, some designed for sheer excitement and thrills and others intended to eulogize national heroes, were extremely common. And although native playwrights were not generally accepted and native themes rarely treated, there were some evidences of an increasing deference to the growing pride in America. In 1765, for example, Douglass changed the name of his theatrical troupe from London Company to American Company.

William Dunlap was the first recognized and accepted American playwright, beginning his dramatic writing in 1789 and continuing to 1815. To Dunlap, "America was the hope of the artist of the future where, unhampered by caste or the dead hand of prestige, the painter, the writer, the musician could develop on the firm basis of his intrinsic worth. His belief in democracy as a stimulant of art is expressed with a hopefulness that not even the bitter experience of years could quite disillusion, for he saw, beyond the accomplishment of democracy, the great principle that survives even the hard disappointments of fact." [31]

But Dunlap found the task of the native playwright extremely difficult. In order to gain a measure of acceptance, he had to resort principally to adapting plays from the German of Kotzebue. The theatre public, or at least so the managers judged, was not yet willing to accept full-fledged dramatic creations by native playwrights. Another case in point is James Nelson Barker's dramatization of Scott's *Marmion*. When this play was first performed (April 13, 1812, at the Park Theatre, New York), it was announced as the work of the British playwright Thomas Morton.

During the period from the close of the Revolutionary War to the War of 1812 there were, none the less, repeated evidences of the romantic temper. Patriotic treatments of the Revolutionary War, expressing the growing faith in the new democracy— for example, Dunlap's *André* (1798)—were not uncommon. The Indian plays, like Barker's *The Indian Princess* (1808), glorifying the "noble savage," were beginning to appear. And in addition to a continued interest in the conventional romantic themes of faraway place and time, there was a new-found interest in the wild actions and mysterious atmosphere of the gothic romance, as evidenced in Dunlap's *Fontainville Abbey* (1795). During this period the theatre undertook the romantic adventure of moving out on to the frontier. In 1790 a production was attempted at Fort Pitt, and in 1798, 1799, and 1801 theatres were erected at Detroit, Lexington, and Cincinnati, respectively.

After the War of 1812, there were two major evidences of romanticism in drama and the theatre. Plays constructed chiefly to praise the new democratic life and to celebrate military actions were increasingly prevalent. Mordecai Noah's *She Would Be a Soldier* (1819) was an example of this type. Theatrical spectacles exhibiting the thrilling sea battles between American and British frigates were repeatedly shown. *The Return from a Cruise* (1812) contained such a spectacle.

The period from 1820 to 1840, in which the high point of romanticism in American drama and theatre was reached, exhibited every phase of the romantic spirit adaptable to the theatre: in *Metamora* (1829), glorification of the "noble savage"; in *Mount Savage* (1822), delight in medieval gothicism; in *The Patriot* (1834), exaltation of the Revolution and its heroes; and above all, in *The Gladiator* (1831), praise for and faith in the democratic fight against political and social tyranny.

In keeping with the move toward more democratic living, the theatre became, during this period, accessible to the masses. The second Park Theatre, in New York, opened in 1821 and seated 2,500 persons; the Bowery Theatre, in New York, was completed in 1826 and accommodated 3,500 spectators. Dramatic entertainment was no longer designed for the few.

Scenic spectacles and panoramic entertainments were extremely frequent prior to 1840, but during the forties they monopolized the theatres. Gaudy displays and striking exhibitions were the order of the day. The forties was the decade of the *tableaux vivants,* the half-nude statuesque groupings representing the *Garden of Eden* or *Neptune Rising from the Sea.* The third tier was flourishing in its most "iniquitous" manner, but for many the lively behavior permitted in this top gallery added romance to the theatre. Two leading performers of the time were Miss Kate and Miss Ellen Bateman, "children of the ages of six and four years, who perform the most difficult Shakespearean characters with a perfect knowledge of the art, and a graceful and correct reading of the great author." [32] P. T. Barnum was getting into full swing with his *Great Model of Niagara Falls with Real Water*. Such dioramas and panoramas as *Six Days of the Creation* and *A Sea Storm and Destruction of an American Packet* were attracting large audiences. Turning the theatre over "to the horses" became a common practice for the managers whose finances were running low. The *Herald* spoke of "Levi North, the famous equestrian, [who] created a greater sensation and collected a greater audience than all the prima donnas from Italy." [33] The forties saw the birth of the Negro minstrel show, in 1842. In 1847, Christy's Ethiopian Minstrels opened at Mechanics' Hall on Broadway. They planned to run for a few weeks, and stayed for nine years and eleven months. Acrobats, dancers, pantomimists, and magicians were seen more frequently than plays. The Astor Place Theatre Riot occurred in May, 1849. Real and horrible as it was, and real as was the quarrel between Macready and Forrest, it nevertheless belongs, as a strange, spectacular, and incredible event, in the history of romanticism in the American theatre.

The drama during this period was devoted principally to sensational actions, weird atmospheric settings, and melodramatic characters. An anonymous moralist of the period found that the theatre "might possibly convey some practical lessons, available hints, and rules of etiquette, to those who expect to pass their lives in a land of ghosts and enchantments, of knights and beggars, of idle dukes, vicious nobles, and obsequious dependents, oppressive aristocracies and oppressed slaves." [34]

Variety entertainments continued through the decade of the fifties, but they were less frequent. The Negro minstrel show was flourishing at its highest peak. But at the same time the decade produced two of the best romantic plays of the nineteenth century: *Francesca da Rimini* (1855) and *Love in '76* (1857). One demonstrated the taste for the conventional romance of remote time and place, the other a predilection for the Revolutionary War theme. Another significant event of the period was the first performance of *Uncle Tom's Cabin,* in 1852. The romantic struggle of the slave against the oppressions of his cruel master became a favored theme.

From the close of the Civil War (1865) to the end of the century, the distinguishing mark of dramatic and theatrical history was the rapidly increasing inclination toward realistic representation. Evidences of the persistent taste for romance were, however, not infrequent. The decade of the seventies produced the significant romantic dramas of the frontier: *Davy Crockett* (1872) and *The Danites in the Sierras* (1877). *Francesca da Rimini* received its deserved success in 1882. The Civil War provided the themes for a number of dramas mixing romantic story and adventure with realistic detail. *Held by the Enemy* was one of the best of these.

Romanticism in the theatre of this period was especially evident in the attitude of the spectator. Even attending a well-authenticated realistic representation, the average spectator looked to the theatre for some form of romantic adventure. He found romance in the stirring spectacle, in the melodramatic story, in the atmospheric effects, or in the highly colored romantic fiction woven around the life of his favorite actor or actress. Actors and actresses were—and to some extent still are—regarded as mysterious creatures who come from another realm and who are endowed with inexplicable beauties of body and soul.

This romantic view of the theatre has prevailed in America certainly up to 1900 and perhaps, in some measure, to the present day. Dunlap observed it in 1837, when he wrote in his *Memoirs of a Water Drinker:*

The music of the orchestra struck up, and although others did not appear to hear it, our hero's delight was increased almost to intoxication. But however much his sense of harmony was captivated by the orchestra, or his eyes attracted to the brilliant company in the boxes, above all he looked at the Green Curtain with interest, for the hidden and unknown is far more attractive than the visible, however beautiful, his eyes lighted on the plain, dull surface of the cloth before him, which told him nothing, but was pregnant with mysterious meaning; for he knew that behind *that* lay something that was to crown all—when *that* should be removed his felicity would be complete. *How* he knew not—but he was sure of it. A bell tinkled and the front lamps rose as if by magic. Another bell rung louder. The curtain vanished. All was dazzling light and many colored brilliance; the silence of breathless expectation succeeded. Then appeared beautiful men and women with fine dresses and sparkling eyes and red cheeks; Surely actors and actresses must not only be the most admired but the best, the most lovely and the happiest of mortals.[35]

To a degree romanticism was evident in drama and the theatre from the beginning to the close of the nineteenth century. It demonstrated itself more markedly in some periods than in others; and, as will be evident in the succeeding chapters, it took on a variety of colorful expressions.

CHAPTER II

Native Themes and Characters

1. Negro Minstrelsy

THE NEGRO minstrel show was the only genuinely indigenous form of American drama. Though American troupes during the fifties and sixties made numerous excursions to England and Germany, blackface minstrelsy remained, during the eighty-odd years of its existence, essentially an American theatrical product. As a musical performance, it had a common heritage with the wandering minstrel and the troubadour, but as a theatrical performance, it had qualities that were distinct from those of any other type.

Brander Matthews traced the origin of the minstrel show to sixteenth-century Paris and the theatrical antics of the quack doctor, Mandor, and his stooge, Tabarin, who were, he believed, the progenitors of the interlocutor and end-men of Negro minstrelsy. In the typically Elizabethan banter between the two Dromios of Shakespeare's *Comedy of Errors,* Matthews found the prototype of the badinage of the minstrel show's Tambo and Bones.[1] Nevertheless, though these apparent resemblances between the Negro minstrel and earlier examples of theatrical entertainment are undeniable, the connecting links, which should presumably be evident during the intervening years, are difficult to find.

Many writers on Negro minstrelsy have traced the source of

the minstrel show to the peculiar character of the Southern Negro, his African heritage, and his life on the plantation: "A Southern gentleman desiring amusement for his guests was wont to call in those among his slaves who could sing and dance, and when he sent out invitations for a party it was often the slaves who played the dance music. Authorities differ as to the exact date when white actors began to realize that there was money to be made by imitating the black man when thus employed." [2] Despite such accounts, it remains doubtful whether the regular minstrel performer ever copied directly from any of these Southern plantation entertainments. Actual descriptions of such entertainments are not available, and the one just recorded was unauthenticated. In the opinion of Charles Sherlock, "You would look in vain in real life for the counterpart of the traditional darkey of the stage as depicted so delightfully by a long line of Negro minstrels." [3]

But even if the Negro of the minstrel show was largely a romantic invention of Northern whites, a fact that will become increasingly apparent as the present investigation proceeds, many characteristics of the real-life Negro unavoidably appeared in the minstrel-stage Negro. Although the minstrel performer was primarily attempting to contrive a lucrative form of theatrical entertainment, irrespective of any historical authenticity, some of the plantation Negro's character crept into the minstrel performance. Without the singularly American romantic notion of a slave-Negro singing and dancing at his work, smiling and joking even under the punishing strokes of his overseer's whip, Negro minstrelsy would never have had the necessary spark to set it burning through the middle years of the last century. Without the peculiar background of American Negro slavery, the minstrel show would never have been founded.

The first actual signs of the budding life of this new theatrical form were found around 1800 in the comic songs sung in blackface at the circus and in the theatre. When rendered on the regular theatre program, they were inserted either between the acts of a play or between the separate sections of the whole

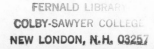

bill. So many of these have been noted with such a diversity of dates and such indefinite descriptions of the actual performances that it is difficult to say which of them came first and which were most directly related to the fully matured minstrel show.

In 1769 Lewis Hallam did an imitation of a drunken Negro during a performance of *The Padlock*. How closely this may have approximated some of the antics of the end-men is impossible to say; or how similar it may have been to such comic songs as the "Song of the Negro Boy," rendered by Mr. Graupner in Boston on December 30, 1799, after the second act of the tragedy *Oroonoko*. There were many of these early singers. In 1815, Andrew Allen, later more famous as a cook and dresser for Edwin Forrest, sang "Back Side of Albany Stands Lake Champlain" between acts at a performance of *The Battle of Lake Champlain* in Albany. Others were "Pot Pie" Herbert, an enterprising pie salesman who peddled his wares with a song; George Washington Dixon, a circus performer usually credited as the author of "Old Zip Coon" (later known as "Turkey in the Straw"); and George Nichols, a clown for Purdy Brown's Theatre and Circus of the South and West, who is said to have sung "Jim Crow" long before Rice made it famous as a dance.

However important an influence these early blackface singers may have been, "Jim Crow" ("Daddy") Rice was unquestionably the most significant figure of these pre-minstrel days. Thomas Dartmouth Rice was born of poor parents in the old Seventh Ward of New York City on May 20, 1808, and received his first theatrical training as a supernumerary at the Park Theatre. He was apparently an excellent comedian, for in a production of *Bombastes Furioso* at the Park his comedy antics attracted so much attention to him and away from the principals that he was fired. After losing this position, he journeyed up and down the Ohio Valley as an itinerant player. For a time he was employed as a property man, lamplighter, and stage carpenter in Ludlow and Smith's Southern Theatre in Louisville. In 1828 he transferred to Samuel Drake's company at the

Louisville Theatre, and it was probably during this engagement, cast as a cornfield Negro in a local drama (Solon Robinson's *The Rifle*), that he sang and jumped "Jim Crow" for the first time.

Like so much of the history of the minstrels the factual history of this famous song and dance is almost impossible to discover. The speculations have been so numerous, and some of the least credible stories occur so frequently that it is difficult to deny them some grain of truth. Only on one thing are all accounts agreed: The date on which Rice jumped "Jim Crow" for the first time was one of the most significant dates in the history of Negro minstrelsy.

Edwin S. Conner, in an article in *The New York Times* for June 5, 1881, attributed the original "Jim Crow" dance to a Louisville stable boy from whom Rice copied the routine. Francis Courtney Wemmys in his autobiography said that the original "Jim Crow" was a native of Pittsburgh and that his real name was Jim Cuff. Marian Spitzer added New Orleans as another in the list of towns that might claim the original "Jim Crow."[4] John Jennings did not mention the stable boy, but favored Louisville as the place of inception and gave 1829 as the date for Rice's first performance of the dance.[5]

One of the most elaborate explanations was that given by Robert Nevin. According to Nevin the dance originated in Cincinnati, and the original performer was a crippled stable boy. In going about his regular chores the stable boy was obliged by his infirmity to walk in a curious jumping fashion. This crippled jump, copied and elaborated by Rice, was the basis for the "Jim Crow" dance. When Rice moved to Pittsburgh, he wanted to insert the dance as part of his performance at the Pittsburgh Theatre. Having no clothes that were appropriate to the "Jim Crow" character, but observing a porter in ragged clothes similar to those of the stable boy, Rice used the porter's clothes for the "Jim Crow" dance. The porter, who seems to have been called Jim Cuff,[6] stood fearfully while Rice removed his clothes, and then waited in the wings practically nude while Rice went out on the stage and sang and danced

"Jim Crow" for the first time. The applause was so overwhelming that Rice was obliged to repeat the dance again and again, while with each repetition the porter became more and more impatient. The next stagecoach was due shortly; and not being at his usual post, the porter was afraid that he would suffer the humiliation of having his competitors do all the toting. Finally in desperation he ran out on the stage and proceeded to strip Rice of his clothes. The applause greeting these antics became so uproarious, according to Nevin, that the exit doors had to be thrown open, signifying the end of the performance.[7]

Of these various explanations of the first jumping of "Jim Crow," the one that associated the original performance with Louisville sometime between 1828 and 1831 seems the most plausible. The music for the dance was composed by Rice and was taken first to the music dealer, Cunning Peters. Peters became a music dealer in Louisville sometime in 1828, but since he did not open his branch in Cincinnati until 1839, it seems quite probable that Rice brought the music to him in Louisville.[8]

In all probability there was some stable boy such as the one already described who furnished the original peculiar walk from which Rice managed to develop a dance step. The original verses and music were written by Rice, and even though an endless stream of verses were added by various later interpreters, the refrain remained the same:

> First on de heel tap, den on de toe,
> Ebery time I wheel about I jump Jim Crow.
> Wheel about and turn about and do jis so,
> And ebery time I wheel about I jump Jim Crow.

The exact nature of the dance, beyond what is implicit in the refrain, is impossible to discover; for the illustrations are few, and limited ordinarily to one pose. They give little more than an indication of the nature of the costume and the curious posture: knees bent, one heel up, one heel down, one arm raised, the other on the hip, and head cocked to one side.[9]

Regardless of any questions about the possible place of origin there is no question about the immediate success of the dance. Rice's reputation was established with that of the "Jim Crow" dance, and he continued "jumping" until his death in 1861.

His first New York appearance was on November 12, 1832, when he jumped "Jim Crow" during the interval between the performances of two serious dramas, *The Hunchback* and *Catherine of Cleves*. The next day he danced between *The Fire Raiser* and *The French Spy;* and on November 15, he was on the bill at the Bowery Theatre following a performance of *Othello*.

At a performance in Washington, Rice introduced Joseph Jefferson to a theatre audience for the first time. Jefferson was just four; Rice carried him on the stage in a sack and sang: "Ladies and Gentleman, I'd have you for to know That I've got a little darkey here that jumps Jim Crow." At this point he dumped the blacked-up boy onto the stage, and Jefferson proceeded to do an excellent child's version of the "Jim Crow" dance. Mrs. John Drew, who was present at this performance, testified that Jefferson's youthful "Jim Crow" was an excellent imitation.

Rice's further distinction in the history of Negro minstrelsy is that he was the first to introduce "Ethiopian Operas." These operas, the first of which were given by Rice as early as January, 1833, when he introduced the Bowery Theatre audience to "Long Island Juba" and "Where's My Head?" were the precursors of the later minstrel burlesques that became essential to the second part of the regular minstrel shows.

Ordinarily Rice was a solo performer, but he made a few appearances in these "Ethiopian Operas" and occasionally in later years performed with two regular minstrel troupes, Charley White's Serenaders and Wood's Minstrels. Although he died in poverty, he commanded at the height of his career as high a salary as any performer of his day. For a single performance in Dublin he received six hundred dollars. His last engagement was at Wood's in New York in 1858, and in September, 1860, he died.

During this whole decade of the thirties preceding the actual founding of the minstrel show proper, Rice had many imitators who were seeking a share in his popularity. Barney Williams became famous for his Negro dances, and Barnum presented Jack Diamond in his famous Ethiopian "break-downs." Bill Keller was singing "Coal Black Rose"; Barney Burns was known for his rendering of "My Long Tail Blue" and "Such a Getting Up Stairs"; and at the Bowery in 1834 Bob Farrell created a stir with "Zip Coon." Negro specialty performers became the popular entertainers of the day in the circus and on the stage.

Perhaps Rice's influence, as Brander Matthews believed, prevented the development of the genuine plantation Negro in the minstrel show; but certainly Rice's influence established the pattern for the individual performers who were to make up the later minstrel show. Although none of these individual performers, Keller, Burns, *et al.*, ever grouped together to found a regular minstrel troupe, the first part of the later minstrel show routine developed as a collection of the songs and dances of these performers. It was "a natural and almost inevitable development from the performance of individual actors who had presented such popular skits and songs as 'Jim Crow,' 'Clare de Kitchen,' 'Lucy Long,' and other favorites." [10]

Although all later minstrel shows stemmed originally from the first "Jim Crow" dance, there was one other first performance that was more directly related to the eventual form of the actual minstrel show, the performance in December, 1842, of Dan Emmett and his group of four. They were the first to attempt a full evening's entertainment of singing and dancing in blackface.

The first meetings of this group were very informal. Frank Bower, Billy Whitlock, and Dick Pelham, all close friends of Dan Emmett, were accustomed to gather several evenings a week in Dan Emmet's boardinghouse room to amuse themselves with singing and dancing to the accompaniment of the banjo, the tambourine, and the bones. Like many such amateur groups in the history of the theatre, they eventually felt compelled to seek an audience. For their first public showing they rounded up a number of their friends who were willing to contribute toward a benefit for Dick Pelham and offered for the first time a regular minstrel-type show in which they played and danced the "Essence of Old Virginny." Pleased with their success, they ventured a regular professional opening at the Bowery Amphitheatre on February 6, 1843,[11] under the name, Virginia Minstrels. Of this performance the *New York Herald* said ". . . an exclusively minstrel entertainment combining the banjo, violin, bone castanets, and tambourine, and entirely exempt from the vulgarities or other objectionable features which have hitherto characterized Negro extravaganzas." [12] After this performance at the Bowery, they appeared at the Park at Welch's Olympic Circus, and then ventured out into the provinces for a brief road tour, stopping for a successful showing in Boston sometime in March of 1843.

As in the history of most theatrical enterprises there were several companies claiming first honors. The Christy troupe, for example, always billed themselves as "founded in 1842"; but this seems to have been rather a typical publicity attempt to antedate the first performance of Dan Emmett and his group than a record of fact. The group assembled by E. P. Christy, however, was one of the most important to the development of the regular minstrel show. Christy established the routine that was for so many years the accepted pattern for all minstrel performances. Probably for this reason the name Christy became almost a synonym for minstrel. In England and on the Continent "Christy" was used as the generic term to describe all Negro minstrels.

E. P. Christy's first appearance (1846) at the Hall of the Mechanics' Society, 472 Broadway, was the first performance at which the regular semicircular line-up was used, a formation that was to become an integral part of the minstrel tradition. This performance established also the custom of placing a man with a tambourine at one end of the line-up and at the other a man with a pair of bones. This pair, the end-men, became known as Tambo and Bones. For many years one Tambo and one Bones was the rule, but in some of the more elaborate performances of the sixties and seventies there were as many as four at each end of the line. As the number of end-men increased, the entire troupe was, of course, enlarged; but in this early group there were only some fifteen to twenty men in the entire line-up. Christy was also the first to give the Interlocutor his central position and to institute the regular pattern of the performance, in which the First Part was devoted to music and to jokes between the end-men and the Interlocutor. In these early performances, however, the Interlocutor had not yet achieved his elegant title; he was known simply as the "middle-man." The First Part of the show ended with a song by the whole company. They sang two choruses, the second one being sung in a very soft and lugubrious manner, and concluded with a "walk-around" by the entire company.[13] This "walk-around," a characteristic feature of all minstrel performances, was executed in the following manner. The whole company stood in a semicircle, and, one at a time, each member of the company "walked around" the inside of the circle several times and then finished by doing his particular specialty in the center of the stage. In general it was very similar to the "finale" associated with vaudeville in the twentieth century and with present-day revue productions.

The Second Part of these early performances was known as the Olio and consisted of specialties: a performer going through the routine of removing innumerable coats and vests or another member of the company whistling Paganini's "Variations on the Carnival of Venice" on a penny tin whistle. The acts of the Second Part were very similar to the regular vaudeville bill of twenty years ago. Many of these specialties, such as the "Jim Crow" dance and Jack Diamond's "break-downs," antedated the minstrel show proper. The "wench character," acted by the female impersonator of the troupe and later established as one of the feature attractions of every minstrel show Olio, was first put on the stage by Dan Gardner in 1835. Gardner was also the first to do the "Lucy Long" routine[14] (a female impersonation in song). The "Juba" dance, well known to latter-day minstrel audiences, was first instituted by Master Juba (William H. Lane) in 1843.

Although probably not originated by Christy, another feature of the early minstrel shows was the street parade, an innovation no doubt borrowed from the circus. Every troupe exhibited either a "silver cornet band" or a "gold cornet band," gorgeously attired in colorful coats and trousers, brass buttons, and striking hats. The band marched in "twos" or "fours," depending on the size of the entire company, from the train to the hotel by the longest possible route. Many a small boy's and young lady's heart beat faster at this first sight of the minstrel troupe coming into town.

As in the case of any type of theatrical performance repeated over and over by different companies and under various circumstances, a traditional and stereotyped minstrel show form was bound to develop. It is impossible to date the development exactly, but it is safe to say that it happened in the late forties or early fifties and that the pattern was first evident in the performances of the Christy troupe.

As the pattern was finally established, the entire company marched on the stage and arranged themselves in the familiar semicircle. The Interlocutor started the performance with the usual phrase: "Gentlemen, be seated. We will commence with the overture." After the overture there was a series of questionings between the end-men and the Interlocutor in which the Interlocutor was always made to suffer at the expense of either Tambo or Bones. The Interlocutor of the minstrel show was really the father of the foil or straight-man of vaudeville and of comedy shows on radio and television. After the first exchanges between the Interlocutor and the end-men, either Tambo or Bones would sing a comic song. The Interlocutor, in his most pompous manner and employing his typically grandiloquent phrases, introduced all of these various numbers. After the comic song there were a series of sentimental ballads sung by the "silver-throated" vocalists and a final song and "walk-around" by the company. This was the First Part.

The Second Part remained much the same as it had been in the performances of Christy's group: special songs, what we term today "vaudeville gags," "wench" numbers, "break-downs," etc. Added to this as a third part, although always identified as a division of the Second Part, was a burlesque of some popular serious drama. This little play "enlisted the whole strength of the company."

Even though this routine, First Part (repartee and song)— Second Part (Olio and Burlesque), became the established form, minstrel actors never felt restricted by this pattern; individual performers were allowed to expand to the extent of their peculiar talents. Even the burlesque plays that were written out in a fairly complete form did not restrain the actors from inserting such remarks of their own as they thought appropriate to the time and occasion. The script was little more than a kind of *commedia dell'arte* scenario; and Jennings was probably not exaggerating in saying that, "A minstrel having a speech of a dozen lines will make it twenty-five times and never make it twice alike." [15]

As the form of the minstrel show became standardized in its two parts, the settings also took on a uniform representation. They illustrated Negro cabins by a cotton patch, a levee piled high with cotton bales, a scene showing boats on a river, or a scene of some particular locale of the South. Not until the later days of the "Gigantic" and "Mastodonic" shows were purely decorative stagings employed.

But the music of the minstrel show, more than the settings, comic repartee, or jig dances, holds the interest of present-day students. The minstrels originated with the comic song sung in blackface, and those who can still recall the days of the old-time minstrel show cherish the many songs that Negro minstrelsy contributed to the album of American folk music. Stephen Foster, America's most distinguished troubadour, wrote a large share of his songs expressly for minstrel performances. Dan Emmett, who has already been noted as one of the founders of Negro minstrelsy, is remembered for many songs that are still popular: "Old Dan Tucker," "Walk Along John,"

"Boatman's Dance," "Early in the Morning," and above all "Dixie," which has probably been sung more widely than any other American song.

Southerners would like to believe that "Dixie" was composed as a patriotic song for the South; but, disillusioning as the fact may be, it was originally composed because Emmett was called upon to furnish Bryant's Minstrels with a snappy "walk-around" with which to finish off their performance. Since the performance at which they expected to use the song had been already announced, Emmett had but two days to write a "snappy tune." "Dixie" was the result. First sung at Merchants' Hall on lower Broadway, September 12, 1859, it was introduced at a burlesque show in New Orleans just before the Civil War, and from this performance it caught on and became the stirring war song of the South.[16] To estimate how many thousands of people at some time or other have thrilled to the singing of "Dixie" would be impossible. In 1860, when Lincoln heard it for the first time at a Minstrel performance in Chicago, he leaned over his box and shouted, "Let's have it again! Let's have it again." [17]

But "Dixie" was not the only favorite that was first sung by some "silver-throated" tenor from the burnt-cork line; "Old Folks at Home," "My Old Kentucky Home," "Tramp, Tramp, Tramp, the Boys Are Marching," and "Marching Through Georgia," to mention but a few, were all originally minstrel tunes.

Although the melodist of minstrel days made a more lasting impression than any of the jokesters, comic dancers, or writers of burlesque, the true comic spirit of Negro minstrelsy is more clearly revealed in the burlesque, introduced as the final number on the minstrel program, than in any other facet of the minstrel's art. It is not only the case that more of the actual working scripts of these burlesques are available today but that in these peculiar exhibitions the blackface performers stretched the theatrical possibilities of their medium to the limit. These undisciplined exaggerations of reality reveal the inherent romantic temper of the entire minstrel performance more clearly than do any of the musical or specialty numbers. White men smeared with burnt cork, their heads covered with wigs of tight curly black hair, and pretending to exhibit the refined manners of Counts, Kings, and Princes—this was at once the romance and the true comic spirit of the minstrel's art.

These "Afterpieces," as they were sometimes called, were not always cast in play form. Sometimes they were stump speeches, burlesques of current oratorical endeavors;[18] such performers as Hughey Dougherty and Billy Rice gained their minstrel fame as stump speakers. These speeches were not composed in any strict rhetorical form, but were, for the most part, merely extended recitals of jokes similar to those of the First Part between the Interlocutor and the end-men.

Sometimes the burlesques were monologues exhibiting the special talents of particular performers. For example, the burlesque of Sarah Bernhardt by "Daddy" Rice and called "Sarah Hartburn" once received the attention of the great Sarah herself. She was delighted at the mimicry of her theatrical mannerisms.

The great majority of these "Afterpieces," however, were burlesques of the popular plays of the day. *Pierre Pathelin* became *The Great Mutton Trail*; *Romeo and Juliet*, *Roman Nose and Suet*; *Othello, Old Fellow; or, The Boor of Vengeance*; *Macbeth, Bad Breath, the Crane of Chowder*; *Camille, Clameel; or, the Feet of a Go-Getter*; *Robert Macaire, Robert Make-Airs; or, the Two Fugitives*.

Even though the minstrel actor followed the skeleton of a popular play, he belonged to that tribe of theatrical performers who were neither impressed nor constrained by a printed text.

In some few instances the minstrels attempted regular full-length plays. *Uncle Tom's Cabin* was one of these, and throughout its long theatrical life the play remained pretty closely associated with Negro minstrelsy. During the first run of the play at Purdy's National Theatre, beginning on August 23, 1852, and continuing for two weeks, T. D. Rice was "engaged to support this pathetic tale of Negro life, with various of his

Ethiopian specialties." One of the longest runs in the history of *Uncle Tom's Cabin* was that of the hundred performances given by the Fox Brothers Minstrels at Troy, New York, in 1853. The history of minstrelsy from the days of Emmett's Virginia Minstrels to the "gigantic" and "mammoth" troupes of the eighties and nineties was filled with similar record-breaking phenomena.

Although a second company, known as the Kitchen Minstrels, was founded by Charley White shortly after the first performance of Emmett's group, in 1843, it was not until 1846, when the Christy Minstrels performed in New York with much success, that the commercial possibilities of minstrel shows were fully realized. George Christy's salary for two and a half years was reported to have reached the astonishing figure of $19,-168.00. During the first year of the company's run in New York a profit of only $300.00 was netted, but during a span of 2,792 performances the receipts mounted to $317,589.30, with profits of over $160,000 for the producers. These figures are even more startling in view of the prevailing admission price, which was twenty-five cents.

After the Christys, the Campbell Minstrels became the leading troupe. They were so popular by the end of the fifties that the country was swarming with companies that called themselves by that name. Often two groups of Campbell's Minstrels would appear in one town at the same time to the great confusion of the public and the respective press representatives.

Rivalling the Campbells was a group organized by Bryant in 1857 that played continuously until June 2, 1866. For the next two years, having no permanent home, they performed in various theatres around New York, and for a brief time in San Francisco. In 1868 they moved into their own house, the famous Bryant's Minstrel Hall in New York, where they continued playing for another seven years. Their total run, counting the period from 1866 to 1868, was eighteen years. Such an engagement is difficult to duplicate anywhere in theatrical history. Nevertheless, although their success was more startling than that of some of the other groups, minstrelsy was flourishing throughout the country in the closing years of the fifties. On April 23, 1859, the *New York Clipper* listed, in the order of their origin, the eleven leading companies then in operation:

1. Sanford's Opera Troupe—Philadelphia.
2. Ordway's Aeolians—Boston.
3. Woods' Minstrels—New York.
4. Campbell's Minstrels (Mat Peel, Manager).
5. Christy Minstrels (in Paris), part of the original company.
6. Campbell's Minstrels (Rumsey and Newcombe, Managers).
7. San Francisco Minstrels (California).
8. Buckley's Serenaders (a Travelling Company).
9. Bryant's Minstrels—New York.
10. George Christy and Hooley's Minstrels (Travelling).
11. Morris, Pell and Trowbridge's Minstrels—Boston.

If minstrelsy owed its inspiration to Negro singing and dancing, it repaid part of that debt by providing a profitable occupation for the members of the first successful all-Negro company, the Georgia Minstrels. Organized in 1865 by Charles Hicks, they were later taken over by Charles Callender and in 1882 went under the management of Daniel Frohman.

Although possessed of genuine dark skins, these Georgia Minstrels employed the same curly-haired wigs and burnt-cork make-up. Not until considerably later did any Negro performers in minstrel shows try to capitalize on their natural color. Sam Jack's Creole troupe that played the Chicago Fair in 1893 and later came to New York for six seasons was one of the first of these. They were also among the first to introduce girls to the minstrel stage, advertising "16 beautiful colored girls" as their chief attraction. In 1895 another all-Negro company, calling themselves "The Octoroons," and in 1896 still another, billed as "Oriental America," appeared without the conventional minstrel make-up.

Just as there were many permanent companies (the Campbell, Christy, and Georgia, for example), there were during the heyday of minstrelsy many theatre buildings devoted exclusively to the presentation of the burnt-cork extravaganzas. Bryant's Minstrel Hall has already been mentioned. Another famous old-time minstrel house was Wood's Minstrel Hall at 514 Broadway (near Broome Street), used principally by Wood and Fellowes' Minstrels. This group made their first showing in New York in 1851 at 444 Broadway and sometime after 1858 moved into their own hall, where they flourished until 1866.

One of the last permanent homes for minstrelsy was that established by Lew Dockstader in 1886. He held forth at his theatre on Broadway for three years; but by this time variety (vaudeville) and musical comedy were beginning to appear, and it became exceedingly difficult for a minstrel show to compete with the beauty and charm of Lillian Russell or the singing ability of Della Fox.

New York was not, however, the only city boasting minstrel theatres. In Philadelphia the first theatre for minstrelsy was built by Sam S. Sanford, in August, 1853. It was destroyed by fire, and in April, 1855, Sanford's Minstrels opened at the Eleventh Street Opera House, where they continued until the spring of 1862. Sanford is remembered principally as the performer who introduced "Carry Me Back to Old Virginny."

In San Francisco, Tom Maguire was the minstrel impresario. In 1850 he built the Jenny Lind Theatre and in 1858 brought George Christy and his company to California; but Californians of the seventies would remember him as the sponsor for Billy Emerson. Emerson became so unquestionably the leading minstrel performer of the Far West that to San Franciscans of the seventies and eighties, a minstrel show without Billy Emerson would have been like *Hamlet* without the Danish Prince.

Brooklyn and Chicago each had its own troupe. In Brooklyn it was Hooley's Minstrels; and in Chicago, J. H. ("Col. Jack") Haverly's Mastodon Minstrels. Throughout the last half of the century Boston was an important minstrel center. The Diamond Minstrels, the Ethiopian Minstrels, and the Sable Harmonists all made their debuts in Boston; and during the fifties and sixties Boston was known as the minstrel's rendezvous. Hartford supported its own local troupe in addition to patronizing the numerous appearances of Buckley's Serenaders and Matt Peel's Campbell Minstrels. In Cincinnati the finest hall,

Pike's Opera House, became the favorite theatre of all the travelling minstrel companies.

With the completion of the first transcontinental railroad in 1869, minstrelsy began to invade the Western towns. In the summer of 1869, Murphy and Mack's Minstrels delighted large audiences for ten days in the famous Salt Lake Theatre of the Mormons. But of all the road companies that toured the country during the last three decades of the century, the most famous were those of Al G. Fields. Fields, a shrewd businessman known as the "Millionaire Minstrel," was the first manager to carry entire stage settings and scenery and the first to build and operate a special train for his troupe. During this period all the companies were enlarged with more performers and were equipped with more elaborate scenery. Two of the largest were the San Francisco Minstrels and Haverly's Mastodon Minstrels. The San Francisco group, famous for its four chief performers, Birch, Bernard, Wambold, and Backus, did not limit its exhibitions to the West coast but played in New York, Australia, and New Zealand. The reputation of this group rested to some extent on the attempt of the performers to make minstrelsy more refined and more closely dependent on genuine plantation models. Haverly's Mastodon Minstrels became identified by the symbol of the big bass drum and the famous legend, "40—Count 'em—40!!!" By 1880, however, Haverly was not satisfied with any mere forty; he travelled with a company of over a hundred performers and with carloads of elaborate stage settings.

Nor were this craze for size and the accompanying demand for extravagant adjectives (anticipating the current practice in publicizing moving pictures) with which to proclaim these attractions limited to Haverly's Mastodons. There were Duprez and Benedict's New Gigantic Minstrels, and Primrose and West's Mammouth Minstrels. Carncross insisted that his company was the Star Troupe of the World, and Hi Henry advertised his as the Superb Operatic Minstrels.

But in spite of their extravaganza proportions, these companies represented the decline of minstrelsy. Our ancestors who really saw the blackface art in its heyday were those who lived through the Civil War era, for from 1850 to 1870 Negro minstrelsy was at its height. During the fifties there were ten theatres in New York City alone devoting themselves almost entirely to minstrel performances, whereas at the beginning of the seventies this number had been reduced to four. Of the hundreds of companies playing throughout the country in the fifties and sixties, there were only thirty still operating in 1880. In 1896 the number had been reduced to ten, and in April, 1919, there were only three.

The decrease in the number of minstrel troupes was due largely to the craze for increase in size. "Bigger and better" was not compatible with the minstrel type of entertainment. When it was enlarged, it tended to become a burlesque or variety bill. For example, the Billy Sweatman, Billy Rice, and Barney Fagan troupe on its tours during the late 1880's carried a company of one hundred and ten members, two bands of fourteen musicians each, a sextet of saxophone players, two drum corps of eight each, two drum majors, and a quartet of mounted buglers. Another troupe of this variety, Gorman's Spectacular Minstrels, playing at the Chicago Opera House in 1887, featured "The Siamese Twins! The Hindoo Ballet Dancers! The Trick Elephants! The Chinese Giants! and the Headless Man!" [19]

These extravagant notions were not solely responsible for the decline of minstrelsy. Several economic factors contributed to the deterioration of the minstrel's popularity. A sharp drop in the number of troupes occurred during the panic of 1873, when eighteen out of the thirty-nine companies on the road failed. But more important was the change in financial structure demanded by the new managers' proclivities for "gigantic and mammouth" shows. Although salaries and the cost of stage settings and advertising had increased, it seemed impossible to raise the admission price from the customary twenty-five cents and still retain an audience. As a result, the minstrel show became a financially unprofitable enterprise. In 1860 one could launch a first-class minstrel company with a weekly salary budget of four hundred and fifty dollars, in the eighties and nineties this had increased to fifteen hundred dollars plus hotel expenses, and in the first decade of this century the costs had risen to about twenty-five hundred dollars. Not only were the performers' salaries increased but stage hands who had formerly been pleased with twenty-five dollars a week were now demanding seventy-five; and the unions were requiring the companies to use three or four stage hands for the job that had formerly been handled by one. Under this economic stress a collapse was inevitable. From the very beginning most minstrel performers had entered the field because of the easy money to be made, and when that attraction disappeared, they saw no reason to continue.

During the years of the rise and decline of the minstrel companies their successes were due chiefly to the popularity of individual performers. Any survey of Negro minstrelsy, however brief, would be incomplete without discussion of the most prominent performers.

Dan Emmett, the first in the long line of regular minstrel performers, composed one of his best known songs, "Old Dan Tucker," before he was sixteen. He organized the Virginia Minstrels and, after they disbanded in Europe, joined Bryant's Minstrels in New York. It was while he was employed by them that he composed "Dixie." In 1870 Al G. Fields brought him back from retirement to tour as the "father of American minstrelsy" and to sing his famous composition, "Dixie." His last appearance was in an amateur minstrel performance for the Elks in Mt. Vernon, Ohio, in 1902. He died on June 28, 1904.

The other members of Emmett's original company were not so well known. Billy Whitlock, distinguished principally for his "Lucy Long," appeared for a time (after his minstrel experience with Emmett) with Barnum's Circus. Dick Pelham and Frank Bower were mainly song-and-dance men. Bower, after concluding his engagement with Emmett, went to England as a circus clown and after his retirement became a saloon-keeper in Philadelphia.

Edwin P. Christy, organizer of the first Christy Minstrels, was at various times an office boy, hotel clerk, and travelling shoe salesman. He organized his first minstrel company in Buffalo and in 1846 brought them to New York. Within twelve years he had accumulated enough money to be in a position to retire in comfort. As already noted, his financial success was largely responsible for the succeeding influx of performers into the field of minstrelsy.

George N. Christy, originally named Harrington, assumed his stage name after appearing as a jig dancer in the Christy Show. He was famous as a female impersonator and as the first performer to introduce the "wench character."

Among the dancers Frank Lynch and Jack Diamond were the best known. Lynch was recognized as the "best representative of Ethiopian break-downs." As early as 1840, Diamond was appearing at Vauxhall for P. T. Barnum, although he achieved his main reputation later as the leading attraction in Barnum's touring shows. Diamond, like so many of these minstrels, was a victim of riotous living and died when he was thirty-four. Bryant's Minstrels donated the proceeds from one evening's entertainment to provide an appropriate marker for Diamond's final resting place.[20]

Charley White, born in New York in 1821, founded the Kitchen Minstrels. He had his own minstrel theatre on the Bowery for many years; and though actually associated with the performances of his troupe, he was more famous for his burlesque adaptations. Just as there were two Christys in the minstrel field there were two Whites. Cool White, whose real name was John Hodges, became a favorite portrayer of the Negro dandy.

Tony Pastor, although better known as a circus performer, started originally as a boy singer at temperance meetings and in 1846 turned to minstrel singing with the troupe then operating at Barnum's Museum.

Dan Bryant, already mentioned in connection with Bryant's Minstrels, was originally Daniel Webster O'Brien. Though he started as a hotel baggage porter, he became one of the favorite dancers and managers of minstrelsy. As a performer he was known mainly for his dancing of "Shew Fly" and "The Essence of Old Virginny."

Ralph Keller, a dancer who devoted three years of his professional career to minstrel road shows, recorded one of the most illuminating accounts of the day-to-day life of the average minstrel performer. Keller started as a dancer of the "Juba" and the "Lucy Long" at five dollars a week. He later joined the Metropolitan Serenaders and in turn played with the Booker Troupe, The Mitchells, and, for a short time, on the Floating Palace show boat. Comments in his journalistic record of life with the minstrels indicated that the minstrel actor possessed many of the characteristics ordinarily associated with the old-time vaudeville actor. "He [the minstrel actor] always talks in hyperbole, uses adjectives for adverbs, and arranges all the minor incidents of his life, as well as his conversation, in the most dramatic form." [21]

Birch, Backus, Bernard, and Wambold were the stars of the San Francisco Minstrels. The comedy patter between William Birch and Charles Backus, the Tambo and Bones of the San Francisco troupe, was probably the best ever heard on the minstrel stage. William Bernard, the Interlocutor for this company, received his early training as a lawyer. David Wambold, the balladist, started as a butcher but deserted his first calling and became a famous blackface singer. During his career he probably toured more extensively than any other minstrel performer. He played in England, France, Prussia, Austria, Italy, and Hungary.

Billy Emerson, the favorite West-Coast minstrel of the seventies and eighties, was an all-round performer, but he was recognized mainly for his singing of such songs as "The Big Sunflower," "Love Among the Roses," and "The Yaller Gal that Looked at Me."

R. M. Hooley, who was long associated with minstrelsy in Brooklyn, came to this country from Ireland and began his career with Christy's Minstrels. In 1860 he organized the Hooley and Campbell troupe and during many years with the

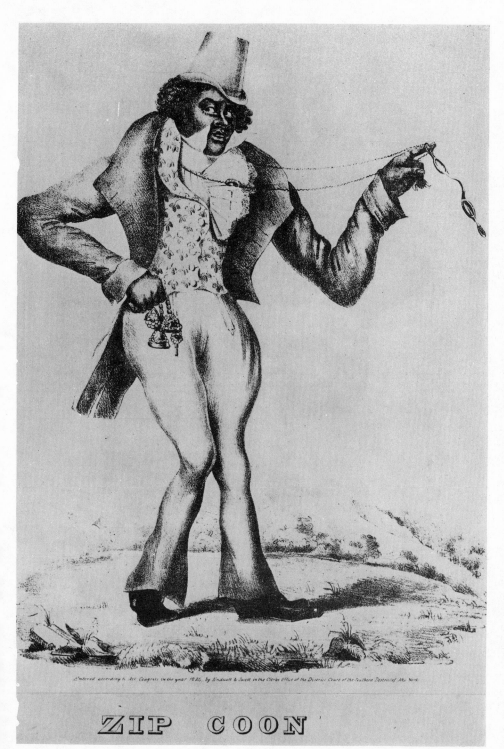

ZIP COON

Plate 1

JIMMY CROW.

Plate 2

JIM CROW.

A
Celebrated COMIC SONG or Ballad,
AS SUNG BY
all the
COMIC SINGERS,
Composed and Arranged
for the
PIANO FORTE.

VOCE

Allegretto

Come listen all you galls and boys, I'm just from Tuckyhoe; I'm goin to sing a

leetle song, My name's Jim Crow. Weel about, and turn about, And do jis so;

Eb'ry time I weel about, I jump Jim Crow.

Plate 3

Plate 4

THE DANDY BLACK BRIGADE

March Song and Chorus

Words and Music by
JAMES A. BLAND
arr. by Charles Haywood

1. We are the Dandy Black Brigade, You've heard so much about,___ We cause such great ex-cite-ment, In the town when we___ turn out;___ Our march-ing is per-fec-tion, that's just what we're taught to do;___ The peo-ple get be-wil-der'd, at the move-ments we___ go through.___ Our mus-kets are the fin-est make, in fact they can't be beat;___ The la-dies wave their hand-ker-chiefs, as we march down the street; The

2. Our u-ni-forms are ver-y rich, How love-ly they do look,___ While drill-ing with the Skid-more Guards, the gold-en prize we took;___ Our guns they out shine dia-monds, and our col-lars white as snow;___ We break the col-or'd la-dies' hearts, as down the street we go.___ We march with such pre-cis-ion you would think it was one man;___ Our no-ble Col-nel Gor-ham he is al-ways in com-mand; He

3. Our balls are held at Tam-'ny Hall, Such crowds are al-ways there,___ The fin-est of the fin-est, And the fair-est of___ the fair;___ The mu-sic of the or-ches-tra is so su-perb and grand;___ You bet we have no e-quals we're the fin-est in___ the land.___ And when the prom-e-nade be-gins, oh, what a love-ly sight;___ To see them glid-ing 'round the room, it fills us with de-light; We

Plate 5

ShewFly!

SHOO FLY!

Waltz 30.
Polka 30.
SONG 35.

Polka Redowa 30.
GALOP 30.
QUADRILLE 40.

ARRANGED BY

ROLLIN HOWARD.

BOSTON:

Published by White, Smith & Perry, 298 & 300 Washington St.

Philadelphia, Pa.:
J. E. WINNER.

New York:
J. L. PETERS.

Cincinnati, Ohio:
JOHN CHURCH & CO.

Entered according to Act of Congress, in the year 1869, by WHITE, SMITH & PERRY, in the Clerk's Office of the District Court for the District of Massachusetts.
MUSIC TYPOGRAPHY BY J. FRANK GILES, 89 WASHINGTON STREET, BOSTON.

Plate 6

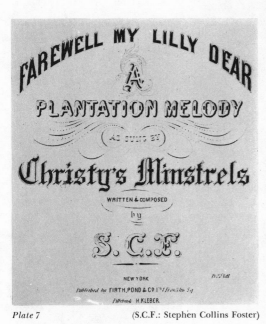

Plate 7   (S.C.F.: Stephen Collins Foster)

Plate 8

JOHN BROUGHAM AS METAMORA

Plate 9

JOHN EDMOND OWENS AS SOLON SHINGLE

Plate 10

burnt-cork art was responsible for the building of several minstrel theatres.

Colonel Jack Haverly is remembered first of all as the man who really started the large-scale shows of the seventies and eighties. After giving up his early occupation as a "baggage smasher," he became first the owner of a small variety theatre in Toledo and then owner and manager of the "40—Count 'Em—40!!!" Haverly's Mastodon Minstrels. With this company he made and lost several fortunes.

Among the famous performers associated with these latter-day extravaganzas were George Evans, George H. Primrose, Lew Dockstader, and Al G. Fields.

George Evans, known as "Honey Boy" Evans for his singing of the popular favorite, "I'll Be True to My Honey Boy," made his first apperance with a quartette in Canton, Ohio, in 1891. After several months of touring with a medicine show, he joined Haverly's Minstrels in Chicago in 1892. Concluding that engagement he appeared for several years with Primrose and West's company.

George Primrose, one of the few well-known minstrel performers who were still playing in the twentieth century, was born in London, Canada, and began his stage career as a juvenile clog-dancer in 1867. He achieved a reputation as one of the greatest soft-shoe dancers of all time; and after appearing for several years with various minstrel and circus troupes, he formed a partnership with William West to organize their own company.

Lew Dockstader concocted one of the most elaborate and topical of the large-scale minstrel productions. He employed leg-men to keep him informed of the local gossip in every town he visited, so that his programs were always alive with topical allusions. One of his most popular exhibitions was his take-off on President Roosevelt, and when Henry Irving was playing *Faust* in New York, Dockstader gave his version, the *Black Faust*.

Dockstader was born in Hartford, Connecticut, in 1856 and

christened George Alfred Clapp. He started his professional
career in Springfield, Massachusetts, as a member of Harry
Bloodgood's Comic Alliance troupe. In 1878 he formed his
partnership with Charles Dockstader—it was then that Clapp
adopted his pseudonym—and the team became known as the
Dockstader Brothers.

Al G. Fields, sometimes called the "Dean of American Minstrelsy," was the last of the large-scale producers. Not until
seven years after his death, in 1921, did the show bearing his
name play its last performance. For forty years his companies
toured the country playing regularly forty-six weeks every year.
During most of these years Fields took an active part in all the
performances either as a monologist or as a foil for the premier
comedian.

There was no definite break between the final spurts of the
minstrel type of performance of Dockstader and Fields and the
new forms, variety, musical comedy, and "burleycue." In fact
many of the players of the new variety theatre achieved their
first reputations in minstrelsy. Many performers on the legitimate stage began their theatrical days as minstrel men, and
even a prize fighter, "Gentleman Jim" Corbett, came from the
blackface ranks. Joseph Jefferson, Edwin Forrest, P. T. Barnum,
Nat Goodwin, Edwin Booth, Denman Thompson, Fred Stone,
Chauncey Olcott, Weber and Fields, Al Jolson, and Eddie
Cantor were all at some time or other associated with the burnt-
cork art.

In its early as well as its later years, with which most of these
names are connected, Negro minstrelsy was above all an entertainment of and for the theatre, presentational in every respect.
The pattern and style of the show grew out of the many specialty numbers of the 1830's combined with the romantic inventions of Dan Emmett and E. P. Christy. At times there may
have been some efforts to draw upon the characteristics of the
plantation Negro, but there was never any genuine attempt to
represent him realistically. The minstrel show resulted mainly
from the combined endeavors of a group of Northern whites
seeking a uniform pattern of entertainment that would be the-

atrically and economically successful. Whether or not it gave
an authentic picture of life on the Southern plantations was of
little concern to them. The minstrel performer never possessed
any representational consciousness, nor was he ever obsessed
with any foresighted attempt to gain the approval of posterity.
He was working in a medium acceptable to the audience of his
day and with songs, jokes, dances, and burlesques that secured
immediate favor.

The material of the show changed from place to place and
from year to year, but the pattern of performance and the general conception of the minstrel-type Negro remained constant
throughout the whole history of minstrelsy. These performers
respected the success of their predecessors and accepted the
blackface Negro of romantic invention without qualification.
If anything, the Negro character of the minstrel show became
farther removed from the Negro of real life as the number of
troupes increased.

Brander Matthews believed that this adoption of a synthet-
ically concocted Negro type was the real reason that the Negro
minstrel form failed to establish itself permanently. "It neglected its opportunity to devote itself primarily to its own peculiar field—the humorous reproduction of the sayings and
doings of the colored man in the United States." [22] This may
be true; but on the other hand, if the minstrel performers had
tried scrupulously to imitate the authentic plantation Negro,
the unique theatrical character of Negro minstrelsy could never
have been established. An attempt to represent the Negro realistically would have frustrated the free, expansive, and inven-
tive comic spirit of the typical blackface performer and denied
him the theatrical freedom that was necessary to his art.

Although Negro minstrelsy has been labelled a distinctively
American contribution in the history of the theatre, the form
exhibits a strong similarity to the Italian *commedia dell'arte*.
As in the *commedia* the special talents of the acting company
determined the nature of the performance. Any limitations
suggested by the script were followed only if compatible with
the creative desires of the particular players. The Negro min-

strel show never developed as many distinct comedy types in
the acting company as the *commedia,* but certainly Tambo and
Bones, the Interlocutor, and the "Wench" performer belong
to the same theatrical family as the *commedia's* Doctor, Captain, and Harlequin. Although the influence of the *commedia*
was never conscious or direct, there are many similarities between the *commedia* Doctor and the minstrel Interlocutor and
between the *commedia* Zannies and the end-men. Furthermore,
the specialty numbers of the Negro minstrel routine in a way
resembled the interpolated comic routines, the *lazzi,* of the
commedia; and like the *commedia* the minstrel show was always
dependent for its success on the talents of the performers, not
on any literary or formal value in the playscript.

The lack of literary value in the minstrel shows no doubt
contributed to their decline. The programs were limited, superficial, and monotonous, always following the routine instituted
by Christy in 1846. The all-male personnel of the company was
another factor contributing to the decline. During the last part
of the century female performers on the variety stage were exceedingly popular, and an entire evening of all-male entertainment featuring a repetition of outworn jokes* between the
end-men and the Interlocutor offered inadequate competition.
The continual recurrence of the same malapropisms, mispro-
nunciations, and conundrums must eventually have deprived
them of any comic value they may once have had.

But though all these factors, plus the economic instability
and the fatal tendency to develop what Quinn calls the "musical and picturesque extravagance," were operating toward the
eventual disintegration of the minstrel show, the reasons for its
great success for a period of fifty or sixty years are of more importance than an explanation of its decline.

---

* Familiar examples are the following:
    Q. When was the theatrical business first spoken of in the Bible?
    A. When Eve appeared for Adam's benefit.
    Q. What language does an Arabian child speak before it starts to cut its
    teeth?
    A. Gum Arabic.

The spontaneity of the performer's art, freedom from the restraint of realistic representation, and above all, the "silver-throated" ballad singer's intriguing melodies were the factors responsible for the hardy life of the minstrel show during the last half of the nineteenth century. Minstrel ballads were, of course, not always good. Sometimes they were, unintentionally, just as incongruous as the regular comedy routine of the show. One song writer, for example, described the St. Lawrence River as a Southern waterway in which his poor Negro was drowned during a violent snow storm; and another sang of the beautiful bananas growing wild in Tennessee.

The songs that really gave distinctive musical life to the minstrels created a romanticized picture of the Southern Negroes on the plantation. The best of these songs were by Stephen Foster. Foster was never thoroughly familiar with the locales about which he wrote his most famous songs, but he was able to endow them with a peculiarly romanticized Southern flavor that made them seem to be genuine.

Foster deserves much more attention in the history of Negro minstrelsy than is ordinarily given him, for he was largely responsible for raising the quality of the Negro minstrel performances with songs which possessed permanent value. From his early years Foster was associated with minstrelsy. As a child he contrived an amateur blackface entertainment in which he sang "Zip Coon," "Long-tailed Blue," "Coal Black Rose," and "Jim Crow." [23] All his early attempts at composition were first shown to "Daddy" Rice, who gave him encouragement and help. Foster never forgot Rice's assistance, and they remained close friends until Rice's death in 1860. Two of Foster's songs, "Long-Ago Day" and "This Rose Will Remind You," were written expressly for Rice. Neither of these songs was well known, for they were not published until 1931.

It is impossible to determine whether the minstrels owed more to Foster or Foster more to the minstrels. Foster contributed the best of the minstrel songs, but without the minstrel show he would not have had an opportunity to present his songs to so large an audience. The interdependence between

Foster and minstrelsy was indicated on the following title page
for one of the volumes of Foster music:

FOSTER'S
ETHIOPIAN MELODIES
as sung by the
Christy Minstrels
Written and Composed by
S. C. Foster

At one time during his career Foster evidently looked upon
the writing of minstrel tunes as a degrading occupation for a
professional song writer; for when "The Old Folks at Home"
was first published, he allowed it to be attributed to E. P.
Christy. From the correspondence relating to this transaction it
is difficult to tell whether Christy paid five hundred dollars or
ten dollars for the privilege, but, judging from Foster's other
financial transactions, the ten-dollar figure seems more likely.
In his letter of May 25, 1852, however, he seems to have
changed his mind about the minstrels.

E. P. Christy, Esq.
DEAR SIR:
As I once intimated to you, I had the intention of omitting my
name from my Ethiopian songs owing to the prejudice against them
by some which might injure my reputation as a writer of another
style of music, but I find that by my efforts I have done a great
deal to build up a taste for the Ethiopian songs among refined people by making the words suitable to their taste, instead of the trashy
and really offensive words which belong to some songs of that order.
Therefore I have concluded to reinstate my name on my songs and
to pursue the Ethiopian business without fear or shame and lend
all my energies to making the business live, at the same time that
I will wish to establish my name as the best Ethiopian song-writer.
. . . I find I cannot write at all unless I write for public approbation and get credit for what I write. . . .

Very respectfully yours,
STEPHEN C. FOSTER.[24]

After making this decision Foster devoted himself wholeheartedly to raising the quality of the minstrel songs and succeeded

in bringing "artistry and sincerity to a medium that before his entry had reeked of the alley and the barroom." [25]

In the history of theatrical affairs there are few forms of entertainment which have achieved a popularity comparable to that of the minstrels during the fifties and sixties of the last century. One writer on the state of the stage during that period summarized the situation in this fashion:

> The great and increasing popularity of Negro minstrelsy since its inauguration as a species of amusement, is a matter of serious concern to the purveyor of dramatic exhibitions in every town or city upon the vast continent of America. How frequently the most eminent in tragedy or comedy, have toiled through the choicest efforts, to scanty listeners; while upon the same evenings, fantazias upon the bones or banjo, has [sic] called forth the plaudits of admiring thousands.[26]

On Februrary 5, 1858, the *Evening Dispatch* of Augusta, Georgia, reported that a splendid company presenting *The School for Scandal* in that city had no audience "in consequence of the Campbell Minstrels." At about the same time the *New York Clipper* stated that the managers were "at a loss for novelties to buck against that improving institution, Negro minstrelsy." [27]

Nor was the popularity of the Negro minstrels limited to the lowbrow theatregoer as is sometimes suggested. Lincoln was a regular patron. Gladstone is said to have liked the sweet singing and the comedy of the end-men, and Thackeray bestowed on minstrelsy one of the highest tributes ever paid to it. Probably with a Stephen Foster melody still singing in his ears he wrote:

> I heard a humorous balladist, not long ago, a minstrel with wool on his head and an Ultra-Ethiopian complexion who performed a negro ballad that I confess moistened these spectacles in a most unexpected manner. I have gazed at thousands of tragedy-queens dying on the stage and expiring in appropriate blank verse, and I never wanted to wipe them. They have looked up, be it said, at many scores of clergymen without being dimmed and behold! a vagabond with a corked face and a banjo sings a little song, strikes a wild note, which sets the heart thrilling with happy pity.[28]

Although considerable space has been devoted to the factual history of the minstrel show, it must be recalled that the chief romantic aspects of Negro minstrelsy were to be found in the sentimentalism of the songs and in the distinctive, romantically evolved structure of the entertainment.

2. *The Negro*

EXCEPT in the minstrel show the Negro never became a figure of major importance in American drama. He had some high days in the ante-bellum abolitionists' plays such as *Uncle Tom's Cabin* and *Dred,* but this success was short-lived. In the half century before this peak, and in the half century after, his stage career was limited to performing the menial tasks of the trusted and faithful family servant and, in his execution of these tasks, to interjecting a bit of comedy relief into the play. Occasionally he was involved with the manipulation of the plot, but never as a principal character.

With a very large Negro population[1] in the Southern states and with the interest in his social welfare becoming more animated north of Mason and Dixon's line, it may seem surprising that the Negro figured so slightly in the history of American drama. The reason was that because of the strong prejudice against the Negro, he was not permitted a place on the stage in a role other than that permitted to him in real life. His position was that of a menial, and there he stayed until late in the nineteenth century. Even the abolitionists who were fighting for his freedom had no clear notion of effecting any radical change in his occupational position. They were fighting for his freedom from bondage, and for the time being that was as far as they wished to go.

If any dramatist had stopped to speculate on the heritage of the Negroes—their ancestors herded together in an African port, family ties broken, shipped in the hold of a tossing boat to a distant and unknown land, set to work in a strange plantation under such oppressive physical conditions that the only pleasantness in life left to them had to be sought in imagination—a stirring romantic drama might have been produced, with the Negro as the principal figure. Unfortunately even the presence in this country of the great Negro actor, Ira Aldridge, offered insufficient stimulation, and grand-scale romantic drama of the Negro was never written. Aldridge was obliged to go to the British Isles to achieve his reputation as the "African Roscius," and the American dramatist turned to Italy and Spain for his romantic themes.

Although American playwrights felt obliged to keep the presentation of the Negro within general occupational limits, the stage Negro was never a close copy of the real-life Negro servant. And though a Negro with any other social status was apparently inconceivable on the stage, the representation of his actual menial tasks never occupied the dramatist. The romantic conception approved by polite society was adopted on the stage: The servant performed the functions of his servitude without ostentation and without comment, and the audience saw only his glorified qualities of loyalty and faithfulness. No realistic investigation of the Negro and his problems concerned the nineteenth-century playwright. The old "darky" was a convenient stage-type embodying certain amusing characteristics that could be employed to inject a bit of comedy into the play. The realistic conception of a slave, working day after day in the fields, deprived of medical attention, scorned for any sentimental devotion to his own family, was completely overshadowed by the romantic stage-type Negro: placid, full of good humor, not easily brought to anger, loyal, faithful, honest, and with a great respect for and a great desire to emulate his master. Many of these qualities he shared with the minstrel Negro, but ordinarily he was less excitable and loquacious than his blackface brother.

That most of the dramatists of the last century were mainly concerned with using the romantic stage-type Negro for his colorful and sentimental values and not with attempting any realistic consideration of the Negro and his problems will become increasingly apparent as some of the plays employing Negro characters are examined.

Oroonoko, a play adapted by Thomas Southerne in 1696 from Mrs. Aphra Behn's novel was, of course, not an American play; but it was the first play that adopted the "noble savage" tradition for the stage Negro and thus is important to the present study as a standard for measuring later Negro plays. Oroonoko, the "royal slave," was of a genuinely heroic stature. Even his captors were fully aware that he was "a prince every inch of him." All of his actions were on a grand romantic level; his sentiments were of the noblest variety, and the major conflict of life for him, resolvable only in death, was that between love and honor. Setting the play in the West Indies colony, Surinam, provided a romantic distance that native playwrights were unable to achieve in treating the American Negro; for surely there was no Negro character in American dramatic literature who approached the romantic standard set by Oroonoko.

Some characteristics of this play were, however, extensively adopted for the American stage. One was the song and dance interpolation inserted in the second act. This began when Stan very abruptly announced: "Hark the slaves have done their work; And now begins their evening merriment" and was followed by an immediate scene change: "Scene III—The slaves, men, women, and children upon the ground; some rise and dance." As already noted, the earliest appearances in this country of the Negro stage character were with specialty songs and dances between the acts of a regular play.

Another similarity between *Oroonoko,* as it was received at the time of Bell's British Theatre edition of the play (1796), and some mid-nineteenth century American plays, was apparent in the preface to Bell's edition, which declared that the performances of *Oroonoko* should have dealt a "death blow to that most infernal of all commerce, the traffic of our Fellow Creatures. . . . Barren as the slave may be of all the trickeries upon which we value ourselves, and to our eye degraded by the unsightly opposition of his colour, he possesses feelings which it is tyranny to wound, and importance which it is treason to annihilate." [2]

Another English play, *The Padlock,* written in 1766 by Isaac

Bickerstaffe[3] and produced frequently in this country during the last few years of the eighteenth century and at the beginning of the nineteenth, had more direct influence than *Oroonoko* on the evolution of the American stage Negro. Mungo was essentially a comic-type Negro who, like the Negro of the minstrel show, frequently took over the stage for his own song-and-dance exhibitions. If Negro minstrelsy had not provided an extensive field for the singing Negro, American dramatists would no doubt have produced some comic operas similar to *The Padlock*.

The date of the first appearance of a Negro character on the American stage is somewhat difficult to establish, for there are varying opinions as to what constitutes a "first appearance." P. L. Ford insisted that the initial introduction of the Negro as a dramatic character in American drama was in the *Fall of British Tyranny* (1796), a play by John Leacock.[4] The Negro slaves in this play were kidnapped by Lord Dunmore. Since they were ignorant and credulous, they readily consented to kill their masters when they were promised release. None of them was very clearly defined, and the entire group were presented as savages with no redeeming nobility.

The appearance, in 1769, of Lewis Hallam as Mungo in *The Padlock* has already been noted (p. 34). In 1770 Colonel Robert Munford wrote a play, *The Candidates,* containing among the dramatis personae a Negro character, Ralpho; but this play was probably never produced.[5]

According to Quinn, the first actual Negro characters on the American stage were those in J. Robinson's *The Yorker's Stratagem; or, Banana's Wedding,* presented on May 10, 1792.[6] Again, however, the first-performance distinction is questionable, for these were not American but West Indian Negroes.

J. Murdock's *Triumphs of Love,* given at the Chestnut Street Theatre in Philadelphia on May 22, 1795, possessed a more justifiable claim. The part of Sambo, played by William Bates, the low comedian in the company, represented a real American Negro; and the play was performed and was definitely of native origin. Evidently pleased with his success in this first venture Murdock included four Negroes, Cato, Caesar, Sambo, and Pompey, in his next play, *The Politicians* (1798).

James Cobb's *Paul and Virginia,* another play of English origin presenting Negro characters, was extremely popular in this country during the early years of the century. Odell dated the first production May 7, 1802.[7] Dominique, Virginia's half-Negro servant, and Alambra, a slave, appeared as the conventionally loyal, humble, and devoted servants. Alambra's devotion was exhibited in an extraordinary fashion in the last scene, in which he swam through a violent sea to Virginia's capsized boat and rescued her. He was then given up as lost, but by some effort of superhuman strength he managed to swim ashore in time for the final tableau.

The major distinction of A. B. Lindsley's *Love and Friendship,*[8] produced at the Park in 1807, was the Yankee character, Jonathan; but the Negro characters, Harry and Phillis, exhibited some stage-Negro characteristics not yet observed. Harry was more completely described than Phillis, whose appearances were brief. Like Mungo, he enjoyed a bit of liquor but knew when to stop; and even while he drank he moralized on the evils of rum: "Heigho! what a wicked worl dis white man worl be for true do! no like de negur country; . . . no do sich ting dere? no had rum for git drunk and fight." [8] Harry was also the first stage-Negro to long for his native soil. He mourned over the evils of the new country, extolled the virtues of his native Africa, and throughout the play was homesick for the land where his mother died. This sentimental romantic quality that became so prevalent in the abolitionists' plays was here exhibited for the first time. In spite of his moralizing, however, Harry had his lighter moments that brought him in line with the typical stage-Negro.

In *Love and Friendship* the attempt to represent the Negro's speech realistically was a distinct innovation; but the curious mixture of Scandinavian, Italian, and stage-Indian that the author recorded could never have been made to sound like the speech of a genuine Negro.

L. Beach's *Jonathan Postfree; or, the Honest Yankee* (1807) was another Yankee play that employed a Negro character. Caesar was the conventionally loyal servant, but unlike his predecessors he provided a running commentary on the action of the play. In his opening speech, the first speech in the play, he explained all the background details of the story.

A dramatization of the Robinson Crusoe story was presented at the Park Theatre, September 11, 1817, with a Mr. Bancker in the part of Friday, played as a Negro. The play, *The Bold Buccaneers; or, The Discovery of Robinson Crusoe,* was evidently a popular melodrama of the time, but nothing more is known of it.

An anonymous and unproduced play, *The Young Carolinians* (1818), dealing with American captives in Algiers, employed a Negro servant, Cudjo. He had the conventionally loyal respect for his mistress and was thoroughly satisfied with his menial status:

I get plenty good ting for eat, and when I sick, ah! my deary misses give me too much nasty stuff for cure me—plenty sweet tea to wash em down;—bye and bye get well again, she look pon me with one kind eye, same like a dove—glad to see old Cudjo well. . . .[9]

Dated the 7th of June (the year is probably 1820), a curious playbill registered the performance of an "African Company" in New York at the "Theatre in Mercer Street, in the rear of the 1 Mile Stone, Broadway," and announced a program consisting of *Tom and Jerry; or, Life in London* and *Obi; or, Three Finger'd Jack.*[10] This very indefinite record was the only one describing the activities of the "African Company"; but since *Obi* was constantly in the repertoire of Ira Aldridge from 1825 to 1848, it is reasonable to assume that there was at least one excellent acting part for a Negro.

The Spy, "a Dramatic Romance in Three Acts," adapted by Charles Powell Clinch from Cooper's novel, was performed for the first time in New York on March 1, 1822, just ten weeks after the publication of the novel.[11] Though the play is mainly of interest for its treatment of a Revolutionary War theme, the

Negro character, Caesar, added some new qualities to the stage-Negro that identified him more closely with the minstrel character than any of the previous stage-Negroes had been. Caesar was the usual devoted servant, but he was more excitable and more easily impressed than some of his predecessors. For example, he was overcome with amazement at the speed of horses galloping; and when he was being questioned by the Judge, his answers sounded like those of a minstrel end-man answering the Interlocutor:

Judge. You know the prisoner?
Caesar. I think I ought.
Judge. Did he give you the wig when he threw it aside?
Caesar. I don't want 'em—got a berry good hair he'self.
Judge. Were you employed in carrying any letters or messages while Captain Wharton was in your master's house?
Caesar. I do what a tell me.
Judge. But what did they tell you?
Caesar. Sometime a one ting—sometime anoder.[12]

Charles Clinch's Negro character was not the first to be favored with such a noble name as Caesar, but he is the first for whom we have the complete record. Although the origin of this romantic practice of christening the Negro with such exalted names is impossible to discover, it must have been in common practice as early as 1788, when Samuel Low inserted the following comment on names into his play, *The Politician Outwitted:* Trueman had just compared the name of Washington to the illustrious names of Alexander the Great, Mark Antony, Kouli [*sic*] Khan, Caesar or Pompey when Humphrey replied: "Caesar and Pompey! Why them is niggers' names." [13]

John Bernard speculated that it might have "gratified the master's own sense of power by exercising mastership over such mighty names," [14] but it seems more reasonable that the burlesque possibilities of the Negro were in the mind of the wag who first named a Pompey or a Caesar. Certainly the incongruity between the Negro servant's humble operations and those of his illustrious namesake provided a good starting point for the romantic type of comedy assigned to the stage Negro.

Another Pompey appeared at the Coburg Theatre in London, December 26, 1829. This character was the invention of the English playwright Thomas Dibdin, writing on an American theme in a play called *The Banks of the Hudson*. The play is important to the present study for demonstrating the difference between English and American attitudes toward the Negro. No American playwright would have dared to present a scene showing the drunken and impertinent Pompey making love to the white girl, Abundance Allright.[15] Nor did any American playwright ever think it advisable to veer from the conventional stage-type to present a Negro as a deceitful villain. Many of the American stage-Negroes lied for comic effect, merely avoiding the truth, but Dibdin's Pompey lied in all seriousness and with fatal consequences to his master. The attitude of the American public even of that time determined what was acceptable in the stage-Negro, and the American playwrights followed their censorship by never allowing a Negro to appear as a villainous character.[16]

Job Jerryson, in William Dunlap's *A Trip to Niagara* (Bowery Theatre, November 28, 1828), was another Negro in the servant category. Jerryson was distinguished mainly for his continuous attempts to emulate the conduct of the white gentlemen and to insist on his rights as a freeman. However, although he explained to the hotel-keeper for whom he was working that the keeper was the manager and that he (Jerryson) was the waiter and that neither of them was master or slave, the issue of slavery did not really figure in the play. Job was very proud to be one of the "gentlemen and ladies of colour," as he was also proud of his thespian abilities. He and "the young coloured gentleman next door" operated a Shakespeare Club for which they brightened up their memories in the morning as they rubbed up the brass knobs and knockers on the street doors. Certainly here were exhibited some of the qualities that distinguished the proud and fancy end-man of the minstrel line-up. However, any interest that the characters of *A Trip to Niagara* may have had was completely overshadowed by the scenery. The play pretended to be nothing more than a scenic spectacle, and the limited attention given to Jerryson's sentiments on freedom from slavery does not warrant classing him as the first of the abolitionists' Negroes.

Cato, in Heath's *Whigs and Democrats* (1839), stood between Dunlap's Job and Mrs. Mowatt's Zeke (in *Fashion*). Cato was more exuberant in his admiration of the man of class than Job, but he did not have quite the fullhearted, unquestioning devotion to the mannerisms of the gentleman that Zeke had. He was, however, clearly a forerunner of Zeke in his attempts to imitate the gentlemen: "I always kept company, myself, with the first class—the servants of Congress-men and great folks."

Sambo in George Lionel Stevens' *The Patriot*, first produced in Boston around 1834, just two years after Rice first jumped "Jim Crow" in New York, demonstrated the influence that the "Jim Crow" dance had on the Negro character in legitimate drama. The Boston audience must have been acquainted with the "Jim Crow" routine, for the whole character of Sambo was built around his interpretation of this dance. On his first entrance: "(singing as he enters) Weel about—turn about—do just so, and eb'ry time weel about jump Sambo." [17] Sambo claimed he was descended from the Lee who had served General Washington, and evidently this heritage and its demands for honesty compelled Sambo to acknowledge his indebtedness to "Daddy" Rice.

Aside from his dancing, Sambo was cast in the pattern of the loyal and trusting servant. With the other characters of the play he expressed his genuine love of freedom, not freedom from slavery, but freedom for his country and his great admiration for Washington; and when he was commissioned by the master to take the bust of Washington out to have it dusted off for the Fourth of July celebration, he replied: "Yes Massa— de big Washington, me lub him massa! were he 'live, me would hug him massa, as him Sambo do—*dis!*" [18]

Of the general type of comic Negro servant who wholeheartedly assisted in fabricating an atmosphere of wealth and gentility around his master, Zeke in Anna Cora Mowatt's *Fash-*

ion[19] (Park Theatre, March 4, 1845), was the best example. He spared nothing, least of all the English language, in performing the functions of a servant to fashionable society. In fact his distortion of language rivalled that of Mrs. Malaprop. Further removed from the tradition of the noble savage than any other Negro character in nineteenth-century American drama, he was just as thoroughly duped by the superficial elegancies of Jolimaître ("Jolly-made-her," as Zeke called him) as was Mrs. Tiffany. To Zeke, Jolimaître was "de genuine article ob a gemman." This complete enslavement to the "gemman" who exhibited the gaudiest external trappings was probably, in a lesser degree than here exhibited, characteristic of some Negroes; but Zeke was willing to go the limit in achieving his proper place in this artificial society, even to the extent of sacrificing his identity by shelving his usual "Zeke" for the more fashionable "Adolph." When Gertrude addressed him as Adolph, he said: "Dat's right, Missey; I feels just now as if dat was my legitimate title; dis here's de stuff to make a nigger feel like a gemman!" [20]

Zeke approached his menial duties with none of the simple humility and devotion of the ordinary Negro servant type, and his manner was so assured and pretentious that the audience's amusement was unaffected by any feeling of sympathy. He was laughed at as an unreservedly and thoroughly ridiculous character.

In some respects Zeke was very similar to the boastful, hightalking Negro of the minstrel show. His continual references to "boss," and the cocksure attitude expressed in some of his speeches ("Yah! yah! yah! I hab de idea be de heel. Well, now p'raps you can 'lustrify my officials?" [21]) might well have been spoken by a minstrel end-man.

If the sentimental aspects of the Negro character were minimized in *Fashion,* in the next play to be considered they reached their fullest expression. Early in August, 1852, just five months after the appearance of the novel by Harriet Beecher Stowe, Taylor's dramatization of *Uncle Tom's Cabin* made its initial bow to the public at Purdy's National Theatre in New

York. This was the first time Negroes were presented as the central figures in an American drama and the first time an abolitionists' document reached the stage. The combination came as something of a bombshell. The critic of the *New York Herald* on September 3, 1852, had this to say about the play: "Here we have nightly represented, at a popular theatre, the most exaggerated enormities of Southern Slavery, playing directly into the hands of the abolitionists." [22] Another contemporary review was even more disapproving: "We would, from all these considerations, advise all concerned to drop the play of *Uncle Tom's Cabin* at once and forever. The thing is in bad taste—is not according to good faith to the constitution or consistent with either of the two Baltimore platforms; and is calculated, if persisted in, to become a firebrand of the most dangerous character to the peace of the whole country." [23] The New York weekly, *The Spirit of the Times,* on August 6, 1853, had, however, some few kind words for the play though even this paper could not extend full approbation: "We do not approve of the spirit of this piece, with all its crudities and absurdities, but what little there is to act is well performed. It is creditably put on the stage, and the little morality which here and there peeps out unexpectedly tells well with the audience." [24]

But whatever the contemporary reviewers may have thought of the play, it was unquestionably the most important abolitionist writing[25] of that time and the most important Negro play of the last century. For the first time the Negro was endowed with a life that spread beyond the humble household tasks of the ordinary slave. He was shown in the company of his own people not only in the day-to-day problems of slave-living but in soul-stirring struggles for freedom and relief from the oppressing strokes of the slave driver and the inhuman commerce of the slave dealer.

This attempted penetration into the whole life of the Negro slave might have produced a searching, realistic study had not the propaganda motive of the dramatist, or rather of the novelist, been the primary aim. As a result, even though the life of the Negro was expanded beyond its usual stage limits, he was built on the conventional sentimental pattern. If as a mere household servant he was humble, loyal, kind, and superstitious, here in his more extended sphere of activity he became completely enveloped by these virtues in a highly sentimentalized form. Nor were these qualities cultivated; they resulted from the natural and inevitable goodness of his character. He belonged unquestionably to the tradition of the noble savage, for whatever assistance or direction he demanded outside his natural sense of right and justice he sought in heaven. He trusted implicitly in the inscrutable ways of the Divine Being and believed that "when all things go wrong to us, we must believe that heaven is doing the very best." Learning that he was going to be thrown into the unmerciful hands of the slave dealer, Uncle Tom humbly submitted to the will of the Divine: "Him that saved Daniel in the den of lions—that saved the children in the firey furnace—Him that walked on the sea and bade the winds be still—He's alive yet! and I've faith to believe he can deliver me." [26] A realistic appraisal of his situation would have demanded that he take his chance to escape to freedom, but Uncle Tom was not a realist.

Romanticism was evident not only in the conception of the Negro character but in the handling of particular scenes. After being sold to Legree, Uncle Tom sat head down, gloomily fingering a lock of Little Eva's hair as the scene opened to the strains of "Old Folks at Home." As he meditated on his sad state, his sentiments were such as might have been lifted from an early nineteenth-century gothic romance: "I have come to de dark places; I's going through de vale of shadows. My heart sinks at times and feels just like a big lump of lead. Den it gits up in my throat and chokes me till de tears roll out of my eyes; den I take out dis curl of little Miss Eva's hair, and the sight of it brings calm to my mind and I feels strong again." [27] The romantic possibilities of a lock of hair were further utilized by Sambo when, after Tom had been severely beaten by Simon Legree, Sambo took the same lock of hair and dangled it before Simon's eyes. The villain was reminded of his cruel treatment of his mother, and the strand of hair turned into a snake that twisted around his fingers and burned him. The romantic atmosphere of such scenes as Eliza crossing the Ohio River on the ice floes, and George, Eliza, Harry, and Phineas, perched high on a craggy hill and shooting down the pursuers one by one as they approached, could have been fully appreciated only by the thousands who were stirred by these scenes during the last half of the past century. Few scenes of that day could approach the romantic sentimentality of the closing scene of the play: "Gorgeous cloud tinted with sunlight. Eva, robed in white is discovered on the back of a milk-white dove, with expanded wings, as if just soaring upward. Her hands are extended in benediction over St. Clare and Uncle Tom who are kneeling and gazing up to her. Expressive music. Slow curtain." [28]

But if Uncle Tom was "a conventional embodiment of patience and meekness rather than a highly individualized character," [29] Topsy was the most unconventional and individualized of all the Negro stage creations. Her naive charm fascinated even those observers who had most severely censored the rest of the play; and it is impossible to imagine an audience that would not be taken with her innocence when she explained to Ophelia that she had not stolen the ribbon, that it had merely gotten caught on her sleeve. And when she recounted her mischievous act of "scunching" ear-rings, and throwing "dirty water on 'em, dat spiles der complexions," and ending each explanation with, "I's so wicked," few ordinary theatre spectators would have hesitated to join with Little Eva in saying "Oh! Topsy, I love you!" If Zeke (in *Fashion*) and Topsy had somehow managed to get into the same play, and if Topsy's innocent pricks at insincerity and sham had been aimed at Zeke's social-climbing maneuvers, American drama might have possessed a truly great Negro comedy.

As the record stands, *Uncle Tom's Cabin* was one of the most important documents in American dramatic history. Although the first dramatization was made without the author's knowledge—she regarded the stage as a place of wickedness—the play has been credited in the final tabulation with as many as three hundred thousand performances, and Montrose Moses mentioned twelve different professional versions of the script.[30] The best-known versions were those by Taylor, Conway, and Aiken. The Taylor version was used for the first performance in New York in August, 1852; the Aiken adaptation, the one referred to in the present study, was used by the Howards at the Troy Museum on September 27, 1852, and the dramatization by Conway was put on the stage by P. T. Barnum at the Bowery on January 16, 1854. This performance, like the first one in New York, enlisted the talents of T. D. Rice for the part of Uncle Tom. Naturally, one can only speculate on how closely Uncle Tom resembled a minstrel character in these productions. With Rice so closely identified with his "Jim Crow" type of exhibition, it was likely that on these occasions there was more of Rice than of Uncle Tom in the part. Even after the abolitionist sentiments had performed their function, the play remained the most persistent attraction in the American theatre from 1852 through the first decade of the twentieth century. In 1902, for example, there were at least sixteen companies touring the country under canvas.[31] Villages and hamlets where a play had never been seen before saw *Uncle Tom's Cabin.*

Mrs. Bateman's *Self,* first produced in 1856, was distinguished for its introduction of a Negro stage-type that has carried down to the present day, the Negro mammy. Aunt Chloe was the first Negro in this tradition and the first to long for "ole Virginny."

The Negro porter in John Brougham's *Life in New York* (1856) was closely allied to the minstrel-type performer, as a small sample of the dialogue will indicate:

Cuff. Ha! Ha! luggage toted boss.
Greene. Toted, boss; what sort of language do you call that?
Cuff. Dat's American language, boss.
Greene. Dear me, I can understand some of it quite well. Just let that be, Mr. Boss, I can tote it myself. (*Writes.—"Language very much like English."*)
Cuff. Guess I'm an American, boss.

Greene. Good gracious! it's an Hindian with his war paint on. Is
    that paint on your face mister?
Cuff. You must be foolish. I guess; this natural color, boss, died in
    de wool.[32]

Cuff may well have been the prototype from whom contemporary railroad porters derived their professional manner.
Curiously enough, the name is used not only here but in a
number of other plays to identify a stage-Negro (see Chap
II, Sec. 1, n. 6).

Brougham was also partly responsible for the introduction
to the stage of the other significant abolitionist novel, Mrs.
Stowe's *Dred*. Two of the adapters of *Uncle Tom's Cabin*, H. J.
Conway and C. W. Taylor, also did adaptations of *Dred*. Taylor's version was the first to reach the stage and was performed
at the National Theatre in New York on September 22, 1856.
Brougham's version arrived at the Bowery on September 29,
and Conway's was performed at Barnum's Museum on October
26, 1856. Of these various dramatizations Taylor's was the most
successful.

The characters in *Dred; or, The Dismal Swamp* were very
similar to those in *Uncle Tom's Cabin*. Old Tif, like Uncle
Tom, had an unbounded faith in the ways of the Almighty.
Any evidences of misfortune were attributed to the temporary
wickedness of the world; eventually everything must turn out
for the best.

Tom Tit borrowed both from Topsy and from the minstrel
Negro. He had the unassumed innocence of Topsy combined
with just a twist of the minstrel's self-conscious awareness of
his own comic turns. Also reminiscent of the minstrel was Tom
Tit's custom of singing a few strains of a song at every entrance
and exit. The whole play demonstrated the growing popularity
of minstrelsy, and the compulsion playwrights felt to introduce
as much singing as possible. At the very opening of the play
the Negroes were grouped on the verandah singing "Pretty
Carolina Rose," and in the first scene of the fourth act the
"Magnolia Grove Troubadours" extolled the "sweet laughter"
of the "North Carolina Rose." Even the suggestions for the

costumes indicated the minstrel performer's type of dress: Old Hundred is to wear a white topcoat with large capes, large black hat, with gold band, white vest and "trowsers" and a large shirt frill; Old Tif a pair of grey "trowsers," profusely patched; and Dred a red flannel shirt with loose, striped pantaloons. Certainly these costumes were not intended to represent the realistic dress of the Negro.

With the introduction of these popular minstrel devices, it might seem that *Dred* should have been more popular than its predecessor, *Uncle Tom's Cabin,* but there were several factors that contributed to its failure. It repeated without variation many of the characters and scenes of the earlier play, the abolitionist sentiments were not as naturally vested in the plot, and the romantic and spectacular representations in *Uncle Tom's Cabin* were more closely connected with the sentimental life of the characters than similar scenes in *Dred.* The romantic outbursts on the glories of freedom must have pleased the abolitionists, but they materially weakened the play. Furthermore, though the theatregoers in the fifties readily accepted theatrical hokum, certain high-flown passages in *Dred* must have evoked unfortunate comparisons with the relative simplicity of *Uncle Tom's Cabin.* An example is the following pronouncement made by Dred: "Wake, O arm of the Lord— awake, put on thy strength—rend the heavens and come down, to avenge the innocent blood. Cast forth thine arrows, and slay them; shoot out thy lightnings, and destroy them utterly." followed immediately by: " (Flash of lightning strikes the tree; the foliage disappears, leaving the naked trunk blased.)" [33] It was apparently evident to the audiences of the day that *Dred* was distinctly an inferior theatrical product intended to profit by the success of *Uncle Tom's Cabin* and the publicity given the Dred-Scott decision.

About three years after *Dred,* on December 5, 1859, Dion Boucicault's *The Octoroon* had its first production, at the Winter Garden Theatre in New York. The main theme concerned the tragedy not of the Negro but of the white girl with slightly Negroid characteristics. Boucicault intensified the pa-

thos of the situation by making Zoe only an eighth Negro. In
Mayne Reid's novel *The Quadroon,* from which the play was
adapted,[34] Zoe had been one-fourth Negro. But even as an
octoroon she was still regarded as a black and as a slave when
the Peyton property was brought to sale at the auction block.

Although Zoe retained a noble and romantic spirit, she was
distinctly a new addition to the Negro stage-type. Not a servant,
she had much the same status in the household as the whites.
Like the typical Southern belle she was gentle, delicate, and
frail, and as Scud said of her: "When she goes along she just
leaves a streak of love behind her." [35] Although the tragedy of
the "one drop in eight that poisons all the blood" was definitely
an advance toward a realistic treatment of the Negro, the
beauty and charm of Zoe had the full flavor of romantic presentation.

In 1862 James McCabe's *The Guerillas* presented the first
view of the slave who, granted his freedom, was unwilling to
travel north "whar de Abulishuners live," a Negro type that
remained popular during the whole last half of the century.

Sam in Augustin Daly's *Under the Gaslight,* first given on
August 12, 1867, was, however, of the opposite view. He was
ready for suffrage when it was ready for him. Sam was an eclectic Negro stage character combining the qualities of the regular
servant and the minstrel performer with the linguistic proclivities of Zeke.

But most of the Negro stage characters of the last decades
of the century were of the type created by James McCabe.
Their sincere and unhesitating devotion to their masters would
not permit them to abandon the homes where they had served
for so many years. In fact the slaves in Herne's *The Reverend
Griffith Davenport* (1899) became incensed when Davenport
offered them their freedom. The social status of the free Negro,
deprived of all his family connections, offered no inducement
to them. There were, however, some later plays, of the type of
David Belasco's *May Blossom* (1883), that employed a minstrel-
type Negro servant for comedy relief.

All the important Civil War plays, set as they were in the South, necessarily introduced Negro servant characters: *Belle Lamar* (1874), by Dion Boucicault; *Held by the Enemy* (1886) and *Secret Service* (1895), both by William Gillette; and *Barbara Frietchie* (1899), by Clyde Fitch.

Uncle Dan in *Belle Lamar* was so completely devoted to Belle that he offered himself to be shot in her place. The half-blind Uncle Rufus in *Held by the Enemy* was of the same stamp, and also offered himself as a human sacrifice. Although the sentimental regard for Uncle Rufus predominated in the play, his proclivity for imitating the words of his mistress made him a more comic character than Uncle Dan.

The two colored servants, Martha and Jonas, in *Secret Service* had the same stalwart and loyal spirit. When the gentlemen in the War Department Telegraph Station refused to send Caroline's message and proposed to refer it to a higher authority, Martha stood in the doorway refusing to let anyone pass. To save Thorne's life Jonas sneaked into the room where the firing squad's rifles were deposited and bit the ball off the end of each cartridge. With Gillette's more compact dramaturgy and his intent to produce a drama of action, it was only natural that the Negro servants were obliged to figure more actively in the play. As usual Gillette wished to get all the details of his production as near to reality as possible, and for the first time in any play he included a specific note about the Negro dialect.

Mammy Lou in *Barbara Frietchie,* elaborating on Aunt Chloe in *Self,* really established the type of the Negro stage-mammy that has persisted to the present day.

The Negro servant in Augustus Thomas' *Alabama* (1891) tended to be slightly more realistic in his scorn for Yankee customs, but essentially he belonged to that group of former slaves who were suspicious of their new-found freedom.

Although in some of these later plays the Negro was emerging as a more realistic figure, he remained essentially in the romantic tradition. Only in such plays as *The New South*

(1893), by J. R. Grismer and Clay Greene, in which the mental processes of a Negro murderer were examined, did the thoroughly realistic Negro begin to appear.

Throughout the century the Negro was exhibited as a romantic stage creation. Sometimes he borrowed comic devices from the minstrel performers, but at the same time he retained his sentimental and pathetic qualities, the nineteenth-century adaptation of his noble-savage heritage. The mixture of Negro comic and sentimental "darky" varied as the taste and interests of the audience changed. With the prevalence of the abolitionists' influence it was inevitable that the pathetic aspect of the Negro's nature should for a time receive first attention, but even here the minstrel note must certainly have crept into T. D. Rice's characterizations of Uncle Tom and Old Tif. In only three plays, *Uncle Tom's Cabin, The Octoroon,* and *Dred,* was the Negro a principal figure in the dramatis personae. No doubt the danger of public disapproval was uppermost in the managers' minds, but that was not the only factor delaying the progress of the Negro drama. American playwrights could not visualize the Negro as a heroic figure; and when they began writing realistic problem plays, they were too occupied with the problems of a higher level of society to perceive the social problems of the emancipated Negro. As a result, the conventional stage-type, the sentimental, lovable, and good-humored old Negro servant, persisted to the end of the nineteenth century.

3. The Indian

DURING the latter part of the seventeenth century and through the entire eighteenth, the numerous treaty meetings between the Indians and white men were essentially the first indigenous American dramatic expression. These "theatre-in-life" dramas, recorded by various secretary interpreters, were solemn and serious in intent; and although the conflicts and problems treated were in the nature of life and death struggles, they were filled with theatrical and dramatic details: the exchanging of wampum belts and strings, the processionals to the treaty, the formal, stage-like form of address, the participation of the spectators as a kind of chorus, and the highly ingenious and romantic figures of speech.*

These romantic and theatrical treaty spectacles did not, of course, belong to the playhouse proper, nor were any of these documents ever transformed into formal drama; but they did provide a stimulating background for further dramatic exploitation.

When American playwrights finally ventured to accept credit for their plays by inscribing them with their own names rather than with pseudonyms, when they allowed their dramatic compositions to appear as native products rather than as foreign importations, it was natural that they should turn from the conventional romantic settings of faraway Greece and Spain to seek dramatic material in local themes and characters. Their choice of subject matter was, however, still prescribed by the romantic temper of the age. They were infected not only by the romantic philosophic theories that reached them from abroad but by the romantic day-to-day life of a bold, free, and expanding society. As a result, they searched for native dramatic substance not with the critical eye of the realistic observer but with the romanticist's predilection for stories that would most closely approximate the remote, colorful, and adventurous dramas to which they had become accustomed. The Indian more than any other native character satisfied their needs.

The Indian furnished the necessary link between the strange and the familiar. For the majority of theatregoers in the thirties and forties—these were the high-water years of Indian drama—the Indian was sufficiently remote from the spectator's everyday life to permit the dramatist to spread the aura of romance around him; at the same time, through family stories and reports from frontier travellers, the Indian was a familiar enough figure to be rendered convincingly in the drama.

* For a detailed study of these treaties, see Drummond and Moody, "Indian Treaties: The First American Dramas," *Quarterly Journal of Speech,* XXXIX (1953), 15-24.

Rousseau's and Chateaubriand's glowing dreams of an American wilderness peopled with a host of nature's noblemen living a perfect life had already found a sympathetic espousal in early American writers. Freneau, writing in *The Picture of Columbus*, extolled the Indian's unspoiled paradise as it was before the encroachment of the white man:

> Sweet sylvan scenes of innocence and ease,
> How calm and joyous pass the seasons here!
> No splendid towns or spiry turrets rise,
> Nor lordly palaces—no tyrant kings
> Enact hard laws to crush fair freedom here;
> No gloomy jails to shut up wretched men;
> All, all are free!—here God and nature reign;
> Their works unsullied by the hands of men.[1]

This Indian's paradise where "nature reigns" became quite naturally one of the important aspects of the Indian drama, not only because of such early descriptions as that of Freneau but because of the prevailing interest during the thirties and forties in the sublime and picturesque aspects of the beautiful. The age of the Indian drama was also the age of the romantic "Hudson River School" of painters. At no other time in the century were the grand, majestic, and awesome expressions of nature so highly regarded. And a word picture of Thomas Cole's canvas, "Scene from the Last of the Mohicans," reads like the dramatist's description of the setting for almost any one of the Indian plays: "Cole laid the scene in a romantic wilderness. Huge crags overlook the rocky platform where the warriors have formed a wide circle round the main actors of the drama. To the left, the mirror of a lake is visible behind the mountains. A dark pond partly fills the right foreground." [2]

The romantic dream of the noble red man was, however, more occupied with the dignity of his moral being than with the picturesqueness of his physical surroundings. The playwright took the figments of this dream and combined them with those conceptions of noble human behavior that had already proved successful in the conventional romantic play, and as a result, the Indian character in American drama became the archetype of human nobility. His natural goodness was so chaste, his heart so incorrupt, that he could safely trust his intuitive judgment on any occasion with no danger of falling into the pitfalls of moral disobedience. By merely obeying his spontaneous inclinations he attained a higher moral plane than the white man could achieve through the most scrupulous observance of a rigid set of moral regulations. By nature, and with no apparent strain of his human frailty, the Indian was endowed with those virtues which were so highly esteemed during the first half of the nineteenth century. He was brave and chivalrous, kind and gentle toward his squaw and children, filled with respect for the honor and accomplishments of his forebears, and unquestioningly trusting in the will of the almighty manitou. Even in his normal day-to-day behavior he was the epitome of the virtuous man. To be sure, not all Indian characters attained this lofty nature. Rum-loving, fierce, and vengeful red men such as Miami and Grimosco (believed by many to represent the Indian of real life) in Barker's *The Indian Princess*—here and there managed to slip into the drama; but compared with their noble brothers, they must have appeared to be products of "nature's journeymen."

The dramatists were not the first, however, to discover the possibilities in a fictional representation of the red man. Nor were the first Indians in American literature, those in Charles Brockden Brown's *Edgar Huntly* (1799), romantic figures. According to Ten Kate they were "patterned after degenerate loafers," [3] a race driven from their hunting ground and filled with a grim and implacable hatred of the white men.

Washington Irving believed the Indians "worthy of an age of poetry and fit subjects for local story and romantic fiction." [4] In *A Tour of the Prairies,* describing his journey to the frontier West in 1832, he acclaimed the glorious independence of the savage red man, who, unencumbered by the enslaving influences of artificial society, really possessed the true secret of personal freedom. It was curious that Irving, when so inspired, did not devote more space to the representation of the Indian in his own writing than the two chapters in the *Sketch*

Book (1819), "Traits of the Indian Character" and "Philip of Pokanoket, an Indian Memoir," although both of these gave a faithful and sympathetic view of the red man.

The writer who really brought the Indian to full maturity was James Fenimore Cooper. He devoted considerable space to the Indian character and exercised a strong influence in conventionalizing the Indian type. Cooper's red men were a composite of the Indian traits described by Heckewelder[5] combined with those derived from his limited acquaintance with Indians and from the tales supplied him by his neighbors. Spiller summed up the characteristics of Cooper's Indians in the following fashion:

. . . the picture which the novelist drew of pioneer and Indian life was almost as romantic to him as it is to us, but more vivid in that there were those still living who had experienced it. . . . He was too late for first hand observation of his Indians—likewise too early for accurate historical and scientific knowledge of their racial characteristics and backgrounds. His Indians are therefore transmuted white men, gone native, and restored to their vanishing wildernesses.[6]

Cooper presented both the light and dark side of the savage nature. In the *Last of the Mohicans,* for example, the Mohican chief Chingachgook and his son Uncas exhibited the Indian's noblest qualities, whereas the Huron villain, Magua, and his fellow tribesmen exhibited him in his dark and depraved aspects.

Although William Gilmore Simms in his romances portrayed border Indians rather than inhabitants of the forest, he endowed them with the conventionally lofty disposition. Unlike Cooper, Simms depended more on his own experience and on the endless stories supplied by his father and grandmother than on source books such as Heckewelder's. Although he did not draw as many Indian characters as Cooper, Simms included them in such novels as *The Two Camps, Lucas de Ayllon, The Yemassee,*[7] and *The Cassique of Kiawah.*

The most widely circulated fictional account of the Indian

was, of course, Longfellow's *The Song of Hiawatha* (1855). Although Longfellow had some acquaintance with a few Indians, most of the native lore in his poem was derived from Schoolcraft,[8] and the meter from the Finnish *Kalevala*.[9] Longfellow depicted the free and independent native who was just entering the dawn of civilization and who was still uncorrupted by contact with the whites.

This cursory glance at a few of the more important fictional treatments of the Indian in American literature during the first half of the century is too brief for any critical analysis, but it does indicate that the Indian was one of the newly discovered characters, valuable to the novelist and poet as well as to the dramatist.

The first play by an American playwright on an Indian theme came appropriately enough from the pen of Major Robert Rogers. As a lad of fifteen, Rogers assisted in defending his home from an Indian attack, and eighteen years later, in 1760, he was commanding the company of "Roger's Rangers" in the siege of Detroit against Pontiac and the French. These experiences must have exerted a strong impression on him; for as a result, he wrote *Ponteach,* the first play on an Indian theme and the first American problem play. It was never produced in Roger's life time, but was published in London in 1766.

Like the first Yankee character, Jonathan in *The Contrast,* the first Indian, Ponteach, was a prototype, embodying most of the noble-savage qualities that were to become the convention for the stage Indian. He was the completely matured type of courageous and self-determined warrior. Yet, like his many stage successors, he was charitable toward his enemies, allowing them surcease from attack if they would mend their evil ways. Once they had refused, however, he summoned the fury of his tongue as well as his sword in attacking his "proud, insulting, and haughty Foes." Even after he had thrown his full strength into the battle and the fate of his tribe lay perilously in the hands of the great manitou, his indomitable will and faith in his own destiny remained unshaken. Ponteach was in fact the complete "Indian," fully possessed of all the romantic and stirring qualities of the noble-savage that were to become the traditional stock-in-trade of the stage type.

Ponteach's sons, however, did not altogether share his loftiness of character. Although Chekiton exhibited an admirable filial devotion, he appeared commonplace and timid in comparison with his father. Early in the play Phillip, the other son, appeared for a time to be a fitter successor to the throne than his brother, but in a soliloquy at the end of the second act, he revealed himself suddenly and without warning as a sinister and revengeful villain seeking to destroy Chekiton and the fair and chaste maiden who was his brother's betrothed. Unfortunately for Phillip, his victims, when left for dead, returned to life, and his evil acts turned against him and sealed his own destruction.

As Ponteach was the first of the stalwart and courageous Indian warriors, Monelia, the betrothed of Chekiton, was the first of the innocent and incorruptible maidens. In true noble-savage tradition, her morality evolved from her own inevitably natural goodness and was not dictated by society. Characteristically, she loathed the white man for his assaults against maidenly virtue:

> He kiss'd, he squeez'd, and press'd me to his Bosom,
> Vow'd nothing could abate his ardent Passion,
> Swore he should die, should drown, or hang himself,
> Could not exist if I denied his suit,
> And said a thousand Things I cannot Name:
> My simple Heart, made soft by so much Heat,
> Half gave Consent, meaning to be his Bride.
> The Moment thus unguarded, he embrac'd,
> And imprudently ask'd to stain my Virtue.
> With just Disdain I push'd him from my Arms,
> And let him know he'd kindled my Resentment;
> The scene was chang'd from Sunshine to a Storm,
> Oh! then he curs'd, and swore, and damn'd, and sunk,
> Call'd me proud Bitch, pray'd Heav'n to blast my Soul,
> Wish'd Furies, Hell and Devils had my Body,
> To say no more; bid me begone in Haste

Without the smallest Mark of his Affection,
This was an Englishman, A Christian Lover.[10]

Monelia's romantic notions of love were even more severely
tested later in the play, and her indictment of the white man
became more vitriolic after the French priest had attempted to
seduce her. Her natural moral fortitude was gauged to with-
stand the most severe assaults, for her belief in the romantic
love of a pure young maiden for her honest and brave warrior
was not contrived from sentimental tales or ministerial admonitions but from the irresistible force of her own nature. Monelia's indictment of the English for their lechery was probably
the play's most severe, though not its only, verbal attack on the
intruders. Chekiton condemned the insincerity and sham of the
English.

The remarkable feature of *Ponteach* as an Indian play was
the extent and degree to which it embodied in a mature form
the qualities that were later to become the stock-in-trade of all
Indian dramas. The romantic natures of the warrior and the
maiden became the archetypes from which all later Indian characters were derived, and the poetic language, crowded with
figurative allusions to the glories of nature, became the pattern
for all the later playwrights. The style is exemplified in the
following:

My Sons, and trusty Counsellor Tenesco,
As the sweet smelling Rose, when yet a Bud,
Lies close conceal'd, till Time and the Sun's Warmth
Hath swell'd, matur'd, and brought it forth to view,
So these my Purposes I now reveal
Are to be kept with You, on pain of Death.[11]

Ponteach was by no means a faultless play, however. Characters and events were neither consistent nor of equal dramatic
intensity. The high and noble Ponteach sometimes sounded
like a petulant child, and the action frequently became
absurdly melodramatic. The critics of the time were more impressed by these deficiencies than by any merits that the play
had. The *Monthly Review* called it "one of the most absurd
productions we have ever seen," and the *Critical Review,* which

had evidently suggested the topic to Major Rogers, pronounced the drama "unreservedly insipid and flat." [12]

The next Indian play for which some record is available is *Tammany*, by Mrs. Anna Julia Hatton. It was first produced in New York on March 3, 1794, under the sponsorship of the Tammany Society. No doubt because of the author's connections with the theatrical profession (she was the sister of Mrs. Siddons) the play was given every possible advantage. A prologue was written by the then popular young New York poet, Richard Bingham Davis; music was composed by James Hewill; and the scenery was painted by Charles Ciceri. Many critics did not subscribe to the political sentiments of the play, but it seems to have been sufficiently popular to warrant an additional production by the Old American Company in Philadelphia on October 18, 1794. Unfortunately, the manuscript of the play has disappeared; and the contemporary comments included no descriptions of the Indian characters in the play which might assist the present study.

During the decade of the nineties the Indian received little attention from the dramatists, but the poets and fiction writers found him one of their most staple materials. Evidence of the popularity of the Indian poetry was apparent in such poems as Royall Tyler's *Death Song of a Cherokee Chief* (1790); Mrs. Morton's *Ouâbi; or, the Virtues of Nature* (1790), and Dunlap's *Cololoo—an Indian Tale* (1793). In the novel Mrs. Rowson's second volume of *Reuben and Rachel* (1798) and Charles Brockden Brown's *Edgar Huntly* (1799), a gothic story in which the Indian supplied one of the sources of terror, were both popular treatments of the red man.

In 1802 Boston theatregoers were presented with a play by Joseph Croswell entitled *A New World Planted; or, The Adventures of the Forefathers of New England, who landed in Plymouth, December 22d, 1620*. Although not strictly an Indian drama, this play exhibited the Indian girl, Pocohante [*sic*], for the first time. But not until James Nelson Barker's *The Indian Princess; or, La Belle Sauvage* had its first performance at the Chestnut Street Theatre in Philadelphia on April 6, 1808, did

Pocahontas appear as the principal figure in an Indian play. Barker's play later became known as "an operatic melo-drame," after, at the request of Bray the composer, Barker introduced Bray's songs into the play. The story was based on the events recorded in Captain Smith's *Generall Historie of Virginia*, which appeared in London in 1624. Barker followed too closely the undramatic order of events of the history. For example, the climax of the story, Pocahontas' rescue of Smith from the execution block, occurred in the first scene of the second act, and all the succeeding action was anticlimactic. Although Miami, the Prince, betrothed to Pocahontas but rejected by her, managed through the machinations of Powhatan's priest, Grimosco, to convince Powhatan of his early mistake in freeing Smith and of the need for inciting his warriors to a retaliatory attack on the whites, this second attempt on Smith's life was dull and feeble compared with the dramatic force of the first encounter.

Most of the Indians in the play were of the same noble-savage variety as those drawn by Rogers. Pocahontas was so gentle and compassionate that she was unwilling to kill a bird. Unlike Monelia, however, she had been favorably impressed by European men and their ways; and the soft and sentimental love scenes between Pocahontas and Lieutenant Rolfe were, even under their romantic coloring, the most genuine of the play.

Nantaquas, the Prince, was similar to his sister, Pocahontas, in his kindliness and understanding of the whites. Their father, Powhatan, although at times appearing auspicious and severe, had the same fundamental kindness. The conservatism of age, however, made him more suspicious of the innovations suggested by the whites. He had even lost faith in his own judgments and followed instead the advices of his war-council.

Unlike Nantaquas and Pocahontas, who believed the white man "is beloved by the Great Spirit," the mass of unidentified warriors of the tribe were certain that the white man had come from some nether region, and that he was a partner to the evils of fire and thunder. They accepted Grimosco's pronouncement that the white man was an "enemy to the Great Spirit."

Barker's play was the first in which the villainous Indian, the unnatural son of the forest, was introduced. Grimosco and Miami were represented as crafty scoundrels who tricked the old and superstitious Powhatan into attacking the whites through the unscrupulous employment of what they insisted were messages from the great manitou. They were as base and depraved as Powhatan was lofty and noble.

The Indian Princess was distinguished more for the general romantic atmosphere that pervaded the succession of events than for the representation of individual characters. The wild and picturesque scenery, the musical interludes, Larry's sentimental wailings for the girl he left behind him, the rapid and unimpeded shift from the scenes among the whites to those in the Indian village, and the climactic build-up of the scene in which Smith was about to be executed were all highly romantic features.

For romantic spectacle and suspense there are few scenes in American drama to rival the scene in which Smith was prepared for his doom. As he was led in, to the accompaniment of music, "his appearance excites universal wonder; [and] Pocahontas expresses peculiar admiration." As Powhatan pronounced the death sentence upon him, Smith turned to the multitude of Indians gathered around him and said:

> Prepare the stake! amidst your fiercest tortures,
> You'll find its fiery pains as nobly scorned,
> As when the red man sings aloud his death-song.[13]

As the first two signals announcing his impending decapitation were sounded, Pocahontas pleaded with her father for his release, and as the third and final signal rang out and the hatchets were swung into the air:

(. . . *the* Princess, *shrieking, runs distractedly to the block, and presses* Smith's *head to her bosom.*) White man, thou shalt not die; or I will die with thee. (*She leads* Smith *to the throne and kneels.*) [14]

Powhatan deliberated to the accompaniment of plaintive music, finally relented, and gave his daughter a string of white wampum, the beads of peace. Pocahontas then turned to Smith and exclaimed: "Captive! thou art free!" [15]

This was, of course, the big scene, but similar spectacular elements were employed throughout the play. The first glimpse into the palace of Powhatan at Werocomoco provided a colorful tableau of Powhatan on his throne surrounded by his many wives and warriors. The festival and ceremonial life of the Indian was frequently introduced, probably for the enchantment it must have held for most members of the audience.

Though Barker was the first dramatist to transfer the Pocahontas story to the stage, it is difficult to determine how much credit is due him for that distinction. When American dramatists turned to native themes, it was inevitable that the innumerable possibilities for elaborating the elements of suspense, intrigue, mystery, adventure, spectacle, character, and love interest, which the bare outline of the Pocahontas story suggested, should become apparent.

Although in the first Philadelphia performance the distaste of the audience for Webster, the singer who played Larry the Irishman, was so strong that the curtain had to be rung down in the middle of the show, the play had a great success. On June 14, 1809, it was given its first New York showing at the Park Theatre; and the London performance at Drury Lane on December 15, 1820, appears "to be the first well authenticated instance of an original American play being produced in London after an initial performance in America." [16]

Indian plays did not begin to appear in any great numbers immediately following Barker's play; but a piece called *Harlequin Panattatah; or, Genii of the Algonquins* (produced at the Park Theatre in New York, January 4, 1809) would appear to have owed its inspiration to *The Indian Princess.*

Barker's next attempt at an Indian theme was a two-act melodrama called *The Armourer's Escape; or, Three Years at Nootka Sound,* which he wrote especially for the armorer John Jewitt, of the ship "Boston"; and in the first production, on March 21, 1817, the part of the hero was acted by the armorer himself. The principal figures of the play were Indians: the treacherous Nootka warriors who destroyed the ship's crew and the peace-loving Klaissat tribesmen who saved Jewitt and Thompson. What distinction the play had rested on the extensive employment of spectacular effects. For example, the fourth and fifth scenes of Act I exhibited (1) a funeral ceremony of the Nootka Indians over the body of their chief, (2) a ship-burning scene, (3) an eclipse of the moon, and (4) an attack by the Acychats. In another part of the play there were a tribal war dance, followed by a dance of young Nootkian girls, and a parade in which the Nootkas were dressed in the costumes of the captured crew. Considered as a whole, however, the play is not comparable with Barker's earlier play.

The Indian in M. M. Noah's *She Would Be a Soldier* was a minor figure who had the conventional distrust of and hatred for the white man. He was a child of the forest and a servant to the will of the "Great Spirit"; but unlike his predecessors he expressed his noble and generous sentiments in a rather cold and straightforward English. His emotional determination to fight against the whites was not very strong; for when he was captured, he easily dismissed his early feelings of resentment and became a close friend of the whites who had captured him. Noah's principal interest was not centered on the red man's character; and the Indian of his play is significant to this study principally as the first Indian part to be played by Edwin Forrest (in 1826), the actor who later became closely associated with the Indian drama through his playing of Stone's *Metamora*.

Lewis Deffebach's *Oolaita; or, The Indian Heroine,* published in Philadelphia in 1821, was a melodrama in which Indians who very closely resembled white men were introduced into a conventional melodramatic arrangement. The heroine, daughter of the Sioux king and possessed of a pure and spotless soul, was so enamoured of the English that she was willing to die for any one of them. Her father, on the other hand, looked on the paleface as a spy, marauder, and thief. The center of interest was the action, which was melodramatic; as a result, the noble red man was characterized only with functional qualities that would further the action.

Logan, The Last of the Race of Shikellemus, Chief of the Cayuga Nation, written in 1821 by Dr. Joseph Doddridge, in commemoration of the exploits of the great chief, was probably the most historically accurate of all the Indian plays; but its colorless prose and its almost total lack of action made it unfit for stage presentation. Logan was represented as having been of the noble stature of Ponteach. He was the friend of the whites; but when they deceived him, he did not hesitate to take arms against them and attack fiercely. When Logan recited the charity of his actions in his well-known and extravagantly praised speech, he adopted the Biblical language of the white man: "I appeal to any white man to say, if ever he entered Logan's cabin hungry, and he gave him not meat; if ever he came cold and naked, and he clothed him not." [17]

Like the conventional romantic play (see p. 193), the Indian drama came to its maturity during the decade of the thirties. The dramatists who were writing about native subjects could not neglect material that was so vital to the life and progress of the country at the time. The West-inspired policy, approved by Jackson, of removing the Indians from the lands which the whites had occupied, the Black Hawk War of 1831–1832, and the ninety-four Indian treaties signed between 1829 and 1837 were historical events that brought the Indian problem to the attention of the people. But in keeping with the accepted romantic practice, the dramatists did not treat the contemporary problem. For the most part their Indian stories were laid in the remote time of the early Colonies and portrayed the Indian in his more glorified aspect.

Although there is only a fragment from which to judge Richard Penn Smith's *William Penn*,[18] first produced at the Walnut Street Theatre, Philadelphia, on December 25, 1829, this fragment is enough to indicate the scope of the play and the general manner in which the Indians were treated. Unlike the plays examined thus far, *William Penn* dealt principally with the

Indians' domestic and intertribal conflicts. The arrival of Penn in the "nick of time" to save Tammany approximated, in its spectacular effect, Pocahontas' rescue of Smith. These were the stage directions that described the scene of Penn's entrance at the end of the first act: "(They lead Tammany to the stake, and having bound him to it, sing the death-song. As they are about to commence the execution, a ship appears at a distance. The Indians start and gaze at it with astonishment. Music. The ship gradually approaches until it arrives in front, when William Penn and his followers descend from it. The curtain drops.)" [19]

The Indians in Smith's play were of the conventional noble-savage type except for their unquestioning and pious faith in the white man, William Penn.

More than any of the plays examined, *William Penn* romanticized the beauty of the Indian maiden. These redskin ladies were more striking than any of their real-life sisters.[20]

One of the most curious features of *William Penn* was the unusual combination of the language of the out-of-door, nature-loving Indian with the speech of the conventional melodramatic stage character. Oulita's description of Manta's attempt to seduce her is a good example: "He wooed me as the panther wooes the fawn. I fled, but he pursued and soon overtook me. He grasped me rudely and cried, 'Thou're mine at last.' I shrieked and struggled. 'It is in vain,' he said; 'your fate is fixed, and if you will not consent, then by force you must become the Sahiccan's bride. . . .' " [21]

The romantic quality of the play rested more on its theatricalizing of the sequence of events than on its representation of the Indian as a romantic figure. Its action was essentially melodramatic, and the characters fitted the accepted classifications of hero, heroine, and villain. Probably the success of the play— it was produced as late as January 1, 1842, at the National Theatre in Philadelphia—rested largely on the melodramatic struggle between two Indian tribes climaxed by the *deus ex machina* arrival of Penn.

That the greatest American Indian drama, *Metamora; or,*

The Last of the Wampanoags, should have been written by a man who was an actor as well as a playwright, John Augustus Stone, is not surprising to those acquainted with theatre history. Nor is it surprising that the play should have achieved its remarkable success because of the special ability of a single actor, Edwin Forrest, who was willing to identify himself with the leading part. *Metamora* first came to Forrest's attention when it was entered in his contest for new native plays.[22] By comparison with present-day playwriting contests the happy fortuity of this contest of 1828 is certainly remarkable. The prize, amounting to five hundred dollars, was awarded to *Metamora*; the judges' decision was approved by the sponsor; and the play was immediately introduced into Forrest's active repertoire. It became one of his most popular vehicles and was an outstanding favorite throughout the country. Almost immediately after its first performance, at the Park Theatre in New York on December 15, 1829, it was played in Philadelphia by Forrest, and in New Orleans and St. Louis by other actors. A careful examination of the Philadelphia theatrical record for the twenty-five-year period following its first production there revealed only two seasons without performances of *Metamora*.[23] A note dated May 11, 1839, from Sol Smith, manager of the theatre at St. Louis, to his partner, N. M. Ludlow, testified to its popularity in that city: *"Metamora* resulted in a house of $951.—Come, not so bad, my master. 'Stocks is riz.' "[24] And E. K. Collier has discovered records of its performance as late as 1887.[25]

Although in *Metamora* the Indians were divided into hero and villain groups as in *The Indian Princess,* the success of the play depended more on the characterization of the kind, honest, and noble Chief, Metamora, than on that of the deceitful and treacherous Annawandah. Metamora was of the same noble-savage stripe as Ponteach and Powhatan; but his vigorous, fierce, and unrelenting verbal and physical attacks upon the whites made him a more striking stage figure. His actions were dictated by a much more rigid and tangible code of morals than those of his predecessors. Although his intuitive sense of right and wrong was as unfailing, he preferred to bring up his proposed actions for a more conscious scrutiny so that the deed might be administered with greater assurance. For example, he spared Oceana from death not because he felt any natural kindliness toward her, but because she was the daughter of the white woman who had once rescued his father from death. "Forgive not a wrong, forget not a kindness" was the creed that defined Metamora's action.

In physical proportions Metamora was the model for all later Indians in painting and sculpture. He was the embodiment of all those qualities that today are immediately brought to mind by the mention of the "noble red man." As Oceana described him, she might have been viewing the painting of an Indian in a twentieth-century parlor rather than gazing up at the noble Metamora who had, with his unfailing marksmanship, just rescued her from the jaws of the panther: "High on a craggy rock an Indian stood, with sinewy arm and eye that pierced the glen. His bowstring drawn to wing a second death, a robe of fur was o'er his shoulder thrown, and o'er his long, dark hair an eagle's plume waved in the breeze, a feathery diadem. Firmly he stood upon the jutting height, as if a sculptor's hand had carved him there. With awe I gazed as on the cliff he turned—the grandest model of a mighty man." [26]

Stone made a strong point of identifying Metamora as literally a child of nature. He "sleeps amidst the roar of a mighty cataract." His heart "is on the hills where his father's shafts have flown in the chase"; and regardless of the specific demands of a particular occasion, his highly colorful speech was always filled with natural figures: ". . . yielding like the willow that droops over the stream, but till with a single arm you can move the mighty rock that mocks the lightning and the storm seek not to stir Metamora when his heart says no." [27]

Metamora actually believed that "the war and the chase are the red-man's brother and sister"; and thus he was revealed as more savage, severe, and bloodthirsty than any of his predecessors in the drama. His unrelenting attack on white men could not be concluded until he had completely annihilated them.

There was no hesitation or apology in his desire for the white man's destruction: "The wrath of the wronged Indian shall fall upon you like a cataract that dashes the uprooted oak down the mighty chasms. The war whoop shall start you from your dreams at night, and the red hatchet gleam in the blaze of your burning dwellings." [28] Even when he was finally captured (having just killed his wife, Nahmeokee, to save her from the white man) and when he realized that there was no escape, he maintained the same determined stand: "My curses on you, white men! . . . And may the wolf and panther howl o'er your fleshless bones, fit banquet for the destroyers! Spirits of the graves, I come! But the curse of Metamora stays with the white man!" [29] Quinn believed that the "similarity of the death scene of Nahmeokee to the death scene in Knowles' *Virginius* showed the kinship of the Indian play with the romantic tragedy of the time." [30]

Although Metamora remained steadfast to his mission and continually asserted his confidence in his own physical prowess in carrying out his task, he was not altogether self-dependent. The mysterious premonitions hinted at in his dreams were his continual guide: "Nahmeokee, the power of dreams has been on me, and the shadows of things that are to be have passed before me. . . . When I sleep I think the knife is red in my hand, and the scalp of the white man is streaming." [31]

But like the highly diversified natural phenomena that surrounded him, his life was not altogether made up of rushing streams and roaring cataracts. He had his moments of quietness and simple devotion. His exuberant love for his tribe and his native land was matched by his intense love for his home, his wife, and his child. His tormented expression of grief: "Ha! Dead! Dead! Cold!" when he discovered the death of his child must have been one of the most stirring moments in the play.

The settings for the play reflected the romantic tendency in the painting of the time and served as supplementary evidence of Metamora's continual allusions to the picturesqueness of his natural surroundings. The author's description of the opening scene indicated the general character of the scenery employed throughout the play: "A wild, picturesque scene; high craggy rocks in distance; dark pine trees, etc. Rocks cross stage, with platform cross behind. Steps, etc., at back. A rude tomb, flowers growing around it. Half dark. Mordaunt discovered leaning on tomb. Slow music." [32] The introduction of the gloomy tomb was reminiscent of the gothic-romantic quality of Monk Lewis' melodramas.

Metamora was one of the significant plays in American dramatic literature. It was the first play to employ a native theme with any great success and to be written expressly to suit the talents of a popular American actor. There can be no doubt that the wide range of emotional expression implicit in the character of Metamora fitted Forrest's tastes and abilities. Of the numerous comments regarding his acting, those of his biographer, Gabriel Harrison, are probably most illuminating: "So accurate had been his observations that he caught the very manner of their breathing. . . . Everything that could be absorbed by one nature from another was absorbed and embodied and represented. In *Metamora* he achieved a piece of acting that seemed to transcend all criticism." [33]

Only one other actor, John McCullough, attempted to play Metamora after Forrest. McCullough dared it only on a few occasions and then with no great success. In fact Forrest was the only actor who ever gained much distinction from acting the noble red man. William Wheatley, a Park Theatre actor, was known as an impersonator of Indian parts, but he never achieved the star ranking accorded to Forrest.

Although George Washington Parke Custis' dramatization of the Pocahontas story in 1830 was his significant contribution to the Indian drama, his earlier play, *The Indian Prophecy*, first produced at the Chestnut Street Theatre in Philadelphia, July 4, 1827, has chronological priority. The play was published in Georgetown in 1828 with this description on the title page: "A National Drama in two acts founded upon a most interesting and romantic occurrence in the life of General Washington." This "romantic occurrence" took place while Washington was on a surveying trip in the Kanawha region of

Virginia, where he met the Indian Chief Menawa. The Chief, who claimed to have been present at Braddock's defeat, related that he had ordered his best marksmen to level their shots at Washington but that some mysterious protective barrier had prevented any of the bullets from reaching their mark. This single incident was used as the climax for Custis' play. In fact it was the whole play; for all that preceded was a lengthy conversation between Woodford, a captain of the rangers, Maiona, his wife, and their Indian protégée, Manetta, the daughter of Chief Menawa. The play was performed in Baltimore and Washington but with no startling success. Unfortunately no manuscript of the play is available from which to judge it more carefully.

Pocahontas; or, The Settlers of Virginia (first produced at the Walnut Street Theatre, Philadelphia, January 16, 1830) had a remarkable stage career. A series of twelve performances, not, however, in a continuous run, was scheduled immediately after the opening. One of these was given on Washington's birthday in memory of Custis' early associations with the great General.[34]

In some respects Custis' dramatization of the story was more realistic than Barker's earlier treatment of the subject and had a greater degree of historical verisimilitude. For example, Pocahontas' affection for the English had been aroused by the teaching of Barclay, a white man who had been left behind by a previous expedition and had married an Indian maiden. Matacoran, the Indian who commanded the opposition to the whites, was motivated, not by any innate villainy, as Miami was in *The Indian Princess,* but by his natural loyalty to the red man's cause.

The romantic and spectacular elements in Barker's play were feeble compared with the colorful pageantry of Custis' *Pocahontas.* The coronation scene, in which Powhatan was crowned King of Pawmunkee, was filled with pomp and ceremony; and after the formal exercise had been completed, a colorful and symbolic dance was introduced.

On the whole Custis' play was also more dramatic than Barker's. From the opening scene, in which the Indians watched Smith's boats arriving and were frightened away by the booming of the ship's guns, the events were arranged in an ascending scale of dramatic intensity to the final scene, in which Smith was to be executed. Custis not only placed the big scene in a more dramatic position, but he increased the tension by indicating that a company of Smith's soldiers were approaching in the distance and might arrive in time to rescue Smith. However, in deference to the accepted story, Pocahontas was given first credit for the rescue. She ran to the execution block, placed her head above Smith's and called "Strike!" Smith was unbound and knelt to the Princess just as "reports of musketry" were heard close at hand.

In general the Indian characters had the same lofty, natural goodness. Namoutac, Pocahontas' brother, was the only one who exhibited a slightly different turn. Having been to England and having lived under the direct influence of civilized society, he was able to compare the virtues of the two ways of living when he returned to his native land. His fervid defense of the Indian's manner of living was in essence an epitomizing of the romanticist's doctrine: "I wish'd to be away from the restraints of civiliz'd society, to throw off the cumbrous dress which fetter'd my limbs, and re-assume my primitive nakedness and liberty; to enjoy the hunt and the dance, and again to become a son of Virginia." [35]

Matacoran was the archdefender of the Indian and his customs against the intruding, civilizing influence of the whites. He was not, however, consistently portrayed. In the early part of the play he exhibited many of the villainous traits of Miami, whereas at the final curtain he was the exalted and unsullied type of the noble savage.

All the Indians were closely identified with their natural surroundings. They were as much a part of the forest as the trees and the wild animals. As Rolfe remarked when he got his first fleeting glimpse of Pocahontas and Omaya: "They have flitted away like nimble fawns which start from the thicket to avoid the hunter's aim." [36] Pocahontas, however, was more highly civilized, and was self-consciously aware of her female frailty in the face of her avowed task of saving the English from destruction. As she embarked on her mission to warn the English against the impending attack, the approaching storm almost unnerved her:

Ha! a storm is brewing, and how will these little hands, us'd only to guide the canoe in sportive race on a smooth and glassy surface, wage its struggling way, when raging billows uprear their foamy crests? Brave English, gallant courteous Rolfe. (*Thunder.*) Night comes on apace— Oh! night of horror! (*clasps her hands and looks up to heaven as if in prayer.*) Thank thee, good Spirit; I feel thy holy influence on my heart. English Rolfe, I will save thee, or Pocahontas be no more. (*Rushes out.*) [37]

Like its predecessors, *Pocahontas* was filled with allusions to the magnificence and sublimity of the natural surroundings. When Rolfe first ventured into the wilds, he was overcome by the picturesque spectacle of "rivers which rush with indescribable grandeur to the sea!" and make the "European pleasure grounds" with which he was familiar seem dull and monotonous. The settings prescribed by the author, woods with an Indian village in the background, or a bank beside a rushing river that "appears agitated," sought to add to the romantic flavor of the play and to explain the noble stature of the Indian in terms of the magnificence of his surroundings. An example is the opening scene with its panoramic view: " (Banks of James river. View of the river—two ships and a sloop at anchor in the distance—on one side of the stage a hut—composed of mats and reeds; on the other rocks and cliffs. Indians on the cliffs gazing at the shipping, and making signs to each other.)" [38]

Carabasset, by Nathaniel Deering, was another of the Indian dramas entered in Forrest's contest. Essentially a closet drama with its main interest focused on the Jesuit priest, Rallé, rather than on the Indian Chief, Carabasset, it offered little competition for *Metamora*. Nevertheless, a production of the play in the Portland Theatre, Portland, Maine, on February 16, 1831, aroused favorable comment from the local press. The *Eastern Argus* of February 15, 1831, called the play "one of much merit, which needed only a more extended circulation to enroll its author among the first of American dramatists." [39] It is very probable, however, that there was an element of local pride in this evaluation.

Carabasset was based on the actual events in the life of the Jesuit missionary, Rallé, on his friendship for the Indians, his distrust of the English, and his final assassination by the English for presumably conspiring against them. To this basic historical structure the dramatist added several imaginary persons and events.

Carabasset was one of the noblest of the noble-savage tribe. Brave, gentle, and just, he fought only in defense of his lawful property, and on one occasion at least his natural goodness stretched beyond all bounds of credibility. After he had been driven almost insane by the sight of his murdered wife and child, he ventured into the white man's land to destroy whatever victims he could find. But when he came upon Agnes, the wife of a white settler, and her small child, they reminded him so vividly of his own family that he was unable to strike the fatal blow that would have extinguished two more innocent lives.

In *Carabasset,* as in the other Indian plays, the physical beauties of nature were highly regarded. There were repeated references to the "rich tints" of nature, the "wild and shadowy glens," and the "noble views." From some of the descriptions given it would seem evident that Deering's motive in writing the play was partly that of extolling the beauties of that particular region of Maine with which he was familiar.

Oralloossa, Son of the Incas, although it dealt with the Indians of South America, requires at least a brief note. It was written by one of the leading early American playwrights, Robert Montgomery Bird; it won a prize in Forrest's contest for native American plays; and it was acted by Forrest at the Arch Street Theatre, Philadelphia, on October 10, 1832.

Bird's avowed purpose in writing *Oralloossa* was, as he stated: "first, the portraiture of the barbarian in which is concentrated all those qualities both of good and evil which are most strikingly characteristic of savage life; the second, to show how the noblest designs of a great man and the brightest destinies of a nation could be interrupted and destroyed by the unprincipled ambition of a single individual." [40] Compared with the North American red man thus far exhibited in the drama, Oralloossa appeared too highly gifted in the ways of civilized society to be called a savage even though he insisted that his craftiness and cunning were but the products of nature's teaching.

Like his northern brother he was "valiant and brave." Though he had a gentle and loving regard for the virtuous Indian maiden, in the face of battle he was filled with the same lust for blood as Metamora. Unlike his northern counterpart, however, he dwelt more on the gloomy, "gothic-romance" aspects of nature than on those of the mighty forest and the rolling plains.

A second play based on the Pontiac theme, *Pontiac; or, The Siege of Detroit,* was, like the first, written by a military man, General Alexander Macomb. Macomb introduced Major Rogers as one of the principal characters in his play and showed further deference to him by maintaining Rogers' sympathetic regard for the Indian's high honor and sense of hospitality. The play was published in 1835, but it received greater attention in Washington in 1838, when the United States Marine Corps participated in its first production.

The famous Indian character Tecumseh appeared on the stage for the first time in 1836 in a play, *Tecumseh; or, The Battle of the Thames,* by Dr. William Emmons. Tecumseh appeared as a high-tempered brave who, like Metamora, was fearless in the face of superior numbers. The other Indians of the play were, however, represented as cold-blooded and cruel.

On July 8 of the same year William Wheatley, the well-known actor of Indian roles, presented the first performance of Emmons' *Sassacus; or, The Indian Wife.* Unfortunately, the script has not survived, and nothing more is known of the play.

Robert Dale Owen, who was born in England but who later became a member of the United States Congress, published his dramatization of *Pocahontas* in 1837. On February 8 of the following year he saw it produced at the Park Theatre in New York. He called the play an "Historical Drama" and accompanied it with an introductory essay and notes. Although Owen had made an extensive study of the historical facts and was intent on presenting the results of his scholarship to the public, the endless parleys between the Colonists and the aborigines made the play too long and involved for stage purposes. Pocahontas had the same kindly regard for the whites as in the previous versions of her story, but her beauty was more extensively noted. Captain Newport's description of her flashing eyes, her slender form, her raven tresses, her wonderful brow, her clear, dusk cheek, her graceful limbs, and her musical voice certainly provided ample motivation for Rolfe's ardent passion. Most of the other Indians in the play reflected the simplicity and purity of their natural environment.

The Forest Princess; or, Two Centuries Ago, by Charlotte M. S. Barnes, presented still another version of the Pocahontas story. First produced on February 16, 1848, at Burton's Arch Street Theatre in Philadelphia, it is more interesting as a typical expression of the romantic temper of the age than as a dramatic presentation of the old legend. Mrs. Barnes was very careful to insist on the historical accuracy of her play, but at times, probably when she remembered her mother in the part of Pocahontas in Custis' play and was carried away by the sentimental fascination of the role, the facts were of minor importance to her. One of the most highly romanticized spectacles in any of the Indian dramas was the "vision of Pocahontas" just before her death:

(A strain of invisible music is heard, and thin clouds obscure the view from the casement. The clouds gradually disperse and discover the open sea across which the "George" is seen to sail. This view fades and gives place to the mouth of the James River with its forest, its rude fort, and its wigwams. On the bank stands Powhatan, awaiting his daughter's arrival in the ship which is seen approaching the shore. Clouds again obscure the scene, and through them a figure of Time passes, beckoning Peace who follows. The clouds partially disperse, and disclose in the distance, the form of Washington—The Genius of Columbia stands near him. Time hovers near, and Peace encircles with her arms the Lion and the Eagle. A mist then conceals the allegorical group, and again dispersing, discovers the view of Gravesend, at Sunset, with the "George" at anchor, as it appeared previous to the vision. The music dies away.) [41]

For dramatic effectiveness the play does not compare with *Metamora* or *Oralloossa*. The dialogue was in dull blank verse, and the events were cast in narrative rather than dramatic form. Even for the theatregoer of the time the strain on verisimilitude must have been rather severe.

The principal difference between Mrs. Barnes' version and those of Custis and Barker lay in her extension of the story to include the episodes in England following Pocahontas' marriage to Lieutenant Rolfe. She also introduced a white man, Volday, as the villain rather than a Miami or a Matacoran.

Mrs. Barnes' Pocahontas was not as vigorous as her predecessors. Perhaps the English climate and her *mal du pays* were responsible for her loss of spirit and finally her death; but like Camille she seemed more suited to this lingering deathwatch than she did to her native habitat along the banks of the James River. Even when she was in full health, her regard for the great out-of-doors was tinged with a more self-conscious pantheism than has yet been observed.

> No classic lore adorns my native lands;
> But rich redundant nature reigns alone.
> Great rivers, giant lakes, in silence sleep,
> And rushing torrents by their solemn voice
> Call man to praise his Maker.[42]

The influence of the *tableaux vivants*, popular in the 1840's, was apparent in most of the spectacle scenes of the play. This curious kind of arrested action furnished a striking contrast to the mobile spectacular scenes in Barker's *The Indian Princess* and Custis' *Pocahontas*. But even with the aid of these tableaux, the play had little chance for success, for it tried to cover the entire Pocahontas legend in the manner of a historian giving just as much emphasis to the ordinary dull details as to the highly colorful dramatic scenes.

Tecumseh, and the Prophet of the West was written by an Englishman, George Jones. Although it had its only publication in London in 1844 and, as far as I have been able to discover, was never performed, it is interesting as a theatrical oddity and for its treatment of one of the principal American Indian characters. In an early work, *History of Ancient America*, Jones had aroused considerable interest in his unique theory that the Biblical Israelites and the Indians were an identical people.[43] Spurred on by some favorable comment on this theory, he resolved to elaborate it further in the form of a play. Tecumseh was endowed with the noble red man's conventional qualities of courage and gentility and was described as a child of the forest, but his conception of the beauties of nature was more sophisticated than the feelings commonly attributed to Indians who were without the advantages of a "Tyrian" heritage.

Although the Indian dramas had continued to appear during the decade of the forties, they were not so numerous as the metrical romances of Indian life. Included among the metrical romances were Seba Smith's *Powhatan* and the Pocahontas poems of L. H. Sigourney, Mrs. M. M. Webster, and William Watson Waldron. These, along with G. H. Colton's *Tecumseh*, P. H. Myers' *Ensinore*, S. A. Barrett's *Black Hawk* and *Maintonomah*, and A. B. Street's *Frontenac* were the predecessors of Longfellow's *Hiawatha*.

One of the first of the few Indian plays brought out in the fifties was a two-act dramatization of Cooper's *The Wept of Wish-ton Wish*. First produced in 1851, the play seems to have had some moderate degree of success and provided a strikingly faithful stage presentation of the events and characters of Cooper's novel.

George H. Miles' *De Soto*, first produced by James E. Murdoch at the Chestnut Street Theatre in Philadelphia on April 19, 1852, was described by Coad and Mims as "one of the best of the lot." [44] The play had a Floridian *mise en scène* and may have derived some of its popularity from the representation of this unfamiliar locale. The principal Indian character was a Pocahontas-like maiden, Ulah, who was distinguished for her beauty. The play was, however, devoted to the tragic and melo-dramatic adventures of De Soto's expedition rather than to a portrayal of the Indian maiden.

By the fifties serious Indian dramas had become infrequent. In fact, James Rees, author of *Charlotte Temple* and *The Invisible Man,* noted the reaction against them as early as 1846, when he commented that the Indian drama "had of late become a perfect nuisance." [45] Certainly the reaction was unmistakably apparent in the burlesques of *Metamora* and *Pocahontas* by John Brougham, and of *Hiawatha* by Charles Walcot. Whether or not these satires, which appeared, respectively, in 1847, 1855, and 1856, initiated the reaction against the serious Indian drama or were merely symptomatic of a growing aversion to that type of theatrical fare is difficult to judge. But whatever the cause, no significant serious Indian plays were produced after this time.

Po-Ka-Hon-Tas; or, The Gentle Savage, by John Brougham, was first produced at Wallack's Theatre, New York, on December 2, 1855, and was by far the best of these burlesques. The record of its performance in New York alone testifies to its popularity. After its initial showing it was repeated at the Bowery in the following July and again at Wallack's in April of 1857. From then until its run at the Bowery Garden, from April 18 to April 23, 1881, it was revived at intervals of every few years.

Brougham's elaborate prolegomenon is indicative of the sprightly spirit and timely satire of the burlesque itself:

The deeply interesting incident upon which this drama is founded, occurred in Virginia, on Wednesday, Oct. 12, A.D., 1603, at twenty-six minutes past 4 in the afternoon, according to the somewhat highly colored and boastful narration of Capt. John Smith, the famous adventurer, backed by the concurrent testimony of contemporaneous history; but subsequent research has proved that either he was mistaken, or that *circumstance* had unwarrantably plagiarized an affair which transpired at a much earlier date; for, upon examining the contents of a wallet found in the vest pocket of the man in armor, dug up near Cape Cod, an entire *epic poem* was discovered upon the very same subject, which was written by a Danish Poet, the Chevalier Viking *Long Fellow* of the Norwegian Academy of Music, who flourished Anno Gothami, 235. This poem contains several square yards of verse, a fragment of which is subjoined to show its peculiar *Finnish*.[46]

The sample of the poem that followed was written in the *Kalevala* rhythm of Longfellow's *Hiawatha:*

> Whence this song of Pocahontas,
> With its flavor of Tobacco,
>
> .   .   .
>
> With the echo of the Breakdown,
> With its smack of Bourbon whiskey,
> With the twangle of the Banjo;
> Of the Banjo—the Goatskinnet,
> And the Fiddle—the Catgutto, . . .[47]

The allusions to the breakdown and the banjo seem to indicate that the play was intended as a burlesque for the Second Part of a minstrel show. In fact, the beginning of the first scene in the play reads like the opening routine of a minstrel performance: The Warriors of the Court of Tuscarora enter and sing the praises of their King. When they have finished, Powhatan congratulates them in a speech that bears a strong resemblance to the opening addresses of the Interlocutors.

Although the play was primarily a burlesque on the Indian dramas, other human foibles and institutions were also satirized. One scene, for example, represented the "Savage Playground of a Tuscarora Finishing Institution" where Poo-Tee-Pet, Lum-Pa-Shuga, Dah-Ling-Duk, and Osa-Charming were playing.

Metamora; or, the Last of the Pollywogs, the earlier of Brougham's two Indian burlesques, was first produced in 1847. *Metamora* was much shorter than *Po-Ka-Hon-Tas* and in the quality of its humor distinctly inferior to the latter; but the satire of the stage Indian, which was aimed at Forrest's portrayal of Metamora, was more direct and severe. Metamora's magnificent bearing, so highly praised by Oceana in Stone's play, was described as follows in the burlesque version:

His hair was glossy as the raven's wing;
He looked and moved a sort of savage king;
His speech was pointed, at the same time blunt—
Something between a whisper and a grunt.[48]

The burlesque imitation of Metamora's raging lust for blood was probably directed more at Forrest's ranting than at Stone's conception of the character.

Although on the whole this burlesque was not nearly as funny as *Po-Ka-Hon-Tas,* the battle scene must have been uproariously amusing to a generation of theatregoers accustomed to the minstrel-type humor: " (METAMORA goes up C, and takes his ground firmly. BADENOUGH advances first, and snaps musket, then crosses to R. corner. WORSER does the same. At each shot, METAMORA jumps and staggers as if shot. VAUGHAN goes up and snaps pistol at him. METAMORA jumps very high and falls, C. BADENOUGH,WORSER, and VAUGHAN go up stage, and shoot him with popguns.)" [49]

The importance of these plays by Brougham as mere burlesques of the Indian drama is overshadowed by their significance as representative specimens of the comic genius of the only fully matured American writer of stage comedy during the last century. His plays and his songs were the only ones from American stage history that might justifiably be placed beside the works of John Gay or Gilbert and Sullivan. As Hutton said of him: "If America has ever had an Aristophanes, John Brougham was his name. His *Pocahontas* and *Columbus* are almost classics. They rank among the best, if they are not the best, burlesques in any living language." [50]

The other burlesque on the Indian drama was *Hiawatha; Ardent Spirits and Laughing Water,* by Charles Walcot. It was also a musical extravaganza, but of inferior quality. Appearing in 1856, just one year after Longfellow's poem, its satire was aimed pretty directly at the Indians in *Hiawatha* rather than at the stage Indians. The jokes and songs were of the minstrel type but less distinguished than those of Brougham. The most interesting speech in the play, from a present-day point of view, was one that described the audience of the time:

It doesn't matter whether it is correct—
That's all played out—the main thing is effect.
Nobody cares about truth now-a-days,
Or who the deuce would stand our local plays? [51]

The Indians that appeared in the drama subsequent to these
burlesques tended to be more realistically represented, for the
dramatists were more concerned with the contemporary problems of the Indian. For instance, in Preuss' *Fashions and Follies
of Washington Life* (1857), Tonawaha pointed out the incon-
sistency in the white-man's treatment of the Indian: "Pale-faces
come, take our land, and drive us away. Pale-faces give us hot
red-water, which make our heart feel bad and burn us up. Ugh!
Den dey bring us good book, to tell 'bout Great Spirit, and
make us good." [52]

Boucicault's Indian, Wahnotee, in *The Octoroon* (1859), was
a mixture of romantic and realistic qualities. Zoe described him
as "a gentle, honest creature . . . with the tenderness of a
woman"; he spoke a curious mixture of broken English and
Indian dialect that was no doubt intended by Boucicault to
be a mark of authenticity.

Wannemucka in Augustin Daly's *Horizon,* first produced at
the Olympic Theatre, New York, on March 22, 1871, had a
similarly mixed nature. He was semicivilized but at the same
time wild and treacherous, and, unlike any of his predecessors,
possessed of a peculiar touch of dry humor.

The last of the plays on the Pocahontas theme was *Pocahontas, a Melo-Drama,* by S. H. M. Byers. Though published in a
stage edition of five acts in 1875, it seems never to have been
acted. The play was more concerned with the complicated and
melodramatic affairs of Helen, the daughter of Governor Wing-
field, and with the ups and downs in Rolfe's courtship of Pocahontas than with a serious representation of the Indian.

Roanoke, the "Indian" in Herne's *The Minute Men of 1774–
1775* (1886), is rather ambiguously relevant to the present
investigation, for at the end of the play he was revealed to be
a white who had been raised as an Indian. Although slightly
more delicate and with a strong sentimental turn, he followed

in the main the conventional stage-type of the noble savage. The attempts to educate him to the ways of civilized society, however, had a fatal effect. Admonished "to shrink from the cruelties of his race . . . to hope that one day he might be something more than a mere Indian," he was deprived of his vigor and his faith in the natural goodness and honesty of his race, and he became a feeble, selfconscious good-for-nothing. Although only a small part of the whole play, this was the first attempt to study realistically the effect of civilizing influences on the character of the Indian.

The last and certainly the least effective Indian drama in the nineteenth century was Alfred Antoine Furman's *Philip of Pokanoket,* published in 1894, but probably never produced. The author no doubt intended to represent the Indians in the noble-savage tradition, and to recount the exciting events of Philip's War; but his inept and uninteresting redskins cannot be compared with a Metamora or a Powhatan. If the serious treatment of the Indian on the stage had not terminated long before this time, *Philip of Pokanoket* would certainly have dealt the finishing blow.

Many factors contributed to the deterioration of the Indian drama in the forties and fifties. The age of "critical realism" was opening up, and audiences were no longer willing to accept the trite and overworked themes that had been popular for so many years. New themes with more realistic representation became the order of the day, and if Herne's slight effort in that direction is excepted, one may say that the Indian was not regarded as a figure worthy of serious critical examination until Mary Austin's *The Arrow-Maker* in 1911.

As with the monotonous pattern of the minstrel show, the sameness of plot in the Indian dramas and the strains on verisimilitude became intolerable. The highly romanticized natural goodness of the Indian was regarded as insufficient motivation for the decisive actions attributed to him, and the stage exaggeration of the physical beauty and prowess of the red man was rejected.[53]

Mark Twain's comments of several years later, that Cooper's

Indians belonged to "an extinct tribe which never existed" and
that the Indian worshippers had been "overestimating the red
man while viewing him through the mellow moonshine of
romance," [54] were already commonplaces to the theatre audiences of the forties and fifties. They were living in an age that
was too critically alive to the prospects of its own future to be
worried about the romantic past of a vanishing race of noble
savages.

4. *The Yankee*

LIKE the minstrel-Negro, the stage-Yankee evolved gradually.
At times he seemed related to his real-life prototype, but as his
appearances in the drama and theatre became more frequent,
he developed into a conventionalized stage-type. The first
writers who introduced the Yankee[1] in the drama found him
an appropriate character through whom to express their nationalistic and democratic sentiments. The goodhearted, simple,
and patriotic New England rustic was endowed with a distrust
of aristocratic formality and sham, and possessed of a wholehearted belief in the ability of the common man to effect his
own destiny. In real life he was a highly romantic spirit; and
when the early writers transferred him to the stage, they took
advantage of this natural inclination. But as the Yankee was
gradually transformed into a stage-type, this phase of his character was neglected, and his realistic eccentricities were exaggerated to make him a stage comic. The stage-Yankee, like
the minstrel-Negro, was essentially a romantic creation designed
for theatrical effect. Even Reed, who was mainly intent on
observing the realistic tendencies in American drama, admitted
that though the Yankee was a "specimen of distinctive American life, [he was] reproduced with obvious exaggeration.
. . . ."[2] Certainly no Yankee drama ever attempted a realistic
psychological study of the Yankee, nor did the Yankee plays
extend into the era of realism.

From 1825 to 1850 the Yankee was one of the popular stage-
types, along with the Indian and the minstrel-Negro. Like the

minstrel shows, the Yankee plays depended on the peculiar abilities of a select group of performers: George Handel "Yankee" Hill, Dan Marble, James H. Hackett, John Edmond Owens, and Joshua S. Silsbee. The numerous Yankee characters in American drama achieved distinction only as they were interpreted by one of these actors.

The acknowledged leader of this group was "Yankee" Hill. The distinction of being the first Yankee actor, however, probably belonged to Alexander Simpson. Simpson was playing Jonathan in Samuel Woodworth's *Forest Rose* at the Chatham Garden in 1825 when Hill saw his performance and was impressed with the comic possibilities of the Yankee character. In 1826 he tried some comic Yankee songs in a theatre in Brooklyn, but shortly after these performances, Hill married and retired from the stage. His retirement was short-lived. On August 30, 1830, he was billed at the New York Museum to recite his famous Yankee story, *Jonathan's Visit to Buffalo and Seneca Village*.[3] In 1831 he was playing a Yankee at the Arch Street Theatre in Philadelphia, probably Jonathan in *The Forest Rose*. His big year, however, was 1832, when he enacted Jonathan at the Park. On November 14, he recited *The Yankee in Trouble; or, Zephaniah in the Pantry* between the play and farce at an engagement of the "classic Kembles" at the "Old Drury" (Philadelphia). And sometime during the same year he daringly ventured several performances of the Yankee, Solomon Swap, in *Jonathan in England*. Since James Hackett had considered this part and the play itself his exclusive property,[4] he immediately protested when he learned of Hill's performances.

On February 25, 1833, Hill opened at the Chestnut Street Theatre, Philadelphia, in the part of Jedediah Homebred in Jones' *The Green Mountain Boy*. Jedediah was a servant and general factotum on a New England farm; the humor depended upon the outrageous expressions with which he answered the stilted remarks of the other characters. During the seasons of 1836 and 1838, Hill appeared in London. He even made some appearances in Paris. In 1838 he was at the Bowery in *The*

Forest Rose, and from then until his death in 1849, he made frequent appearances in New York, alternately as Jonathan and Jedediah.

Like Hill, James H. Hackett made his early success as a Yankee storyteller. He was known particularly for his rendering of the "Uncle Ben" story. In 1827 he took his Yankee impersonations to England. While on this visit, he got the idea for the Solomon Swap character already mentioned.

On December 10, 1829, he created another Yankee character, Industrious Doolittle in *The Times; or, Life in New York.* One of his most popular characters was that of Major Joe Bunker in *Down East; or, The Militia Training,* first produced at the Park, April 17, 1830. Hackett was not known exclusively for his Yankee impersonations. His King Lear and Hamlet were not, however, as popular as his Jonathan Ploughboy and Lot Sap Sago.[5]

Dan Marble, like the other Yankee actors, made his start with Yankee stories. During the years from 1833 to 1836 he was occupied in rendering these stories, but sometime during the 1836–37 season in Buffalo he discovered the Yankee character Sam Patch, and constructed a play, *Sam Patch,* in which this character was the central figure. In 1838 he made his debut at the Park, and in 1844 he appeared at the Strand Theatre, London, in the character of Deuteronomy Dutiful in *The Vermont Wool Dealer.* In 1846 he offered a $500.00 prize in a contest for Yankee plays. The prize was awarded to J. M. Field for *Family Ties,* produced unsuccessfully on June 19, 1846, at the Park.

Marble was always more closely associated with the part of Sam Patch than with any of the other Yankee characters. Some hints as to the nature of his performances in this part can be derived from the program description: "Sam takes a wonderful leap over Niagara Falls, in a 'union of courage and virtue— proving, some things can be done as well as others!' Mr. Marble will leap from the extreme height of the theatre, a feat never attempted by any one but himself, and prove that 'cold water don't drown love.'"[6] In 1838 the young Jefferson saw Marble act in Buffalo, and as he recalled the performance in later years, the nature of Marble's costume was particularly clear in his memory: "His costume was much after the present caricature of Uncle Sam, minus the stars but glorifying in the stripes." [7]

Joshua S. Silsbee, who was born in Steuben County, New York, on December 1, 1813, started his acting career in Natchez, Mississippi. In 1840 he started telling Yankee stories, and on June 16, 1843, in New York at the New Chatham Theatre,[8] he played his first Yankee character. For the most part he depended upon the repertoire of his predecessors: *The Yankee Peddler, The Vermont Wool Dealer, The Green Mountain Boy,* and others. In 1850 he made a successful tour of the country followed by a greater triumph in England. According to Quinn, Silsbee developed a quieter and more restrained manner, pointing toward the later schools of acting.[9]

Chronologically John Edmond Owens belongs somewhat outside this group. His first performance of Solon Shingle in *The People's Lawyer,* by J. S. Jones, was at the Broadway Theatre in 1864. He continued playing the part at frequent intervals until his death. In 1865 he played *The People's Lawyer* in London, and in 1882 he gave his last performance of it at the Harlem Theatre in New York. Winter described Owens' acting as being always "rosy with health and redolent of enjoyment." [10]

Denman Thompson was the last of the Yankee actors. His style was considerably changed from that of the earlier impersonators, and when he performed Joshua Whitcomb in *The Old Homestead* (1886) in Keene, New Hampshire, the people wanted their money back. They insisted "It warn't no actin'; it was jest a lot of fellers goin' around and doin' things." [11]

Unfortunately the present study can only echo Odell's wish for a magical power to enable one to get a glimpse at these Yankee actors, for the Yankee belongs more to a history of the theatre than to a history of the drama. There are, however, just a few scattered impressions of actual performances, providing only suggestive hints to the nature of the interpretations; and one must turn to the plays, those that are available for examination, for further light on the nature of the Yankee character.

How much direct influence Royall Tyler's *The Contrast* (first produced at the John Street Theatre by the American Company on April 16, 1787)[12] exerted on the characters created by the later Yankee actors is impossible to determine. But there is no doubt that Jonathan, the forerunner of all the later "Jonathans," was the first and certainly one of the best Yankee characters in American drama. Jonathan displayed the admirable qualities of the "true American" in contrast to the outmoded foreign artificialities of Dimple, Jessamy, Charlotte, and Letitia. The play rejoiced in the emergence of "an independent, National culture." The prologue began:

> Exult, each patriot heart!—this night is shewn
> A piece, which we may fairly call our own;[13]

.   .   .   .   .

Jonathan was an independent "true blue son of liberty," as he labelled himself. He was filled with a homely good humor, distrustful of any appearance of sham, and faithfully devoted to his master, Colonel Manly. He was careful to insist that he was Manly's waiter and not his servant. He was imbued with the typical New England puritanic condemnation of the theatre as the "devil's parlor"; and when he discovered that he had, by accident, paid a visit to the playhouse he exclaimed: "Mercy on my soul! did I see the wicked players?—Mayhap that 'ere Darby that I liked so was the old serpent himself, and had his cloven foot in his pocket. Why, I vow, now I come to think on't, the candles seemed to burn blue, and I am sure where I sat it smelt tarnally of brimstone." [14] Like so many of his successors he had a weakness for the ladies; he liked "to buss" them. But after his first encounter with Jenny—she slapped him when he kissed her—he vowed: "If this is the way with your city ladies, give me the twenty acres of rock, the bible, the cow, and Tabitha, and a little peaceable bundling." [15]

Jonathan introduced the picturesque colloquial language

that was to become closely identified with the stage-Yankee. When, after singing a few verses of "Yankee Doodle," [16] he had finally screwed up enough courage to kiss Jenny, he exclaimed: "Burning rivers! cooling flames! red-hot roses! pig nuts! Hasty-pudding and ambrosia!" [17]

He had the same shrewdness and materialistic turn that even today is regarded as a typical Yankee quality. Before he left home he "broke a piece of money" with Tabitha as a promise of mutual fidelity. When Jessamy proposed to make him acquainted with Jenny, Jonathan wondered how he could contrive "to pass this broken piece of silver—won't it buy a sugar-dram?" [18] In fact, most of the Yankee characteristics that became the stock-in-trade of the later Yankee actors were apparent in Jonathan.

Like Jonathan, Humphry Cubb in Samuel Low's *The Politician Outwitted* (1789) was a country bumpkin who was bewildered by the ways of the city folk, the "monstrous sight of people a scrouging backwards and forwards." Humphry was more broadly caricatured than Jonathan, for Low was more intent on exhausting all the comedy possibilities inherent in Humphry than in exhibiting his sterling qualities of honesty, loyalty, etc. Although the picturesque language was similar to that in *The Contrast,* the comedy scenes seemed less sincere. In fact, some of Humphry's speeches anticipated the style of the minstrel end-men. Humphry was awkward, droll, and exceedingly loquacious, and during most of the play he wandered about trying to discover the meaning of the curious new word "constitution."

Susannah, the comic serving maid in Dunlap's *Father of an Only Child* (1788),[19] had no specific Yankee characteristics although she called herself a Yankee. She was a loud-talking country girl, suspicious of the ways of society, and inclined to blurt out whatever came into her head. The comic effect of her speeches depended mainly on the incongruity arising from her inability to understand fully the remarks addressed to her. Although Susannah appeared absurdly stupid as a citizen of a growing democracy, Dunlap expressed through the other characters a fervent sympathy for the ideals of the newborn republic, as opposed to the detested customs of the parent country.

The anonymous "operatical, comical farce," *The Better Sort; or, The Girl of Spirit* (1789), gave only secondary attention to the good-natured Yankee, Yorick. The typical Yankee shrewdness was, however, apparent in Yorick; for when he was challenged to a duel with Captain Flash, he saved himself by making the Captain his friend.

Several plays during the nineties apparently employed the Yankee character; but how closely they followed the pattern established by Tyler in *The Contrast* is impossible to determine from the limited evidence available. The leading character in *The Yorker's Stratagem; or, Banana's Wedding* (1792), by J. Robinson, was apparently a Yankee trader whose trade had carried him to the West Indies. Here he became entangled in a melodramatic adventure involving a native West Indian, a French soldier of fortune, and a villainous scoundrel, Mr. Fingercrash. *The Little Yankee Sailor*, first produced on May 4, 1795, appears to have been an English nautical ballad piece, localized with the introduction of a Yankee and some American Indians. Obadiah in *The Traveller Returned* (1796) was an awkward country fellow who had the characteristic Yankee distrust for such "new-fangled" contraptions as "the glass thing by which folks find out when we should be cold and when we should be warm."

Another Jonathan appeared in John Minshull's *Rural Felicity* (1801), but as a very minor character. He had only three speeches in the entire play. In these he bemoaned the loss of his truelove, who had been enticed away from him by a Scottish bagpiper in spite of Jonathan's vigorous rendering of "Yankee Doodle."

The honest, patriotic, and uncompromising Yankee received his most sincere treatment in Dunlap's *The Glory of Columbia* (1803). When William and his rustic comrades captured André and discovered the large quantity of money that André was carrying on his person, William remarked that there was "more in that there purse, than father's farm's worthy stock and all! but somehow or other there is a sort of something here [pointing to his chest] that we Yankees don't choose to truck for money." [20] And when André tried to bribe them by offering them British uniforms, William answered: "An American soldier *wears an uniform*, to show that *he serves his country*, and never will *wear a livery or serve a master*." [21]

The same unabashed honesty was evident in L. Beach's musical farce, *Jonathan Postfree; or, The Honest Yankee* (1807). Beach's Jonathan was a goodhearted soul who was willing to help anyone who needed help. He particularly enjoyed carrying notes, letters, and memorandums "post-free." Like Tyler's Jonathan, he expressed his disgust with social convention in picturesque language, liked to sing "Yankee Doodle," and was repeatedly getting into the wrong establishments. Unlike the earlier Jonathan, he was possessed of an embarrassing physical awkwardness. When he entered the Ledger's house, he slipped on the carpets—or "kiverlids," as he called them—and fell flat on his face. Although he was lured by money to assist Fopling in the abduction of Maria, he refused to continue with it, in spite of Fopling's entreaties, when he discovered the underhanded nature of the assignment.

Nathan Yank, Rangely's pugnacious and energetic servant in J. N. Barker's *Tears and Smiles*,[22] in many respects followed the "Jonathan" convention. Yank blundered about ashamedly, asking whatever straightforward questions he thought might assist him in finding "Cognita"—his master having explained to him that she was travelling incognito. He was unruffled by any small details of meaning that evaded his grasp as long as he got the general sense.

Still another "Jonathan" appeared in A. B. Lindsley's *Love and Friendship; or, Yankee Notions* (1809), which Lindsley says in the Preface was "designed for a farce, but being considered too long [was] printed as a comedy." Lindsley's Jonathan was a New England merchant who had come South to peddle his wares. Like the other Jonathans, he rendered a few verses of "Yankee Doodle," and like Tyler's Jonathan, Lind-

sley's was sent into paroxysms of amorous delight by the sight
of girls. When he saw Portrain kissing Charlotte's hand, he
could hardly contain himself: ". . . if it don't beet the old
Nick and all nater! Kissen the gals right afore folks. O'ny 'e
dot dewe it right; 'e don't kiss the place we Yankee boys dewe.
. . . What a nation fine thing it is tewe have a pretty wife, by
gun! darned 'f I don't git straight along back tewe Suffield
again and marry along 'f my sweet Polly Perkins, and we'll kick
up sich a rotten dust on't, never fetch me! Bunker hill and the
Yankee gals for ever, for the Yankee boys, says brother Jonathan." [23]

David Humphreys' *The Yankey in England* (1815) was the
first play to introduce the Yankee in an English scene, and the
first to provide a glossary of Yankee terms. That Humphreys'
Doolittle was constructed in the "Jonathan" tradition is evident
from the description Humphreys gave of him in the Introduction. In fact, this description provides an excellent composite
picture of the typical stage-Yankee: "He is made of contrarie-
ties—simplicity and cunning; inquisitive from natural and
excessive curiosity, confirmed by habit; credulous, from in-
experience and want of knowledge of the world; believing
himself to be perfectly acquainted with whatever he partially
knows; tenacious of prejudice; docile when rightly managed;
when otherwise treated, independent to obstinacy; easily betrayed into ridiculous mistakes; incapable of being overawed
by external circumstances; suspicious, vigilant, and quick of
perception, he is ever ready to parry or repel the attack of
raillery by retorts of rustic or sarcastic, if not of original and
refined, wit and humour." [24]

In Joseph Hutton's *Fashionable Follies* (1815), the Yankee
characters, Mr. and Mrs. Ploughboy and their son Robert, were
more sentimental than the conventional stage-Yankee in their
devotion to the ideals of peace, liberty, and Christian charity.
Unlike the other Yankee plays, *Fashionable Follies* exhibited
a lively affection for the romantic aspects of the pastoral scene
and the glory of the growing America. Dorriville, looking out
over Lake Champlain, exclaimed: "Hail! my country; once

more I press my natal soil and breathe thy purer air, America, thou sole abode of liberty and peace. Welcome, ye grassy fields, ye shady arbours, and ye limpid streams that flow meandering through the winding dell; and thou, pellucid Champlain, whose unruffled bosom reflects the radiance of the morning sun." [25]

Samuel Woodworth's *The Forest Rose; or, American Farmers* (first performed at the Chatham Garden, New York, October 6, 1825) was the first Yankee play to become associated with the principal Yankee actors. As already noted, the part of Jonathan was first performed by Alexander Simpson. According to Ludlow, Simpson played Jonathan as a New Jersey country boy; and the part did not take on the Yankee peculiarities until Henry Placide, G. H. Hill, and Dan Marble assumed the role. The author indicated in his Preface, however, that "Simpson's Jonathan was every way equal to my hopes and wishes." [26] The success of the Yankee actors in the part has already been mentioned. In the Preface to the 1854 edition of *The Forest Rose* it was noted that J. S. Silsbee had played Jonathan in London for over one hundred consecutive nights, and in California Louis J. Mestayer had played the part for forty or fifty nights.

Woodworth was no doubt influenced by the earlier Jonathans of Tyler and Lindsley. He had already attempted a somewhat minor Yankee booby, Daniel Briggs, in his *Deed of Gift* (1822). But Quinn believes that Woodworth was influenced most of all by Henry Placide's playing of the part of Zekiel Homespun in Coleman's *The Heir-at-law*, the play that had introduced that great comedian to the Park Theatre audiences in 1823.[27]

The Forest Rose was loosely constructed and designed to satisfy the theatrical tastes of the audience. Specialty numbers were introduced at frequent intervals, and such speeches as Miller's eulogy of the American farmer were no doubt expected to evoke a cheer from the audience: "If I thought her in earnest, William, I should regret that you ever bestowed a thought on so worthless an object; for the girl who would reject the honest heart and hand of an American farmer for a fopling of any country is not worthy of affection or confidence." [28]

Like his predecessors, Woodworth's Jonathan blurted out what he had to say regardless of circumstances. He was "a little in the merchant way, and a piece of a farmer besides"; and his eyes were sharp to see a bargain. When Bellamy asked him to assist in arranging an assignation with Harriet, Jonathan replied that he could if it "pays well." But after he had received the money, and realized that he had promised to surrender Harriet to a villainous fop (Bellamy), he was faced with a dilemma: "I don't calculate I feel exactly right about keeping this purse; and yet I believe I should feel still worse to give it back. Twenty-three dollars is a speculation that ain't to be sneezed at, for it ain't to be catched every day. But will it be right to keep the money when I don't intend to do the job? Now, if I was at home, in Taunton, I would put that question to our debating society, and I would support the affirmative side of the question." [29]

Like the other Jonathans, he was susceptible to female charms; and many of the comedy sequences in the play arose from the manner in which the ladies contrived to dupe him.

There was, however, less humor in Jonathan's colloquial speech than in that of his predecessors; and aside from the comedy in the love-making scenes the play followed a semi-serious sentimental pattern. The comic effect of the play must have been derived from the mannerisms of the Yankee actors, although even they probably made no attempt to shade over the sentimental passages. The text of the play is comparatively short, but it was probably expanded in performance to include additional specialties and to admit extemporaneous comic interludes.

Although no author's name appeared on the title page of the copy of *Jonathan in England* which I examined, this was probably the play by Charles Mathews (performed at Drury Lane in 1826) from which Hackett took the title for his play. Unquestionably the play was of English authorship, for the allusions to liberty and freedom in America contained bits of British satire. Jonathan, for example, concluded that England "cannot be a land of liberty where a man can't beat his own Nigger without being brought to account for it. Ah! there is no independence to equal that of America; there a man may have twenty Niggers, he may beat them every hour of the day he pleases, and no person will dare call his humanity in question." [30] Jonathan had many of the characteristics of the typical stage Yankee. He worried about "that trifle" of money his Uncle Ben owed him, he was no respecter of formality, and he shook the hand of everyone he met. But whereas the American Jonathans were ingenuous, Mathews' Jonathan was calculated to show the Yankee in an unfavorable light.

William Dunlap in his *Trip to Niagara* (1830) borrowed directly from the Mathews play and from an anonymous play, *The Times* (1820). The character name, Jonathan Doolittle, was taken from *The Times*; and Jonathan's Uncle Ben, who never appeared in either play but who was repeatedly alluded to, was derived from *Jonathan in England*. Dunlap's Jonathan[31] was represented as a tricky business man who insisted that he used to make nutmegs "out of pine plank, and sold the whole cargo to a grocer in York." [32] In Dunlap's play the Yankee proclivity for exaggeration was so extended that Doolittle became the first stage-Yankee to appear as a teller of tall tales. The following passage illustrates this characteristic:

Bull. Nathan and I were out duck shooting on the Connecticut river in father's skiff. We had meazing fine sport, we had; but just as I was priming my gun, some how or 'nother I drops my powder horn, and the curst thing went right over, plump into the river, and pop down to the bottom. . . . "Nathan," says I, "lend me your powder horn to prime." And would you believe it? The stingy creetur wouldn't. "Well then," says I, "you're a good diver—Nathan—there it is—I see it—dive down and fetch it—and I'll give you some." Well—he did so. Down he went—and there he staid.
Dennis. For what would he stay?
Bull. That puzzled me. But I look'd down—the water was meazing clear—and what do you think he was doing?

Dennis. How should I know.

Bull. There I saw the tarnal creetur emptying my powder into his
own powder horn.[33]

The thirties and forties were the decades of highest popularity for the Yankee actors, just as they were the decades of the
celebrated "down east" humorous philosophers such as "Jack
Downing." Seba Smith created this illiterate and naively humorous critic of manners and political life, but he was imitated
almost immediately in Charles A. Davis' *Letters of Jack Downing* (1834). During the forties these homespun philosophers
became more numerous. In addition to Downing, there were
Ethan Spike, Obadiah Squash, Uncle Toby, and Sam Slick.
J. W. McClintock's *Sleigh Ride* and Ann Stephens' *High Life
in New York* were typical of the literature in which these
characters were presented.

Two of the best known of the Yankee plays, *Yankee Land*
and *The Vermont Wool Dealer,* were written by Cornelius A.
Logan. Unfortunately neither of these was available for the
present study. *Yankee Land,* first produced at the Park in 1834,
introduced the character of Lot Sap Sago, the part in which
Hackett achieved his greatest success. *Yankee Land* was slightly
altered in 1846 by Leman Rede and appeared under the title
of *Hue and Cry. The Vermont Wool Dealer* was first produced
at the Bowery on April 11, 1840. Danforth Marble played the
part of Deuteronomy Dutiful in this opening performance,
toured the country with it during the following seasons, and
took it to London in 1844.

Jonathan Seabright in George Lionel Stevens' *The Patriot;
or, Union and Freedom* (1834) was the first seafaring Yankee,[34]
and all of his utterances were interspersed with nautical terms.
His weakness for the female sex and his forthright manner of
speech identified him with the other Yankees, but as a sailor
he was not a typical stage-Yankee.

Solon Shingle, the "country teamster" in J. S. Jones' *The
People's Lawyer* (1839), was played at various times by Burke,
Hill, Hackett, Silsbee, and Owens. Hill, Hackett, and Silsbee,
the first actors to play Solon Shingle, interpreted him as the

conventional ruddy-faced and youthful rustic. Charles Burke, the half-brother of Jefferson, was the first to make Solon "a simple-minded, phenomenally shrewd old man from New England with a soul which soared no higher than the financial value of a ba'l of apple sass." [35] When Owens took up the role, he continued in the tradition established by Burke; and until Owens' death, in 1886, "the drivelling old farmer from Massachusetts was as perfect a specimen of his peculiar species as our stage has ever seen." [36]

During the forties and fifties *The People's Lawyer* was the favorite Yankee play. The sentimental story of how Charles was unjustly jailed because he refused to be dishonest, and of how he was brought to trial and finally acquitted through the efforts of the "people's lawyer," Howard Enters, would certainly have had no distinction without the introduction of Solon Shingle, the Yankee, whose straightforward, down-to-earth, and unashamed colloquialisms were totally and entertainingly incongruous with the sentimental speeches of the other characters.

Solon's principal comedy scene occurred in the courtroom during Charles' trial. Having gone to sleep during the proceedings, Solon woke up suddenly believing that whoever was on trial was being tried for stealing his "apple-sass," which Solon had lost out of the back end of his wagon that morning. He was put on the stand, and he related his troubles: "That's what I'm coming to—my team did go; for I couldn't bring up into the shop; so I was talking with Mr. Ellsley there about matters and things—my Nabby's getting married and soon, and how things worked—Squire, I wish you'd hand me a pen there to pick my tooth, I eat three cents worth of clams, afore I come into court, and really believe there's a clam atween my eye tooth, and tother one next to it." [37] Like the other Yankee characters, Solon was unabashed by any attempts to intimidate him. His particular style of honest straightforward attack on sham and artificiality in society was really a forerunner of the ingenuous and deflating manner of Will Rogers.

Solon was not an integral part of the plot structure, his comic interludes having been merely inserted into the play.

Even the suggestions for costumes indicated that Solon was a specialty performer. The other characters were to be dressed in "costumes of the present day," whereas Solon was to wear "dark drab old-fashioned surtout with capes, Sheep's grey trowsers [*sic*], lead colored striped vest, old style black-cloak, cow-hide boots, broad-rimmed low-crowned hat, bald-headed flaxen wig." [38]

Hiram Dodge, the peddler, in *The Yankee Peddler; or, Old Times in Virginia*, by Morris Barnett, was one of the most colorful of the Yankee characters. He was certainly much shrewder, if a little more underhanded in drawing a bargain, than previous Yankees. And unlike his predecessors, he had no sentimental affection for independence and liberty. He did not object to becoming a parasite when such a position appeared to be profitable.

He had, however, the same uprushing of emotion at the sight of a young lady. When he spied Jarusha for the first time, he was overcome: "There's another on 'em. Oh, Lord, I'm a goner! If she'll only let me kiss her in the meouth, I'll give her all my sassingers for nuthin!" [39] Few of the Yankee characters could rival the racy, robust, and vividly colloquial speech of Hiram Dodge. He was a master of this form of expression as the following examples indicate:

He's a dreadful cross old creeture; he's bout as cross and crooked as our old brown heifer's tail was—and that was so universal crooked dad used to bore hoes with.[40]

　　·　　　·　　　·　　　·　　　·

Anything squire to make money. I'll swallow one of your niggers hull, if you'll grease his head and pin his ears back.[41]

　　·　　　·　　　·　　　·　　　·

Four niggers carryin' one table! They're bout as weak as old Granny Dobson was—she was so weak that she was obliged to have three or four mustard plasters applied to help her draw her last breath.[42]

Two other Yankees, Captain Chunk and his son Curtis Chunk ("Cur Chunk," as he called himself), were, unlike Dodge, neither grasping nor selfish. They appeared in O. E. Durivage's *The Stage Struck Yankee,* first produced at the

Eagle Theatre, Boston, 1845. Curtis was a young man who had been completely bowled over by the attractions of the stage and had fallen in love with an actress, Fanny Magnet. Like Jonathan in *The Contrast* he described his impressions of the performance of *Richard III* he witnessed:

I never see such handsome sights. There was a bloody tyrannical sojer, King Richard Three, that made nothing of chopping off heads by the dozens. But then he got rowed up Salt Creek at last; for there was another chap, that must have been a colonel or a major, tackled him, and fit like murder, and bime-by he run his sword right through his body, so that it stuck out on t'other side, and that ere was the death of King Richard Three.[43]

His affectionate note to the actress, Miss Fanny, was probably one of the earliest masher notes recorded in American drama:

I write, dear Fanny, for to tell
How in love with you I fell.
Except Jedidah, you're the fust
That ever made my heart to bust.
Jedidah, I have quit and cussed her,
All for you, you little buster!
Your eyes like lightning bugs do glitter,
You most consummate, beautiful critter,
And I shall be in tarnal torture
Till you let me come and court your.
I guess you'll find a lad of spunk
Is Curtis, called for short Cur Chunk.[44]

Both Curtis and his father were strong-spirited and pugnacious but good-humored, generous, and honest. That they were intended as representatively independent, liberty-loving, and patriotic Americans was evident from their costumes: Curtis was to wear a long-tail drab coat, a showy vest, trousers with *red, white,* and *blue* checks, a bell hat, a fancy cravat, a long flaxen wig, and a large dickey.

One of the best known of the Yankee characters was Adam Trueman in Mrs. Mowatt's *Fashion* (1845). Although he was not strictly of the comic stage-Yankee type, he displayed the same direct, incisive, and colorful speech. But he was cast in a more serious and sentimental mode than the previous Yankees. He took a similar delight in knocking the foundations from under artificially constructed social conventions, but not so much for the sheer pleasure of seeing them collapse as for the evangelical interest he had in reforming society. He sincerely wanted his city cousins to see the error of their ways and to return to the happiness of the simple and noble rustic life. He urged Tiffanny to have his daughter and wife shipped off to the country where they can learn "true independence, and home virtues, instead of foreign follies."

Frequently Trueman has been interpreted as a satire on the farmer type, but from Mrs. Mowatt's comments in her *Autobiography,* it seems certain that she intended his sentimentality to be taken seriously: "The only character in the play which was sketched from life was that of the blunt, warm-hearted, old farmer. I was told that the original was seen in the pit vociferously applauding Adam Trueman's strictures on fashionable society. It was not very wonderful that his sentiments found an echo in my friend's bosom. I longed to ask the latter whether he recognized his own portrait; but we have never met since the likeness was taken." [45]

Jonathan Peabody, in James Kirke Paulding's *The Bucktails; or, Americans in England* (1847), added nothing new to the story of the American stage-Yankee. Paulding's Jonathan was plain, democratic, and blunt-witted. He insisted on the distinction between serving and being a servant, as the earlier Jonathan had in *The Contrast.* He sang his stanzas of "Yankee Doodle," uttered the conventional denunciation of the foreign and imposed culture, and, like all of his "Jonathan" predecessors, was completely confused by the big city.

Our Jeminy; or, Connecticut Courtship (185-), by H. J. Conway, introduced the first Yankee woman in a major role. Her qualities were not strictly Yankee. She was a country girl of high spirits and good humor who delighted in humbling the refined and high-mannered Honorable Gas. However, her picturesque figures of speech ("fidgetted like a hen on hot cinders") and her tall-tale descriptions were reminiscent of such Yankees as Dunlap's Jonathan Doolittle. Conway wrote another play, *Hiram Hireout* (1852), that introduced a Yankee servant in the name part, but nothing further is known about it.

That Mr. and Mrs. Barney Williams were successful in playing Pat, the Irishman, and the Yankee girl, Nancy, in the anonymous *Irish Assurance and Yankee Modesty* is evident from the number of theatres that housed this attraction during the 1850's.[46] Nancy, like "Our Jeminy," was not strictly of the Yankee stage-type. As she describes herself, she was "an all fired tiger when she [got] her dander up." Again like "Our Jeminy," Nancy loved a tall tale: "You Irishers do laugh all over your face. . . . Pop once had a Irish pig, and the crittur—he was such a good natured clever little soul—he youst to come in the house and set down, and get up, and go out, and come in again, and go into the barn, and whistle Paddy Carey, and come in the house again, and kick over the swill pail, and stick his feet through the window, and spit tobacco juice all over the carpet, and wipe his nose in the buck wheat cakes, and make himself so sociable, such a crittur you never did see." [47]

Like Adam Trueman, Zachary Westwood in *Nature's Nobleman* (1853?), by Henry Oake Pardey, had a distaste for fashion and for imitations of foreign manners. Zachary was direct and blunt, if not so picturesque as Adam, in his condemnations of artificiality. And like many of his Yankee predecessors, he was possessed of a fervent democratic spirit: "Aristocrats! It riles me to hear that word—it hadn't ought to pass American lips, we are borrowing the notions as well as the fashions of foreigners. By and by plain honest republican feeling will be unknown in our rich families." [48]

The two Yankees in *Uncle Tom's Cabin* (1852), Gumption Cute and Ophelia, had little in common with the typical stage-Yankees. Gumption, the Vermont overseer on the Southern plantation, had a tricky, sharp-witted, and speculating nature, untempered by any Yankee kindness or geniality. Ophelia, the old-maid housekeeper, was energetic, easily vexed, and puritanic. She was not in the vein of "Our Jeminy" or

Nancy, but rather the forerunner of the realistic New England spinster.

Although the costume directions indicated that Trueman Smelts in Lucien B. Chase's *Young Man About Town* (1854) was to be dressed "like a raw Yankee," he had none of the typical stage-Yankee qualities. He was a policeman who was primarily concerned with getting votes and who refused to give assistance to anyone who did not vote the right ticket.

Though a minor character, Jasper, in *The Irish Yankee* (1856?) by John Brougham, possessed the typical Yankee desire for straightforward picturesque speech. His observation on drums seems remarkably astute: "The fellow that invented drums knew something about human nature. I'm a man of peace, myself; but by the shield of Bellona, there's something about that darned sheepskin that echoes through a fellow's heart in a most surprising way." [49]

Neighbor Jackwood (1857), by Trowbridge, introduced four Yankee characters though none of them was of the conventional stage-type. The name character, a Vermont farmer, was a strong abolitionist and great lover of humanity. Enos Crumlett was a "speculating Vermonter"; Mrs. Jackwood, "a great fretter"; and Grandmother Rigglesty, a crotchety old lady with a "crick in her back." [50]

In Ballou's *Miraldi* (1858), Seth Swap was a Maine Yankee who had just returned from the Mexican silver mines, but nothing more is known about the play or the Yankee character. [51]

Salem Scudder in Boucicault's *The Octoroon* (1859) was too well integrated in the plot structure to be considered a typical stage-Yankee. He had, however, the honest and energetic nature associated with the type and the same love for picturesque description: "Ten years ago the judge took as overseer a bit of Connecticut hardware called McClosky. . . . The judge drew money like Bourbon whisky from a barrel, and never turned off the tap. . . . So it went, till one day the judge found the tap wouldn't run. He looked in to see what stopped it, and pulled out a big mortgage." [52]

With the growing realism in drama during the sixties, the

Yankee character became a more direct copy of his New England prototype. Tarbox in Curtis' *Change of Base* (1866), a "seedy" down-East farmer who had just returned from the War; and Hiram Beers in Daly's *Legend of Norwood* (1867), the village teamster and oracle, were both of this type. The last of this type of Yankee, and by far the best, was Joshua Whitcomb in Denman Thompson's *The Old Homestead* (1876).[53] Joshua was a direct copy from the real-life character, Joshua Holbrook of Swanzey, New Hampshire. Thompson evidently portrayed the simple, lovable old farmer as a faithful copy of the real-life prototype; for the Keene, New Hampshire, audience (already referred to) would not believe that Thompson's performance was acting.

The Yankee appeared early in American drama but matured slowly into the accepted and popular stage-Yankee type who held the boards roughly from 1825 to 1855. As a simple, sentimental, liberty-loving, patriotic, goodhearted critic of artificial society, he was a romantic figure. As a shrewd, bargaining, blunt sort of rustic and as a lover of tall tales and picturesque speech, he was no doubt intended to be a copy of the real New England Yankee. But even this second aspect of his nature as exhibited on the stage was a romantic exaggeration of real life. During the last years of the eighteenth and the early years of the nineteenth century, the Yankee was generally represented as an ingenuous, blundering, and amorous youth on his first visit to the big city. But after Charles Burke had discovered in the early forties that Solon Shingle in *The People's Lawyer* was more theatrically effective when played as a sharp-tongued, mercenary, shrewd old man, with enough good humor, geniality, and honesty to be sentimentally acceptable, the final pattern for the stage-Yankee was set for the rest of the nineteenth century. After 1840 the young "Jonathan" type of character appeared only twice.[54]

Although the Yankee was remarkably well characterized in his first appearance in American drama in *The Contrast*, he would probably not have achieved the success that he had as a theatrical figure had it not been for the playing of the Yankee actors. In their early years these actors no doubt studied the peculiar mannerisms of the New England Yankee; but they were certainly more concerned with creating a physical manner, a striking costume, and an individual way of speaking that would draw laughs, applause, and cheers from an audience than they were in giving a faithful rendering of a real-life New England farmer.

5. *The Wars*

No OTHER events in the history of the United States are so heavily enveloped with romance as are the wars. The War of Independence (1775–83), the wars against the Barbary States (1785–1816), the War of 1812, the Mexican War (1846–48), and the Civil War (1861–65) all became romantic adventures in the life of a growing democracy. The heroic battles, adventurous forays of scouting parties, lovers' meetings behind the enemy lines, high-spirited young Rebels defying the commands of Tory fathers, or the sheltered and delicate young Southern belle deserting the Confederate home fire for love of a Yankee soldier—these and other war incidents were ready-made romance for the poet and dramatist. There were no tanks, airplanes, armored cars, or battleships. These wars were won by the small companies of common foot soldiers, ill-equipped and often ill-nourished, and by light hand-hewn frigates, at the mercy of the wind and guided by the skill of Yankee sailors. The causes for which they fought ran high in the blood of American soldiers. Superhuman strength in the face of apparently insurmountable opposition made heroic excursions the order of the day. Ten men dead, one officer captured, an outpost lost, a hill surrounded were significant battle communiqués in these struggles. The world of battle was smaller, and the common man was at the center of the fight. He knew his purpose. He was fighting to preserve the democratic ideals of the new country. Right or wrong, as one might now judge the Tory or Rebel, the Confederate or Unionist, in 1776 and 1861 each knew and believed in the cause for which he was fighting.

The romantic spirit of freemen fighting for what they held dear prevailed in all the American wars. And the events of battle, the behind-the-line incidents, and the struggles for reconstruction after the war became full-fledged romantic adventures.

REVOLUTIONARY WAR

Why the events preceding, surrounding, and following the Revolutionary War, what Charles Angoff called ". . . the most romantic events in history," [1] never came alive on the stage sometime during the last century in a significant play is difficult to determine. The explanation offered by Eaton in 1908 was probably near the truth: "In the early days of the last century, when memory of the struggle was still fresh and the nation was still trying its young limbs with the tingle of novelty in every leap and blow, grateful for its release, there were no American dramatists with the technical skill to write any sort of drama. And now, when our dramatists have acquired or are acquiring the technical skill, the present is too full of problems, the future too engrossing, the past too remote, for them to be interested in the Revolution. We are at once too old and not old enough as a nation to make copy of our past. Perhaps that is the real reason why the historical drama of 1776 does not get written." [2] But even though most of the Revolutionary War plays belong in a minor bracket of dramatic history, many of them became colorful, romantic, and stirring theatrical presentations.

The recent critical analyses of the Revolutionary War, such as Carl Van Doren's *Secret History of the American Revolution* and Kenneth Roberts' novel *Oliver Wiswell*, emphasizing the realistic, selfish, and unattractive traits of the men who led, fought, and governed during the War years, would have been fiercely condemned in the nineteenth century. Then, as now, the War of Independence was for most persons the blooming of the romantic ideal, representing faith in the power of individual man to shape his own destiny. These freemen of the

Colonies were not naturally rebellious. Their first desire was for allegiance to their mother country. But when the infringements on their rights as freemen became too oppressive, the flames of fighting opposition were readily kindled; and the struggle that began with the handful of ill-trained but high-spirited "minute-men" at Lexington and ended six years later with the surrender of Cornwallis at Yorktown had the elements of a brilliant romantic pageant that cannot be shadowed or discolored by any amount of critical inquiry. Whether one searches the minds of the Revolutionary Rebels for the causes that moved them to civil strife—for it was a civil war and not a war against an invader—or merely looks on at the unfolding spectacle of farmers, blacksmiths, and grocers hastily grabbing their rifles and trying to assume unfamiliar military formations, or views the more colorful and correct troops of Washington executing the orders of their revered and noble commander in chief, the romantic aspect of this broad and expansive canvas is unavoidably apparent. This conception of the war became the accepted standard for all writers. William Dunlap, as a boy in his early teens, had seen the War and its soldiers in New York and in New Jersey. He remembered them in this way:

As I walked on the road leading from Princeton to Trenton, alone, for I ever loved solitary rambles, ascending a hill suddenly appeared a group of cavaliers, mounting and gaining the summit in my front. The clear autumnal sky behind them equally relieved the dark uniforms, the buff lacings, and the glittering appendages. All were gallantly mounted. All were tall and graceful, but one towered above the rest, and I doubted not an instant that I saw the beloved hero. I lifted my hat as I saw that his eye was turned to me, and instantly every hat was raised, and every eye fixed on me. They passed on, and I turned and gazed as at a passing vision. I had seen him. All through my life, used to the pride and pomp and circumstance of glorious war, to the gay and gallant Englishman, the tartaned Scot, and the embroidered German of every military grade, I still think that old blue and buff of Washington and his aides, their cocked hats worn side-long, with the union cockade, the whole equipment as seen at the moment was the most martial thing I ever saw.[3]

The war was glorious to the men who participated in it and to the poets and dramatists who recorded it during the succeeding century. The soldiers were nature's noblemen as they fought in battle and as they were represented on the stage.

The present examination, however, must begin with those plays that appeared before and during the War, when the romantic aspect of the struggle for freedom was not yet clearly defined, and when Tory sentiments found frequent expression in the drama.

The first play that had any relation to the conflict, *A Cure for the Spleen,* appeared in Boston in 1755. So far as can be determined, it was never produced and probably was not written for stage performance. The outspoken Tory appeal to the Colonists for sanity of action was evidently found to be very persuasive in its pro-British feeling, for it was reprinted in New York. Like so many of the plays that appeared preceding the war, it was little more than "a conversation of the times over a friendly Tankard and Pipe."

Among the many satires that were printed immediately preceding the Declaration of Independence, those of Mrs. Mercy Otis Warren were the most incisive. Mrs. Warren, sister of James Otis, the patriot statesman and writer, was closely associated with the events leading up to the Revolution and was well acquainted with the leading political figures.

Mrs. Warren's *The Adulateur* (1773) was a satire directed chiefly against Thomas Hutchinson. Hutchinson was open to attack; he had held at once the three offices of Member of the Council, Chief Justice, and Lieutenant Governor of Massachusetts. By describing *The Adulateur* as, "A tragedy, as it is now acted in Upper Servia" and assigning her characters such names as Brutus, Junius, Portius, she was able to give her play the romantic distance required by the prevailing standards for playwriting and to provide a token concealment of the persons satirized. The satire in this play was not, however, as severe as in her later play *The Group* (1775), in which her attack was levelled against the men involved with the abrogation of the charter of Massachusetts and against the appointment by the King of a Council, the Upper House of Massachusetts, through a royal mandamus instead of through election by the Assembly. The list of characters in *The Group* was, of course, printed without interpretation, though to anyone familiar with the historical personages the intended representations were unmistakable. Her treatment of most of the royalists was pretty severe, but she portrayed Gage sympathetically. Although Mrs. Warren's pieces were dialogues rather than dramas, *The Group* clearly represented "the outcry of democracy against oligarchy, of liberty against prerogative, of the descendant of the Puritans against the upholders of kingcraft and oppression." [4]

The Blockheads; or, The Affrighted Officers, an anonymous prose farce published in 1776 recording an imaginary conversation between British officers and Tory refugees lamenting their starvation in Boston, has often been erroneously attributed to Mrs. Warren. The play was evidently intended as an answer to General Burgoyne's farce, *The Blockade,* which had been performed in Boston, 1775–76. Burgoyne's play ridiculed the patriot army which was then blockading Boston.

One of the most romantic incidents of Revolutionary War theatrical history was associated with a production of *The Blockade.* While the British officers were performing the farce, a sergeant walked out on the stage announcing that "the Rebels [had] attacked the lines on the Neck." The soldiers in the audience believed the speech was a part of the play; they applauded with great spirit until a continual repetition of the announcement, supported by the orders of their commander, General Howe, who was present at the performance, convinced them that the sergeant's report of an attack under Major Knowlton upon the British lines in Charlestown was authentic. The performance was stopped, and the soldiers returned to their stations.[5]

In 1774 an anonymous play, *A Dialogue Between a Southern*

Delegate and His Spouse on His Return from the Grand Continental Congress (subtitled "a Fragment Inscribed to the Married Ladies of America by their most sincere and affectionate Friend and Servant Mary V. V."), reiterated the Tory sentiments earlier expressed in *A Cure for the Spleen.*

Most of the dramatic activity during the War years was carried on by the British soldiers. In 1774 Congress recommended suspension of all public amusements and four years later issued a more stringent decree prohibiting play acting in any form. Thus, from 1775 to 1784 the American stage was in full control of the British military. There were some few plays from that period which belong in the present study; but for the most part the British soldiers produced the Elizabethan, Restoration, and contemporary plays which were currently appearing in London.

One of the lustiest Tory farces, *The Battle of Brooklyn,* possibly from the pen of a British soldier, was published in New York in 1776 by J. Rivington, a known Tory. The play was conspicuous for its scurrilous attack on Washington and his generals for their immorality, stupidity, and military ineffectiveness. Most of the play was devoted to a satirical representation of the Continental Army, but it concluded with a Tory plea for allegiance to the Crown that had a ring similar to the Whig pleas for revolution: "O almighty . . . open the eyes of my deluded fellow subjects, in this once, happy country; encourage them to a free exercise of that reason, which is the portion of every individual, that each may judge for himself: then peace and order will smile triumphant; over the rugged face of war and horror; the same hand that sows shall reap the field; and our vines and vineyards shall be our own." [6]

Probably the first time a military action of the War was represented in the drama was in Hugh Brackenridge's *The Battle of Bunkers Hill,* published by Robert Bell in Philadelphia, 1776. It was also the first play devoted almost exclusively to glorifying the cause of freedom and the fight against tyranny and despotism. The fight for liberty was strongly championed in word and deed by General Warren. The British soldiers were not represented as villains but as the dupes of their superiors. The soldiers were, however, fully aware of the tyranny of their cause, and, unlike their predecessors in *The Battle of Brooklyn,* they had a wholehearted respect for the courage of the Americans.

The lack of action in the play and the too frequent repetition of the odes to freedom were explained by Brackenridge's dedication: The play was "first drawn up for an Exercise in Oratory, to a number of young Gentlemen in a southern Academy." There is no authenticated record of a production of the play, but it seems quite probable that it was performed at the Somerset Academy, in Maryland, where Brackenridge was teaching.[7] The general tenor of the play was no doubt partly inspired by Brackenridge's association with Freneau. They had been schoolmates and in 1772 had collaborated on a poetic dialogue entitled *The Rising Glory of America.*

Freneau, however, in his Revolutionary War satires, 1775–1776 and 1779–1780, treated the British with less gentility than Brackenridge. In his rough satire, "General Gage's Soliloquy," he pilloried Gage for his incompetence, and in "The Midnight Consultation" he burlesqued a British staff meeting. In his later period, 1779–1780, he continued his attack on the British with "George the Third's Soliloquy" (1779) and "The British Prison-Ships" (1780).

The year following the publication of *The Battle of Bunkers Hill,* another Brackenridge play was printed, *The Death of General Montgomery.* The patriotic purpose was again immediately evident. The title page contained this explanation: "a tragedy with an ode, in honour of the Pennsylvania Militia and the small band of regular Continental Troops, who sustained the campaign in the depth of winter, Jan., 1777, and repulsed the British Forces from the Banks of the Delaware." [8] There is no record of a performance of the play, and it seems unlikely that it was ever produced; for Brackenridge insisted that the play was intended only "for the private entertainment of gentlemen of taste."

As in *The Battle of Bunkers Hill,* the historical event, Montgomery's attack on Quebec, was used as a background against which to display the noble sentiments of the American heroes who had no fear of death when they were dying for the cause of freedom. The American soldiers were of true heroic stature and of high romantic spirit; but unlike the British soldiers in the Bunker-Hill play, the English in *The Death of General Montgomery* were pictured as despicable villains whose "dark hearts" were filled with "black poison."

In general the same criticism can be applied to this as to Brackenridge's earlier play. Too much attention was given to a recital of the cause of freedom and too little to creating verisimilar dramatic action.

John Leacock's *The Fall of British Tyranny*, published in Philadelphia in 1776, was broader in scope than either of the Brackenridge plays. It was a sweeping chronicle satire in which the action shifted back and forth between England and the Colonies. Not only the military actions at Lexington, Bunker Hill, and Quebec but also the struggles within the English Parliament were included, and for the first time in the drama General Washington was represented on the stage. Although the play attempted to cover too much ground and although some of the speeches were frequently allowed to run on for pages at a time without interruption, the action was more dramatic, and there were stronger climaxes than in either *The Battle of Bunkers Hill* or *The Death of General Montgomery*.

The odes on the glory of freedom were not so frequent as in Brackenridge's play, although they did appear. Leacock's play offered a timely caution to the newly established Congress to beware of the "internal enemies [who] are worse than open foes." The author was, however, intent mainly on providing a satirical view of the British rulers in Parliament. So far as I have been able to discover, there was never any attempt to produce the play.

The Motley Assembly, like *The Blockheads*, has often been attributed to Mrs. Warren but without any substantial evidence to support such a claim. Printed in Boston in 1779, it ridiculed the Boston group who were unsympathetic to the Revolution for social reasons. The Rebels were not thought to be socially acceptable.

A bit of Tory propaganda that seems to have had some measure of success was contained in an anonymous two-act opera called *The Blockheads; or, Fortunate Contractor* (not to be confused with *The Blockheads; or, The Affrighted Officers*). First performed in New York and reprinted in London in 1782, it dealt with the conflicting opinions in America as to whether a closer alliance with France or with England was to be preferred after the War.

Immediately following the War there appear to have been no plays celebrating the final victory in the fight for Independence or glorying in the newly established democracy. The theatre was not prepared to celebrate military victory or contemporary events as it was to do during the War of 1812.

The next play based on events of the Revolutionary War was John Burk's *Bunker-Hill; or, The Death of General Warren.* This was first performed in Boston on February 17, 1797, and was repeated at the John Street Theatre in New York on September 8, 1797. In spite of some unfavorable contemporary comments, the play was successful enough to pay the author the astonishing sum of $2,000. Like the earlier play on General Warren and Bunker-Hill by Brackenridge, the espousal of the cause of freedom received the primary emphasis. Just before he was killed, Warren rallied his troops with the following:

> *Courage Americans!*
> The spirits of those heroes, who expir'd
> Massacred at Boston and at Lexington,
> Are this day witnesses of your renown;
> Suspended o'er this hill, let them behold
> Vengeance inflicted on their murderers;
> Let's give them in their names another fire,
> And in their ears shout, LIBERTY OR DEATH.
>   *(Americans shout.)* [9]

And as he expired, he had a vision of the glorious future of America:

O might I look into the womb of time
And see my country's future destiny!
Could I but see her proud democracy,
Founded on equal laws, and stript entire
Of those unnatural titles and those names
Of King, of Count, of Stadtholder, and Duke.[10]

The introduction of the love scenes between Elmira and Abercrombie and the love and honor struggle constitute the chief difference between this version of the story and the earlier one by Brackenridge. On the whole Burk's play was cast in a more theatrical form, more of the action occurring on the stage. For example, at the very beginning, "A party of English fly across stage as if pursued." There were no violent battle scenes even in this version, but there was a striking tableau representing the funeral of General Warren:

American army moves slowly to the sound of solemn music. Second, the troops out of uniform who fought in the hill. Third, children bearing flowers. Fourth, the Bier is brought in, on one side Prescott, on the other Putnam, at proper intervals the standards decorated with republican emblems, and popular devices.

1st Standard	Rights of Man.
2nd Standard	Liberty and Equality.
3rd Standard	He Died for His Country.
4th Standard	Boston, Parent of the Revolution.
5th Standard	Hatred to Royalty.
6th Standard	A Federal Constitution.

The Bier is laid down. Two Virgins advance to it, and leaning over it, sing.[11]

On February 9, 1798, the City Theatre in Charleston presented an anonymous masque-like spectacle devoted exclusively to a patriotic celebration of the fight for freedom. It was called *Americana; or, A New Tale of the Genii.* The scene was laid in the Allegheny Mountains and represented "an airy and unbounded prospect, wings and back flat representing a clear sky, light clouds but low and near the floor—by this means the stage will very naturally represent the summit of the vast rock on which the Masque is represented." [12]

The Candidates and *The Patriots,* the two plays by Colonel
Robert Munford of Mecklenburg, Virginia, published in the
same year, 1798, were undoubtedly written much earlier. They
were distinguished from the other Revolutionary War plays for
their peculiarly nonpartisan view of the struggle. *The Candidates* was in all probability written before the War, for there
were no references to the conflict. It was a satire on the methods of conducting elections for the Assembly. *The Patriots* was
a pacifist play. Trueman, the character who expressed the sentiments of the author, detested the "opprobrious epithet of Tory,
as much as . . . the inflammatory distinction of Whig." There
is no indication that either play was acted.

Of greater importance than either of these was William Dunlap's *André,* produced and published in 1798. It was not the
first play on this favorite theme. On April 16, 1796, the Old
American Company of Philadelphia had given the only known
performance of Mrs. Marriott's *Death of Major André; or, The
Land We Live In;* and in the same month a year later *West
Point Preserved,* by a Mr. Brown, was played for six successive
nights. Neither of these earlier plays, nor even any of the many
later ones, treated the subject with as much dramatic effectiveness as did Dunlap.

Dunlap's selection of incidents and his disregard for historical accuracy were responsible for the success of his *André.* The
initial bargaining between Arnold and André, Arnold's be-
trayal of his country, and the subsequent capture of André
have occurred before the play opens. Though André's imprison-
ment and execution were the only strictly historical events used
by Dunlap, he built several dramatic scenes around them. A
large portion of the play, however, was narrative rather than
dramatic. Only in the scene in which the younger Bland
pleaded madly with Washington for André's release, and the
one in which Washington received the note from the elder
Bland entreating him, "Do *your* duty," did the dramatic substance receive proper dramatic treatment.

A major part of the play was devoted to romantic poetizing
on the dignity of man, the cause of freedom and liberty, and

the awakening of the new national spirit. Dunlap championed the romantic revolt of the common man wherever such revolt was manifest:

> And hence, from our success (which by my soul,
> I feel as much secur'd as though our foes
> Were now within their floating prisons hous'd,
> And their proud prows all pointing to the east),
> Shall other nations break their galling fetters,
> And re-assume the dignity of man.[13]

Dunlap's play was by far the best of the many dramas dealing with André and is remarkable in the history of American drama for the fact that when it was first performed, on March 30, 1798, just eighteen years after André's execution, both Washington and Arnold were still living.

On July 4, 1803, Dunlap presented a reworked version of *André* under the title of *The Glory of Columbia—Her Yeomanry.* Many of the scenes from the earlier play were repeated verbatim, but on the whole *The Glory of Columbia* was more realistic and yet less serious in its intent. Comic characters and songs were introduced, and there was throughout a confusing mixture of the serious and comic.

Arnold, who had not appeared in the earlier play, was given a short and unimportant scene with André. Washington appeared as he had in *André,* but he spoke in a more realistic, down-to-earth manner. A spectacular tableau closed the play: "a transparency descends, and an eagle is seen suspending a crown of laurel over the commander in chief, with this motto— IMMORTALITY TO WASHINGTON." [14] That Dunlap contrived *The Glory of Columbia* for a Fourth-of-July celebration probably explains its curious hodgepodge quality. Such "occasional" pieces as *The Glory of Columbia,* prepared for special "rhetorical" occasions, should not, however, be judged by the same standards that are applied to regular drama. The technique was not, nor did it pretend to be, the technique of drama. And for the purpose of celebrating particular events, these pieces were undoubtedly more suitable than regular plays.

Their long speeches extolling freedom and liberty and their unrestrained and elaborate use of scenic displays were appropriate to the general tenor of the occasion.

Since none of the later dramatizations of the "André-Arnold" theme were particularly meritorious or related to the period in which they were written, they are mentioned only in connection with Dunlap's two plays on this theme.

For almost fifty years after *The Glory of Columbia* no dramatists attempted to treat the story. In 1847 Horatio Hubbell's *Arnold; or, The Treason of West Point* was published in Philadelphia. Brander Matthews says its "construction is rambling and scattering, and its blank verse is unspeakable." [15] The play was not performed. Similarly, Elihu G. Holland's *The Highland Treason* (1852) was not intended for the stage. The play was a chronicle history of Arnold's career from Ticonderoga, Quebec, and Saratoga to his declining years in London. Holland was intent on a literal rather than an artistic representation of events. For example, the actual reprimand delivered by Washington to Arnold was incorporated into the play.

Jason Rockwood Orton's *Arnold* (1854) attempted a similar all-inclusive chronicling of Arnold's life. Orton was sympathetic to Arnold's early breaches of conduct and attempted to explain them away, but after his treasonable action, Arnold was regarded as an unpardonable villain. Whereas Holland related most of the story through the conversation of two or three citizens or soldiers, Orton included in his dramatis personae all the principal figures associated with Arnold: Washington, Greene, Gates, De Lafayette, Hancock, Jay, Clinton, Miss Shippen, *et al.* It appears unlikely there was ever a performance of Orton's play.

In 1856 Scribner published *André*, a tragedy in five acts, by William Wilberforce Lord. Like the preceding plays this was also in blank verse and was not intended for the stage. But unlike the others, it was not in chronicle form. The dramatic setting of the treason occupied the entire play. And even though not intended for the stage, its closely knit structure would have made it more theatrically acceptable than the plays of Holland

and Orton. Unlike the other "André" plays, it possessed a high romantic coloring.

André was the central figure in Lord's play, but he did not assume quite the heroic proportions allowed him in George Henry Calvert's *Arnold and André* (1864). In this version Arnold was drawn definitely as villain and André as hero. Washington made two appearances in Calvert's play but never spoke. The first time he merely crossed the stage, and in the final scene he was shown in pantomime signing the sentence of death on André. The play contained very little dramatic struggle and not much dialogue; it appears to have been intended as a poem rather than as a drama.

Three other versions of the theme were noted by Matthews which I have been unable to examine. *Washington* (1875), by Ingersoll Lockwood, assigned important parts both to Mr. and Mrs. Arnold, but gave no attention to André. Martin Farquhar Tupper's treatment of the story in *Washington* (1876) was labelled by Matthews, "an unnecessary and ineffective play." And for P. Leo Haid's *Major John André* (1876) Matthews had even less regard: "That this turgid trash should ever have been acted, even by amateurs, is almost incomprehensible. . . ." [16] In seventy-eight years no treatment of the theme had equalled Dunlap's *André*.

Following Dunlap's *Glory of Columbia,* the next play to deal with a Revolutionary War theme was William Ioor's *Battle of Eutaw Springs,* printed in 1807 and first produced at the Southwark Theatre in Philadelphia on June 9, 1813. This was another chronicle-type play with little effective dramatic action.

M. M. Noah's *Marion; or, The Hero of Lake George,* first performed by the Park Theatre Company on November 25, 1821, was the first Revolutionary War play to utilize the War merely as a background for the simple romantic story of a comparatively insignificant War hero. In a way, *Marion* was a precursor of the Civil War dramas which almost invariably dealt with the domestic struggle resulting from opposing allegiances within the same family. None of the battle scenes of Saratoga were represented on stage. In fact, they were hardly mentioned until the final scene of the play, when Marion received a commission from General Washington for his acts of bravery in that encounter.

Noah's intention in the play was indicated in his dedication to William Coleman:[17] "Some of the incidents of this play are taken from a popular French piece, and it was written for the stage, and not for the closet, with the view of placing in a strong and effective light the dangers and sacrifices of our revolutionary soldiers—the hazards they encountered—the privations they suffered—the pains and penalties of their devotion to the sacred cause of liberty and their animating efforts to secure to you and I [sic] and their posterity the freedom we so happily enjoy." [18] The glory of the common man's fight for freedom and the hope for the future prosperity of the country received Noah's first attention.

Marion must have been a convincing stage piece. The action was well integrated: There were few superfluous scenes, and the nationalistic sentiments were comparatively unobtrusive. Along with Dunlap's *André,* it is outstanding among the early War plays.

Late in December, 1821, James Fenimore Cooper published his popular novel of the Revolution, *The Spy.* Ten weeks later, on March 1, 1822, the Park Theatre presented Charles Powell Clinch's dramatization of it. The sequence of events was the same in the play as in the novel, and the romance of mystery, intrigue, and adventure enveloping the leading figure, Harvey Birch, predominated in both. Birch's connection with Washington and the Continental Army was hinted at from time to time early in the play but was not clearly understood until the end. There were no major campaigns or even battles. Instead, attention was focused on Birch's behind-the-lines espionage and his thrilling captures and sensational escapes.

The romantic and benevolent power of fate guided the destinies of the hero. He was continually in danger, but he always miraculously avoided the impending fatality. In the accepted patriotic manner, the play ended with fullhearted praise for the misjudged patriot, Birch, and for General Washington:

"Rest in peace, injured patriot. Thy country and the world shall know that hearts like thine beat and break to serve it! Comrades! Friends! let it be our most cherished pride throughout this struggle, and our proudest boast to Heaven—our consolation whenever death may overtake us—that the approbation of the 'Father of his Country' is ours, ours the confidence of WASHINGTON!" [19]

Samuel B. H. Judah's *A Tale of Lexington,* first performed at the Park Theatre, July 4, 1822, was a formless affair that served no longer than for a Fourth-of-July celebration that year.

Montgomery; or, The Falls of Montmorency by H. J. Finn, was first performed at the Boston Theatre on February 21, 1825. The play is interesting for its introduction of the nationalistic note into domestic comedy. Contrary to the implication of the title, General Montgomery was an unimportant figure in the drama. The action centered on the successful efforts of Sergeant Welcome Sobersides to save Altamah, a half-breed Indian wife of Chevalier LaValle, from the villain, L'Araignée.

According to Quinn, Samuel Woodworth's *The Widow's Son; or, Which Is the Traitor?* "ranks easily next to *André* as the best of the Revolutionary plays of this period." [20] First produced at the Park Theatre on November 25, 1825, the play dealt with the domestic tragedy of Margaret Darby. Although the daughter of a British officer, she was loyal to the Rebel cause. When her son, accused of being a Tory, sought to avenge the insult by betraying Fort Montgomery to Sir Henry Clinton, Margaret offered her services to Washington to procure valuable military information from Sir Henry Clinton. *The Widow's Son* pictured more vividly than any other play of the period "the bustle and confusion that marked the irregular warfare of that period of the Revolution." [21] Judged by later standards, however, such plays of the twenties as *Marion* and *The Widow's Son* seem shallow and unimportant, though they were definitely superior to previous Revolutionary War plays.

In the novels of the period the Revolution was also a dominant theme. Cooper's *The Spy* appeared in 1821, John Neal's

Seventy-Six in 1823; and in 1825 there were "seven novels . . . utilizing such events as the battle of Lexington, the battles of White Plains, Camden, and others." [22]

It is not surprising that 1825 should have been the peak year. The country was celebrating fifty years of national life and fortune. On June 17, 1825, General de Lafayette, two hundred veterans of the Revolution—forty of them survivors from the Battle of Bunker Hill—and several thousand common citizens gathered to hear Daniel Webster's stirring patriotic oration on the occasion of the laying of the cornerstone for the Bunker Hill Monument.[23] This semicentennial celebration, although it brought the memorable heroic events of the Revolution into a sharper focus, seems not to have inspired any War plays or, for that matter, to have had any effect on patriotic plays in general.

George Lionel Stevens' *The Patriot; or, Union and Freedom* was exactly what it professed to be: "A Drama, in Three Acts. Wherein is Introduced A National Chant, Containing the Names of the Signers of the Declaration of Independence, Adapted to be represented in all Theatres of the Union, on Public Days of Rejoicing." It was printed in Boston in 1834, but no performance was given there or in New York. Unlike the previous plays, there were no Revolutionary war figures, fictional or historical, among the dramatis personae. The events of the War were related secondhand by Moreton, the son of a War hero. The plot, involving Henry Wythe's attempts to win the hand of Emily against the wishes of her father, had little connection with the patriotic purpose of the play. The elaborate spectacles, such as the five-page chant at the end of the first act, gave a theatrically forceful expression to the author's nationalistic sentiments. As far as I have been able to discover, *The Patriot* was never performed.

Another of the many closet dramas based on Revolutionary War incidents was Delia Bacon's *The Bride of Fort Edward* (1839). The play was filled with allusions to the great natural beauty of the new country that were similar to those encountered in the Indian drama.

H. N. Bannister's *Putnam, the Iron Son of '76,* first produced at the Bowery Theatre, August 5, 1844, was a vigorous play, noteworthy for the spectacular escape scene in which Putnam rode down the precipice at Horse Neck Hill.

The thirties and forties were lean years for Revolutionary War drama; nor were the treatments in the novels greatly superior. William Gilmore Simms got a hearing with his *The Partisan* (1835) and *Mellichampe* (1836), and Hoffman's *Greyslaer* (1840) went through four editions in its first decade. But these were not in the same rank with Hawthorne's *Twice Told Tales* (1837) and Cooper's *The Deerslayer* (1841).

John Brougham in *The Irish Yankee; or, The Birth-Day of Freedom* wove the historical events of the Battle of Bunker Hill into the structure of his play more cleverly than any of the previous dramatists who had used this theme. But at the same time he presented the conventional glorification of American liberty. Although the major portion of the play was devoted to the domestic struggles resulting from opposing Tory and Whig loyalties, the nationalistic sentiment prevailed throughout. The play ended with a typical patriotic tableau:

(*Hail Columbia played—guns fired—general shout as scene changes. Procession of the thirteen original States, with banners.*—Ebenezer and Jasper *enter, the former with green banner, having harp and joined hands painted on it, surmounted by the thirteen stars.*)
Eben. Now, boys for a shout that will be heard across the water.
Liberty all over the world, and where it is not given with a good will may it be taken by a strong hand.
(*Three cheers are given—joy bells ring—drums, and scene changes to the Temple of Liberty—clouds—*Washington *takes place on a low pedestal—curtain.*)[24]

The play was performed at the Broadway Theatre, New York, probably during the 1856–57 season and during succeeding seasons at the St. Charles Theatre, New Orleans, and at the National Theatre in Boston.

A Southern battle scene was introduced into the drama for the first time in Clifton W. Tayleure's *Horseshoe Robinson; or, The Battle of Kings Mountain,* first performed at the Holiday Street Theatre in Baltimore, April, 1856. The story and characters were taken directly from John Pendleton Kennedy's novel of the same name. As was customary, the "sacred sentiments of resistance to oppression" were frequently reiterated.

Love in '76, by Oliver Bell Bunce, first performed for the benefit of the Shirt Sewers' Union on February 28, 1857, at Laura Keene's Theatre in New York, was the best of the nineteenth-century Revolutionary War plays. As in the Civil War dramas, the interest was focused on the household split between Tory and Whig sentiments. The young sentimental heroine, Rose, was in love with Captain Armstrong of the Rebel forces, though her father and brother were staunch Tories. Rose exhibited the graciousness and courage of the later Civil War heroines as she addressed Major Cleveland, of the British Army, and Capt. Armstrong: "Let me see you shake hands, gentlemen, for here, you know, you must be friends. If you like to cut each other's throats elsewhere, so be it; but, of course, you sheathe your swords, and swear peace in the presence of a lady." [25] Contemporary critics approved the play because it was not loaded down with obtrusive patriotic eulogies, and twentieth-century critics have admired it for the same reason.

The next year at the same theatre (Laura Keene's) J. G. Burnett, who had played the part of Major Cleveland in *Love in '76,* produced his dramatization of George Lippard's novel, *Blanche of Brandywine.* The captures and escapes of Frazier and his adopted daughter, Blanche, were the main adventures of the play; but the leading Revolutionary War figures, Washington, Greene, and Howe, were also introduced into the plot. Howe was captured and brought before Washington. He tempted him with the offer of a dukedom to desert the American cause, but Washington refused the offer and magnanimously allowed Howe to depart unmolested. A tableau of the Battle of Bunker Hill, representing the historical characters in the attitudes of Trumbull's painting of the battle, was used to close the second act.

Mrs. W. L. Wheeler's *A Cup of Tea Drawn from 1773* merits attention only as the present survey is intended to be as complete as possible. Aside from the brief description of the Boston Tea Party, there was little reference to the War, and the sentimental story of Mercy and Warren Hasty's breaking-off over a cup of tea and of their reconciliation over a cup of tea twenty-seven years later was related in narrative rather than dramatic form.

Although James A. Herne's *The Minute Men of 1774–1775* has already been mentioned in the chapter on Indian plays, the War background of the play requires some further attention. Actual events of the War were not introduced into the plot structure, but were inserted as separate tableaux of the Battles of Lexington, Concord, and Bunker Hill. The author insisted that the rehearsals of the tableaux were to be in keeping with the historical pictures of these battles. Frequent patriotic outbursts were included in the text, but they were on a more realistic level than similar expressions previously encountered.

The most ponderous drama on the Revolutionary War was written by Ethan Allen. It was simply and monumentally entitled *Washington; or, the Revolution*. The first edition of the play (1894) was in prose, and the second (1899) in blank verse. In the Introduction, Allen needlessly stated: "It was no part of the author's intention to prepare this drama for actual presentation upon the stage." The action began with General Gage and the Boston Massacre and covered *all* the events of the War down to Washington's inauguration in New York City. There were ninety scenes in the play.

The last play of the century to employ a Revolutionary War theme was Clyde Fitch's *Nathan Hale*, first performed in Chicago, January 31, 1898. Although much more realistic in treatment than any of the previous plays, it retained the romantic qualities of Hale's heroic mission. The play had a greater popular success than most of the War plays, because Fitch did not hesitate to introduce fictional characters and events that would increase the dramatic intensity.

The Revolutionary War plays that have found the greatest success in the theatre have covered a limited span of historical events and have unhesitatingly sacrificed historical accuracy to dramatic effectiveness. Many of the War plays were intended merely as theatrical demonstrations to give voice to the prevailing patriotic sentiments. In these plays dramatic verisimilitude gave way to spectacular tableaux and commemorative eulogies. All the War plays to some extent followed the romantic urge to glorify the revolutionary spirit and the heroic actions of the fight for freedom.

WARS WITH THE BARBARY STATES

From 1785 to 1816 the United States was involved in a continual struggle with the pirates of the Barbary States. These pirates—the Algerians seem to have been the most vicious—preyed on all shipping that passed through the Mediterranean, seizing the vessels and placing the crews in slavery. Thomas Jefferson was in Paris as early as 1786 trying to negotiate peace with the Barbary States, but he concluded that naval action was the only possible course that would secure United States shipping in that region. Until 1801 the country was unable to put Jefferson's suggestion into action. American naval forces were occupied with the more urgent problem of dealing with France's violations of our neutrality. But immediately preceding and during the War of 1812, American naval vessels were battling in the Mediterranean against the States of Algiers, Tripoli, Morocco, and Tunis. And with the vigorous naval attack of Stephen Decatur in 1815, the United States was finally freed from this piratical menace.[26]

The romantic adventures of American and English sailors, captured and put into slavery in the mysterious, faraway land of Algeria, was ready-made material for the romanticists.

The first theatrical reference to the Algerian trouble seems to have been in *Shelty's Travels,* an interlude which Dunlap put on for Hodgkinson's benefit (Hodgkinson was the manager of the John Street Theatre) on April 24, 1794. The text has not survived, and nothing is known of how extensively the Barbary States figured in the action.

The first extant play on the subject was *Slaves in Algiers; or, a Struggle for Freedom,* by Susanna Haswell Rowson. It was performed at the Chestnut Street Theatre in Philadelphia, December 22, 1794. Although the title suggested a patriotic motive, the text of the play offered no perorations on the glory of the "struggle for freedom," such as those which have been observed in the Revolutionary War plays. The exciting escape of the Americans from their Algerian captors by the use of disguise was the principal incident of the play.

Frequent allusions to the struggle with the pirates are to be found in plays which did not deal directly with the subject. For example, in John Minshull's *Rural Felicity* (1801), Margaret remarked: "Sailors are coming fast into fashion. By their skill we shall suppress the pirates, and secure our trade." [27] And in James Nelson Barker's *Tears and Smiles* (1807), the General instructed the crowd: "Go welcome the prisoners from the dungeons of Tripoli with that sentiment! dry with it the tears that are shed for those who fell in attempting their deliverance, or generously give it in thanks to the brave survivors of *that* action which accomplished it!" [28]

In 1812 James Ellison wrote a play for the Boston Theatre entitled *American Captive; or, The Siege of Tripoli;* this was based on the capture of Americans and their treatment by the Tripolitan leader, the Bashaw. Ellison gave one new turn to the usual story by having the native girl, Immonina, become infatuated with the American, Anderson. The play was revived by J. S. Jones in 1835.

In 1818 an anonymous play, *The Young Carolinians; or, Americans in Algiers,* was published in Charleston. Evidence within the text indicates that the play was written several years earlier while Colonel David Humphreys, the United States Minister to Portugal, was still trying to negotiate with the Dey of Algiers by offering him a tribute of $800.00, a frigate, and a treaty of peace. Before the close of the play, the navy was in action, and the captives were rescued and returned safely to Carolina. Spectacular scenes were repeatedly introduced: the sea fight and eventual capture of the American ship; a grand procession to the accompaniment of Turkish music with the

Turkish princess, Selima, borne on a sedan chair and followed by a colorful train of attendants.

The text of M. M. Noah's *Siege of Tripoli,* first produced at the Park Theatre on May 15, 1820, has not survived. But even if it had, the manuscript would probably not be of as much interest as the historical record of the third performance of the play at the Park. Just after the audience had left the theatre, the building burned to the ground. As was the custom, the third night had been the author's benefit night, and Noah, with the magnanimity so often exhibited in the theatrical profession, devoted his entire profit of $400.00 to assisting the distressed members of the company. On January 25, 1822, the play was repeated in Philadelphia with new scenery and under the new title, *Yuseff Caramalli.*

Printed in 1823 but never produced, J. S. Smith's *The Siege of Algiers; or, The Downfall of Hadgi-Ali-Bashaw* was labelled by the author "a Political, Historical and Sentimental Tragi-Comedy in five acts." The play was distinctive only for the curious symbolic and "expressionistic" figure, Christian Monitor, who served as a kind of collective conscience for all the characters. Though he never actually appeared, he repeatedly uttered admonitions to the other characters.

John Howard Payne's *The Fall of Algeria* had its first production at the Drury Lane Theatre in London, 1825, and was first produced in this country in Philadelphia in 1827. There was a striking similarity between Payne's play and Mrs. Rowson's *Slaves in Algiers,* particularly in the scene in which Timothy Tourist, disguised as a woman, was borne off by Coigi, who mistakenly believed he was saving Lauretta. The play celebrated the British attack on Algiers, but the principal action involved the adventures of the two lovers, both of whom, unbeknownst to each other, were prisoners of the Algerians. The Algerian locale provided merely a colorful and exotic background for their repeated attempts to escape.

The Bombardment of Algiers (1829), by Richard Penn Smith, was never played and remained unpublished until it was included in the thirteenth volume of *America's Lost Plays.*

It was an adaptation of the French melodrama *Le Bombarde-ment d'Alger ou le Corsaire Reconnaissant,* by Frederic du Petit-Mère, and bore a marked resemblance to Payne's play. In Smith's play the story of husband and wife captured by the pirates on separate occasions and, unknown to each other, placed in the custody of the Dey, became an exciting romantic adventure in the remote and picturesque splendor of the Dey's court. There was little patriotic feeling for the American cause in the fight against Algerian barbarity.

Naval Glory; or, Decatur's Triumph (1844) was the last of the plays dealing with the Mediterranean pirates. Although Decatur had also participated in the War of 1812, his adventures in the battles with the Barbary States were far more distinguished. In 1815 the ships under his command finally cleared the Mediterranean for American commerce. The play was successful in its day mainly for the spectacular scene of ships being blown to bits. Decatur is remembered for his famous toast which was probably incorporated in the text of the play: "Our Country! In her intercourse with foreign nations may she always be in the right; but our country right or wrong."

There were no first-rate plays dealing with this phase of American history, and on the whole the dramatists used the exotic grandeur of the North African locale merely as a romantic background for melodramatic adventure. Patriotic praise for the naval heroes or glorification of the fight for freedom of the seas was only infrequently hinted at.

WAR OF 1812

None of the other military engagements of the United States was as quickly reflected in the drama as the War of 1812. From 1812 to 1815, the Park Theatre in New York, the Chestnut Street Theatre in Philadelphia, and the Federal Street Theatre in Boston were re-enacting in miniature the brilliant American naval victories over British frigates. In a way, these representations were the precursors of the current newsreels. On December 8, 1812, news reached Philadelphia of the capture of the *Macedonia* by the United States. On December 11, the Chestnut Street Theatre offered a patriotic sketch, *The Return from a Cruise,* commemorating this event. The victory of the *Constitution* over the *Guerrière* occurred on August 31, 1812. On September 9, Dunlap's *Yankee Chronology* was given its first performance, at the Park in New York.

That Dunlap's play was intended merely as a patriotic interlude prepared especially for the occasion is evident from his advertisement of the play: "The song of Yankee Chronology was written for the Fourth of July last, excepting the last verse. Upon the arrival of the news of the victory obtained by Captain Isaac Hill of the *Constitution,* over the English frigate, the *Guerrière,* Mr. Cooper, the manager of the Park Theatre, called upon the writer and requested an additional verse, and an introductory interlude. My wishes were too much in unison with his to allow of hesitation. On the anniversary of the evacuation of this place, another verse was requested and given; and the writer should be happy to evince his gratitude to every defender of his country's rights, by adding for each a tribute of applause till his song outdid chevy-chase in number of verses." [29] This exceedingly brief one-act interlude, although written in dialogue, was more narrative than dramatic. There were only three characters, Old Bundle, his son Ben, and O'Blunder. Ben Bundle had been on board the *Constitution* during the engagement with the *Guerrière* and had just returned to recount the battle to his father. When he had finished his story, he sang a series of verses chronicling the major events of American history from the early colonization up through the War of 1812. To the published version of *Yankee Chronology,* Dunlap added two other songs: one, "Freedom of the Seas," had been sung at the New York Theatre on July 4, 1810, and the other, "Yankee Tars," had been sung by Mr. Yates at the same theatre on December 10, 1812.

Philip Freneau also gave a spirited account of this naval battle in "On the Capture of the Guerrière." Freneau's hatred of the British had not abated since the days of his Revolutionary War poems, and his attacks in such poems as "On the British

Invasion" and "On the British Commercial Depredations" were more relentless and severe than any sentiments expressed in the War of 1812 drama.

That the practice of commemorating in the theatre events of the War continued until the last battles had been fought is evident from Ireland's notation of the following performance. On February 20, 1812, *The Festival of Peace* celebrated the ratification of peace between Great Britain and the United States.[30] Something of the nature of this spectacle can be derived from a list of the dramatis personae: Old Fearnought, Young Fearnought, Julius Caesar Babble, Columbia, Genius of Columbia, Peace, Plenty, and Commerce. Evidently *The Festival of Peace* was intended as a hopeful forecast of the future of America.

The plays of the War of 1812 did not, of course, cease appearing in 1815. Old ones were repeated from time to time, and new ones were introduced. On July 4, 1818, St. Louis saw a performance of *Yankee Chronology*. And in this instance the patriotic spectacle was carried even to the exterior of the theatre: "In front of the theatre will be exhibited an elegant transparency representing the Genius of America crowning with laurels the tomb of the immortal Washington." [31]

Like many other plays dealing with the War of 1812, G. E. Grice's *Battle of New Orleans* was produced on July 4. A stilted drama in which General Jackson appeared as a heroic figure, it had its first performance at the Park Theatre on July 4, 1816. Unlike most of the War of 1812 plays, Mary Clarke's *Fair Americans* (1815) expressed an undercurrent of Federalist criticism of the War. It seems not to have been acted.

Naval encounters were not easily adapted to the stage except as spectacular scenic representations, yet no land operation of the War was used as dramatic material until M. M. Noah's *She Would Be a Soldier*, first presented on June 21, 1819, at the Park. Noah's play was based on the battle of Chippewa, July 5, 1814, in which the American Army under General Jacob Brown and General Winfield Scott redeemed the earlier defeats of the Canadian campaign. Although the account of the battle given in the play was fairly accurate according to historical records, it furnished only the background for the main theme, the sentimental story of Christine and Lenox.

A strong nationalistic sentiment pervaded the play, but with less bitterness toward the enemy than was common in the patriotic sympathies expressed in Revolutionary War plays. The final speech, for example, in tune with the prevailing spirit of good will that followed the War, pleaded for tolerance: "When old age draws on apace, may you remember the Plains of Chippewa, and feel towards Britain as freemen should feel towards all the world—Enemies in war—in peace, Friends!" [32] There were, however, frequent thrusts at the English gentleman soldier who was annoyed at being deprived of the refinements of his London life, of his Bond street clothes and anchovies.

Noah wanted chiefly to preserve in the drama a record of the Battle of Chippewa. As he said in the Preface: "National plays should be encouraged. They have done everything for the British nation, and can do much for us; they keep alive the recollection of important events, by representing them in a manner at once natural and alluring. We have a fine scope, and abundant materials to work with, and a noble country to justify the attempt. The Battle of Chippewa was selected because it was the most neat and spirited battle fought during the late war, and I wish I was able to do it more justice." [33]

According to the author's Preface, Richard Penn Smith's *Eighth of January,* first performed at the Chestnut Street Theatre on January 8, 1829, was written much in the same manner and for the same reason as Noah's play: "*The Eighth of January* was merely intended to serve the occasion on which it was produced, and so little time was allowed for its composition, that it was sent piecemeal to the theatre to be copied and the last act was not written until after the piece was announced, and within a week of its performance. . . . It is time that the principal events in the history of our country were dramatized, and exhibited at the theatre on such days as are set apart as national festivals, and that there are few more deserving of commemoration than that herein slightly touched upon." [34] Ostensibly the play was intended to celebrate the triumph of Jack-

son at New Orleans in 1815, but more immediately it celebrated the ascendancy of popular government in Jackson's
election to the Presidency in 1828. Jackson was represented in
the same romantic light in which his followers of the time saw
him: He was straightforward and "tough as a hickory"; he was
possessed of a charitable disposition and an unfaltering belief
in the power of right and justice to prevail; and he was convinced that all men were created with equal rights and that it
was the duty of every man to sacrifice private gain for the welfare of his country.

Whereas *The Eighth of January* dealt with a battle of the
far South, Penn Smith's other War of 1812 play, *The Triumph
at Plattsburg,* sought its material from a Northern battleground.
It was first produced at the Chestnut Street Theatre on January
8, 1830, and was based on the victory of MacDonough's fleet in
Plattsburg Bay, September, 1814. The dramatist's interest centered on the escape of Major McCrea from the British, but the
audience was probably more interested in the scenic representation of the fleet. The second act closed with the naval spectacle.

Most of the major events of the War of 1812 were at some
time or other recorded in drama. And although in a strict view
of acceptable dramatic structure, none of these plays can be
classed as good drama, they were eminently successful as theatrical spectacles and reportorial representations.

MEXICAN WAR

The events of the Mexican War were reported in the theatre
very much as were the events of the War of 1812. Historical
battles were represented on the stage almost immediately after
they occurred. Durang, writing about the Philadelphia stage,
says that the Mexican campaign was "on and off all season at
the Arch Street Theatre";[35] and some Mexican War dramas
continued to be played during the fifties. As late as 1858 a *Battle of Buena Vista* was being played in New York.

Although several titles of plays dealing with the Mexican

War are known, none of the plays has survived.[36] The literary
record of the Mexican War is to be found rather in such poems
as Whittier's "The Angel's of Buena Vista," Theodore O'Hara's
"Bivouac of the Dead," and William Simms's "Lays of the Pal-
metto."

CIVIL WAR

The first shock of the Civil War naturally disrupted the normal
routine of the theatre: Niblo's Garden was closed from April
29 to December 23, 1861; the Bowery was dilapidated by military occupation in May, 1862; and the Boston Theatre closed
on April 6, 1861, after a short season of only sixteen weeks. But
following the early disturbances these theatres regained their
equilibrium and continued uninterrupted for the remaining
War years. Naturally the conflict changed the course of life for
many actors. Some entered the service, others devoted themselves to giving patriotic recitations, and many performed for
the camp Amusement Associations. Steele Mackaye, for example, acted Shakespeare in a camp in Baltimore.

The transcending tragedy of the period was, of course, the
shooting of Lincoln, on April 14, 1865, at Ford's Theatre in
Washington during Laura Keene's production of *Our American Cousin*. Of all events in American theatrical history the
assassination was certainly the most indelibly marked.

In the drama of this period War themes began to appear
even before the first shot was fired on Fort Sumter. *Our Union
Saved; or, Manon's Dream,* an anonymous play in which the
part of "the President" was played by D. J. Maguire, was first
performed at the Olympic Theatre on January 16, 1861. On
February 11, a national tableau entitled "Uncle Sam's Magic
Lantern" was inserted into the spectacular *Seven Sisters,* a play
by George H. Miles which had been having an excellent run
at Laura Keene's Theatre, but which, until the insertion of the
tableau, had had no relation to the coming conflict.

As in the other wars, actual events were represented on the
stage almost immediately after they had occurred. The Battle

of Bull Run, for example, was fought on July 21, 1861, and on August 15, *Bull Run; or, The Sacking of Fairfax Courthouse,* by Charles Gayler, was on the stage. *Hatteras Inlet; or, Our Naval Victories,* also by Gayler, was performed at the New Bowery on November 2, 1861, just three months after the event. And Harry Seymour's *Capture of Fort Donelson,* performed at the New Bowery, February 22, 1862, celebrated Grant's triumph of February 16.

Not all the War plays celebrated specific events. Two anonymous plays performed in 1862, *The National Guard,* at Niblo's Garden, and *How to Avoid Drafting,* at the Bowery, were more general in their scope.

On December 22, 1862, the Richmond Varieties Theatre presented *The Guerillas,* the first original drama to be produced in the Southern Confederacy. Written by James D. McCabe, Jr., it exhibited a vigorous patriotic feeling though it was not a first-rate play. During 1863 there seems to have been a lull in Civil War plays; but in January, 1864, the Bowery Theatre presented *The Unionist's Daughter; or, Life in the Border States.*

After the War there was a lively spate of plays dealing with the conflict.[37] In December, 1865, John F. Poole's *Grant's Campaign; or, Incidents of the Rebellion* was performed at the New Bowery. In December, 1867, Milnes Levick's *The Union Prisoner* was at Barnum's Museum. In the same year, 1867, Augustin Daly's *Norwood* presented the first stage version of the Battle of Gettysburg. *British Neutrality,* by T. B. DeWalden, was at the Olympic in July, 1869; *Ulysses; or, the Return of U. S. Grant* was at the Union Square Theatre in September, 1871; and in October, 1871, *Returned Volunteer* was being presented at the Academy of Music. Alfred R. Calhoun's *The Color Guard,* although not definitely dated, is said to have been popular with the Union soldiers after the War.

None of these plays was available for the present study, and few of them are extant. Their loss is felt principally in theatrical history, however, for they were not comparable dramatically to the later treatments of Civil War themes.

Just as Dunlap's *André* was the first play to transform the Revolutionary War into creditable drama, Boucicault's *Belle Lamar* was the first noteworthy play dealing with the Civil War. The first appeared eighteen years after the Revolutionary War and the second nine years after Lee's surrender at Appomattox, receiving its first performance at Booth's Theatre on August 10, 1874. Unlike *André, Belle Lamar* had little foundation in historical fact. Except for "Stonewall" Jackson, the characters were fictitious, and the battles and troop movements were created to fit Boucicault's dramaturgy. Although the play gave indications of the growing tendency toward realism in the theatre—introducing Belle as Philip's divorced wife, for example—the pervading tone was romantic: troops arriving in the nick of time, sentries calling out in the darkness, spies slipping through the enemy lines, the colored servant, Old Dan, giving himself up to save Belle, distant bugles, councils of war, and mysterious troop movements. In fact, Boucicault introduced practically all the romantic details that could be employed in a Civil War play.

Belle was the first of the romantic Southern heroines, a type that was to become indispensable in the succeeding War plays. She was undeniably in love with Marston Pike, an officer in the Northern Army, and yet she was willing to use information procured from him to aid the Confederate cause. "Stonewall" Jackson was also cast in the romantic mold. An heroic soldier born to the tradition of romantic warfare, he always warned his enemies of their imminent destruction, giving them an opportunity to surrender before he attacked them. With its romantic natural background and with the growing intensity of battle action, these scenes must have provided some exciting moments. Boucicault described the background and the climactic rescue action as follows:

The White Stone Gap. A gorge in the Shenandoah Mountains. An hour before daylight. At the back, in the distance is seen the range of mountain tops, and in the half distance a plateau, cut by a chasm in which a river flows across the picture. The river is visible only L. H., where it bends toward the spectator; here it is spanned by a bridge. In front, a rocky ledge, with a rude log cabin. Military works have been thrown up, to turn the place into a redoubt. . . .[38]

.   .   .   .   .

The head of a column of National troops is seen coming rapidly across the distant bridge. It disappears for a moment behind a grove of trees; then spreads out, and lines of troops appear. At the same time at the plateau in the center above, from the line of woods, other columns appear moving down and forward. Distant rifle firing is heard in the valley. Guns appear on salient points, and their rapid flash and report is mingled with the drums, bugle calls, and regimental music; distant cheers—which grow louder. Several field officers and men mount the bastions, leap over, and greet Philip. The men wave their hats on their rifles.

Tableau.
Guns—Music—Shouts
Quick Curtain.[39]

For ten years following *Belle Lamar* there were no significant Civil War plays. Belasco's *May Blossom* (first produced in New York at the Madison Square Theatre on April 12, 1884) was an alteration of his earlier play, *Sylvia's Lovers* (first produced in Virginia City, Nevada, in 1875) and belongs in the present study only to complete the record. The War served merely as an indefinite background for the love-triangle story of Richard Ashcroft, May Blossom, and Steve Harlan.

Allatoona, by Major General Judson Kilpatrick and J. Owen Moore, was first produced on October 22, 1877. This was a chronicle play beginning at West Point, where the hero, Harry Estes, and his classmate, Charles Dunbar, took up opposite sides of the struggle. It had some vigorous moments and was supposed to have been historically accurate in the rendering of details, but it was not in the first rank of Civil War dramas.

William Gillette's *Held by the Enemy,* first produced at the Criterion in Brooklyn on February 22, 1886, was the next important play of the War. Though it was a military play, it was not concerned with any major campaign, dealing primarily with the struggles between officers of the Union Army over the love of a Southern girl, Eunice McCreery, and secondarily, with the escape and capture of her brother, a Southern spy. All the subsidiary action, however, and all the backgrounds were given a romantic military atmosphere; and every scene carried as high an emotional tone and as much melodrama and dramatic suspense as it could without seeming to be too artificially contrived. Gillette was more intent on avoiding the appearance of artificiality than any of the dramatists previously encountered.

Held by the Enemy was full of realistic details. One of the characters, a magazine illustrator, had his battle pictures already drawn, ready to be sent off as soon as an appropriate battle occurred; and the court-martial scene and the scene in the military hospital were rich in realistic particulars. But Gillette was insistent that no details of setting should seem to be planned specifically for theatrical effect.

The play was especially distinguished by the swift-moving and continually changing melodramatic action. For sheer dramatic suspense the hospital scene is unequalled in American drama. Colonel Brant and Eunice McCreery in trying to effect Hayne's escape from the hospital, where he was being held prisoner by Brigadier Surgeon Fielding, had contrived, during Fielding's absence, to have Hayne pronounced dead. With Hayne laid out on a stretcher, impersonating a dead man, they were just on the point of removing him from the hospital when Fielding, who was in love with Eunice and the sworn enemy of Colonel Brant, returned. For several moments they were able to divert Fielding's attention from the departing procession. But finally Fielding suspected he was being tricked and was just about to throw back the sheet uncovering Hayne's body when Eunice whispered to Fielding that she would marry him if he would allow Hayne to escape. Fielding hesitated for a moment, bent over the body, and looked at Eunice; then he agreed that Hayne was dead and allowed the cortege to proceed. In the final scene of the play, however, Colonel Brant forced Fielding to release Eunice from her promise.

As in most of the Civil War plays, the basic causes of the conflict were never hinted at. The military allegiances of the

Northern and Southern fighters to their respective armies provided the motivation to action.

On November 19, 1888, an early version of Bronson Howard's *Shenandoah* was performed at the Boston Museum.[40] This first production was not a success, but Charles Frohman saw it and made suggestions to Howard for revision. Howard accepted the suggestions and returned to his study; and on September 9, 1889, a rewritten *Shenandoah* was performed at the Star Theatre in New York. The play achieved a great success not only because of its dramatic effectiveness but because of its historical and technical accuracy.

Although not a spy drama, Howard's play had many striking similarities to Gillette's *Held by the Enemy*. There was, for one thing, the same realistic representation of romantic adventure. Unlike Gillette's drama, however, *Shenandoah* had a strong element of intrigue and suspicion and was closely related to actual military events. For example, the play opened in a "Southern Residence overlooking Charleston Harbor," and during this first scene one witnessed the firing on Fort Sumter.

As in most of the Civil War plays, however, the focus of attention was romantic love and conflict, in this case the love of a Northern soldier, Kerchival West, for a Southern maid, Gertrude Ellingham, and the conflict between their love and honor. The conflict was brought to a point of uncomfortable strain when Gertrude was captured as a spy by Union soldiers and placed in the custody of Colonel West.

The soldiers in *Shenandoah*, particularly Colonel West, were highly romanticized figures. They were noblemen of strong hearts and strong bodies and were unyielding in their resolve to fight to preserve the Union. Colonel West, for example, arose from his sick bed to lead his regiment. Even the ladies were endowed with strong and active spirits. They were not frail and delicate Southern belles; Gertrude was like "Another Evangeline! Searching for her lover through the wilderness of this great war!" [41]

The growing tendency toward realism both in stage presentation and in character drawing was apparent in *Shenandoah*.

Captain Thornton, for example, was despicable enough to have been a typical melodramatic villain; but instead he was portrayed realistically, his badness relieved by some touches of goodness. The backgrounds (the "shore of Charleston Harbour," "the Ellingham Homestead in the Shenandoah Valley," with its magnificent view of the mountains) were romantic in the grandeur of their conception but realistic in their attention to detail. The military aspects of the production observed a scrupulous regard for historical accuracy. Howard had read extensively from Civil War records before he wrote *Shenandoah,* and the bugle calls, for example, were to be the actual bugle calls used in the War.

Undoubtedly a considerable share of the success of the play resulted from the acting. Frohman had assembled a magnificent company for the play: Wilton Lackaye appeared as General Haverill, Henry Miller as Colonel Kerchival West, Viola Allen as Gertrude Ellingham, and Effie Shannon as Jenny Buckthorn.

Augustus Thomas' *Surrender,* first produced in Boston on November 21, 1892, was laid in or near Richmond during the last days of the Confederacy. The main incident was based on the historically obscure attempt to free the Confederate prisoners at Johnson's Island in Lake Erie and to launch an attack on New York.

Gillette's other drama of the War, *Secret Service,* was first produced at the Broad Street Theatre in Philadelphia on May 13, 1895, under the title *The Secret Service.* The first presentation of the revised text, the text as it now stands, was at the Garrick Theatre in New York on October 5, 1896, where it continued playing until March, 1897. Few plays of this last decade of the century achieved such widespread success as *Secret Service.* In May, 1897, Gillette played it in London, and a French version was prepared by Pièrre Decourcelle. Up to the date of the publication of his *History of the American Drama* (1917), Quinn tabulated 1,799 performances of the play over this twenty-year period.

In *Secret Service* the interest was centered directly on the romantic adventurous life of the spy. Henry Dumont, alias

Captain Thorne, was a daring, quick-thinking, and quick-acting Northern spy who risked everything to attempt to transmit a telegraphic report to the Northern headquarters. The romance of the "Secret Service" was the predominating tone. As Thorne said near the end of the play: "We fight our battles alone—no comrades to cheer us on—ten thousand to one against us—death at every turn! If we win we escape with our lives—if we lose—dragged out and butchered like dogs— no soldier's grave—not even a trench with the rest of the boys —alone—despised—forgotten! These were my orders Miss Varney—this is the death I die to-night—and I don't want you to think for one minute that I'm ashamed of it." [42] Thorne certainly made a realistic appraisal of his situation, but he still maintained the romantic honor of his calling. When Edith contrived to get a special order from President Davis permitting Thorne to use the Confederate telegraph office, thus protecting him from seizure by Southern officers, he refused to use the order to further his own interests, for it went against his sense of honor.

Secret Service like *Held by the Enemy* was rich in realistic detail. No other play of the period provided such elaborate and carefully planned suggestions for stage movement as those which Gillette supplied for the scene in the War Department Telegraph Office. The slightest twitching of the mouth was indicated in the text. Actions rather than words were frequently used to convey meaning. Such directions as "Scarcely more than a movement of the lips—'Yes.'" occurred repeatedly, and interrupted and dovetailed speeches were extremely common. But even with all this attention to detail (Thorne jumping over balustrades, whisking about from one telegraph key to another, poking his cigar in his mouth, and sliding down in his chair to simulate composure) the grand sweep of the romantic adventure still held the major attention.

Belasco's *The Heart of Maryland,* first produced at the Grand Opera House in Washington on October 9, 1895, was more notable as Belasco's first substantial success and as the drama which introduced Mrs. Leslie Carter to the theatre than as a

Civil War play. The Southern atmosphere was admirably suggested; but the introduction of the spectacular scene in which Maryland saved her lover by swinging on the clapper of the bell, the artificiality of the situation in which the rebel, General Kendrick, was forced to court-martial his son, Colonel Kendrick, of the Union Army, the utterly villainous nature of Colonel Thorpe, and the would-be "grave-diggers" scene made the play a theatrical hodgepodge. Belasco was evidently trying to combine all the elements that had been found successful in previous Civil War plays, with the result that the romantic love story and the attempts at realistic representation were overshadowed by the melodrama.

Although the increasingly frequent occurrence of realism has been noted in several plays, it was not until *The Reverend Griffith Davenport,* by James A. Herne, was produced at the Lafayette Square Theatre in Washington on January 16, 1899, that a Civil War play received an almost completely realistic treatment. The problem of slavery had hardly been mentioned in previous Civil War dramas, whereas in Herne's play it was the starting point. The military operations in the earlier plays had been clearly defined actions, depending for success only on the skill and fortitude of the men and their commanders, but in *The Reverend Griffith Davenport* the enormous complexity of the military problems was at the center of the drama. Where motives and feelings had been clear and unmistakable in the plays of Howard and Gillette, the emotions and thinking of Herne's characters were complex and confused. Katherine Davenport was an ardent believer in the Southern cause, but her feeling of loyalty to her husband was so strong that not until the final scene was she able to break from him and act in behalf of her Southern compatriots.

The Reverend Griffith Davenport was one of the most intricate realistic character studies of nineteenth-century American drama. He was opposed to slavery, but his own slaves, whom he had acquired through marriage, were devoted to him. When he finally got enough courage to act on his convictions and free them and when his neighbors discovered that he had also voted for Lincoln, he was driven from his home, although he had been a respected member of the community. When he moved to Washington and was asked by Lincoln to assist in planning the difficult military campaign into the Shenandoah Valley, he at first hesitated because he felt physically incapable of such a momentous task and emotionally incapable of launching a campaign into his wife's home country. But even though this essentially realistic tone persisted throughout the play, there was a suggestion of grand-scale romanticism in the attribution to Davenport of the sole power to effect the success or failure of the Shenandoah campaign.

Clyde Fitch in *Barbara Frietchie*, first produced at the Broad Street Theatre in Philadelphia on October 10, 1899, made no pretense to historical accuracy. The story Fitch concocted was purely romantic invention. Barbara, a young Southern girl, had fallen in love with Captain Trumbull, a wounded Northern soldier who had sought refuge with the Frietchies. Although her father at first refused to consent to their marriage, he finally relented, and they were married shortly before Trumbull died. Barbara, in honor of her dead husband, hung a Union flag from her window just as Jackson and his Rebel soldiers marched by. Jackson had given orders that no man was to shoot at Barbara's Union flag. In disobedience of the order, Jack Negly, Barbara's former suitor, shot at the flag and killed Barbara. Negly's father, Colonel Negly, was then obliged, in accordance with Jackson's commands, to sentence his son to be shot. The incidents of the play were romantic in their aspects and arrangement, but the dialogue and the portrayal of character were, in general, realistic.

The Civil War provided the theme for some of the best American dramas of the nineteenth century. These plays were not closely related to actual events of the war, but they were historically accurate in rendering details which were suggestive of real happenings. For the most part they depended upon a combination of realistic details with romantic stories. Slavery as the underlying cause of the War received little attention. The fight to preserve the Union was given some consideration;

but on the whole, the plays depended, for their dramatic action, on the conflict between loyalties to the North and South. The causes for which the armies were fighting were only hinted at. There were no eulogies of the War heroes or spontaneous patriotic outbursts. In this respect the Civil War plays differed markedly from the plays of the other wars.

Practically all Civil War plays were set in the South. Since they were intended for Northern consumption, this removal of locale from the realm of immediate acquaintance provided an initial romantic tone. Furthermore, the Southern battleground was more dramatic. The dangers to the cities and domestic establishments were more harrowing; the pathos of losing all material possessions in fighting for a lost cause was more stirring. A Northern scene would of necessity have exhibited less military action, and the conflict would have seemed remote.

In the Civil War plays one perceives the beginnings of a style of playwriting that, judging from its later popularity, seemingly suited the tastes of the American public. The result was a play with realistic details imposed upon a romantic story or situation.

6. *The Frontier and the Folk*

FROM THE earliest days in America until the last decades of the nineteenth century, the westward-moving outposts of civilization offered the adventurous spirits of the country a bountiful share of excitement and romance. Men and women from the older states were repeatedly seeking a freer life in the vast expanses of the West. They found it successively in the backwoods country from New York to Georgia, in the "beautiful" Ohio Valley, and along the banks of the Mississippi. Then, following precarious and ill-marked trails, they discovered the "promised land" in Oregon and California; and finally, traveling along these same Western trails in Conestoga wagons, they stopped to set up the cow-towns in Kansas and Wyoming and the mining camps in Colorado, Nevada, and California.

These frontiersmen were imbued with the romantic spirit in its fullest intensity. The very nature of their wild and undisciplined surroundings demanded adventurous, romantic living. And although they were too occupied with subduing the unsympathetic forces of nature to record their adventures in the drama, they took the theatre with them onto the frontier.

One of the earliest recorded dramatic performances on the frontier was given in 1797 by the inhabitants of the hamlet of Washington, Kentucky. In 1810 a professional troupe from Montreal was transported to Lexington to perform on a theatrical circuit that included Lexington, Frankfort, and Louisville; but owing to internal dissension and disagreement with the local promoters, the group did not last out the season. Early in 1815 the local Kentucky promoters opened negotiations with Drake's company in Albany, and in December a group of actors from that company arrived in Lexington. This group was more successful probably because they made a conscientious effort to adapt themselves to the accepted social practices of the frontier inhabitants.

In 1801 a theatre was opened in Cincinnati, in 1814 a thespian society was organized in Vincennes, and in 1815 an amateur theatrical group gave performances in St. Louis. In Detroit a theatre was being operated in 1816 by the officers from General MacComb's garrison. And, following the example of Vincennes, thespian societies were rapidly being organized in Lafayette, Indianapolis, Logansport, New Harmony, Dayton, and Springfield.

Noah Ludlow was the first of the theatrical managers on the frontier. The success of his ventures, beginning in 1817, as manager and promoter was largely dependent on his careful and sympathetic study of the men and women on the frontier. In 1880 he wrote: "For the greater part of my life I have entertained the opinion that the pioneers on the various roads of the world's broad highways were among the most interesting objects for the study of the coming generations of men." [1] Sol Smith, who had been a member of Drake's company in Albany, was Ludlow's principal competitor in the managerial realm in the Ohio and Mississippi valleys until the two joined forces in 1835 in Mobile. From then on they practically controlled the entertainment field in that region. Their only opponent was a Mr. Caldwell. Caldwell had started his theatrical enterprises in New Orleans in 1820 and had then moved up the river to offer his attractions to the inhabitants along the Ohio.

About 1830 showboats began to appear on the Ohio River. William Chapman's *Floating Theatre* was one of the first. During the forties such gaudy and spacious boats as the *Snow Queen* or the *Fanny Elssler* were tied up every night at village landings to present their dazzling visions of the outside world to the local gentry. Many of the regular river steamers had facilities for theatrical and musical entertainments and, in addition to their gilded concert-saloons, more intimate saloons for gambling. Asbury estimated that in 1850 there were two thousand professional gamblers operating on the river boats.[2]

During the thirties the Eastern actors were coming to the West by boat; Joseph Jefferson III remembered vividly his trip to Chicago on "The Pioneer." When he wrote his *Autobiography* in 1889, he still recalled the striking impression this journey through the Erie Canal and across the Great Lakes had made upon him. He still saw the romantic vision of his first sight of the energetic and expanding village of Chicago with its "bright and muddy streets, gaudy colored calicoes, blue and red flannels, and striped ticking hanging outside the dry-goods offices."[3] His uncle had urged his father to join him in the management of the new theatre in Chicago, but the Jeffersons made only a brief stay in Chicago, moving west to play in Galena, Illinois, and in Davenport, Iowa. Through most of the nineteenth century practically every town was a one-night or a week stand for the itinerant actor.

Often the pioneers set up a theatre wherever they stopped. When Joseph Smith led his group of Mormons to Nauvoo on the banks of the Mississippi, they founded a dramatic company. In 1850, shortly after their arrival in Salt Lake City, they began again to perform plays; and in 1861 Brigham Young erected the Salt Lake Theatre at a cost of more than a hundred thousand dollars.

The nineteenth-century frontier theatre was a thriving and vital institution in the community. The frontier drama and the drama of the folk were, however, slower to develop. Most of the companies maintained the conventional repertoires: *Romeo and Juliet, Richard III, Pizarro,* and other similar plays.

Joseph Jefferson III was only nine years old when his father struck out for Chicago in 1838, twenty-one years before he made his first appearance in *Rip Van Winkle.* Yet Ludlow's Cincinnati company had played a *Rip Van Winkle* as early as the fall of 1828. And although Ludlow's performance was the first west of the Alleghenies, it was not the first performance. According to Phelps, the first dramatization of Irving's story was made by "an Albanian" and performed by a Thomas Flynn in Albany in May, 1828.[4]

The first version of *Rip Van Winkle* which has survived was that by John Kerr, produced at the Walnut Street Theatre in Philadelphia on October 30, 1829. James Hackett, the Yankee actor, played a modification of Kerr's version at the Park Theatre in New York on April 22, 1830. While in London, Hackett became acquainted with still another dramatization of the story which had been prepared by W. Bayle Bernard for the English actor, Yates. Hackett persuaded Bernard to alter Kerr's dramatization, and on September 4, 1833, Hackett appeared again as Rip at the Park in this composite Kerr-Bernard version. It seems, however, to have been little changed from Kerr's original. That Hackett succeeded in capturing some of the pathos for which Jefferson's final scene became so famous is evident in Sol Smith's comment: "I should despair of finding a man or woman in an audience of 500 who could hear Hackett's utterance of five words in the second act, 'but she was mine vrow' without experiencing some moisture in the eyes."[5] On January 7, 1850, at the National Theatre, New York, Charles Burke, half brother of Jefferson, acted in yet another version. Hackett recognized the superiority of Burke's dramatization and proceeded to adopt it for his performance of *Rip Van Winkle* at the Broadway Theatre in 1855. Still another, but less known, *Rip Van Winkle* was the London adaptation of Kerr's play which Thomas Hailes Lacy prepared.

By far the best dramatic treatment of Washington Irving's story was, however, that which was finally evolved by Joseph Jefferson III. Jefferson stated in his *Autobiography* that the idea of acting Rip came to him suddenly in 1859. He had had, however, some acquaintance with the play before that time. His father, Joseph Jefferson II, had acted Rip at various times; his uncle had played the part of Knickerbocker; his aunt had played Alice; his first cousin had played Gustaffe; and Jefferson himself had played Seth Slough, the Innkeeper, in the production put on by his half brother, Charles Burke, in Philadelphia in 1850. In the fall of 1859 Jefferson completed his three-act version of the play, compiled from the older texts, and with himself in the leading part presented it at the Carusi Hall in Washington. He was not satisfied with the script, however, and while in London in 1865, he commissioned Boucicault to rewrite the play for him. Boucicault's version was performed at the Adelphi Theatre, in London, on September 5, 1865. It ran for 170 nights. The following year, on September 3, 1866, it received its New York *première* at the Olympic Theatre. From then until 1904, a year before his death, Jefferson acted the part. Hutton estimated that Boucicault's version was played by Jefferson upward of 1,400 times.[6]

The two other dramatic treatments of the story never achieved any particular distinction. An operatic version was produced at Niblo's Garden, September 27, 1855. The libretto was by J. H. Wainwright and the music by George F. Bristow. In 1874 (*ca.*) James Herne prepared a version of *Rip Van Winkle* which Belasco praised for its fidelity to the Dutch quality in the character.

Rip Van Winkle was an important play in nineteenth-century American dramatic and theatrical history on the frontier and in the theatrical centers. It was the only extant drama of the nineteenth century based chiefly on folk material. Although the various versions differed somewhat in the sequence of events and in the treatment given the minor characters, they all depended essentially on Washington Irving's original conception of the central character. Rip was at the heart of the story. And as Rip became an actor's star-part, beginning with Burke's version and culminating in the dramatization prepared by Boucicault for Jefferson, the stage effectiveness of the play was immeasurably increased. The hearty, quick-witted loafer, loved by everyone excepting his wife, was a stage figure known and cherished by every theatregoer of the last half of the century. The pathos of the scenes in which his wife drove him out into the rain, in which he wakened after his twenty years' sleep and returned to the village to find that he had been forgotten, and in which his little girl, Meenie, finally recognized him, brought the stoutest audiences to tears.[7]

Although, strictly speaking, no other American dramas in the nineteenth century were devoted to folk material, many of the frontier plays were derived from the folk legends which had been built up around real-life characters.

Frontier plays did not appear early in American dramatic literature. They followed almost by a decade the first frontier novels of James Fenimore Cooper. Cooper was not only the first American to establish the novel as a literary form but the "first to discover and chart out our great romantic hinterland."[8] In 1823 he published his romance of the forest, *The Pioneers*. Natty Bumpo, who was to become the representative frontier hero, was introduced by Cooper in *The Last of the Mohicans* (1826) and in *The Prairie* (1827). Cooper was not, however, the only novelist of this period to treat the frontier. Timothy Flint, following Cooper's pattern, used his frontier experiences in such novels as *George Mason, the Young Backwoodsman* (1829), *Arthur Clenning* (1828), and *Shoshonee Valley* (1830). In the decade of the thirties, novels of the Western region became more frequent with the works of William Leggett, Charles Fenno Hoffman, Albert Pike, *et al.*

Travel books and nonfictional retrospections such as James Hall's *Sketches of the History, Life, and Manners in the West* (1835) also began to appear.

The first noteworthy frontier character in the drama was Colonel Nimrod Wildfire in James Kirke Paulding's *The Lion of the West*. Paulding's play was written especially for James Hackett and was first played by him on April 25, 1831, at the Park Theatre, New York. On his trip to London, Hackett took the character with him but not the play. And just as he had got W. Bayle Bernard to assist in preparing a new *Rip Van Winkle*, he got him to write a new play incorporating the character of Nimrod Wildfire. Bernard's play, *A Kentuckian's Trip to New York in 1815*, was first performed with "enormous success" at Covent Garden, April 1, 1833, and later at the Haymarket.

Nimrod, clad in buckskin clothes, deerskin shoes, and coonskin hat, was an unpolished but generous son of "old Kentuck" who was always "primed for anything, from a possum hunt to a nigger funeral." He was a pugnacious "crittir," and if he failed to find a fight every ten days, he began to feel "a might wolfy about the head and shoulders." At the end of Paulding's play, Wildfire introduced his wife, Miss Patt Snap of Salt Licks. As he described her, she must have been a suitable companion for his rough-and-ready life: "There is no back-out in her breed for she can lick her weight in wild cats and she shot a bear at nine years old." [9]

The craze for sensational "blood-pudding" frontier stories such as William Gilmore Simms' *Richard Hurdis* (1838), *Border Beagles* (1840), and *The Kinsmen* (1841) was never adopted by the dramatists. But the exciting adventures of the Argonaut's trek to California in '49 were treated in such plays as the anonymous *A Trip to the California Gold Mines,* played by Charles Burke at the Arch Street Theatre in Philadelphia on January 10, 1849.

Theatrical performances were instituted in California during the forties. The first legitimate English play was produced by American soldiers at Sonoma, California, in 1847; and the first professional company appeared at the Eagle Theatre, in Sacramento, on October 18, 1849. Theatrical events moved rapidly in the late forties. In December, 1850, Tom Maguire opened his first Jenny Lind Theatre in San Francisco. It burned down the next year, was rebuilt immediately, and was reopened on October 4, 1851. From then on through the early days of Belasco's productions in the sixties and seventies and the minstrel performances of Billy Emerson in the seventies and eighties, San Francisco was the theatrical center of the West. Junius Brutus Booth, Edwin Booth, Laura Keene, Lola Montez, and California's own star, Lotta Crabtree—who had first played as a child actress in mining-camp barrooms—appeared at the Jenny Lind. But San Francisco was not the only Western town to boast of a theatre. In the flush days of Virginia City (Nevada) there were five legitimate theatres and six variety houses running at the same time. When Adah Isaacs Menken made her famous ride on the wild horse in *Mazeppa,* Virginia City miners went mad: "When the horse clashed up the rocky mountain trail with her beautiful, almost naked body lashed to its flank, pandemonium broke loose . . . Virginia City had never been so thrilled. It christened a new mining district The Menken and organized a Menken Shaft and Tunnel Company. When their dazzling heroine finally left, she was laden down with bars of bullion, silver nuggets, and certificates of mining stock." [10]

The next contribution to the frontier drama was Dr. Thomas Dunn English's *The Mormons; or, Life at Salt Lake City,* first given at Burton's Theatre in New York City in March, 1858. The story of the play involved the adventures of a New York politician, Timothy Noggs. Noggs had gone West to instruct the Danites (Mormons) in political manipulation but he discovered that they were his masters in manipulation and, when he retired, found himself bound to thirteen wives. Among the other characters in the play, Walter Markham exemplified the high-principled type of frontier character and Whiskey Jake the plains scout. Jake, a more representative type than Markham, was faithful to his friends, unmerciful to his enemies, and addicted to whiskey and gaming.

Not to be outdone by Burton's production, Wallack in May, 1858, presented the anonymous *Deserted; or, The Last Days of Brigham Young.* The play began in New York with the Irishman, Luny O'Flab, and the fireman, Tom Scott, preparing to go West in search of wives. But the scene shifted immediately, not to the Western region, but to the imaginary "paradise of Mahomet," to which Brigham Young had departed. It then became a burlesque of Mormonism and included even an unrelated parody of Poe's "The Raven."

The anonymous play, *A Live Woman in the Mines; or, Pike County Ahead* (1857), exhibited a number of the conventional Western types. Pike County Jess was the rough, uneducated, yet dependable and generous miner who favored the natural justice of the West to any city-type law courts. His wife was an honest and kindhearted soul who could see the miners' admirable qualities beneath their rough exteriors. Cash and Dice were outlaw gamblers from Sacramento, and High Betty Martin was the illiterate yet resourceful and fearless "Amazonian of the Western plains."

Fast Folks; or, Early Days of California, by Joseph Nunes, was another favorite frontier play of the period. It appears to have been acted by Mr. and Mrs. Wallack in San Francisco, and by John Dolman and Mrs. Drew in Philadelphia during the 1858-59 season.

Across the Continent, by J. J. McCloskey, was first produced in New York at the Park Theatre on November 28, 1870. Doud Byron acted the leading part, Joe Ferris, in this performance, and continued playing it repeatedly during the next thirty years. Although the last scene of the play used the Station House of the 47th Station on the Union Pacific Railroad as a background, no frontiersmen were introduced. McCloskey made no pretense of providing a serious portrayal of frontier life, and the Indian raid that closed the play was introduced merely for its spectacular effect. Some of the romance of the early days of the railroad was inherent in the thrilling episodes of calling back the train and having the troops arrive just at the right moment. And the conception of the West as the place where men go to forget their pasts or start new lives was to become one of the popular romantic ideas about the frontier.

Only a few plays dealing with frontier subjects were significant markers in the history of American drama and theatre. All of these appeared on the stage during the decade of the seventies, when the literary scene was changing rapidly. The young men from the West, Howells, Harte, and Twain, were beginning to dominate the new literature. They wrote of the regions they knew with a curious blend of romantic impulse and realistic technique. The dramatists followed the same pattern; romantic adventure was enacted in the costume and manner of the real-life frontiersman.

One of the favorite plays of the seventies was T. B. DeWalden's *Kit the Arkansas Traveller*, first played at the Boston Theatre on February 14, 1870. The leading part in the play, Kit Redding, was interpreted by F. S. Chanfrau; and from that time on, Chanfrau's manner of playing the pioneer character became the standard for all succeeding pioneers.

Augustin Daly's *Horizon*, produced at the Olympic Theatre in New York on March 21, 1871, was the first drama that drew its inspiration directly from Bret Harte's stories of the Western frontier. Harte had caught the picturesque aspects of the frontier characters and the exciting episodes of their melodramatic life; and although some critics objected to his interpretation of the West, he became the model for succeeding frontier writers.

Daly's characters were stage adaptations of Harte's fictional characters. They were an independent lot of free-speaking and free-acting men who had no regard for traditional legal authority. Rowse's grant of land from Congress, for example, was to them a mere scrap of paper. And yet their justice could not be said to have been hastily or inconsiderately administered. It was merely the inevitable and inscrutable law of the frontier. As Rowse insisted: "We are here proceeding according to law. Not the musty statutes of effete systems and oligarchies of the

Old World, but the natural law implanted in the bosoms of man since our common ancestors were washed, wrung out and hung up to dry by the universal flood." [11]

Such a fervent appeal to democratic doctrine was certainly reminiscent of similar sentiments expressed repeatedly in the war plays and the Yankee plays. In these early plays the complaint had been directed against the oppressions of a tyrannical King and his officers. Now it was directed against the vestiges of that same authority which had been taken up by the aristocratic Easterners.

In Daly's play frontier coarseness was contrasted with Eastern artificiality, just as New England Yankee bluntness had been contrasted with urban blandness. And just as Mrs. Tiffany in *Fashion* bowed to anyone who was fully acquainted with the "fashion," Columbia Rowse in *Horizon* worshipped anyone who was "prominent." Daly's satire was not as clever as Mrs. Mowatt's, but it probably made its cuts.

A romantic view of nature, similar to that in the Indian drama, persisted in *Horizon*. The strongest elements of the romantic were, however, in the spectacular scenes. One was the scene in which the women, left alone in the fort, were overpowered by the Indians. Another was the stirring climactic spectacle of the final scene in the deep ravine. Sundown Rowse, Columbia Rowse, and the Widow were held captive by the Indians and were awaiting their execution. High above on the bridge one could see their friends and would-be rescuers, Alleyn, Sergeant, and Mrs. Smith, but they did not perceive the prisoners. The prisoners were afraid to signal for fear of being killed instantly. The trio up above moved on, and all hope was lost. Then suddenly and unexpectedly, Loder, who had entered in the disguise of an Indian, threw off his disguise and held the Indians at bay while the troops stumbled down the rocks into the ravine and effected the rescue.

Loder was in most respects a typical frontiersman, but he was drawn with a more realistic turn of mind than most frontier characters. He recognized that although he loved Med deeply, she belonged to another class of society. As Quinn said, the

scene in which Loder renounced her, "for simplicity of language and restraint of passion [went] far to establish Daly's
claim to be the first of the modern realists in American playwriting." [12]

Generally, the frontier plays dealt with life in Nevada,
Colorado, and California; yet the most popular frontier play,
Davy Crockett, dealt with the frontier days in Tennessee.

The real Davy Crockett was born in Hawkins County, Tennessee, in 1786. His father, who had fought at Kings Mountain,
had crossed the mountains from North Carolina into Tennessee,
probably some ten or fifteen years after Daniel Boone had gone
to Kentucky. Crockett's remarkable adventures in Tennessee
and later his startling actions and pronouncements in Congress
—he had gone to Washington as a Congressman just before
Jackson went as President—were all recorded in an incredible
series of books, purported to have been written by himself,
but actually written by smart journalists in Washington. One
of these books, however, gave some evidence of authenticity;
this was the *Autobiography,* published in 1834. In it Davy remarked that it was strange indeed that a fellow who "can't
scarcely read and write" should be one of the most popular
authors in America. In this one instance, however, he certified
that the book really was his, "every sentence and sentiment,"
although he had allowed someone to correct the spelling and
grammar. No semimythical or mythical frontier hero received
such an elaborate and complete literary record as did Davy
Crockett. Daniel Boone, the bold, simple, and honest woods-
man; Paul Bunyan, the mythical frontier strongman; and Mike
Fink, the mythical, red-haired, hard-fighting and hard-loving
boatman—although the legends of all three were endless—
never achieved in literature and on the stage the heroic stature
destined for Davy Crockett.

The play *Davy Crockett* was written by Frank Hitchcock
Murdoch and was first performed at the Opera House in
Rochester, New York, September 23, 1872, thirty-six years after
the real Davy Crockett had died in defense of the Alamo. In
the first performance, as in the last, the leading role was

assumed by Frank Mayo. Mayo had begun his career at the American Theatre in San Francisco in 1856; but not until he became manager of the Rochester Theatre and persisted in playing *Davy Crockett* did he reach his full stride. Few actors have ever hung to a play so tenaciously as Mayo did after *Davy Crockett*'s cold reception in Rochester. Years later in recounting these events Mayo wrote: "For a year and a half the play received no encouragement beyond the good-natured comment that is bestowed indiscriminately by some of the kind-hearted critics. It was not until the third year that it began to be regarded with high favor, and since that time it has been dubbed an 'idyl,' a 'pastoral,' an 'epic' in five acts. . . . I have now been playing it eight years, and am conceited to the extent that I think I have made a very good piece of dramatic workmanship by my personation of *Davy,* but I would rather have written the play in all its crudeness, than have acted it ten times better than I have done." [13] From the opening in Rochester until his death, Mayo played the part almost continuously. He kept count of his performances up to 2,000 and then stopped. The last performance was given at the Broadway Theatre in Denver, June 6, 1896. Mayo died two days later.

Davy was a "natural gentleman" who stuck to the motto his father had followed: "Be sure you're right, then go ahead." He was bold but unassuming, gentle but strong-willed, shy and sensitive but capable of any sacrifice for love. The sight of Eleanor overwhelmed him: "Great Lord, that gal could buy me out, body and soul, for next to nothing, and I ain't for sale generally. I ain't neither." [14] Although she had been his childhood companion, she had lived since childhood among the refinements of London. But even though she had experienced the delights of the civilized society of the Old World, she still loved the simple folk of the frontier. When Davy rescued her from the cold and brought her to his cabin, she read to him the ballad of Young Lochinvar. Davy listened rapturously, but he was still embarrassed by his own awkwardness: "I ain't fit to breathe the same air with you. You are scholared and dainty, and what am I, nothing but an ignorant backwoodsman, fit

INTERIOR OF PARK THEATRE

Plate II

DROP CURTAIN OF FIRST BOWERY THEATRE

EXTERIOR AND INTERIOR OF BROUGHAM'S LYCEUM

Plate 13

WILLIAM BRADY'S PRODUCTION OF "UNCLE TOM'S CABIN" (1901)

Plate 14

Plate 17

Courtesy of Museum of the City of New York

"THE FOREST ROSE"

Plate 18

"THE CONTRAST"

Plate 19

Plate 20

SCENES FROM "SHENANDOAH"—A GREAT COMEDY DRAMA.

THE PLAY OF THE CENTURY—SUCCESS HERE—EVERYWHERE.

300 NIGHTS IN NEW YORK—LOVE-MAKING ON THE STAGE.

only for the forests and the fields where I'm myself hand in hand with nature and her teachings, knowing no better." [15] When the light of the fire grew dim and the menacing howls of the angry wolves were heard around the cabin, Davy braced himself for the struggle; all through the night he stood with his weight against the door barring the ravaging wolves as he watched Eleanor sleeping by the fire. When Eleanor awakened and realized Davy's devotion, she was overcome: "Yes, look at my tears—my soul is welling through my eyes. This night has shown me all your noble self—your loyalty, your unselfish devotion. I read your nature, as you cannot, for in the greatness of your heart, you depreciate those qualities which in my eyes raise you far above your kind, to where, rugged and simple but still pre-eminent, you stand a man. Fate seems to have linked our lives, but the world divides us. We must part here, and both must learn to forget." [16] This was certainly one of the most sentimentally moving scenes in the frontier drama. *Davy Crockett* was an exciting play, but it was cherished mainly for its sympathetic portrait of the noble frontiersman.

The Gilded Age, by Mark Twain and C. D. Warner, dealt realistically with a more stabilized frontier and exposed the brazen profiteering carried on by politicians in Washington. The hero, Colonel Sellers, perennially young and filled with the spirit of adventure, represented that class of frontiersmen whose ambition and energy led to the feverish, and often corrupt, exploitation of the Western regions.

The first dramatization of the novel was prepared by Gilbert S. Densmore and performed at the California Theatre, April 23, 1874. Twain, however, revised Densmore's dramatization for the performances at the Park, which began on September 16, 1874, and continued for one hundred and nineteen nights.

Joaquin Miller and Bret Harte were the leading "local colorists" of the Western lands during the seventies and eighties. Miller wrote four plays: *Forty-nine,* first played at Haverly's Theatre, New York, on October 1, 1881, dealt with the story of the pioneer who stuck to his tunnel even after hope was gone and finally found gold; *Tally-Ho*[17] was based on Horace

Greeley's account of his crossing of the Sierras with Hank Monk, the dashing stagecoach driver; *An Oregon Idyll,*[17] Miller's favorite play, focused attention on the natural glories of the mountains and forests of the Pacific Northwest. It was his first play, however, that was the most vigorous and exciting; this was *The Danites in the Sierras,* produced in the Broadway Theatre, New York, on August 22, 1877.

The Danites dealt with the mysterious and vigilante-like activities of the Danites (Mormons) in trying to effect an unexplained revenge on Nancy Williams. It was a play of strong passions and emotions, of quick thinking and action; and the characters were of genuine frontier extraction. In fact romantic figures of the West similar to those created by Miller are still employed with slight variations as the stock characters for the moving pictures of Western romance. Typical among the Danites were: Sandy, "A king, this man Sand; a poet, a painter, a mighty moralist; a man who could not write his own name"; the Parson, "So-called because he could outswear any man in Camp"; the Judge, "Chosen because he was fit for nothing else in this Glorious climate of California." In other respects the play predated the conventional movie treatment of the West. The Widow came as a missionary and managed to institute sufficient reforms to get most of the bachelors married; and the Judge meted out justice in the impromptu frontier manner.

The glorification of natural beauty was, however, the principal romantic aspect of *The Danites.* Miller was known as the "poet of the Sierras," and certainly in this drama one felt that the mountains, "the white watch towers of the Sierras," were more than mere theatrical background.

As Billy (Nancy Williams)[18] and the widow came out of Billy's cabin and gazed over the magnificent expanse of mountain peaks, Billy was overcome with admiration.

> How beautiful! The whole moon's heart is poured out into the mighty Sierras. O what a miracle; the moon and golden stars; and all the majesty and mystery of this calm, still world to love. O, life is not so hard now.

Widow. And you love the world, with all your sad, hard life?
Billy. And why not? Is it less beautiful because I have had troubles?
My sweet friend, it seems to me the highest, the holiest religion that we can have, is to love this world, and the beauty,
the mystery, the majesty that environ us.[19]

Such a spiritually romantic view of nature has not been observed in any of the previous frontier plays that have been considered.

No writers knew the Western frontier better than Bret
Harte, and few had a passion for the stage equal to his; yet his
plays were not stage successes. His dramatizations of *Thankful
Blossom, The Luck of Roaring Camp, Clarence,* and *A Blue
Grass Penelope* were never produced; and his *Two Men from
Sandy Bar,* based on his story, *Mr. Thompson's Prodigal,* had
only a moderate success. It was first performed at the Union
Square Theatre, New York, on August 28, 1876. *Ah Sin,* on
which Harte and Twain collaborated, had somewhat better
luck. It opened at the National Theatre, Washington, May 7,
1877, and was sufficiently successful to induce Augustin Daly
to produce it in New York on July 31 at the Fifth Avenue
Theatre. Harte's greatest stage success came in 1896, when
Sue was first performed at Hoyt's Theatre in New York. *Sue*
was not, strictly speaking, a frontier play.

Two Men from Sandy Bar, although too long, rambling, and
diffuse to become an effective stage play, did treat frontier life
with vigor and sympathy. Harte was principally occupied with
the story, but his characters were appealing frontier types,
rough and ready but "clar grit all through." Even the city-
born Miss Mary preferred the rough miners to her overrefined
cousin. Sandy was a hard drinker, but he reformed; and John
Oakhurst, who appeared through most of the play as an impos-
tor, turned out finally to be a "pretty decent sort."

The typically Western and romantic notion of partner loyalty was displayed for the first time in Harte's play. Sandy explained to Concho: "Look ye, Concho, he has wronged me in
a private way; that is *my* business, not *yours;* but he was *my*
partner, no one shall abuse him before me." [20] The introduc-

tion of Spanish characters was another Western detail that had not been used before in the frontier drama.

Romantic exterior scenes with vistas of the "snow-capped" Sierras were used as backgrounds, but they were never viewed with the romantic and religious fervor noted in Miller's play. In *Two Men from Sandy Bar* there was a mixture of the romantic spirit with realistic detail that often resulted in unfortunate incongruities in the dialogue. For example, when Miss Mary was soliloquizing on Sandy, she remarked: "Crime and Sandy! No! shame and guilt do not hide themselves in those honest but occasionally somewhat bloodshot eyes." [21]

In *Ah Sin,* Harte and Twain were merely trying to capitalize on the popularity of the Chinese character Hop Sin. Hop Sin had appeared as a minor figure in *Two Men from Sandy Bar.* *Ah Sin* was entirely built around him at the expense of probability, and the conglomeration of miners and townspeople served only as a background for his antics.

Bartley Campbell was more successful than either Harte or Miller in transferring the Western mining region to the stage. He was, however, indebted to both these earlier writers. In 1875, when he became a member of California's famed Bohemian Club, he met Harte and Miller and borrowed freely from their extensive Western experiences.

Campbell's first play of the West was *How Women Love; or, The Heart of the Sierras,* first produced at the Arch Street Theatre, Philadelphia, on May 21, 1877. It was based on Harte's *Outcasts of Poker Flat* and was rewritten later under the title *The Vigilantes; or, The Heart of the Sierras.* When Campbell died, he was at work on another frontier play entitled *Romance of the Rockies.* *My Partner,* performed at the Union Square Theatre, New York, from September 16 to October 18, 1879, was, however, his best play of the West, and certainly one of the best of the frontier dramas.

My Partner leaned heavily toward realism. In fact, the story of the fallen heroine who later achieved a happy marriage in spite of her early transgression was more realism than most audiences of the time were willing to allow. Many communities and critics censored the play for its unorthodox views on sin. On the other hand, the realistic comments on politics salted in with the mellifluous phrases from the mouth of the silver-tongued orator and legislator, Major Britt, must have delighted most audiences. When Ned remarked to Britt that "Politics are not what they were in California," Britt replied: "Nothing like it! Those were the days when a man was as proud of the hue of his nose as of the color of his meerschaum, when a fellow could throw out a string of adjectives baited with patriotism and haul in enough votes to elect him every time." [22] As in many of the Western plays the characters were not distinctly endowed with specific traits and manners; and except for the villainous Josiah Scraggs, most of them lived in accord with the nobility of their surroundings, as loyal, kind, and gentle folk. Campbell like Miller felt the overpowering moral influence of the great Sierras. It was almost impossible for men to be bad with these glorious monuments of nature, "the green groves of God," looking down on them.

Another play that employed romantic scenic beauty as a background was Augustus Thomas' *Arizona*, first performed in Chicago on June 12, 1899, at Hamlin's Grand Opera House. Thomas' play was not essentially frontier drama, however, and is not otherwise relevant to the present discussion.

In the nineties frontier drama was overshadowed by the spectacular shows of such real-life Western heroes as "Wild Bill" Hickock and "Buffalo Bill" Cody. This phase of American theatrical history has been well described by Dulles: "[These famous characters] re-enacted for cheering audiences saloon brawls, stage-coach hold-ups, and blood-curdling Indian attacks. Trusty rifles and murderous six-shooters barked continuously in *The Gambler of the West*, and at every bark another red-skin bit the dust. Between the acts Jack Dalton threw bowie-knives at Baby Bess, the Pet of the Gulch, and Rattle Snake Oil was sold at a dime a bottle in the lobby." [23]

Except for the startling success of Frank Mayo in *Davy Crockett*, the frontier character in the American theatre never achieved a popularity comparable to the stage-Yankee. The bulk of the frontier drama appeared during the seventies, but even during that period playwrights with sufficient skill were not making a sustained attempt to interpret the romance of the frontier. Harte, Miller, and Campbell, to be sure, did treat the romance of the miner, with his frantic quest for gold, his natural honesty and good spirits, and his love of drinking and shooting, but they invariably directed their attention to the melodramatic story rather than to the development of character. As a result, the Western dramas did not exhibit any characters of sufficient vitality and completeness to become enduring figures in the American theatre.

In the seventies the turn of drama was toward realism, but an atmosphere of romance still hung over the frontier regions. The dramatist could not treat a frontier theme forthrightly; and in his attempt to retain the spirit of romance and yet to introduce realistic turns in character, action, and dialogue, he created a drama that was for the most part feeble and erratic.

CHAPTER III

Romanticism in Acting
and in the Traditional Drama

ALTHOUGH the present investigation has been focused primarily on the romantic aspects of the plays which employed native themes and characters, some attention must be given to those plays which adopted the conventional romantic pattern, treating the universal passions of love, revenge, jealousy, and hatred, as demonstrated in the lives of heroic personages in faraway places and times. Of course, even the conventional romantic drama was frequently not altogether divorced from contemporary life. In the twenties and thirties, for example, when romantic plays were dominating the dramatic scene, the spirit of the growing democracy was reflected in their condemnation of tyranny and glorification of the rights of the common man even though they dealt with distant places and times. During the decade of the seventies, however, the conventional romantic plays by native playwrights were almost totally unrelated to the life of the time.

Three general types of conventional romantic drama were popular in the American theatre during the nineteenth century. One of these types, probably the most prevalent, presented a dramatis personae of quasi-historical characters against a colorful romantic background of some distant locale. An example of this type is John Howard Payne's *The Last Duel in Spain*. The second type differed from the first in that it treated historical figures. Such plays as Robert T. Conrad's *Jack Cade* and William Dunlap's *Peter the Great* belonged to this category. The third group consisted of gloomy gothic presentations of the mysterious and sinister adventures of medieval nobility; *Fontainville Abbey,* by Dunlap, and *Mount Savage,* by Payne, were typical. Many of the plays in these three groups were not, of course, original creations. Adaptations of French and German plays and English novels were extremely common in the first quarter of the century. In fact, most of the successful plays up to 1825 were by English playwrights or were adaptations from the French and German.

In the early years of the American theatre, 1760–1800, when English companies dominated the scene, the repertoires were made up almost entirely of conventional romantic plays drawn directly from the London theatre. Shakespeare, Farquhar, Otway, Congreve, and Addison were performed repeatedly, and even in the mid-nineteenth century, when native plays were being accepted, the leading actors still maintained their reputations and sustained themselves by playing Richard, Othello, and Macbeth.

The nineteenth-century American theatre, on the whole, was a theatre of actors. The audiences looked for the next performance by Forrest, Booth, and Barrett rather than for the next plays by Bird, Stone, or Boker. It is fitting then that the present discussion of plays should include concurrently some allusions to the romantic actors who were responsible for keeping romantic drama on the stage.

The preponderance of conventional romantic plays in early American theatre repertoires has already been noted. In keeping with this prevailing taste, it was natural that *The Prince of Parthia,* the first American play to be performed in the Colonies (April 24, 1767) should have been a romantic tragedy. It drew heavily on Elizabethan tragedy. The scene was laid in Parthia sometime about the beginning of the Christian era; the play dealt with events that were supposedly drawn from history and dwelt only on grand passions and noble sentiments. But even in this early romantic tragedy of faraway place and time the growing protest of the Colonists against the oppression of King George found expression in such lines as these:

> Jove's thunder strikes the lofty palaces,
> While the low cottage, in humility,
> Securely stands, and sees the mighty ruin.
> What King can boast, tomorrow as today,
> Thus happy will I reign? The rising sun
> May view him seated on a splendid throne,
> And setting, see him shake the servile chain.[1]

Seventeen years later (1784) Peter Markoe's romantic tragedy, *The Patriot Chief*, was written to warn the people against the dangers of another oppression, that which resulted from aristocratic rule. In his judgment "the most odious and oppressive of all modes of government" was that in which the aristocracy had control.

Mrs. Warren, whose major dramatic efforts were discussed in the section on Revolutionary War plays, wrote two romantic tragedies in verse, *The Sack of Rome* and *The Ladies of Castile*. They were published in 1790, but neither has survived. On May 7, 1790, the American Company presented *The Widow of Malabar*, by David Humphreys, at the Southwark Theatre, Philadelphia. Laid in India and based on a French play, *La Veuve de Malabar*, by LeMierre, it was one of the first of the native romantic plays to be produced.

Native drama employing accepted romantic materials did not appear in quantity until William Dunlap began his series of adaptations from Kotzebue. Kotzebue's influence on domestic tragedy has so often been noted that one is inclined to forget that he also wrote plays of the conventional romantic type. Dunlap's *Count Benyowski* (first performed April 1, 1799) and his two South American plays portraying the romantic tradition of the noble savage, *The Virgin of the Sun* (March 12, 1800) and *Pizarro in Peru; or, the Death of Rolla* (March 26, 1800), were adaptations from Kotzebue. *Pizarro* was the first native play to find a place in the accepted repertoire of the leading romantic actors, Thomas Hamblin, J. W. Wallack, and Edwin Forrest.

Dunlap did not limit his adaptations to Kotzebue. A blood-and-thunder romantic melodrama, laid in Venice, *Abaellino, the Great Bandit* (February 11, 1801), was derived from the German of Johann Heinrich Daniel Zschokke. And *Peter the Great* (November 15, 1802), one of the first American plays to employ a real historical figure, was taken from the German *Die Strelizen,* by Joseph Marius Babo.

During the nineties and the first years of the new century, the sentimental novels of Richardson and the themes of horror used by William Godwin and Mrs. Radcliffe were widely popular in the States. Richardson's sentiment had little effect on the American theatre, but the themes of Godwin's and Mrs. Radcliffe's gothic romances were found to suit the taste of the theatre public. Dunlap drew on Mrs. Radcliffe's *Romance of the Forest* for his gloomy *Fontainville Abbey* (February 16, 1795). All the accepted devices of melancholy and fear were introduced: bats blowing out candles with the flap of their wings, mysterious murders, skeletons covered with cobwebs, dim light, and dark and foreboding passageways leading to unfathomable caverns. Even in this atmosphere, however, the love for liberty was again extolled: "But this, compar'd with prisons, is a palace—for here I've liberty." [2]

No native writers of the early nineteenth century produced as many plays as Dunlap, but some other examples of conventional romantic plays of this period are to be found. Dr. Elihu Hubbard Smith, following the example of Schiller, introduced a robber as the romantic hero of his *Edwin and Angelina; or, the Banditti* (December 19, 1796). John D. Turnbull's *Rudolph; or, the Robbers of Calabria* (Boston Theatre, 1807) was also influenced by Schiller's *Die Räuber. Rudolph* was one of the first American plays to specify a sympathetic musical accompaniment, "music expressive of suspicion," and "music expressive of agitation." Charles Jared Ingersoll turned to the historic struggle between King Edwy and Bishop Dunstan for his *Edwy and Elgiva* (Chestnut Street Theatre, Philadelphia, 1801). Burk, although better known for his *Bunker-Hill,* found the story of Joan of Arc admirably suited to express his fervent love for freedom. His *Female Patriotism; or, the Death of Joan d'Arc* was first produced at the Park, in April, 1798.

The Charleston playwrights during the first decades of the nineteenth century produced a variety of conventional romantic plays. *Foscari; or, the Venetian Exile,* by John Blake White (Charleston Theatre, 1806), was set in Venice and followed the pattern of Elizabethan tragedy. Isaac Harby chose fifteenth-century Florence for his *Alberti* (1819); and Frances Wright in *Altorf* (February 19, 1819) found fourteenth-century Switzerland best suited to express her love for freedom. Edwin Clifford Holland drew from a more contemporary scene, presenting the romantic story of Lord Byron in a drama entitled *The Corsair* (Charleston, 1818). Several plays from this Charleston group were written in the tradition of gothic romance. Two of these were John Blake White's, *The Mysteries of the Castle; or, the Victim of Revenge* (Charleston Theatre, 1806), and Isaac Harby's *The Gordian Knot; or, Causes and Effects* (1807).

During the second decade of the century the picturesque romances of Scott were widely read, and on April 13, 1812, James Nelson Barker's dramatization of Scott's *Marmion* was played at the Park Theatre. Although it was presumably recording historical grievances, the words of King James in addressing Marmion were timely echoes of the immediate complaints against England that preceded the War of 1812:

. . . England's constant agents,
Roamed through our land, and harboured in our bays!
Our peaceful border sacked, our vessels plundered.
Our abused liegemen robbed, enslaved and slaughtered,
My lord, my lord, under such injuries,
How shall a free and gallant nation act?
Still lay its sovereignty at England's feet—
Still basely ask a boon from England's bounty—
Still vainly hope redress from England's justice?
No! by our martyred fathers' memories,
The land may sink—but, like a glorious wreck,
'Twill keep its colours flying to the last.[3]

One of Scott's romances, *Kenilworth*, was antedated by Dunlap. Dunlap drew the Earl of Leicester as an ideal figure in his *The Fatal Deception; or, the Progress of Guilt*, April 24, 1794. A leading American dramatist of the second and third decades of the nineteenth century was John Howard Payne.[4] In *Mount Savage* (May 27, 1822), which he had adapted from the French of Pixérécourt, Payne followed the fad for the atmosphere of medieval romance. He combined the gothic mood with the romance of adventurous love in *Mazeppa; or, the Wild Horse of Tartary*[5] (July 22, 1833), an adaptation from the French of Leopold and Cuvelier; and he employed the romantic atmosphere of Renaissance Spain and Italy in *The Spanish Husband; or, First and Last Love* (Park Theatre, November 1, 1830).

His best romantic drama was *Brutus; or, the Fall of Tarquin*. In constructing the play, Payne sifted all the pertinent historical facts from previous Brutus plays and molded them into a striking and enduring drama. Given its first American performance at the Park Theatre on March 15, 1819, it became one of the most successful plays in the repertoires of such actors as Junius Brutus Booth, the elder Wallack, Edwin Forrest, John McCullough, and Edwin Booth; and it set the pattern for all later historical romantic plays. Payne endowed his heroic figures with an exuberant fascination for fulfilling the commands of their destinies, and he never allowed them to stoop to the level of petty domestic intrigue.

In the mid-twenties liberty-loving Americans were stirred by the Greek fight for freedom. The name of Greece was on every tongue in America; newspapers and magazines dwelt on the struggle. On the floor of Congress, Webster insisted that the liberty of "Greece was of Moment, of high moment, to the cause of political liberty in all countries."

The Grecian Captive; or, The Fall of Athens, by Mordecai M. Noah, performed at the Park on June 17, 1822, was the first play to echo these sentiments. Such passages as the following recurred at frequent intervals: "Constancy will do for us what it has already done for the western world—broke the chains of tyranny, and liberated the fairest portion of the globe, . . ." [6] Noah, as he said in his preface, arranged the events of the war to fit his dramatic structure without regard to factual accuracy: "The privilege of imagination is the peculiar property of the dramatist . . . if eventually the Greeks should not recover Athens, it will not be my fault, it was necessary to my play, and so I gave them possession of that interesting spot with a dash of the pen." [7] Noah also wrote two melodramas after the conventional French pattern, *The Mountain Torrent*, 1820, and *Rose of Arragon* [sic], 1822.

The full flood of the romantic outburst in American drama followed almost immediately the rise of French romanticism in the plays of Hugo and Dumas. The performance of *Hernani* (in English) in Philadelphia during the season of 1831–32 may even have had a direct influence on Richard Penn Smith, for Smith in all probability saw the performance. Five years later he derived the incidents for his *The Actress of Padua*, performed on June 13, 1836, from Hugo's *Angelo*. Smith's greatest play, *Caius Marius*, first produced at the Arch Street Theatre, January 12, 1831, by Edwin Forrest, was, however, an original creation based on Roman history. The manuscript, unfortunately, has been lost although the play was continually in Forrest's repertoire.

The leading dramatist of this period, and, with the possible exception of Boker, the best proponent of the conventional romantic play, was Robert Montgomery Bird. Bird's first romantic dramas, *The Cowled Lover* (1827; set near Lake Como and somewhat reminiscent of *Romeo and Juliet*), *Caridorf* (set near Vienna), and the three unfinished plays, *Giannone, The Fanatick,* and *Isidora,* were all immature essays in the dramatic form; but in *Pelopidas* and *The Gladiator* he produced two of the best conventional romantic dramas by a native author. *Pelopidas* was based on the account in Plutarch of the revolt of the Theban city against the tyrants of Sparta. *The Gladiator* dealt with the Romans' persecution of their slaves; and although the events of the story were not drawn from an historical source, Bird caught the gaudy and spectacular coloring of the Roman life with which he was dealing. Few plays during the past century exhibited such strikingly dramatic scenes as the closing scene of Act Two in *The Gladiator*. Spartacus was thrown into the gladiatorial ring to fight his brother, Pharsarius; but instead of proceeding to slaughter each other, they summoned their army of sympathizers who had been expectantly waiting outside the gates and turned fiercely against their bewildered Roman oppressors. Spartacus cried:

> Death to the Roman fiends, that make their mirth
> Out of the groans of bleeding misery!
> Ho, slaves, arise! it is your hour to kill!
> Kill and spare not—for wrath and liberty!
> Freedom for bondmen—freedom and revenge! [8]

The Broker of Bogota, laid in Santa Fe de Bogota sometime in the eighteenth century, dealt with characters on a domestic level; but Bird raised the play to the accepted romantic plane by making them heroic rather than sentimental. This play was first produced at the Bowery (February 12, 1834) and later, with Edwin Forrest in the leading part, in Philadelphia (June 11, 1834).

The plays of Bird cannot be fully appreciated without some attention to the actor, Edwin Forrest, who performed the leading part in all of them. In fact, all the conventional romantic plays of the period are better understood in relation to the audience's preferences in actors.

Pelopidas was the first play by Bird that Forrest accepted; *The Gladiator* was the first that he produced (September 26, 1831, at the Park). It was his tremendous success in the part of Spartacus that prompted Forrest to make his bow before the London public. He performed *The Gladiator* at the Drury Lane Theatre on October 17, 1836. Forrest retained the play in his repertoire till his retirement from the stage in 1872. Performed for the thousandth time in 1853, it is thought to have been the first play in English to be given a thousand performances during the lifetime of the author. After Forrest's death the play continued on the boards until early in the 1890's.

Edwin Forrest was the first great American romantic actor, and he was also the only nineteenth-century actor who devoted a large share of his repertoire to plays by native playwrights. His English predecessors had relied upon the romantic plays of the London repertoire. For example, George Frederick Cooke, the first outstanding theatrical star to come to America, made his first appearance at the Park on November 12, 1810, in *Richard III*. Cooke was considered to have a picturesque appearance, and even though his voice was high-pitched and intense, his playing of Shakespeare was violent and thunderous. Some years later, on September 7, 1818, the "elder Wallack," James William Wallack, made his American debut at the Park in *Macbeth*. He became known for his graceful manly bearing, his musical voice, and his energetic manner. Wallack like Cooke limited his repertoire almost exclusively to Shakespeare.

But neither of these early romantic actors influenced Forrest. Forrest's style of acting was 'derived almost directly from Edmund Kean and the Kembles, though the Kemble influence was the less marked. Charles and Fanny had come to the United States in 1832; and as in England, they soon became known for the highbred quality of their performances. They were elegant, dignified, and in perfect taste, but to the American audience the generally languorous manner of their performances made the Shakespearean scenes of violent passion seem too tame. Fanny and Charles were not, of course, twins in the manner of their playing. Fanny had a certain impetuosity and fervor that Charles lacked. They were both, however, grand elocutionists, and it was this quality that Forrest borrowed from them.

Edmund Kean was at the opposite pole from the Kembles. His playing, as Coleridge said, was "like reading Shakespeare by flashes of lightning." He was tempestuous and passionate. Alger gave the following description of Kean's acting:

. . . no effort of the will, no trick or art of calculation, but nature itself uncovered and set free in its deepest intensity of power, just on the edge, sometimes quite over the edge of madness. . . . It came not from the surface of his brain, but from the very centers of his nervous system, and suggested something portentous, preternatural, supernal, that blinded and stunned the beholders, appalled the imagination, and chilled their blood.[9]

This preternatural, passionate, and intense manner was adopted by Forrest. Kean made his first appearance in America at the Anthony Street Theatre on November 29, 1820, in *Richard III*.

Edwin Forrest made his New York debut at the Bowery on November 6, 1826, in *Othello*. He had, however, appeared in Philadelphia as early as 1820. During his apprentice years in the New York theatre, he was under the tutelage of Thomas T. Cooper, an ardent Kemble disciple. But after he had gone West to play on the "river circuit" for a few seasons, he returned East to fulfill an engagement with Kean at the Albany Theatre. He was to play Iago to Kean's Othello, Titus to his Brutus, and Richmond to his Richard III. Forrest was so completely dazzled by Kean's genius that from that time forward he fashioned all his performances in imitation of the wild and tempestuous Kean. Forrest had a robust physique, a fine voice, and a manly bearing. He was physically well equipped for his wild tirades. His performances were never graceful and polished or refined and delicate; and, according to many observers, he was overinsistent on displaying his physical prowess. His acting, especially of the turbulent moments in the dramatic lives of Metamora, Spartacus, Lear, Othello, and Jaffier, was usually vigorous and sustained but not infrequently irregular and spasmodic. If romantic acting demands a free, spontaneous, unstudied, and frenzied performance, Forrest was unquestionably the leading American romantic actor of the nineteenth century.

In some respects Junius Brutus Booth's performances were even wilder and more verging on insanity than Forrest's, but Booth's intense and impassioned nature fitted well with the style of playing inaugurated by Kean. Booth depended on the inspiration of the moment, and usually this inspiration carried such intensity into his sonorous voice and into the flash of his eyes that audiences forgot his imperfections. His first appearance in America took place at Richmond, Virginia, on July 13, 1821, in *Richard III*.

Thus, early in the twenties the romantic tradition of free, expansive, and tempestuous acting was established as the mode for American actors. And through most of the century acting was accepted as an art which was not confined by rule, but which allowed the actor with a fiery and vigorous personality to follow the insistent urge of his own spirit. The leading actors, to the average nineteenth-century audience, were idols and heroes off the stage as well as on. The romantic life they portrayed in the theatre was thought to be merely a vivid reflection of their own lives. J. B. Booth, Forrest, Wallack, Barrett, and Edwin Booth lived and acted in an atmosphere of perpetual romance.

Ordinarily J. B. Booth did not perform in native plays, but on December 14, 1830, he appeared at the Chestnut Street Theatre in David Paul Brown's *Sertorius; or, the Roman Patriot*. This romantic drama was written by a Philadelphian, a contemporary of Bird, and was laid in Spain during the Roman Republic at the time of the victory of Sertorius over Pompey. To the present study *Sertorius* is important not as a vehicle for Booth but as one of the earliest romantic dramas from the Philadelphia school. In fact it antedated most of Bird's plays.

John Augustus Stone was another Philadelphia playwright of this period who contributed to the romantic historical drama. Although the Indian drama, *Metamora*, was his best-known work, he also wrote an unacted chronicle play, *Tancred; or, the Siege of Antioch*, dealing with the Christian attack on Antioch during the First Crusade. Another romantic historical drama by Stone, using the same title but a different subtitle, *Tancred; or, The King of Sicily*, was acted at the Park on March 16, 1831. Robert T. Conrad was, however, the leading Philadelphia exponent of the romantic historical drama. His *King of Naples*, first performed at the Arch Street Theatre, was written for the rising young star, James E. Murdoch. Conrad's best play was *Jack Cade*, or *Aylmere*, as it was frequently called. Historically, the Kentish rebellion of 1450 had been strictly political, but for dramatic purposes Conrad transformed it into a moral revolt against oppression. Jack Cade became the symbol for any attempted rebellion against the arbitrary powers of a princely caste. A rewritten version of the play was acted by Forrest at the Park on May 28, 1841.

The foremost New York writer of romantic tragedy was Nathaniel Parker Willis. His two romantic tragedies, *Bianca Visconti* and *Tortesa, the Usurer* were among the best of American plays of this type. *Bianca Visconti,* laid in Milan in the 14th century, was written in competition for a prize offered by Josephine Clifton. Miss Clifton wanted a play that would suit her particular talents. Evidently she found *Bianca Visconti* to her taste, for she performed it at the Park on August 25, 1837. *Tortesa, the Usurer,* first performed at the National in New York, April 8, 1839, was set in Florence and bore marked resemblances to *Romeo and Juliet.*

One of the most curious American romantic tragedies, and an indisputable testimony to the popularity of this form of dramatic writing, was Mrs. Charlotte Barnes Connor's *Octavia Bragaldi; or, the Confession,* first produced at the National, November 8, 1837. The story of the play was taken from a well-known incident of honor that occurred in Frankfort, Kentucky, in 1825. Colonel Beauchamp had murdered Colonel Sharpe when he discovered that Sharpe had seduced his wife. Beauchamp was convicted and sentenced to death. A few days before his execution, he and his wife attempted a double suicide in his cell, but the attempt was unsuccessful and he was finally hanged. This story had frequently been treated in fiction retaining the authentic historical locale;[10] but Mrs. Connor felt compelled to transfer her drama to fifteenth-century Milan.

In Boston, Epes Sargent was the leading exponent of romantic tragedy. His first play, *Bridge of Genoa,* concerned with the struggles of the patrician and plebeian orders in fourteenth-century Genoa, was first played at the Tremont Theatre on February 13, 1837. *Velasco,* performed at the Tremont on November 20, 1837, with James E. Murdoch as Velasco and

Ellen Tree as Izidora, was, however, a more mature play. It dealt with the colorful career of the Spaniard Rodrigo Díaz de Bivar, the Cid. The story followed a pattern similar to that in Corneille's *Le Cid;* but love, in Sargent's version, prevailed over honor without the external machinations that were necessary to Corneille. It was impossible for Izidora to resist the romantic love she felt for Velasco even though honor commanded her to refuse him:

> Revenge and love and duty and despair!
> The fury of the elements! the shock
> Of adverse fleets on a tempestuous sea!
> But, over all, riding the topmost wave,
> Love's bark still floats triumphant! [11]

Most of the other romantic tragedies written during this period were not intended to be performed, but such closet dramas as Rufus Dawes's *Athenia of Damascus* (1839) and Longfellow's *The Spanish Student* (published serially in 1842 and in book form in 1843) might have been stage successes had they ever been tried in the theatre.

From 1820 to 1850 a romantic atmosphere pervaded all art expression, but the conventional romantic play on the American stage during this period represented more than a taste for faraway time and place and a romantic view of historical events. It was not mere coincidence that so many of the plays celebrated the revolts against tyranny. They reflected the growing democratic spirit of attack on all institutions that would suppress the lives and will of the common man.

In the fifties some vestiges of the accepted romantic play were apparent in such dramas as Anna Cora Mowatt's *Armand, the Child of the People,* and Lester Wallack's *The Veteran.* George H. Miles's *Mohammed* won $1,000 in one of Forrest's contests; and although never acted by Forrest, it was played at the Lyceum Theatre, New York, on October 27, 1851.

In the main the romantic tragedy of the mid-century turned in another direction. Instead of the romance of the struggle against oppression, Boker presented the tragedy of the patrician. It is quite likely, however, that Boker's dramas were the result of his natural bent for the exotic, his taste for Scott's novels, and his persistent fascination with Spanish history. His early tragedies were merely forerunners of his great romantic play, *Francesca da Rimini,* but even in them his mastery of the tragic form was evident. His first play, *Calynos,* dealing with the Spaniard's aversion for Moorish blood, was first performed in this country at the Walnut Street Theatre, Philadelphia, on January 20, 1851. *Anne Boleyn* was never produced. His romantic comedy, *The Betrothal,* laid in Tuscany at an indeterminate time, was given at the Walnut Street Theatre on September 25, 1850. His next play, *Leonor de Guzman,* was a powerful and successful drama laid in Castile in the fourteenth century. *Leonor de Guzman* was played at the Walnut Street Theatre on October 3, 1853.

Boker's masterpiece, *Francesca da Rimini,* was the best romantic tragedy written in America up to 1900. It was first performed at the Broadway Theatre, New York, on September 26, 1855. The dramatic story was taken from the fifth Canto of Dante's "Inferno" and was, as Boker explained, composed at "white heat." He seems to have been so inspired by the romantic and tragic story of Francesca and the two brothers, Lanciotto and Paolo, that the blank verse came to his mind as fast as he could record it. Compared with the later dramatic versions of the same story by D'Annunzio and Stephen Phillips, Boker's tragedy stands out as a strikingly virile piece of dramatic writing.

None of the romantic dramas that followed *Francesca da Rimini* reached the high mark set by Boker. During the fifties, however, several romantic dramas appeared. Charles James Cannon's *The Oath of Office* (Bowery Theatre, March 18, 1850) was laid in Ireland near the close of the fifteenth century and Oliver Bell Bunce's unacted romantic tragedy, *Fate; or, the Prophecy* (1856), in "Altenburg in the Early Feudal Times."

Julia Ward Howe wrote two plays in the vein of romantic tragedy: *Leonora; or, the World's Own* (Wallack's Theatre,

New York, March 16, 1857) and *Hippolytus* (1864). The latter was written for Edwin Booth, and if the scheduled production, in which he was to play Hippolytus to Charlotte Cushman's Phaedra, had reached the stage, the performance would no doubt have been a distinguished one.

Hippolytus and *Francesca da Rimini,* with their lofty sentiments and sustained emotional tone, were comparable to the distinguished New England literature of the same period: Hawthorne's *The Scarlet Letter* (1850) and *The House of the Seven Gables* (1851), Melville's *Moby Dick* (1851), *et. al.* Boker and Mrs. Howe were not in close touch with the popular theatre of their day. Like Longfellow, Boker lived under the spell of European culture and mysticism. His ideals of refinement permitted no sympathy with coarseness or frankness. And the plays of Julia Ward Howe offered a striking contrast to such popular sentimental outbursts as Fanny Fern's *Fern Leaves from Fanny's Portfolio,* which sold 100,000 copies in its first year.

During the sixties and seventies there were no new romantic dramas in the theatre. Forrest retained *The Gladiator, The Broker of Bogota,* and *Jack Cade* in his repertoire, but the newly arrived English and Continental actors exhibited only the standard romantic dramas of their home countries. Actors, not plays, were the chief attraction in the theatre during this era.

Tommaso Salvini, Italy's illustrious tragedian, made his debut in America on September 16, 1873, in *Othello,* bewildering the audience with his murderous attack on Desdemona, in which he appeared to one observer as "bereft by maniacal jealousy of mercy and reason, [and] reduced to primeval savagery." [12]

On January 10, 1870, Charles Fechter, the French tragedian, made his first appearance in America at Niblo's Garden in Hugo's *Ruy Blas.* He fascinated his audiences with his polished style, which exhibited all the culture of the Comédie Française. His compatriot, Sarah Bernhardt, inaugurated her illustrious American appearances at Booth's Theatre in 1880 in *Adrienne Lecouvreur.* She was high-strung, temperamental, and eccentric and was in this way endowed with qualities that were then regarded as essential to great romantic acting.

Adrienne Lecouvreur was also the play in which Helena Modjeska, the distinguished Polish actress, had made her bow to the American public at the California Theatre in San Francisco on August 20, 1877. Her poetic power was more graceful and refined than that of the great Sarah.

Henry Irving began his first American tour on October 29, 1883, at the Star Theatre in New York as Mathias in a maniacal melodrama called *The Bells,* although during his tour he also played Hamlet, Richard III, Richelieu, and Becket. Irving was a brilliant actor, intellectual rather than emotional; and he thrilled his audiences with his subtle and moving intensity.

John McCullough was not an American-born actor although he performed most of his life in this country. He made his first appearance in America at the Arch Street Theatre on August 15, 1857. He had a powerful physique and a voice "like a ring of a trumpet." It was not surprising, in view of his physical aptitude, that he borrowed some of his roles from Forrest's repertoire: Spartacus, Lear, and Metamora.

Edwin Booth was, of course, the leading American actor of the last half of the nineteenth century. His first noteworthy appearance was as Richard III in 1851, when his father was unable to appear because of illness. During the decade of the Civil War he was the foremost tragedian in New York, playing such parts as Richelieu, Shylock, Lear, Romeo, and Hamlet. His spectacular success led him to attempt some theatrical adventures that were, for the time, almost unbelievable. In 1868 he laid the foundation stone for his million-dollar playhouse, and in 1871 he opened his magnificent production of *The Winter's Tale* at a cost of $40,000. Such financing was too high for the theatre of the time, and in 1873 he was bankrupt and obliged to surrender his New York management. For the next twenty years he was on the road. In contrast to Forrest he was an intellectual and spiritual actor. He approached his task reverently and thought of himself not as an entertainer but as an interpreter of great dramatic literature. He tried always to subjugate his own individuality to the idealized reality he was attempting to portray.

Lawrence Barrett attempted to follow in the footsteps of Booth. He also undertook his roles with a "tremendous earnestness," and as a result became, according to Winter, "one of the noblest figures of the modern stage." Barrett was the first actor to give a successful performance of *Francesca da Rimini.* He gave the Boker play the attention it deserved, and after its first performance (with Barrett as Lanciotto and Otis Skinner as Paolo), at Haverly's Theatre in Philadelphia, September 14, 1882, it became one of the standard romantic tragedies in Barrett's repertoire. Boker, pleased that his play was now receiving recognition, wrote two more tragedies for Barrett. Both of these, *Nydia* (1886) and *Glaucus* (1886), were drawn from incidents in Bulwer-Lytton's *Last Days of Pompeii,* but neither of them was ever produced. In 1887 Barrett joined forces with Booth, and the two of them toured the country with *Julius Caesar, Othello, Hamlet,* and *Macbeth.*

Two of Barrett's leading roles during the eighties were in plays by William Young. *Pendragon,* a blank-verse play dealing with the Arthurian story, was first produced by him in 1881, in Chicago. *Ganelon,* dealing with the tragic story of the traitor who betrayed Roland at Roncesvalles, was first presented in New York in 1891. Neither of these plays was published; but Young's two spectacular dramas were: the romantic comedy, *The Rajah,* which opened at the Madison Square Theatre on June 5, 1883, and ran for two hundred and fifty performances; and his popular dramatization of Lew Wallace's *Ben Hur,* which became a perennial favorite after its opening at the Broadway Theatre on November 29, 1899.

The romantic tragedies of the last two decades of the century achieved a modicum of success when they were adopted by the leading actors. Richard Mansfield, for example, was responsible for the attention given to Henry Guy Carleton's romantic melodrama *Victor Durand* (1884) and Thomas Russell Sullivan's *Napoleon Bonaparte* (1896). Neither of these, however, attained the success of Mansfield's own romantic dramas, *Monsieur* (1887) and *Don Juan* (1891).

Thomas Bailey Aldrich wrote one prose tragedy for the stage, *Mercedes,* a short romantic play that was set in Spain in 1810 and related the tragic story of a French soldier and a Spanish *señorita* who were compelled by the exigencies of war and national loyalty to drink poison and die in each other's arms. *Mercedes* was produced at Palmer's Theatre on May 1, 1893.

As mentioned above, some substantial examples of the romantic drama, *Ganelon* and *Monsieur,* for instance, appeared during the nineties; but even such exciting spectacular shows as *Ben Hur* and *The Rajah* were far outdistanced in popularity by the historical romances in printed fiction: *The Prisoner of Zenda, Quo Vadis, To Have and to Hold, Richard Carvel,* and *When Knighthood Was in Flower.* In the twentieth century most of these historical novels were dramatized and became exciting theatrical spectacles.

American drama exhibited a noteworthy progress from *The Prince of Parthia* to *Francesca da Rimini;* but aside from *Francesca* and *The Gladiator,* as representative of the two great periods of the conventional romantic drama, there were no American plays worthy of being ranked with the classics in the dramatic literature of the world. And although there were significant performances of native romantic tragedies by the leading nineteenth-century actors, these performances did not differ from their English and Continental counterparts. The dramatists followed the established European patterns for the romantic play, and the actors were schooled in the old-world traditions of romantic acting.

CHAPTER IV

Romanticism in Scene Design

THE preceding examination of plays has repeatedly revealed romantic elements in scenic representation and display which bear a marked similarity to the romantic characteristics noted in American painting. The scene painter found his most theatrically stimulating backgrounds in the wild glories and incomprehensible sublimities of natural scenery—there was hardly a play that did not require at least one exterior. Cataracts, sharp declivities, deep forests, moonlit streams, and distant mountain vistas were represented by him in their most striking and awesome aspects. And, like the Hudson River painters, he particularly delighted in the tempestuous and destructive manifestations of nature on the rampage. Fires, thunder and lightning, rain, snow, and tornados became indispensable accompaniments to the scenic display. In this respect the scenic artist had an advantage over the mere painter. With the assistance of the stage mechanic, he was able to produce "real" fire, water, rain, snow, and what appeared to be real thunder and lightning. Ships were brought out to sail the tempestuous seas and be dashed to bits on the rocks; historical battles were represented in striking tableaux scenes; whole buildings were levelled to the ground by terrific explosions. But the scenic artists did not limit themselves to such stormy displays. Brilliant pyrotechnic exhibitions and extensive panoramic views such as "Jerusalem," "The Battle of Waterloo," and "A Trip up the Hudson" were favored types of scenic manifestation.

At times these spectacles were integrated with the representation of a drama; at times they were inserted between the play and the farce, or as the concluding feature of the evening's program; but as often as not they were exhibited by themselves as the feature attraction, much in the fashion of the seventeenth-century court masques. Scenic exhibitions were one of the chief attractions in the American theatre. When plays were being announced to the public, the splendor of the "new" scenic decorations was as highly "puffed" as were the abilities of the leading actor. The names of Ciceri, Reinagle, Lehr, and Audin were as prominently displayed in the old playbills as were Douglass, Hallam, or Dunlap. The scenic artist and his mechanics were, through the entire period of the present study, respected and admired.

Although the falsity of arbitrary chronological divisions invariably becomes apparent after thorough investigation, scenic art in American theatrical history can roughly be divided into four periods. Before 1820 the notable scenic displays were not integrated with the drama. The fireworks, the transparencies, and the apotheoses were exhibited on the same program with the drama, but were ordinarily unrelated to it. From 1820 to 1840, during the high tide of the Hudson River landscape painters, the romantic exterior scenes of deep woods, bald mountain peaks, rushing cataracts, and mysterious caverns served as the principal backgrounds for the drama. During this period, scenic spectacles, notably the panoramas, were sometimes directly related to the drama; but more frequently these gigantic displays of historical and natural phenomena were exhibited in their specially designed exhibition rooms. From 1840 to 1860 spectacular shows, not always primarily scenic, were again largely disassociated from the legitimate drama. Equestrian shows, *tableaux vivants,* striking musical exhibitions, circuses, startling and freakish shows, such as that exhibited at Barnum's Museum, and panoramic displays were attracting the largest crowds to the theatre. From 1860 to 1900, realistic details began to appear more frequently in scenic representations. Romantic backgrounds still persisted, but they tended to be more closely related to the context of the drama. Three-dimensional properties became more prevalent, and interior scenes became more frequent and more specifically localized. Prior to this time, interiors had ordinarily been limited to palace halls, gloomy caverns, and conventional parlor scenes. After 1860, restaurants, banks, boudoirs, gambling dens, and barrooms were repeatedly represented and with varying degrees of authenticity. Yet, at the same time, the romantic impulse to represent the mysterious, the distant, and the incomprehensible still persisted. Moonlit lakes, snowcapped peaks, and indistinct vistas were repeatedly introduced as backgrounds. Nor were spectacular exhibitions totally lacking in this latter-day theatre. Marine displays, battle scenes, and cataclysmic destructions were by no means uncommon. The ships, trains, sawmills, avalanches, etc., were no doubt more realistically represented than similarly spectacular devices in the early American theatre, but even at this later date, they appealed to the audience not as realistic representations but as spectacles. The average spectator was attracted to the theatre not to appraise the degree of realism in the representation of a locomotive on the stage but to delight in the striking and thrilling melodramatic action in which the locomotive played its part.

Again it must be emphasized that these chronological divisions are merely rough indications of the pattern of scenic display in American theatrical history. A more detailed examination of some of the specific scenic representations and displays will make the pattern clearer.

Plays, actors, and scenic backgrounds in the theatres of pre-Revolutionary America were imported from England. But just as the typical Colonial troupe of actors was smaller than the typical London acting company, the scenery in the early American theatre was comparatively meager. Whereas the London theatre might boast of five or six sets of wings and backdrops, the American theatres of the period had to be satisfied with two sets: an exterior combination and an interior combination. Nor were these settings of a high quality, judging from Brown's description of the scenic equipment in Hallam's New Theatre in New York in 1752: "The scenes, curtains, and wings were all carried by the managers in their property trunks. A green curtain was suspended from the ceiling. A pair of paper screens were erected upon the right and left hand sides for wings. Six wax lights were in front of the stage. . . . Two drop scenes representing a castle and a wood, bits of landscape river and mountain, comprised the scenery." [1] With such meager facilities, spectacular displays were not to be expected at this date.

But although the country was slow to develop and accept native drama, innovations in scenic splendor were readily encouraged and approved. On December 9, 1768, Douglass offered at his Southwark Theatre in Philadelphia, "at no extra charge" and as an addition to the regular program, a fireworks display. The spectacle, arranged by "two Italian brothers" was comprised of a "large wheel illuminated with brilliant fire; a triumphal arch with a globe in the middle; a tornant with variegated fire and several fountains of different composition." [2] Evidently the show was successful, for it was repeated on the 14th with new pyrotechnic combinations.

Two factors contributed materially to the development of scenery in the American theatre: (1) Audiences were not long satisfied with a single change, from wood to interior and back to the same wood; (2) such fragile equipment as that described above could not have endured many performances and certainly not many journeys. Furthermore, when the scenery, originally imported from England, had to be replaced, local artists were naturally engaged to do the painting.

One of the first scenic backdrops painted in America, however, was executed not by a native but by a British soldier (later a spy), Major John André. It was painted in 1778 for the Southwark Theatre in Philadelphia and was described by Durang in the following words: "It presented a distant champaign country and a winding rivulet extending from the front of the picture to the extreme distance. In the foreground and centre was a gentle cascade—the water exquisitely executed—overshadowed by a group of majestic forest trees. The perspective was excellently preserved, the foliage, verdure and general coloring artistically toned and glazed. . . ." [3] The distant vista, the "winding rivulet," the "gentle cascade," and the "majestic forest trees" anticipated by half a century the stock romantic ingredients of the typical Hudson River painting.

The gothic influence was also evident in the drama and thus in scenic backgrounds many years before it was apparent in painting and architecture. The first act of Dunlap's *Fontainville Abbey* (1795), for example, was set in the large hall of a gothic abbey. In the back of the scene there was a "dark passage, stones from the walls and fragments of pillars partly choaking [sic] it." Similarly, the set for Dunlap's *Ribbemont* (1795) was an "Antique Castle with Turrets and Battlements, and a distant view of a Convent."

During the post-Revolutionary period, the spectacular scenic representations were, however, of more interest than mere scenic backgrounds. On July 4, 1786, the Old American Company at the John Street Theatre instituted the first theatrical celebration of the Fourth of July, a theatrical custom which persisted through the first two decades of the nineteenth century. Seilhamer's description of the spectacle was as follows:

Hallam and Henry exhibited on the stage a piece of painting representing two Corinthian columns, one on each side of a monument. On the monument were inscribed the names of Warren, Montgomery, Mercer, and Wooster. Under these was a spread eagle with a sword in one claw and thirteen arrows in the other. From his beak issued the label LIBERTY, inscribed with the names of Washington, Greene, Knox, and Wayne. At the top of the monument were two angels, and a flame issuing heavenward—at the foot on each side were placed the genii of Agriculture and Liberty, and in the center between them were thirteen stars in a circle. At the foot of the pedestal on the right were three sheaves and on the left a ship under full sail. "Thus," it was said, "have these gentlemen given a reiterated and expensive proof that they are by principle well-wishers to the United States of America." [4]

Many of the early theatrical spectacles were designed to honor national heroes. Benjamin Franklin died in 1790. On April 22, 1796, a scenic production by Audin, the *Apotheosis of Franklin,* was displayed. The romantic quality of the presentation is evident from a description of the scenes:

I. Houdon at work on tomb of Franklin.

II,i. A gloomy cavern through which were seen the river Styx and the banks of the Stygian lake.

II,ii. Elysium revealed, the Goddess of Fame descended and proclaimed the virtues of Franklin, who was then conducted by Philosophy to the abodes of Peace, where Diogenes, the cynic, introduced him to all the wise and learned men who inhabit the abodes of eternal rest.

II,iii. Temple of Memory, statues and busts of all the deceased philosophers, poets, and patriots. As the curtain fell on this scene, Franklin's statue was placed on a vacant pedestal facing that of Sir Isaac Newton.[5]

On December 14, 1799, the nation was shocked by the death of Washington. On the 28th, the Chestnut Street Theatre in Philadelphia exhibited the following solemn scene:

The Curtain slowly rising, discovered a tomb in the centre of the stage, in the Grecian style of architecture. In the centre of it was a portrait of the General, encircled by a wreath of oaken leaves; under the portait, a sword, shield, and helmet, and the colors of the United States. The top was in the form of a pyramid, in the front of which appeared the American Eagle, weeping tears of blood for the loss of her General, and holding in her beak a scroll on which was inscribed: "A Nation's Tears." The sides of the stage were decorated with black banners, containing the names of the several States of the Union.[6]

Performances of this kind were not limited to the commemoration of heroes. Historical events were also represented. For example, on May 3, 1797, between the play and the farce, the Park Theatre presented a "Dramatic Sketch" called *Naval Gratitude; or the Generous Tar"* in the course of which will be introduced an exact representation of the TELEGRAPHE, explaining the mode of conveying intelligence by it, as now practised in Europe. . . . To conclude with a View of Frigates United States, Constellation, and Constitution, fitted completely for sea; the frigates will each fire three broad-sides." [7]

This was a forerunner of the popular marine spectacles of the second decade of the nineteenth century.

Some spectacular scenes were, of course, introduced directly into the drama. The striking scene representing the storming of Bunker-Hill by the British in John Burk's *Bunker-Hill* (1797) was minutely described in a letter from Burk to Hodgkinson, the manager of the John Street Theatre. Although this letter has frequently been quoted, a part of it probably should be set down here; for no other document of the period indicates so explicitly the manner in which such scenes were contrived on the stage:

The hill is raised gradually by boards extended from the stage to a bench. Three men should walk abreast on it, and the side where the English march up should, for the most part, be turned towards the wings; on our hill there was room for eighteen or twenty men, and they were concealed by a board painted mud-color, and having two cannon painted on it—which board was three feet and a half high. The English marched in two divisions from one extremity of the stage, where they ranged after coming from the wings; when they come to the foot of the hill, the Americans fire—the English fire—six or seven of your men should be taught to fall—the fire should be frequent for some minutes. The English retire to the front of the stage—second time of English advance from the wing near the hill—firing commences—they are again beaten back—windows on the stage should be open to let the smoke out. Again the English make the attack and mount the hill. After a brisk fire the Americans leave works and meet them. Here is room for effect, if the scuffle be nicely managed. Sometimes the English fall back, sometimes the Americans—two or three Englishmen rolling down the hill. A square piece about nine feet high and five wide, having some houses and a meeting-house painted on fire, with flame and smoke issuing from it, should be raised two feet distance from the horizon scene at the back of your stage; the windows and doors cut out for transparencies—in a word, it should have the appearance of a town on fire. We had painted smoke suspended—it is raised at the back wing, and is intended to represent Charlestown, and is on a line with the hill; and where it is lowest, the fire should be played skillfully behind this burning town, and the smoke to evaporate. When the curtain rises in the fifth, the appearance of the whole is good—Charlestown on fire, the breastwork of wood, the Americans appearing over the works and the muzzles of their guns, the English and the American music, the attack of the hill, the falling of the English troops, Warren's half descending the hill, and animating the Americans, the smoke and confusion, altogether produce an effect scarce credible. We had a scene of State Street— if you had one it would not be amiss—we used it instead of the scene of Boston Neck—it appears to me you need not be particular, but the hill and Charlestown on fire.[8]

Another type of scenic display which was to achieve an ascending popularity during the first half of the ninteeenth century, the panorama, made its first appearance in New York during the last decade of the eighteenth century. At times these panoramas were exhibited in the regular theatres, but ordinarily they were shown in their own halls. Some indication of the fascination these displays had for the general populace can be derived from Dunlap's remarks on them: "Panoramic exhibitions possess so much of the magic deceptions of the art as irresistibly to captivate all classes of spectators . . . for no study or cultivated taste is required fully to appreciate the merits of such representations." [9]

On January 28, 1790, a panorama entitled the "Holy City; a Panorama of Jerusalem" was exhibited from 10:00 A.M. to 10:00 P.M. at Lawrence Hyer's Tavern in Chatham Street, New York.[10] In 1794 a panorama of "Westminster and London, including the Three Bridges" was shown in Greenwich Street, "next door to Mr. Rhinelander's." [11] In 1797 Gardiner Baker advertised a panorama of the "City of Charleston" which was to be 110' long by 20' high.[12]

After the turn of the century, romantic backgrounds glorifying natural phenomena became more frequent. *A Tale of the Mystery* at the Park Theatre in 1802 had a scene representing a "wild mountainous country . . . with pines, and mossy rocks. A rude wooden bridge on a small height thrown from rock to rock; a rugged mill stream a little in the background; . . . a steep ascent by a narrow path to the bridge . . . the increasing storm of lightning, thunder, hail and rain becomes terrible." [13]

A similar desire for the romantic background was apparent in James Nelson Barker's *The Indian Princess* (1808) even though no detailed setting descriptions were included in the text. Barker suggested simply a "wild and picturesque" view of the Powhatan River. Samuel B. H. Judah's *The Mountain Torrent* (1820) demanded the following romantic details in setting:

overhanging rocks; masses of crags are strewn around; . . . a fig tree felled and resting on each end of the bridge, and two crags projecting over the precipice makes the crossing; a fall of water rushes over some rocks beneath the bridge, and joins a rapid stream. . . . The scene is nearly dark, and the glare of lightning at intervals discovers the masses of rocks; and gleams on the waters which are swollen and violently agitated by the wind; the storm becomes more terrible every moment.[14]

The most spectacular scenic representations of this period occurred in the dramas dealing with the War with the Barbary States and the War of 1812. For striking effect, these marine battles were unrivalled in the nineteenth century American theatre. The following scene from the anonymous *The Young Carolinians* (1818) was typical:

Scene. The ocean—a ship sailing—a gun is fired—American ship hoists the U. S. flag.—An Algerine corsair approaches under Hamburg colors—fires another gun— Hoists the bloody flag and puts out a boat, which rows to the ship—they attempt to board but are for sometime repulsed by the Americans . . . (The Americans are finally overpowered.) Algerines hoist the crescent on board their prize, leaving some of the pirates to keep possession—the rest with the American sailors row to the corsair, and as soon as taken on board, the vessel sails off.[15]

The naval engagements between the British and American frigates in the War of 1812 influenced even the interior decorations of theatres. When in the early summer of 1814 Mr. Worrall was commissioned to redecorate the Providence Theatre, he demonstrated his patriotic spirit in his designs:

Over the proscenium was an Ionic entablature, the frieze adorned with a gold scroll ornament. On the centre, resting on the tablet, were the sterns of three ships, viz.: the *Independence,* supported by the *United States* on the right, and the *Constitution* on the left. . . . The dados around the upper tier of boxes were adorned with three tablets; those on the right and left contained representations of vessels which had signalized themselves; the *Wasp,* the *Hornet,* the *Enterprise,* and the *Peacock;* that in the centre contained the *Lawrence,* and the *Niagara.* . . .[16]

Panoramas did a flourishing business during the first two decades of the century. The pictures of Jerusalem and of London and Westminster continued to be exhibited, and innumerable new paintings were added. Battle panoramas and panoramic views of American and European cities were particularly popular. Typical battle panoramas were "Battle of Alexander in Egypt" (1804; painted by Robert Kerr Porter and covering 3,000 square feet of canvas), "Naval and Land Engagements on Lake Champlain and at Plattsburgh" (1815), and "Battle of Waterloo" (1818). Among the views of cities were a panorama exhibiting an entire circular view of New York, Governor's Island, and part of New Jersey (1808), "City of Rome" (1811), and "Panorama of Baltimore" (1814). Generally, the painters' names were not conspicuously advertised with these pictorial shows. However, when John Vanderlyn's "Panorama of the Gardens at Versailles" was exhibited at the Panoramic Rotunda in 1819, the audience must have been attracted as much by his name as by the subject matter of his painting. The success of these panoramas led other artists to exhibit their regular-sized canvases in similar public shows. For example, Francis Guy's paintings were "lighted every evening" and shown with a musical accompaniment. John Trumbull's "Surrender of Cornwallis" was given a similar showing at Washington Hall, July 6, 1820.

Theatres of the early nineteenth century in America were, on the whole, designed to accommodate large audiences. The Chestnut Street Theatre in Philadelphia (1791) seated 2,000; the Park, New York (1798), 2,000; the second Park, New York

(1821), 2,500; and the Bowery, New York (1826), 3,500. And as the houses became larger, prices were lowered. At the turn of the century the customary price was $2.00 in the boxes, $1.50 in the pit, and $1.00 in the gallery. By mid-century the general scale was "50-cent top" and gallery seats for 12½ cents. Obviously the entertainments offered in these theatres were intended to reach the popular audience. It was inevitable that spectacular displays, with their simple appeal to the uninitiated, should constitute a prominent part of the repertoire. An emphasis on sensuous appeal was evident in all representational and decorative aspects of the theatre.

The drop curtains in the twenties were designed not only to fit in with the classical mood of the interior decorations of theatres but to suggest the romantic spirit of the scenic representations that were concealed behind the curtain. The drop curtain at the New Park (1821), for example, represented "a rich damask crimson curtain drawn up by gold cords and tassels into festoons of drapery, a porch of Mosaic workmanship, with a ballustrade [sic] in the centre, and beyond the ballustrade is an equestrian statue of Washington; the background seen under the folds of the curtain is a distant prospect . . . of the Hudson River. . . ." [17] Similarly, the drop curtain at the Bowery (1826) represented the ruins of a Greek temple, a fountain of Greek statuary, a pool of clear water, and mammoth trees with luxurious foliage. Perhaps the most spectacular curtain was that which the Park added in 1822, a two-ton, gilt-framed looking-glass curtain that permitted the members of the audience to view themselves before and after the performance.

In the decade of the twenties, romantic scenes of rugged cliffs, mountain summits, deep forests, dark caves, and gothic castles furnished the backgrounds for a large share of the popular dramas. The new scenes painted by Reinagle and Evers were typical: "cliffs rugged and broken; Sea Shore. Castle of Ellangower in the Distance; a Cavern . . . a broken lofty entrance at the summit of the stage, from which descends a rugged path . . . ; Frozen mountain of the Caucasus." [18]

John Howard Payne's *Mount Savage* (1822) employed the

characteristic romantic backgrounds and spectacular devices of the period. A glance at a few of the scenic representations suggested for this drama will indicate the prevailing taste: "I. i.— The parlor of an old monastery in ruins. The back is entirely formed of three large ogive windows of colored glass, but so broken that it is easy to see through them in the most distinct manner Mount Savage, covered with fir trees, larch trees, and whose ridge surmounted by eternal snows, is lost in clouds. On the swell of the hill, on the point of a perpendicular rock, rises a humble cottage. On the right, a road in the rock conducts to the arch of an old bridge. Snow falls abundantly." [19] Later in the scene: "The tempest, which had appeared to relent, revives, and increases to a frightful pitch of terror. The waters of the lake are prodigiously agitated. The lightnings flash. The thunder bellows. The trees are uprooted and fall with a crash. One of them overturns in its fall and draws with it a little cottage placed on the bend of the hill and the ruins of which are precipitated in the lake." [20] These early scenes were, however, merely preludes to the grand spectacle which concluded this gothic melodrama.

(*The* Baron, Eloi *and all the villagers enter a sort of cavern at the left. The* Unknown *remounts to the summit. The* Count, Michieli, *and soldiers scale all the sides at once. In an instant the mountain is covered with soldiers.*)

Count. (*Before he appears*). Follow me, soldiers.

Unknown. 'Tis death thou callest on them as on thyself. Who permitted thee to violate this asylum?

Count. Love and vengeance. I came to seek for Elodie.

Unknown. Approach. I am going to restore her to thee and avenge her. Behold— (*With one hand he lifts up the mantle* (*the body of* Elodie *is under the mantle*) *and with the other, seizing the flambeaux, which he had placed behind a rock, he fires the mine. A terrible explosion takes place; the quarters of the rock, launched into the air, fall with a horrid crash.* Palzo *and* Michieli *are thrown down and crushed, as well as their suite. The* Unknown *is fallen dead by the side of his beloved. After the explosion the* Baron *and all those who were in the hollow come out.* Herstall *shows them the body of* Elodie. *All express their grief and their regrets.*) [21]

Mount Savage responded to the public taste for wild and tempestuous spectacle, and *A Trip to Niagara* featured a picturesque native landscape. This play by Dunlap, first performed on November 28, 1828, at the Bowery Theatre, New York, gave the audience a graphic description of the trip from New York to Buffalo by way of the Hudson River and the Erie Canal. Since its diorama [22] represented most of the scenes along this route, persons who had not made the journey were permitted to do so vicariously, and those who had could recall each scene as it was exhibited to them. As Dunlap indicated in his Preface, the play made no pretense at being anything more than a scenic display: "The following Farce, for, be it remembered it makes pretensions to no higher character, was written at the request of the Managers, and intended by them as a kind of running accompaniment to the more important product of the Scene-painter." [23]

The 25,000 square feet of moving scenery showed only that part of the trip from the Bowery to Catskill landing and consisted of eighteen faithful reproductions of views along the Hudson painted on the spot by competent artists. The following scenes were represented:

1. Harbour of New York, Governor's Island. Ships at anchor.
2. Frigate at anchor. Jersey City.
3. Hoboken.
4. Weehawk.
5. Palisades.
6. Approaching storm.
7. Storm.
8. Boats passing through a fog.
9. Clearing away and rainbow. Caldwell's landing. Boat stops.
10. Highlands.
11. Buttermilk Falls.
12. West Point. Sun setting.
13. Highlands continued.

14. Newburgh by moonlight.
15. Island near Newburgh.
16. Catskill Mountains in distance, and Mountain House.
17. Continuation of Scenery.
18. Catskill landing.[24]

The remainder of the journey to Buffalo was shown by a series of non-moving picturesque backgrounds culminating in a stupendous view of Niagara Falls from the American side. The descriptions of the pictures in the diorama and others from the later section of the play ("The little falls of the Mohawk. A view of the stupendous rocks, through which the river flows. A part of the town. The canal and the aqueduct crossing the river." [25]) are also of interest. Reading them, one is struck by the strong similarity between these canvases and those painted by the Hudson River painters during the same period.

The dioramas which were painted to be shown in specially designed halls were exhibited in a slightly different fashion. For these showings the spectator stood or sat on a moving platform and viewed the pictures through two large framed openings. At one moment he was looking through one of the frames, and at the next moment the platform had been turned so that he was viewing another picture through the second frame. By the time the platform moved him back to the first frame another picture was in place in that position. The framed openings were placed at a sufficient distance from the pictures, and the horizon of the painting was extended out of "sight-lines"; thus the spectator had the impression that he was looking at an unframed picture.

Strictly speaking, dioramas were transparencies. By control of the light behind the picture the view seemed to change before the eyes of the spectator. Small profile figures, often articulated figures, were frequently used to help the illusion. For example, ships were made to seem to disappear in the distance by the use of three or four ship models successively reduced in size as the ship sailed away. At the conclusion of the diorama in *A Trip to Niagara* "the boat stops, and passengers are seen putting off in a small boat, and landing at Catskill, at night." [26]

Although common usage has tended to make panorama the generic term for describing all such spectacles, strictly, the panoramic exhibition differed from the diorama. In the panorama hall the spectator stood on a stationary circular platform completely surrounded by the painting. The railing on the platform kept the bottom of the painting out of sight, and a canopy above, stretching out over the edges of the platform, masked the uppermost edge of the canvas. Thus, the spectator had the impression of an unframed landscape. In this type of exhibition the spectator was sometimes provided with binoculars, so that he could pick out the details in the distant landscape.

The cosmorama was still another popular variety of scenic exhibition. The term, unfortunately, seems to have been used to describe two distinct types of scenic display: (1) that in which the spectator looked at a picture through a window of magnifying lenses; and (2) that in which three-dimensional wax figures were set against a panoramic background.

The important distinction to be kept in mind for the present discussion is that the diorama was a transparency showing views which changed while one looked, whereas the panorama, lighted from in front, completely surrounded the spectator with a continuous but non-changing picture. One is struck by the similarity of interest in this nineteenth-century scenic show and the present-day excitement over cinerama and other comparable moving-picture devices.

The specially exhibited panoramas also continued to be popular during the thirties. In 1825 another "Battle of Waterloo," using 20,000 square feet of canvas and exhibiting 10,000 painted figures, was exhibited at the Rotunda. A "Panorama of Athens" (1826), painted by Barker of London, and a "City of Paris" (1827) were also exhibited at the Rotunda.

Romantic scenic vistas and romantic spectacles were indispensable to the drama of the 1830's, for this was the age of romanticism in full bloom. In the backgrounds for the conventional romantic plays and the Indian plays—these were the popular dramas of the period—three varieties of picturesqueness were discernible. There were (1) the wild and untamed natural beauty of the American landscape, (2) the gloomy and mysterious atmosphere of medieval gothic, and (3) the exotic and misty picture of faraway place and time.

Of the natural scenery backgrounds, those for Custis' *Pocahontas* (1830) and for Stone's *Metamora* (1829) were typical: "Banks of James' river—View of the river—two ships and a sloop at anchor, in the distance—on one side of the stage a hut—composed of mats and reeds; on the other rocks and cliffs. Indians on the cliffs gazing at the shipping. . . ." [27] "Sunset. A wild, picturesque scene; high, craggy rocks in distance; dark pine trees, etc. . . ." [28] The gothic settings were customarily combined with romantic natural vistas as, for example, in two of the scenes from Payne's *Mazeppa* (1825):

A Gothic apartment. In the flat, three glazed doors, which open on a picturesque country seen through an iron rail fence. At the horizon a craggy mountain terminating at the left extremity with a foaming torrent.[29]

.   .   .

In front, the interior of a grotto or cavern, open at the back, through which appears a wild and ragged prospect of the desert plain, or steppes of Tartary, crossed by an extensive lake. In the grotto, right hand, is the entrance of another cavern which seems to descend deep into the mountain. This entrance is closed with a barrier of unhewn wood. At the side, a natural bank covered with moss and detached. Several groups of horses are discovered grazing at large in the steppes beyond the lake. . . .[30]

The romantic backgrounds of distant place and time were of two varieties. One delighted in the romance of antiquity, representing such scenes as were familiar through the reading of classical literature. An example is Robert Montgomery Bird's *Pelopidas* ("Athens. The Acropolis"). In the other variety there is the romantic atmosphere which surrounded distant, totally unfamiliar places: "A public square, terminating in a quay which borders on the sea shore. Left hand, splendid mansion of Don Diego de Cardona, magnificently illuminated. Right hand, on the sea shore, a headland surmounted by a lighthouse. Same side, galleys moored. In the offing, a galley, all sails spread, lying to." [31]

Spectacular scenes of battles, demolitions, and processionals were common theatrical accoutrements during this period. Typical stage directions were "Thunder and lightning," "The river appears agitated," "Ship on fire," "Boat approaching in the distance," "A storm is raging."

The processional scene in Smith's *Bombardment of Algiers* (1829) and a scene in Custis' *Pocahontas* (1830) will illustrate the tendency toward this type of spectacle. *Bombardment of Algiers:* "Guards in advance; these are followed by black eunuchs, and then Valentine carried in a rich palanquin. Slaves playing on various instruments. Before the palanquin an officer bearing the Dey's standard. The procession terminates with a platoon of guards. . . ." [32] *Pocahontas:* "Palace of Powhatan at Werocomoco. Powhatan seated on a throne which is covered with bear skins, a spear in his hand; on his right the Princess, on his left, Omaya, with fans of feathers, double rows of guards with spears, bows, and arrows." [33] Of the many scenes of destruction, none was more exciting than the second-act spectacle of *Bombardment of Algiers:*

While the strokes of the axes, etc., continued to augment, and the firing of the cannon becomes more frequent, all at once a bomb crashes the roof of the hut and falls into the chamber whither Valentine has fled. She rushes out in great alarm. The bomb bursts and the explosion is terrible. The hut, already undermined by workers, falls down with a terrible noise. It is entirely destroyed; but the fragments fall in the direction of the bomb, near the bottom of the stage, leaving the actors untouched who are in the scene. The falling in of the hut shows to the spectators the whole extent of the port of Algiers. Beyond the sea, the western pier and one of the vessels on the roadstead are seen in flames. [34]

With the taste for spectacular effects and for scenic beauties still prevailing, it was natural that the panorama should continue to flourish during this period. In 1834 a panorama of the "Liverpool and Manchester Railroad" was shown in Brooklyn. From June, 1838, to May, 1840, the Panorama Building at

Prince and Mercer Streets in New York exhibited "Jerusalem," "Niagara Falls," "Lima," "Rome," and "The Bay Islands in New Zealand." A diorama, the "Battle of Bunker Hill," was at the Masonic Hall in 1839, and Daguerre's "Panoramas from Paris" were at Lockwood's Room in 1840. William Dunlap, who, in spite of his frequent success as painter, dramatist, and historian, was often penniless, attempted to capitalize on the public taste for panoramic displays by preparing a special showing of his monumental Biblical paintings with lecture accompaniment. This display, consisting of "Christ Rejected," "The Bearing of the Cross," "Calvary," and "Death on the Pale Horse," was opened at the National Academy in February, 1832, and continued for several weeks.

Through the forties and fifties picturesque backgrounds of natural beauty were still evident: "Picturesque Valley in Virginia, through which the Rock-fish River passes. Beyond the river lofty verdure-covered hills." [35] Distant places were still represented: "Mountain Plateau near Athens, with a distant view of the Mediterranean Sea." [36] Gothic scenes of "Grottos" and "Crypts" were not infrequent. Thrilling spectacular sequences such as Eliza crossing the Ohio on the ice floes with the bloodhounds in close pursuit were exciting the popular audiences. But the distinguishing feature of the scenic representations of the period was the emphasis on magnificence and splendor.

In this respect no previous productions could have equalled Charles Kean's *Richard III* and *King John*. They were said to have cost $10,000 and $12,000, respectively. It was the first time in America that entirely new scenery had been prepared for a Shakespearean production. It had been the custom when Shakespeare was presented to use whatever happened to be available. The romantic details in Kean's settings were not essentially different from similar details in previous settings, but they were more elegantly rendered. A scene description will illustrate: "The Cloisters of Old St. Paul's with a view of the Cathedral, prior to the great fire. The scene is strikingly effective. The gloomy cloisters in the foreground, with their open gothic arches, affording a view of the tombs and the churchyard, and the lofty and massive cathedral—stretching hugely in the distance, make the representation highly imposing." [37] The taste for sumptuousness and elegance was also evident in other productions. *The Count of Monte Cristo* (1858) exhibited a dazzling spectacle: "Interior of the Grotto, profusely hung with Crimson and Gold Brocade—curtains overhanging the arches gorgeously decorated. Magnificent Chandelier, Divans, Furniture, Statues, and appointments of the most unique and costly description, presenting a *coup d'oeil* of more than Eastern Gorgeousness." [38] Another scene of this type was shown in Heister's grand display in *The Vision of the Sun* (1851): "Bridal procession to the Lake, with distant city of Cusco. Oultanapac plunges Koran into the lake . . . the waters become agitated and rise, and in their progress to the whole height of the stage, they assume various tints, till a most Brilliant Palace rises out of the Water." [39]

Panoramas appeared early in America and continued to provide their peculiar type of entertainment even into the twentieth century, but their years of greatest popularity were from 1840 to 1860. Battle scenes were exceedingly popular during this period: "Battle of Bunker Hill" (1844), "Battle of Mexico" (1847), and "The Bombardment of Vera Cruz" (1848), accompanied by a pyrotechnic display. Religious representations were frequent: "Creation of the World and the Deluge" (1848), "Pilgrim's Progress" (1850), and "Panoramic Mirror of the New Testament and Scenes in the Holy Land" (1853). Views of distant cities and scenes seem to have been exceedingly popular: "Holyrood Chapel" and "City of Brest" (1849); "A Voyage to Europe, showing Boston, its Harbour, the Ocean, Liverpool, London, the Thames, etc." (1850); "London" (1851); "World Panorama" (1854), which a "Professor" Hart advertised by announcing that he would distribute $300.00 worth of gifts at each showing; "100 Views of Europe" (1855); "China and Japan" (1856); "River Rhine" (1857); and "Arctic Regions" (1857). Sea voyages were popular, particularly those dealing with whaling. Among these were: "Whaling Voyage"

(1851), "Great Nautical Exposition of the South Sea Whaling Voyage" (1861), and "Voyage to California around Cape Horn" (1859). Views of the Hudson, the Great Lakes, Niagara Falls, and other inland scenes were common; for example: "American Scenery, from the Atlantic Ocean to Lake George" (1849), "Seven Mile Mirror of Scenery of the Lakes, Niagara, and the St. Lawrence" (1849), and what seems to have been the most popular of them all, Banvard's "Panorama of the Mississippi" (1848).

Beginning with Augustin Daly's productions in the sixties and culminating with David Belasco's in the late eighties and nineties, there was, in the drama and in scenic representation, an increasing tendency toward stage realism. Drama in general turned from romantic themes and characters to realistic appraisal of man and his environment. As a result, dramatic action tended to be represented within the confines of interior settings rather than in the broad and unlimited expanses of the open country. Nor were these interior scenes, as noted above, standardized locales such as the "parlor scenes" of the early nineteenth century. Familiar interiors, hospitals, telegraph offices, etc., were so represented that the spectator could judge of their authenticity. Realistic detail was at a premium.

But even though this steadily increasing desire to transfer actual scenes to the stage was the distinguishing mark of scenic representations in the late nineteenth century, many of the romantic elements in scenic display still persisted. Backgrounds glorifying the beauties of the great out-of-doors were not infrequent. Spectacular displays were essential ingredients to the innumerable melodramas of the period; and panoramic exhibits, although less numerous, were still being shown.

Expansive mountain regions demonstrating the sublime and morally elevating aspects of nature were indispensable to the dramas of the far-western frontier. The exterior scenes in *Horizon* (1871) and *Danites in the Sierras* (1877) were typical. *Horizon:* "A ravine, in which the Indians have camped for the night. High ground at sides and at back surmounted by bushes and thick shrubbery. A path, quite high at the back across from right to left. Path down from right and left to center, at back. Mountainous perspective." [40] *Danites in the Sierras:* "Moonlight on the Sierras. Rocky Run crossing stage; ledge overhanging; set cabin, practical door, foot of run; background of distant snowcapped peaks." [41] The background suggested for Howard's *Shenandoah* (1889) was in the same tradition: "Ellingham Homestead in the Shenandoah Valley. . . . Three top Mountain in the distance.—A road across the stage. . . . When curtain rises it is sunset. As the act proceeds this fades into twilight and then bright moonlight." [42]

With the perfection of realistic lighting effects, it was natural that the romantic aspects of light changes, particularly through sunset, twilight, and moonlight, should become the principal means for enveloping the action in the atmosphere of romance. Realistically rendered gardens and even interiors could, by the turn of a valve (during the latter days of the century by the turn of a switch) be transformed into misty and shadowy recesses, alive with the expectancy of romantic adventure. Love scenes were almost invariably given the benefit of moonlight—a custom that has persisted to the present day. Such directions as "distant view of the city by moonlight," "lake view by moonlight," "mountain background in moonlight" were particularly common.

Spectacular displays during the last forty years of the century often attempted to satisfy simultaneously the spectator's taste for realistic representation and for striking and unusual effects. This tendency was particularly noticeable in the frequent use of trains on stage. The first transcontinental railroad was completed in 1869. Railroad travel was still, for the mass of the population, an exciting adventure. And it is evident from the manner in which train scenes were employed on the stage that they were introduced for their romantic and sensational rather than for their realistic appeal. One of the most stirring train scenes occurred in Augustin Daly's *Under the Gaslight* (1867). The hero is tied to the tracks. The sound of the approaching train is heard in the distance. The beam of the headlight stretches across the stage. The heroine is locked in the station, unable to save her lover. Finally, when by superhuman strength she breaks down the door, and "takes his head from the track, the train of cars rushes past with a roar and whistle. . . ." [43] In *Across the Continent* (1870) the train speeds into the station with United States troops just in time to prevent an Indian massacre. *The Main Line* (1887), by Henry C. DeMille and Charles Bernard, dealt entirely with the "romance of the rails"; and one of the thrilling scenes in Frederic Book's *The Living Age* (1881) represented the "horseshoe bend" on the Pennsylvania Railroad.

Other equally spectacular phenomena were frequently introduced. For example, in Daly's *The Red Scarf* (1868) a thrilling sawmill scene was presented in which the heroine narrowly escaped being sawed in two. Fight scenes ("Terrific Combat between a Man, a Horse, and a Bear," in E. A. Locke's *Nobody's Claim*, 1883) and marine spectacles ("Hudson River Steamboat on Fire," in Daly's *A Flash of Lightning*, 1868) were very common.

An interesting account of two action scenes (in Paul Merritt's *The World*, 1881) is given by Jennings.

Next came the explosion scene, when the vessel was, by the supposed use of dynamite, sent flying in splinters in mid-ocean, and all save four souls went down to the briny depths. The mere ship setting, with its boilers, its hatches, its galleries, spars and guys, was worthy of admiration. While the performers were leading up to the point where the awful and fateful moment comes, a man sat quietly behind the scenes ready to fire an anvil of guns, each charged to the muzzle; men stood at the numerous openings in the rear, and men with chemical red-fire occupied the side-scenes, while others with powdered lycopodium were under the stage beneath a half-dozen grated openings. At the left, in the wings, stood an array of "supers," to rush on and increase the commotion when the shock came. When the heavy villain announced that there was a dynamite machine on board, and the captain gave orders to his men to overhaul everything below and try to find it—then the thunder came. Bang went the young cannons in the rear. The stage shook, and the theatre seemed ready to fall about our ears; the females shrieked;

the "supers" rushed on and shouted; then came the leaping flames from below and from the sides, until, finally, the whole picture was one burning glow and whirl of smoke, and the curtain came down in time, I suppose, to prevent a panic, for women shrieked, and men got up from their seats to flee from the theatre. Act three brought the grandest illusion of all—the great raft scene. This picture shows a raft tossing on a rolling ocean with a vast stretch of sea on all sides, the sky and waters apparently meeting as far away as if they were realities and not mere attempts at nature. This scene always struck me with awe until I saw it from the stage. The second act at an end, the stage manager has the stage cleared in a short time; then the carpenter and his assistants go to work. A "ground piece" of sea is placed across the stage at the first entrance. All the side scenes are removed and a huge curtain of light blue is hung in a semicircle from one side of the stage, up around to the rear and then down to the other side. A couple of men now came down to the centre of the stage bearing something that looks like an old barn-door with four swinging legs, one at each corner. A pivot is fastened on the stage; the barn-door is balanced on it and down through four small openings in the stage go the four arms or legs, at points corresponding with the four corners of the door. I can see now that the upper side of the door bears a slight resemblance to a rude raft, the timber being artistically painted upon its surface. Somebody sticks a pole in the side up the stage. A box is placed at one end for the villain who is among the saved; a cushion is furnished at the other end for the young lady who plays the lad, *Ned; Old Owen,* the miner, lies along the lower side and *Sir Clement Huntingford,* the hero, takes his stand at the mast, pale and haggard with hunger and anxiety. The sea cloth, covering the stage except for a rectangular aperture that goes around the raft and has its edges fastened to the raft, is spread; boys crawl under the sea and lie upon their backs; men stand in the side scenes holding the ragged edges of the already white-crested sea. Everything is ready now, and amid the right kind of music the curtain goes up on the magnificent raft scene. Four men under the stage have hold of the four pieces hanging from the corners of the raft, and by pulling in exact line give it the motion of the heaving sea; the men in the side scenes agitate the blue cloth and the boys beneath it toss and roll the cloth with hands and feet.[44]

Thunder and lightning, roaring cataracts, and rain and snow were standard props for melodramatic action, and new and ingenious spectacular effects were continually being invented. There was, for example, the extraordinary scene in *Heart of Maryland* (1895), in which Maryland swings on the clapper of the bell; and in *A Prisoner for Life* (1885) the heroine is heroically saved from a "great avalanche." Fireworks were extremely popular. Paine's *The Bombardment of Alexandria* (1884) showed five hundred troops (undoubtedly profile figures) in action and the "ocean ablaze." Byron's *Sardanapalus* was presented in 1876 with a conflagration by Randle, pyrotechnist to the Queen of England. Nor was the taste, notable in the 1840's, for sheer splendor and richness in abeyance. Ornate fireplaces, crystal chandeliers, rich furniture, and delicately painted screens were common properties. Few scenes in the American theatre equalled in brilliance "the Palace of Dew Drops" painted by the Brother's Brew of London at a cost of $15,000 for *The Black Crook* (1871).

Special mention must be given to the master spectacle-maker of the American theatre, Steele Mackaye. Although his great show—and what would have been the greatest show in American theatrical history—the *Spectatorium* was never completed, his plans for this project and the many theatrical projects which he did complete give him first rank among American scenic artists and stage engineers. His folding chairs, his elevator stage at the Madison Square Theatre (allowing one stage to be set up while the other was in view of the audience), and his elevator stage for the orchestra at the Lyceum Theatre, to mention only a few of his inventions, were incomparable advances in stage mechanics.

His theatrical work was not limited to engineering. He was an actor, a designer, a teacher, and a playwright. His *Rose Michel* (1875), *Hazel Kirke* (1880), and *Paul Kauvar* (1887) were among the most popular plays of their time. Although most of the settings for his dramas were, in keeping with the custom of the time, rich in realistic detail, evidences of Mackaye's taste for romantic backgrounds were not infrequent. For example:

Paris, 1765. A quay on the Seine, opposite the Isle of St. Louis. In background, steps leading down to the river and old Paris in the background.[45]

• • •

Garden of Professor Tracy's house on the seashore. . . . Throughout the scene in background, view of sky and ocean. Night. The garden is illuminated with Chinese lanterns; the moon is seen through the trees, shining upon the ocean. . . .[46]

• • •

The old stone seat in the wood, at the foot of an old pine, C., on each side of which are three pines. In background, Cenci Lake is seen, and the Convent of St. Rosalia in the distance. Time, twilight. . . .[47]

Before Mackaye became a theatrical artist, he was a painter, a pupil of Inness; and like Inness "he was . . . a lover of serene nature—a painter of dreamy landscapes and browsing cattle." [48] In later years he found the theatrical, panorama-like paintings more to his taste. In 1886 he consented to prepare and deliver an oration as an accompaniment for Matt Morgan's cycloramic exhibit of famous scenes of the Civil War.[49] Later in the same year he prepared a scenario of scenes which were to serve as backgrounds for Cody's "Wild West Show." These backgrounds, painted in the panorama style, later became the basis for his *Drama of Civilization* (1886).

Even when Mackaye first suggested his proposal for the *Spectatorium* at the Chicago World's Fair (1893), it is evident from his letter to the Director that he thought of it as a kind of panoramic display: ". . . to erect a building completely equipped for the exhibit of all the latest inventions, machinery, and appliances, connected with electricity in its practical application to Panoramic and Dramatic Art." [50] No spectacular display, proposed or realized, ever approached the magnitude of his *Spectatorium*. The intricacy of the theatre and the scenic construction forbids a satisfactory brief description,[51] but an excerpt from Mackaye's explanation of the structure and its function will help to indicate its general nature:

The Spectatorium was 480 feet long, 380 feet wide, and from the foundation to the apex of the dome 270 feet high.—In the front of the house were the entrance lobbies, and an immense roof garden, running the full length of the structure from east to west, overlooking the whole of Jackson Park.—There were also two large restaurant floors with a grand cafe, 80 feet square, in the central pavilion. Above this were to be the observation floors of the immense dome. . . . The rear of the building was a vast semi-circular reservoir, the surface dimensions of which were over 100,000 square feet. From the foundation of the reservoir to the gridiron of the scenic department, the height was 170 feet, making the cubic measurement of the Scenitorium or Scenic department alone, over 1,700,000 cubic feet. Here was to be placed all the newly invented machinery for a startling advance in realism.

There were to be twenty-five telescopic stages, all of which were to be furnished with *scenery of an entirely new species* devised by myself. The frame of the stage pictures was 150 by 70 feet, and the full range of the vision of the public, at the horizon of the picture, would have been over 400 feet. It would have required over six miles of railroad track for these stages to move upon, and their aggregated weight would have been over 1,200 tons. In making a change of scene, the machinery of the building would have easily controlled over 600 tons, and would have made each change within forty seconds. . . . An *entirely new system of lighting* was to be used in connection with these stages, the aim being to arrive at as close a reproduction of the subtle light effects of nature as modern mechanism made possible. It would have required, to produce these effects, an amount of light equal to over 500,000 candle power, and *all the mechanism by which this light was to be managed was entirely new in design and character.*[52]

The project was never completed. The financial panic of 1893 wrecked the Columbian Celebration Company, the organization which had sponsored Mackaye's undertaking. The failure of this venture, however, did not subdue Mackaye's indomitable spirit. He immediately set to work on his *Scenitorium,* a fragmentary version of the *Spectatorium* employing many of the scenic devices of the original project, but on a smaller scale. The *Scenitorium* was opened in Chicago on February 5, 1895, with *The World Finder,* the dramatic spectacle relating the story of Columbus which Mackaye had prepared as the first production for the ill-fated *Spectatorium.* Even though the opening date at the *Scenitorium* was repeatedly postponed because of Mackaye's illness and the difficulties encountered in preparing the machinery, and even though many of the special devices (the wind machine, for example) were not in operation at the opening, contemporary newspaper accounts indicate that the production was well received. The ingenious lighting effects in particular seem to have amazed the audiences. A short excerpt from the article by the critic of the *Chicago Times* indicates the elaborateness of the spectacle:

In the first scene . . . a beautiful incident was the celestial vision which illumined the darkest hour in Columbus' struggle. At this point, the sky was suddenly darkened; then from it burst a great congregation of angels, and Christ was seen, amid a number of the world's rejected, pointing to the earth floating in space, with the western hemisphere dimly outlined. . . . The curtain of light blotted out the scene as effectually as any curtain ever devised. When the lights were again lowered, the witching outline of the city of Santa Fe came into view, its palaces lit up in the foreground, while behind twinkled the lights of the watchful moslem in the minarets of the mosques at Granada. Gradually the moonlight gave way to rosy dawn, that revealed a superb vista of city and plain, running back in far distance to the snow-capped Sierra Nevadas. To the scene which succeeded this gorgeous pageant was added the mystical poetry of the ocean.

It is the little town of Palos, but at first we can see only the lights in the church on the hill and some houses on the shore. From the church comes the glorious melody of a Gregorian mass which mingles strangely, ever and anon, with the boisterous song of sailors drowning their fears before the awful voyage. . . . Day breaks on the quaint outlines of caravels lying at anchor in the bay. Light grows and out of mist emerge the windmill on the hill, the wide stretch of sea, the low-lying line of the shore. . . . Signal is given; anchor weighed; the tiny barks set out to sea; we go with them.

The town slips away—we are abreast the lighthouse at the harbor mouth—at last (splendid realism it is!) the coast sinks down the horizon and naught but the great, green desert of waters meets the eye. The missing wind-apparatus could hardly have heightened the wonder of this scene.[53]

Certainly no other theatrical artists of the last century approached the magnificent and lofty conceptions of Mackaye, and his genius for creating theatrical wonders remains unequalled.

During the latter part of the century, panoramas and panorama-like backgrounds were frequently associated with regular plays. *Horizon* (1871) showed a panorama of a Western river and a surprise attack at night by an Indian band upon a company of United States troops. Telbin's "Panorama of Old London" was shown in connection with a performance of *Henry VIII* at Booth's Theatre in 1878.[54] The Panoramic tendency was evident in the third scene of the third act in *Under the Gaslight*: "Foot of Pier 30, North River. Sea Cloth down and working—A pier projecting into the river. A large cavity in front. Bow of a vessel at back, and other steamers, vessels, and piers in perspective on either side. The flat gives view of Jersey City and the river shipping by starlight. . . ."[55]

Many of the old panoramic displays continued to be shown during this period: "Panorama of the World" (1864), "Pilgrim's Progress" (1864), and "Panoramic Mirror of Ireland" (1882). The religious panoramas, for the most part, had been moved into the churches; and a number of panoramic paintings, "The Progress of a Nation" (1867), for example, were exhibited in connection with minstrel shows. A "Panorama of the War" was on view at the Madison Square Hall on April 6, 1868, and a "Cyclorama of the Battle of Gettysburg" was exhibited in New York during the 1890's. Some new canvases, "Franco-Prussian War" (1875), "Shooting by Communists of the Archbishop of Paris" (1875), "The Surrender of Yorktown" (1885), and a magnificent panorama of Yosemite (1890), seem to have had a degree of popularity; but, on the whole, panoramic shows became comparatively infrequent.

Elements of romanticism persisted in scenic backgrounds and displays through the entire century. Vistas of natural beauty, decaying antique ruins, dark and unfathomable caverns, and distant, exotic locales, exciting spectacles of battles at sea, thundering railroad trains, and explosions and avalanches were all essential scenic accompaniments to nineteenth-century theatrical performances. Scenic representations in the theatre were directly related to the prevailing tastes in art. In fact, the Hudson River painters, with their renderings of the sublime and awesome aspects of natural beauty, were foreshadowed by the early panoramic and scenic artists. And during the last half of the century, when audiences in the theatre and art gallery alike were unquestionably delighted with a higher degree of realistic representation, there still persisted a strong yearning for the remote and the unfathomable beauties of nature. Distant mountain peaks bathed in moonlight became synonymous with romance.

Throughout the century, and in spite of the growing tendency toward realism, the theatre was regarded as the assured place for romantic adventure, for escape from the troubles and problems of ordinary society to a world of magnificent and irrefutable make-believe.

CHAPTER V

The Panorama in Perspective

IF THE manifestations of romanticism in American drama and theatre seem less robust and virile than similar expressions in England, France, and Germany, it must be recalled that there were in America no traditional artistic canons against which the romantic artist was rebelling. He partook indirectly of the European revolt against outmoded rules as the romantic theories filtered in from abroad; but more directly, he responded to the romantic spirit in the life around him, the romanticism of the growing democracy. In order to appreciate the peculiar character of the romanticism in America, it is necessary to understand this duality of influence.

Having no established tradition against which to rebel, American dramatists and theatrical artists adopted from the beginning a romantic attitude toward the formal qualities of drama and theatre. Form was dictated by the immediate subject matter and the momentary inclination of the artist. Classical admonitions regarding the unities, the climax, the denouement, and the number of acts were avoided if, indeed, they were ever considered. Nor was the province of the drama limited by any strict concept of appropriateness. There was little attempt, for example, to distinguish between comedy, farce, melodrama, and tragedy; and many plays were so filled with interpolations of songs, dances, and scenic effects that they were little more than variety entertainments. This was particularly true in the interval from 1865 to 1875, when the variety shows of the mid-century had died out and vaudeville as such had not yet started.

Formal details of organization and design were rarely employed for their own effectiveness either in the drama or the theatre. Audiences, in general, were too unacquainted with and uninterested in dramatic and theatrical technique to derive satisfaction from these alone. Subtlety of expression was sacrificed to direct presentation of striking and suggestive actions and settings.

The expanding life of the new democracy was clearly reflected on the stage from the beginning of the nineteenth century. Through most of the century, the theatre was viewed as a vast panorama-like spectacle, stretching out to include whatever materials the dramatist chose to introduce; nothing was too large or too complex. Dramatic action was set against a seemingly unlimited and ennobling exterior background or against the regal splendor of a princely hall. Expansiveness and freedom were invariable ingredients in all dramatic representations, at least during the first half of the century. Not until the sixties were audiences willing to accept dramatic action represented within the limits of a narrow and familiar scene.

The continual search for new shapes, ingenious devices, and strange and unusual presentations was also in keeping with the prevailing spirit of a democratic society; and the firm conviction that distance would "lend enchantment to the view" was a doctrine which most theatre artists accepted implicitly. Various aspects of these general romantic tendencies have been observed both in drama and theatre.

In drama the urge to seek romance in the distant and remote was noted particularly in the conventional romantic plays. The locales and heroic actions, remote in place and time, of Italy, Greece, and Spain, were favored subjects. In the early part of the nineteenth century, the taste for gothicism, inspired by the novels of Radcliffe and Godwin, led the romantic artist to seek remoteness in the gloomy, mysterious, and sinister actions of medieval dukes and commoners. The effects were similar to those achieved by Poe in the short story and poetry, though the gothic dramas never rivalled in artistry the works of Poe.

Romantic adventure was the chief ingredient in the plays of the wars and of the frontier. Compared with the novels of James Fenimore Cooper, these dramas appeared feeble in spirit and expression. Only in the Civil War plays of the eighties and the frontier plays of the seventies were the dramatists markedly successful in picturing a convincing romantic atmosphere. The Civil War plays of Howard and Gillette not only caught the exciting atmosphere of the War but succeeded in suggesting the romantic Southland of the ante-bellum period. The frontier plays of Joaquin Miller were particularly striking in their representation of the ennobling effect of the sublimities of nature on man's character.

The ever-increasing faith—increasing at least until the middle of the century—in the rights and abilities of the common man was repeatedly reflected in the drama. The Indian dramas represented the noble savage as the ideal "nature man"; and the implication was that any man similarly unencumbered by the civilizing and restraining influences of society could achieve his rightfully free and noble destiny. The prevailing confidence in the democratic ideal was more directly evident in the war plays, particularly in those of the War of 1812 and in the conventional romantic dramas of the twenties and thirties, which, in spite of their remote locales, glorified the struggle of man against tyranny and oppression. The celebration of the democratic spirit of America was, however, never as sustained and irresistible in the drama as it was in the poetry of Walt Whitman.

The romantic urge to sentimentalize certain characters and aspects of character was evident in the treatment of the Negro and, to a degree, of the Yankee. The distinguishing aspects in the representation of these characters were theatrical rather than dramatic. The Negro minstrel show was undoubtedly the most peculiarly American demonstration of theatrical romanticism; and the stage-Yankee, created by the "yankee actors," was a mixture of realistic detail, gathered from observation of real-life Yankees, and stage exaggeration.

The manifestations of romanticism in the theatre were on the whole more striking than those in the drama. Scenic representations of faraway places, ancient locales, mysterious and exotic regions, and awe-inspiring natural wonders demonstrated a vigorous romantic spirit. The panorama shows and the panoramic tendency in scene painting combined realistic rendering of detail with romantic design and concept. Although the realistic aspects of the panoramas and scenic backdrops were greatly admired, the average spectator viewed them with romantic curiosity. He was more interested in discovering and delighting in the elegancies of Venice and the sublimities of the Mississippi or Niagara Falls than he was in appraising the authenticity of the rendering. The scenic artists were undoubtedly attempting to paint realistically; but when the observer raised his spy-glass to pick out the minute details in the landscape of Yosemite, for example, he was searching for the hidden wonders in the landscape. The sublime, the awe-inspiring, the unusual, the "godlike" were the qualities that were looked for and found in the panoramas, in the paintings of the Hudson River School, and in the backgrounds for the conventional romantic plays, the Indian plays, and the frontier plays. These were the aspects of romantic visual representation that were persistently enjoyed by the theatre spectator through the nineteenth century.

Closely allied to this taste for striking scenic backgrounds was the taste for thrilling, incredible, and spectacular theatrical displays. Scenes of destruction, marine battles, and pyrotechnic exhibitions were common properties of the nineteenth-century theatre. Just as in the drama there was a striving after new forms and new materials, there was in theatrical art a persistent search for new and startling displays; and, as in the background paintings, there was an attempt to achieve realistic representations of trains, ships, fire scenes, and other similar effects. But again, it was the sensational aspect of the representation rather than the realistic that appealed to the spectator. That these effects managed to combine the elements of realism and romanticism accounts, at least in part, for their remarkable popularity in an age when the romantic taste for the strange and spectacular had not yet been supplanted by the realistic taste for the factual.

In the last half of the century realism and romanticism were simultaneously in evidence and are indeed difficult to appraise. The gradual movement from romantic technique and attitude toward twentieth-century "critical realism" was in progress, and we find in the theatre and drama of this period a searching for realistic detail to be exhibited within a general romantic design. In some degree, however, the atmosphere of romance was to be found in all theatrical performances of the nineteenth century. Certainly throughout the century the average spectator of American theatre and drama delighted in the larger-than-life representations of the romantic imagination.

NOTES

CHAPTER I

1. F. L. Lucas, *The Decline and Fall of the Romantic Ideal* (New York: Macmillan, 1936), p. 3.

2. Arthur O. Lovejoy, "On the Discrimination of Romanticisms," *PMLA* XXXIX (1924), 229–53.

3. Quoted from Freneau in G. Harrison Orians, *A Short History of American Literature* (New York: F. S. Crofts, 1940), p. 38.

4. Vernon Louis Parrington, *The Romantic Revolution in America* (New York: Harcourt, 1927), pp. 161–62.

5. Calvin Colton, *Junius Tracts*, VII (New York, 1844), quoted by Carl Russell Fish, *Rise of the Common Man*, Vol. VI in *History of American Life*, eds. Schlesinger and Fox (New York: Macmillan, 1927), dedication page. Quoted by permission of the Macmillan Co.

6. H. J. C. Grierson, *Classical and Romantic* (Cambridge: Cambridge Univ. Press, 1923), p. 19.

7. Fish, *Rise of the Common Man*, p. 255.

8. Russell Blankenship, *American Literature* (New York: Holt, 1931), p. 242.

9. Ralph Waldo Emerson, "The American Scholar," *Complete Essays and Other Writings of Ralph Waldo Emerson* (New York: Random House, 1940), p. 63.

10. Percy H. Boynton, *Literature and American Life* (New York: Ginn, 1936), p. 469.

11. Quoted by Oskar Hagen, *The Birth of the American Tradition in Art* (New York: Scribner, 1940), p. 47.

12. Each of these paintings covered two hundred square feet of canvas.

13. The separate canvases were entitled: "The Savage State or Commencement of Empire," "Arcadian or Pastoral State," "The Consummation of Empire," "Destruction," and "Desolation."

14. Modern art critics have not, to date, been able to evaluate Cole's paintings properly. Of the eighty-two canvases assembled for the memorial exhibition to Cole in 1848, a third are not now to be located.

15. Walter L. Nathan, "Thomas Cole and the Romantic Landscape," in *Romanticism in America,* ed. George Boas (Baltimore: Johns Hopkins Press, 1940), p. 24.

16. Homer Saint-Gaudens, *The American Artist and His Times* (New York: Dodd, Mead, 1941), p. 83.

17. *Ibid.,* p. 126.

18. *Ibid.,* pp. 126–27.

19. Quoted by Roger Gilman, "The Romantic Interior," in *Romanticism in America,* p. 112.

20. *Ibid.,* p. 114.

21. *Ibid.,* p. 117.

22. Lubov Keefer, "The Beethovens of America," *Romanticism in America,* p. 149.

23. Heinrich was born in Germany, but he became an American citizen.

24. The original "Hail Columbia" was written by Joseph Hopkins in 1798 to the tune of the "President's March," by Philip Phile.

25. Keefer, "Beethovens of America," p. 184.

26. Even Paganini was said to have been unable to perform this maneuver.

27. Keefer, "Beethovens of America," p. 182.

28. Quoted from *The Dial,* as excerpted in "Beethovens of America," p. 189.

29. Foster Rhea Dulles, *America Learns to Play* (New York: Appleton-Century, 1940), pp. 48–49.

30. J. Barzun, "To the Rescue of Romanticism," *The American Scholar,* IX (1940), 157.

31. Arthur Hobson Quinn, *A History of the American Drama From the Beginning to the Civil War* (New York: Harper, 1923; Appleton-Century-Crofts, 1943), p. 74.

32. Quoted by Meade Minnigerode, *The Fabulous Forties* (New York: Putnam, 1924), p. 221.

33. *Ibid.,* p. 148.

34. "The Theatre, A Voice to the Friends of Morality in Large Towns and Cities, Remonstrating against its Patronage," *Tracts for Cities* (New York, 1849), IV, 1–8.

35. William Dunlap, *Memoirs of a Water Drinker* (New York, 1837), I, 76.

CHAPTER II, 1

1. Brander Matthews, "The Rise and Fall of Negro Minstrelsy," *Scribner's Magazine,* LVII (1915), 757.

2. Mary Caroline Crawford, *The Romance of the American Theatre* (New York: Halcyon House, 1940), p. 356.

3. Charles Reginald Sherlock, "From Breakdown to Ragtime," *Cosmopolitan*, XXXI (1901), 631.

4. Marian Spitzer, "Lay of the Last Minstrels," *Saturday Evening Post*, CXCVII (March 7, 1926), 197.

5. Jennings, *Theatrical and Circus Life* (St. Louis, 1886), p. 368.

6. The name "Jim Cuff" must have been associated with some real-life or stage Negro, for it occurred again in connection with Sol Smith's play, *Tailor in Distress,* in which Edwin Forrest played the part of "Cuff" at the Globe Theatre, Cincinnati, on July 17, 1823. A similar name, "Cuffy," was used for the Negro character in Samuel Low's *The Politician Outwitted* (1788). Brougham's Negro character in *Life in New York* (1856) was also called "Cuff."

7. Robert P. Nevin, "Negro Minstrelsy and S. C. Foster," *Atlantic Monthly*, XX (1867), 608.

8. John Tasker Howard, *Stephen Foster, America's Troubadour* (New York: Crowell, 1934), p. 124.

9. See illustration, Laurence Hutton, *Curiosities of the American Stage* (New York, 1891), p. 116. See also a contemporary painting of Thomas D. Rice on the fifty-seventh night of his sensational success at the American Theatre, New York, November 25, 1833. Reproduced in Dulles, *America Learns to Play*, p. 126.

10. Carl Wittke, *Tambo and Bones* (Durham, N. C.: Duke Univ. Press, 1930), p. 41.

11. Sigmund Spaeth and Dailey Paskman, *Gentlemen, Be Seated* (Garden City, New York: Doubleday, Doran, 1928), p. 15.

12. Quoted by Wittke, *Tambo and Bones*, p. 45.

13. Olive Logan, "The Ancestry of Brudder Bones," *Harper's New Monthly Magazine*, LVIII (1879), 692.

14. Edwin LeRoy Rice, *Monarchs of Minstrelsy* (New York: Kenny, 1911), p. 26.

15. Jennings, *Theatrical and Circus Life*, p. 374.

16. Matthews, "Negro Minstrelsy," p. 356.

17. Quoted by Wittke, *Tambo and Bones*, p. 209.

18. There was a great vogue for lectures during the forties and fifties. The lyceum movement provided a platform for speakers on every conceivable topic: history, philosophy, and geology; women's rights; prison reform and insane asylums; temperance and abolition.

19. Wittke, *Tambo and Bones*, p. 106.

20. *Ibid.*, p. 218.

21. Ralph Keeler, "Three Years as a Negro Minstrel," *Atlantic Monthly*, XXIV (July, 1869), 72.

22. Matthews, "Negro Minstrelsy," p. 756.
23. Howard, *Stephen Foster*, p. 120.
24. *Ibid.*, p. 196.
25. *Ibid.*, p. 120.
26. Wittke, *Tambo and Bones*, pp. 58–59.
27. *Ibid.*, p. 59.
28. Quoted by Matthews, "Negro Minstrelsy," p. 759.

CHAPTER II, 2

1. The following table, selected from *Negro Population—1790–1915* (Washington, D. C.: Department of Commerce, 1918), gives an indication of the Negro population trend during the last century:

| | | *Number of Negroes* *per thousand whites* | |
DATE	TOTAL POPULATION	WHOLE COUNTRY	SOUTH
1800	5,308,483	233	539
1820	9,638,453	225	592
1840	17,069,453	203	613
1860	31,443,321	165	582
1880	50,155,783	152	564

2. Thomas Southerne, *Oroonoko,* in *Bell's British Theatre* (London, 1797), XIX, 30.
3. Isaac Bickerstaffe, *The Padlock* (Boston, 1795).
4. P. L. Ford, "Beginnings of American Dramatic Literature," *New England Magazine,* n.s. IX (1894), 682.
5. Hutton, *Curiosities,* p. 96.
6. Quinn, *History of American Drama, Beginning to Civil War,* p. 132.
7. George C. D. Odell, *Annals of the New York Stage* (New York: Columbia Univ. Press, 1928), II, 137.
8. A. B. Lindsley, *Love and Friendship; or, Yankee Notions* (New York, 1809), p. 35.
9. *The Young Carolinians; or, Americans in Algiers* (Charleston, 1818), p. 96.
10. Hutton, *Curiosities,* p. 96.
11. *America's Lost Plays* (Princeton: Princeton Univ. Press, 1940–41), XIV, 59.
12. *Ibid.*, p. 97.
13. Samuel Low, *The Politician Outwitted,* in Montrose Moses, *Representative Plays by American Dramatists* (New York: Dutton, 1921), I, 398.
14. John Bernard, *Retrospections of America, 1797–1811* (New York, 1887), p. 132.

15. Jonathan, the country bumpkin in *The Forest Rose* (1825), was blindfolded and enticed into hugging the Negro girl, Rose; and later in the play Rose was substituted for Harriet to keep an assignation with the fop, Bellamy, but both of these scenes were entirely on the comic level.

16. A similar censorship applied to most of the types on the American stage. The Irishman was always a jovial good-natured jokester; the Indian was a "noble savage" and a son of the forest; the Yankee was a shrewd but honest and unassuming New England farmer; and the frontiersman was rough and ready but at the same time gentle and just. There were some slight deviations from these types—as will be noted later in the present study—but on the whole, once the stage type was established, the audiences insisted that the essential qualities of the character be retained.

17. George Lionel Stevens, *The Patriot* (Boston, 1834), p. 36.

18. *Ibid.*

19. Anna Cora Mowatt, *Fashion,* in Allan Gates Halline, *American Plays* (New York: American Book, 1935).

20. *Ibid.,* p. 262.

21. *Ibid.,* p. 241.

22. Quoted by Montrose Moses and John Mason Brown in *The American Theatre as Seen by Its Critics, 1752–1934* (New York: Norton, 1934), p. 75.

23. *Ibid.*

24. Odell, *Annals,* VI, 311.

25. This was, of course, the decade of the great antislavery orations: Wendell Phillips' "Public Opinion," "Harper's Ferry," and "Burial of John Brown"; and Charles Sumner's "Freedom National, Slavery Sectional" and "The Crime Against Kansas."

26. George L. Aiken, *Uncle Tom's Cabin* (New York: Samuel French, n.d.), p. 8.

27. *Ibid.,* p. 46.

28. *Ibid.,* p. 60.

29. Benjamin Brawley, *The Negro in Literature and Art in the United States* (New York: Duffield and Co., 1918), p. 98.

30. Moses, *Representative Plays,* II, 605.

31. Arthur Hornblow, *A History of the Theatre in America* (Philadelphia: Lippincott, 1919), II, 69.

32. Quoted by Helen de Rusha Troesch, "The Negro in English Dramatic Literature and on the Stage" (Doctoral dissertation, Western Reserve Univ., 1940), Chap. IV.

33. John Brougham, *Dred; or, The Dismal Swamp* (New York: Samuel French, n.d.), p. 35.

34. Boucicault did not limit himself to this one novel as a source for his play. The scene in which McClosky steals the mail, kills the Negro,

and is photographed in the process was taken directly from *The Filibuster*, by Albany Fonblanque.

35. Dion Boucicault, *The Octoroon*, in Arthur Hobson Quinn, *Representative American Plays* (New York: Century, 1930), p. 376.

CHAPTER II, 3

1. Quoted by Albert Keiser, *The Indian in American Literature* (New York: Oxford Univ. Press, 1933), p. 22.

2. Nathan, "Thomas Cole," p. 33.

3. Herman F. C. Ten Kate, "The Indian in Literature," *Annual Report of the Board of Regents of the Smithsonian Institution* (Washington, Government Printing Office, 1921), p. 508.

4. Quoted by Keiser, *Indian in American Literature*, p. 53.

5. John Heckewelder, *An Account of the History, Manners, Customs of the Indian Nations Who Once Inhabited Pennsylvania and the Neighboring States* (Philadelphia, 1819).

6. Robert Spiller, *James F. Cooper—Critic of His Times* (New York: Minton, Balch and Co., 1931), p. 11.

7. This novel was adapted for the stage by an unknown dramatist in the same year (1835) in which it was published.

8. Henry Rowe Schoolcraft, *Algic Researches, Comprising Inquiries Respecting the Mental Characteristics of the North American Indians* (New York, 1839).

9. The peculiar rhymeless trochaic tetrameter was derived from the Finnish national epic, *Kalevala;* although some of the incidents of *Hiawatha* can be compared with similar events in the Finnish epic, Longfellow repeatedly maintained that they were not taken from that source.

10. Major Robert Rogers, *Ponteach*, in Moses, *Representative Plays*, I, 155.

11. *Ibid.*, p. 141.

12. Quoted by Keiser, *Indian in American Literature*, p. 66.

13. James Nelson Barker, *The Indian Princess*, in Moses, *Representative Plays*, I, 595.

14. *Ibid.*

15. *Ibid.*

16. Quinn, *History of American Drama, Beginning to Civil War*, p. 139.

17. Quoted by Keiser, *Indian in American Literature*, p. 93.

18. *America's Lost Plays*, XIII, iii.

19. *Ibid.*, p. 91.

20. George de Forest Brush, defending his portrayal of the Indian in his paintings, admitted that the casual traveller to the West would probably

see only dirty and degenerate warriors and "fat, pre-maturely wrinkled squaws," but insisted "it is a mistaken notion to suppose that Indians are all homely." Even he owned, however, that a "really handsome squaw is rare" and that the "superb and symmetrical physique" associated with Indians belonged solely to the warriors.—George de Forest Brush, "An Artist Among the Indians," *Century,* VIII (May, 1885), 55–57.

21. Smith, *William Penn,* in *America's Lost Plays,* XIII, 87.

22. Forrest was not prompted by an altruistic desire to aid American playwrights. He wanted to secure roles that suited his particular talents. When his salary took a sudden jump from forty to four hundred dollars per week (he was twenty-three at the time), he had printed in the November 22, 1828, issue of the *Critic* this announcement: "To the author of the best Tragedy, in five acts, of which the hero or principal character shall be an aboriginal of this country, the sum of five hundred dollars, and half of the proceeds of the third representation, with my own gratuitous services on that occasion. The award to be made by a committee of literary and theatrical gentlemen." The committee to judge the plays was composed of William Cullen Bryant, Fitz-Greene Halleck, James Lawson, William Leggett, Prosper M. Wetmore, and J. G. Brooks. In 1836 R. M. Bird was commissioned by Forrest to revise the play. Forrest later claimed, however, that he never used this revision, and he did not pay Bird for his work.

23. *America's Lost Plays,* XIV, 306.

24. Quoted by William G. B. Carson, *Theatre on the Frontier* (Chicago: Univ. of Chicago Press, 1932), p. 281.

25. Thomas Allston Brown, *History of the New York Stage* (New York: Dodd, Mead, 1903), III, 227.

26. John Augustus Stone, *Metamora,* in *America's Lost Plays,* XIV, 10.

27. *Ibid.,* p. 17.

28. *Ibid.,* p. 23.

29. *Ibid.,* p. 40.

30. Quinn, *History of American Drama, Beginning to Civil War,* p. 272.

31. *America's Lost Plays,* XIV, 16.

32. *Ibid.,* p. 9.

33. Gabriel Harrison, *Edwin Forrest: The Actor and the Man* (Brooklyn, 1889), p. 37.

34. George Washington Parke Custis' father, John Parke Custis, was George Washington's stepson.

35. George Washington Parke Custis, *Pocahontas,* in Quinn, *Representative Plays,* p. 176.

36. *Ibid.,* p. 177.

37. *Ibid.,* p. 185.

38. *Ibid.,* p. 173.

39. Quoted by Leola Bowie Chaplin, *The Life and Works of Nathaniel Deering* (Orono: Univ. of Maine, 1934), p. 85.

40. Quoted by Clement Foust, in *Life and Dramatic Works of Robert Montgomery Bird* (New York: Knickerbocker Press, 1919), p. 53.

41. Charlotte M. S. Barnes, *Plays, Prose, and Poetry* (Philadelphia, 1848), pp. 262–63.

42. *Ibid.*, p. 243.

43. The Mormon religion also holds this view as a result of a sacred record inscribed on golden plates and revealed to Joseph Smith by the Angel Moroni in 1827.

Although Jones' *History of Ancient America* (New York, 1843) appeared just thirteen years after the *Book of Mormon* had been published (1830), Jones does not seem to have drawn his inspiration from it. The Mormons held that America had been settled first by Jaredites who came directly from the Tower of Babel and later by Israelites, descendants of Joseph, who were thought to have come to America in about 600 B.C. Jones believed that the history of America began in 332 B.C. with the settlement of the Western continent by Tyrians. Both Smith and Jones were agreed, however, that the Indians were direct descendants of these early inhabitants.

44. Oral Sumner Coad and Edwin Mims, Jr., *The American Stage* (New Haven: Yale Univ. Press, 1929), p. 96.

45. Quoted by Hutton, *Curiosities,* p. 18.

46. John Brougham, *Po-Ka-Hon-Tas; or, The Gentle Savage* (New York: Samuel French, n.d.), p. 3.

47. *Ibid.*

48. John Brougham, *Metamora; or, The Last of the Pollywogs* (Boston: R. W. Swett, n.d.), p. 4.

49. *Ibid.*, p. 17.

50. Hutton, *Curiosities,* p. 164.

51. Charles Walcot, *Hiawatha; or, Ardent Spirits and Laughing Water* (New York: Samuel French, n.d.), p. 17.

52. Quoted by Perley Isaac Reed, *Realistic Representation of American Characters in Native American Plays Prior to 1870* (Columbus: Ohio State Univ., 1918), p. 61.

53. Dunlap was of this opinion as early as 1832. "How these sons of the forest must have despised the sorry imitation of barbarism, who followed in their train, with painted cheeks, rings in their noses, and bladders smeared with red ochre drawn over their powdered locks."—William Dunlap, *History of the American Theatre* (New York, 1832), p. 200.

54. Quoted by Keiser, *Indian in American Literature,* p. 297.

CHAPTER II, 4

1. The etymology of the word "Yankee" has never been satisfactorily explained. The most concerted effort to trace its origin and history was that undertaken by Oscar Sonneck in his Report on "The Star-Spangled Banner," "Hail Columbia," "America," and "Yankee Doodle" (Washington: Government Printing Office, 1909).

Sonneck, though not fully convinced, preferred the suggestion that "Yankee" was derived from the Dutch name Jan (John) which frequently added the diminutive cke and became Jancke. This explanation became more plausible if one accepted the customary meaning of "doodle" as a "simpleton, noodle, silly, or foolish fellow," generally of a rural type. Thus Sonneck concluded: "If these derivations of 'Doodle' be adopted, all difficulties of explaining the meaning of 'Yankee Doodle' vanish. Whatever the origin of 'Yankee' might have been, after 'Yankee' was preferably applied to the New Englanders, 'Yankee Doodle' would simply mean a New England doodle, and it is not to be wondered at that the New Englanders did not take kindly to this nickname 'Yankee,' especially not if it meant 'Johnny'." For a more complete account of this interesting etymological problem see Sonneck's Report, pp. 79–95.

2. Reed, American Characters in Native American Plays, p. 48.

3. Odell, Annals, III, 476.

4. How Hackett felt about Hill's "piratical" performance was evident in the following letter to Mr. Wemyss from Philadelphia and under date of November 5, 1833: "During my absence in England, Mr. Hill had had the impudence, as well as injustice, to perform, without my permission, my best Yankee character, Solomon Swap (well known as unpublished and of my own originating) at the Park (some dozen times) and elsewhere. I have, of course, a remedy at law against him and the managers who permit it, but a resort to it would be looked upon, perhaps, by the public (who don't understand these matters) as a kind of ill nature on my part, and beneath me; and therefore to prevent my property being thus further hacknied, after being taken down from my mouth, or otherwise surreptitiously obtained, I have notified managers generally of the fact, and shall consider their permitting such an infringement of the most unalienable of literary rights (the spinning of one's own brains), an act of open hostility to me, and proceed accordingly. Mr. Hill has characters enough of his own without carrying on that species of Yankeeism; and if I cannot protect myself from having my character made stale by such depredations, I will resort to rigorous measures against both him and managers wherever the infringement transpires.

"Of course, I do not fear your countenancing such dishonesty, but I thought I would drop you a line, as you might be ignorant of the fact of Solomon Swap being, in every respect, my own exclusive property. I have stopped him in Boston, New York, and here, but understand that he has been trying it in Albany; and though he will not attempt it again here, if I can catch him in New York, where I am returning tomorrow, I must clap 'Grace' upon him, for example's sake. . . ."—Crawford, *American Theatre*, pp. 480–81.

Hill evaded the injunction by adopting the original name of the character and the original play title, Solomon Grundy and *Who Wants a Guinea*.

5. Jonathan Ploughboy in *Fashionable Follies*, by Joseph Hutton. Lot Sop Sago in *Yankee Land*, by Cornelius A. Logan.

6. Quoted by Odell, *Annals*, IV, 321.

7. Joseph Jefferson, *Autobiography* (New York, 1889), p. 20.

8. During this season, 1842–43, Hill, Marble, and Silsbee were playing Yankees in New York simultaneously.

9. Quinn, *History of American Drama, Beginning to Civil War*, p. 302.

10. William Winter, *The Wallet of Time* (New York: Moffat, Yard, and Co., 1913), I, 218.

11. Quoted by Hutton, *Curiosities*, p. 44.

12. This was the first American comedy to be produced by a professional company in this country.

13. Royall Tyler, *The Contrast*, in Moses, *Representative Plays*, I, 444.

14. *Ibid.*, p. 475. His description of his visit to the playhouse is one of the classics in American drama:

Jenny. Well, and how did you find the place?
Jonathan. As I was going about here and there, to and again, to find it, I saw a great crowd of folks going into a long entry that had lanterns over the door; so I asked a man whether that was not the place where they played *hocus-pocus?* He was a very civil kind man, though he did speak like the Hessians; he lifted up his eyes and said, "They play *hocus-pocus* tricks enough there, Got knows, mine friend.
Jenny. Well—
Jonathan. So I went right in, and they shewed me away, clean up to the garret, just like meeting-house gallery. And so I saw a power of topping folks, all sitting round in little cabins, "just like father's corn-cribs:" and then there was such a squeaking with the fiddles, and such a tarnal blaze with the lights, my head was near turned. At last the people that sat near me set up such a hissing—hiss—like so many mad cats; and then they went thump, thump, thump, just like our Pegleg threshing wheat, and stampt away, just like the nation; and called out for one Mr. Langolee,—I suppose he helps act the tricks.

Jenny. Well, and what did you do all this time?

Jonathan. Gor, I—I liked the fun, and so I thumpt away, and hissed as lustily as the best of 'em. . . .

Jenny. Well, and did you see the man with his tricks?

Jonathan. Why, I vow as I was looking out for him, they lifted up a great green cloth and let us look right into the next neighbor's house. (pp. 473–74.)

15. *Ibid.*, 478.

16. This was the earliest use of "Yankee Doodle" for dramatic purposes although the song had first been introduced on the stage in Andrew Barton's *The Disappointment; or, The Force of Credulity, a new American comic-opera of two acts* (1767).

After canvassing all the various explanations of the origin of "Yankee Doodle," examining carefully the evidence for each claim, Sonneck (his *Report*, pp. 79–156) reached a few limited conclusions: Whatever its original form might have been, "Yankee Doodle" passed through many hands before it became fixed in the popular mind in its present form. "Indeed the assumption is not at all far fetched that 'Yankee Doodle' in its modern form is a composite tune, formed out of at least two different tunes of different age." (p. 125.) A chorus refrain with "Doodle-Doodle, do" existed in England as early as the middle of the seventeenth century. That "Yankee Doodle" is possibly identical with this air "has become so probable that this probability obliges the historian to move with caution and skepticism. . . ." (p. 145.) Nevertheless, the text of the song clearly revealed an American origin. "It is so full of American provincialisms, slang expressions of the time, allusions to American habits, and customs, that no Englishman could have penned these verses." (p. 141.) But finally, in his summation, Sonneck was obliged to admit that all the explanations offered are inadequate: "The origin of 'Yankee Doodle' remains as mysterious as ever, unless it be deemed a positive result to have eliminated definitely almost every theory thus far advanced and thus by the process of elimination to have paved the way for an eventual solution of the puzzle." (p. 156.)

17. Tyler, *The Contrast*, p. 477.

18. *Ibid.*, p. 469.

19. Dunlap had used a Yankee servant in an earlier, but nonextant play, *The Modest Soldier; or, Love in New York* (1787).

20. William Dunlap, *The Glory of Columbia* (New York, 1817), p. 15.

21. *Ibid.*, p. 17.

22. In the Preface to his play Barker included some illuminating comments on the reception accorded a native playwright's work in 1808. After submitting his manuscript to a friend for examination, he received this reply: " 'You meant to have written a comedy? . . . and you have produced nothing, absolutely nothing but a collection of Columbianisms,

in five parts.' 'And pray,' asked I, 'what may a Columbianism be?' 'The term,' replied my good natured friend, 'was invented and applied by certain hypercritics of our own, who, perhaps from being placed too near the scene, cannot discover the beauties of their own country and whose refined taste is therefore better pleased with the mellow tints which distance gives to every foreign object. This term of derision they apply to every delineation an American may attempt to make of American manners, customs, opinions, characters, or scenery. Thus, while they rapturously applaud the sentiments of a foreign stage patriot, the lover of his country, in an American play, utters only contemptible Columbianisms. . . . In fine this unaccountable prejudice extends to every thing here; the farther, therefore you rove from America, the nearer you approach to their favour. Take my advice, then, burn your book, write a melodrama, and lay your scene in the moon.' "—J. N. Barker, *Tears and Smiles* (Philadelphia, 1808).

23. Lindsley, *Love and Friendship*, pp. 56–57.

24. Quoted by Quinn, *History of American Drama, Beginning to Civil War*, p. 114.

25. Joseph Hutton, *Fashionable Follies* (Philadelphia, 1815), p. 26.

26. Samuel Woodworth, *The Forest Rose; or, American Farmers* (Boston, 1855), Preface.

27. Quinn, *History of American Drama, Beginning to Civil War*, p. 295.

28. Woodworth, *Forest Rose*, p. 10.

29. *Ibid.*, p. 25.

30. Charles Mathews (?), *Jonathan in England* (London: Hodgson and Co., n.d.), p. 9.

31. It should be kept in mind that Dunlap's Yankee was not a genuine Yankee but John Bull's impersonation of a Yankee character.

32. William Dunlap, *A Trip to Niagara; or, Travellers in America* (New York, 1830), p. 36.

33. *Ibid.*, p. 48.

34. Jonathan in Lindsley's *Love and Friendship* was servant to a sea captain, but he had not picked up the nautical lingo.

35. Brander Matthews, "The American on the Stage," *Scribner's Monthly*, XVIII (1879), 331.

36. *Ibid.*

37. J. S. Jones, *The People's Lawyer* (Boston, 1856), p. 30.

38. Montrose J. Moses, *The American Dramatist* (Boston: Little Brown, 1911), p. 51.

39. Morris Barnett, *The Yankee Peddler* (New York, 1877), p. 347.

40. *Ibid.*, p. 346.

41. *Ibid.*, p. 349.

42. *Ibid.*, p. 350.

43. O. E. Durivage, *The Stage Struck Yankee* (New York: 184-), p. 28.

44. *Ibid.*, p. 28.

45. Anna Cora Mowatt, *Autobiography of an Actress; or, Eight Years on the Stage* (Boston, 1854), p. 203.

46. It opened at Wallack's on July 4, 1852, and then played at the Broadway, in New York; at the National and New Boston, in Boston; at the Walnut Street, in Philadelphia; and at the National, in New York.

47. Barney Williams, *Irish Assurance and Yankee Modesty* (New York: Samuel French, n.d.), p. 9.

48. Henry Oake Pardey, *Nature's Nobleman* (New York, 1853), p. 16.

49. John Brougham, *The Irish Yankee; or, The Birth-day of Freedom* (New York, n.d.), p. 19.

50. Reed, *American Characters in Native American Plays,* p. 113.

51. *Ibid.*, p. 114.

52. Boucicault, *The Octoroon,* p. 376.

53. The play had first appeared as a variety sketch at Harry Martin's Varieties in Pittsburgh, February, 1875, under the title *Joshua Whitcomb.* The first full-length version, written with George W. Ryer, retained the above title and had its first performance at the National Theatre, New York, April 3, 1876. The first performance of the play under the title *The Old Homestead* was at the Boston Museum, April 5, 1886. See also Arthur Hobson Quinn, *History of the American Drama From the Civil War to the Present Day* (New York: Harper, 1927), p. 398.

54. Curtis Chunk in *The Stage Struck Yankee;* and Jonathan Peabody in *The Bucktails.*

CHAPTER II, 5

1. Charles Angoff, *Literary History of the American People* (New York: Knopf, 1931), II, 399.

2. Walter Prichard Eaton, "Where is our Drama of '76?" in *The American Stage of Today* (Boston: Small Maynard, 1908), p. 259.

3. Quoted by Marjorie Barstow Greenbie, *American Saga* (New York: Whittlesey House, 1939), p. 175.

4. Quinn, *History of American Drama, Beginning to Civil War,* p. 46.

5. Dunlap, *History of American Theatre,* p. 88.

6. Anonymous, *The Battle of Brooklyn* (New York, 1776), p. 45.

7. The custom of presenting plays in the schools was important to the development of early American drama.

8. Hugh Brackenridge, *The Death of General Montgomery* (Norwich, 1777).

9. Quoted by William Clapp, *Record of the Boston Stage* (Boston, 1853), p. 53.

10. *Ibid.*, p. 79.

11. *Ibid.*, p. 81.

12. Quoted by Quinn, *History of American Drama, Beginning to Civil War*, p. 127.

13. William Dunlap, *André*, in Halline, *American Plays*, p. 55.

14. Dunlap, *Glory of Columbia*, p. 56.

15. Brander Matthews, "Introduction" to Dunlap's *André* (New York, 1887), Ser. I, IV, xvi.

16. *Ibid.*, p. xxii.

17. Coleman was editor of the *New York Evening Post;* he had severely condemned the opening performance of *Marion* without having seen it.

18. M. M. Noah, *Marion* (New York, 1822), pp. 5–6.

19. Charles Powell Clinch, *The Spy*, in *America's Lost Plays*, XIV, 105.

20. Quinn, *History of American Drama, Beginning to Civil War*, p. 156.

21. *Ibid.*, p. 157.

22. Orians, *Short History*, p. 81.

23. Webster also delivered an oration on the occasion of the completion of the Monument, June 17, 1843.

24. John Brougham, *The Irish Yankee*, p. 28.

25. Oliver Bell Bunce, *Love in '76*, in Moses, *Representative Plays*, III, 215–16.

26. See *Naval Documents Related to U. S. Wars with the Barbary Powers* (Washington: United States Government Printing Office, 1939), Foreword by Franklin D. Roosevelt.

27. John Minshull, *Rural Felicity* (New York, 1801), p. 53.

28. Barker, *Tears and Smiles*, p. 9.

29. William Dunlap, *Yankee Chronology; or, Huzza for the Constitution* (New York, 1812).

30. Joseph N. Ireland, *Fifty Years of a Playgoer's Journal* (New York, 1860), p. 234.

31. Carson, *Theatre on the Frontier*, p. 25.

32. M. M. Noah, *She Would Be a Soldier* (New York, 1819), p. 73.

33. *Ibid.*, Preface, p. 4.

34. Quoted by Quinn, *History of American Drama, Beginning to Civil War*, p. 207.

35. *Ibid.*, p. 286.

36. See Play List.

37. There was a comparable outburst in fiction. Orians indicated that there were no less than fifty novels on the War theme between 1865 and 1870. Whitman's poems dealing with the War were, however, the distinctive contribution to post-War literature. His "O Captain! My Captain!" and "Hush'd Be the Camps To-day" are practically the only Civil War poems remembered today.

38. Dion Boucicault, *Belle Lamar*, in Garrett H. Leverton, *Plays for the College Theatre* (New York: Samuel French, 1934), p. 143.

39. *Ibid.*, p. 146.

40. The play was evidently based on an even earlier comedy of Howard's which had been produced in the late sixties at Macauley's Theatre in Louisville.

41. Bronson Howard, *Shenandoah*, in Moses, *Representative Plays*, III, 439.

42. William Gillette, *Secret Service*, in Quinn, *Representative Plays*, p. 614.

CHAPTER II, 6

1. Quoted by Coad and Mims, *The American Stage*, p. 123.
2. Dulles, *America Learns to Play*, p. 154.
3. Jefferson, *Autobiography*, p. 22.
4. H. P. Phelps, *Addenda to Players of a Century, a Record of the Albany Stage* (Albany, 1889), p. 1.
5. Quoted by Hornblow, *History of Theatre in America*, II, 17.
6. Laurence Hutton, *Plays and Players* (New York, 1875), p. 208.
7. Even a present-day audience, accustomed to look coldly on such sentimental displays, finds it difficult to resist the pathos of the final reunion of Rip with his daughter. The present writer played the part for a dozen or more performances in 1934 and found that few in the audience were unaffected at the final curtain.
8. Orians, *Short History*, p. 85.
9. Quoted by Crawford, *American Theatre*, p. 482.
10. Quoted by Dulles, *America Learns to Play*, pp. 173–74.
11. Augustin Daly, *Horizon*, in Halline, *American Plays*, p. 356.
12. Quinn, *History of American Drama, Civil War to Present Day* (New York: Harper, 1927; Appleton-Century-Crofts, 1943), I, 14.
13. Quoted by Phelps, *Players of a Century*, p. 334.
14. Frank Murdoch, *Davy Crockett*, in *America's Lost Plays*, IV, 125.
15. *Ibid.*, p. 133.
16. *Ibid.*, p. 135.
17. I have found no record of performance for either of these plays.
18. Nancy is dressed as a boy, and to everyone except the Danites she is known as Billy Piper.
19. Joaquin Miller, *The Danites in the Sierras*, in Halline, *American Plays*, p. 389.
20. Bret Harte, *Two Men from Sandy Bar* (Boston, 1876), p. 81.
21. *Ibid.*, p. 64.
22. Bartley Campbell, *My Partner*, in *America's Lost Plays*, XIX, 65.
23. Dulles, *America Learns to Play*, p. 216.

CHAPTER III

1. Thomas Godfrey, *The Prince of Parthia,* in Moses, *Representative Plays,* I, 45–46.
2. William Dunlap, *Fontainville Abbey* (New York, 1807), p. 162.
3. Quoted by Quinn, *History of American Drama, Beginning to Civil War,* p. 144.
4. Although Payne did much of his work in England, he was born in America, and his plays were always produced here immediately following their London openings.
5. A version of this play became the famous equestrian drama of the forties in which Adah Isaacs Menken, playing the part of Mazeppa, was tied to the wild horse and sent riding on a runway out over the audience with her scanty garments flying in the wind.
6. M. M. Noah, *The Grecian Captive* (New York, 1822), p. 25.
7. *Ibid.,* p. iii.
8. Robert Montgomery Bird, *The Gladiator,* in Foust, *Works of Bird,* pp. 354–55.
9. Quoted by Garff Wilson, "American Styles and Theories of Acting from Edwin Forrest to David Belasco" (Doctoral dissertation, Cornell University, 1940), pp. 38–39.
10. For example, William Gilmore Simms's *Beauchampe* (1842).
11. Epes Sargent, *Velasco* (New York, 1839), p. 99.
12. Quoted by Hornblow, *History of Theatre in America,* II, 229.

CHAPTER IV

1. Quoted by Hornblow, *History of Theatre in America,* I, 46.
2. G. O. Seilhamer, *History of the American Theatre* (Philadelphia, 1888), I, 246.
3. Quoted by Hornblow, *History of Theatre in America,* I, 155. Presumably it was this background which was used to represent the scene on the banks of the Hudson in the production of Dunlap's *Glory of Columbia* at the South Street Theatre in Philadelphia, July 4, 1807. It is a curious irony of theatrical history that Dunlap's play dealt with the capture and execution of André.
4. Seilhamer, *History of the American Theatre,* II, 189–90.
5. *Ibid.,* III, 287–91.
6. Hornblow, *History of Theatre in America,* I, 256–57.
7. Odell, *Annals,* II, 24.

8. Brander Matthews, Introduction to John Burk's *Bunker Hill* (New York, 1891), pp. 7–9.

9. Alan Burroughs, *Limners and Likenesses* (Cambridge: Harvard Univ. Press, 1936), p. 145.

10. Odell, *Annals*, I, 286.

11. *Ibid.*, I, 298.

12. *Ibid.*, I, 443.

13. *Ibid.*, II, 224.

14. *Ibid.*, II, 558.

15. *The Young Carolinians*, in *Essays, Religious, Moral, and Poetical* (Charleston, 1818), II, 70.

16. George Willard, *History of the Providence Stage 1762–1891* (Providence, 1891), p. 75.

17. Odell, *Annals*, III, 5.

18. *Ibid.*, pp. 8, 146.

19. John Howard Payne, *Mount Savage*, in *America's Lost Plays*, V, 59.

20. *Ibid.*, p. 63.

21. *Ibid.*, pp. 88–89.

22. Eidophusicon or Moving Diorama was the name for this new scenic device. The principle of operation was simply that of indicating motion by having the scenery rather than the object move. The long canvas was unrolled from a roller on one side of the stage and rolled up on a roller at the other side.

23. Dunlap, *A Trip to Niagara*, Preface.

24. *Ibid.*

25. *Ibid.*, p. 42.

26. *Ibid.*, p. 27.

27. George Washington Parke Custis, *Pocahontas*, in Quinn, *Representative Plays*, p. 173.

28. John Augustus Stone, *Metamora*, in *America's Lost Plays*, XIV, 9.

29. John Howard Payne, *Mazeppa*, in *America's Lost Plays*, V, 176.

30. *Ibid.*, V, 181.

31. John Howard Payne, *The Spanish Husband*, in *America's Lost Plays*, V, 236.

32. Richard Penn Smith, *The Bombardment of Algiers*, in *America's Lost Plays*, XIII, 50.

33. Quinn, *Representative American Plays*, p. 185.

34. *America's Lost Plays*, XIII, 81.

35. Clifton W. Tayleure, *Horseshoe Robinson; or, The Battle of King's Mountain* (New York, 1856), p. 4.

36. Quoted by Odell, *Annals*, VII, 379.

37. Odell, *Annals*, V, 174.

38. *Ibid.*, 422.

39. *Ibid.,* VI, 13. This was undoubtedly a dioramic or transparency transformation scene.

40. Augustin Daly, *Horizon,* in Halline, *American Plays,* p. 371.

41. *Ibid.,* p. 388.

42. Bronson Howard, *Shenandoah,* in Quinn, *Representative American Plays,* p. 487.

43. Augustin Daly, *Under the Gaslight* (New York, 1867), p. 43.

44. Jennings, *Theatrical and Circus Life,* pp. 190–93.

Further information regarding the manipulation of similar spectacular scenes can be found in Albert Hopkins, *Magic, Stage Illusions, and Scientific Diversions* (New York, 1897), pp. 251–362.

45. Steele Mackaye, *Rose Michel,* in *America's Lost Plays,* XI, 3.

46. *Won at Last, ibid.,* p. 57.

47. *An Arrant Knave, ibid.,* p. 203.

48. Percy Mackaye, *Epoch, The Life of Steele Mackaye* (New York: Boni and Liveright, 1927), I, xviii.

49. He did not carry out this project.

50. Mackaye, *Epoch,* II, 300.

51. For a complete description see *Epoch,* II, 311–437.

52. *Ibid.,* II, 346–47.

53. *Ibid.,* pp. 443–44.

54. Odell, *Annals,* X, 568.

55. Daly, *Under the Gaslight,* p. 30.

SELECTED BIBLIOGRAPHY

Angoff, Charles. *A Literary History of the American People.* New York: Knopf, 1931.

Atkinson, F. W. *Early American Plays, 1756–1830. Later American Plays, 1830–1900.* MSS. in Huntington Library and in libraries of Harvard Univ., Univ. of Chicago and Univ. of Pennsylvania.

Balch, Marston. "Jonathan the First," *Modern Language Notes,* XLVI (1931), 281–88.

Barzun, J. "To the Rescue of Romanticism," *The American Scholar,* IX (1940), 147–58.

Bernard, John. *Retrospections of America, 1797–1811.* New York, 1887.

Blake, Charles. *Historical Account of the Providence Stage, 1762–1891.* Providence, 1868.

Boas, George, ed. *Romanticism in America.* Baltimore: Johns Hopkins Press, 1940.

Bradley, Edward Sculley. *George Henry Boker.* Philadelphia: Univ. of Pennsylvania Press, 1927.

Briggs, E., and H. E. Briggs. "The Early Theater in Chicago," *Illinois History Journal,* XXX (1946), 165–78.

Brown, Thomas Allston. *A History of the New York Stage from 1732 to 1901.* 3 vols. New York: Dodd, Mead, 1903.

Brush, G. de F. "Indians as Art Subjects," *Century Magazine,* VIII (May, 1885), 55–57.

Burroughs, Alan. *Limners and Likenesses.* Cambridge: Harvard Univ. Press, 1936.

Caffin, C. H. *The Story of American Painting.* New York: Doubleday Page and Co., 1907.

Carson, William G. B. *Managers in Distress.* St. Louis: Historical Documents Foundation, 1949.

———. *The Theatre on the Frontier.* Chicago: Univ. of Chicago Press, 1932.

258 *America Takes the Stage*

Chaplin, Leola Bowie. *Life and Works of Nathaniel Deering.* Orono: Univ. of Maine, 1934.

Clapp, William W. *Record of the Boston Stage.* Boston, 1853.

Clark, Barrett, ed. *America's Lost Plays.* 20 vols. Princeton: Princeton Univ. Press, 1940–41.

————, ed. *Favorite American Plays of the Nineteenth Century.* Princeton: Princeton Univ. Press, 1943.

Cline, J. "Rise of the American Stage Negro," *The Drama*, XXI (Jan., 1931), 9–10.

Coad, Oral Sumner. "The American Theatre in the 18th Century," *South Atlantic Quarterly*, XVII (July, 1918), 190–97.

————. *William Dunlap.* New York: Dunlap Society, 1917.

————, and Edwin Mims, Jr. *The American Stage.* New Haven: Yale Univ. Press, 1929.

Cooper, James Fenimore. *Notions of the Americans.* London, 1828.

Crawford, Mary Caroline. *Romance of the American Theatre*, rev. ed. Boston: Little, Brown, 1927.

Curvin, Jonathan. "Realism in Early American Art and Theatre," *Quarterly Journal of Speech.* XXX (1944), 450–55.

Damon, S. F. "Providence Theatricals in 1773," *Rhode Island History*, IV (April, 1945), 55–58.

Downer, Alan S. "Players and Painted Stage—19th Century Acting," *PMLA*, LXI (1946), 522–76.

Duerr, Edwin. "Charles Ciceri and the Background of American Scene Design," *Theatre Arts Monthly*, XVI (1932), 983–90.

————. "Early Stage Decoration in the American Theatre, 1772–1872." Cornell Univ. Thesis, 1931.

Dulles, Foster Rhea. *America Learns to Play.* New York: Appleton-Century, 1940.

Dunlap, William. *Diary of William Dunlap (1766–1839).* New York Historical Society, 1930.

————. *History of the American Theatre.* New York, 1832.

————. *A History of the Rise and Progress of Design in the United States.* 3 vols. Boston: C. E. Goodspeed and Co., 1918.

————. *Memoirs of a Water-Drinker.* New York, 1837.

Eaton, Walter Prichard. *American Stage of Today.* New York: Small, Maynard and Co., 1908.

Eich, Louis M. "The Stage Yankee," *Quarterly Journal of Speech*, XXVII (1941), 16.

Emerson, Ralph Waldo. *Complete Essays and Other Writings.* New York: Random House, 1940.

Firkins, Ina Ten Eyck. *Index to Plays, 1800–1926.* New York: H. W. Wilson, 1927.

Ford, P. L. "Beginnings of American Drama," *New England Magazine,* n.s., IX (1894), 673–87.

———. *Washington and the Theatre.* New York: Dunlap Society, 1899.

Foust, Clement Edgar. *The Life and Dramatic Works of Robert Montgomery Bird.* New York: Knickerbocker Press, 1914.

Gafford, Lucille. "The Boston Stage and the War of 1812," *New England Quarterly,* VII (1934), 327–35.

Gagey, Edmond M. *The San Francisco Stage, a History.* New York: Columbia Univ. Press, 1950.

Gates, Lewis E. "The Romantic Movement in the 19th Century," *The Critic,* XXXVI (1900), 172–80, 268–75.

Gergenheimer, A. F. "Early History of the Philadelphia Stage," *Pennsylvania History,* IX (1942), 233–41.

Gilbert, Douglas. *American Vaudeville, Its Life and Times.* New York: Whittlesey House, 1940.

Graham, Philip. *Showboats.* Austin: Univ. of Texas Press, 1951.

Greenbie, Marjorie Barstow. *American Saga.* New York: Whittlesey House, 1939.

Grierson, Herbert J. C. *Classical and Romantic.* Cambridge: Cambridge Univ. Press, 1923.

Hagan, John S. G. *Records of the New York Stage from 1860–1870.* New York, 1880.

Hagen, Oskar. *The Birth of the American Tradition in Art.* New York: Scribner, 1940.

Halline, Allan Gates. *American Plays.* New York: American Book, 1935.

Hamar, Clifford E. "American Theatre History: a Geographical Index," *Educational Theatre Journal,* I (1949), 164–94.

———. "Scenery on the Early American Stage," *Theatre Annual,* VII (1949), 84.

Harrison, Gabriel. *Edwin Forrest, The Actor and the Man.* Brooklyn, 1889.

———. *The Life and Writings of John Howard Payne.* Albany, 1875.

Hazard, Lucy Lockwood. *The Frontier in American Literature.* New York: Crowell, 1927.

Heckewelder, John. *An Account of the History, Manners, Customs of the Indian Nations Who Once Inhabited Pennsylvania and the Neighboring States.* Philadelphia, 1819.

Hill, Frank Pierce. *American Plays Printed, 1714–1830.* Stanford, Calif.: Stanford Univ. Press, 1934.

Hoole, William Stanley. *The Ante-Bellum Charleston Theatre.* Tuscaloosa: Univ. of Alabama, 1946.

Hopkins, Albert A. *Magic, Stage Illusions, and Scientific Diversions.* New York, 1897.

Hornblow, Arthur. *History of the Theatre in America from its Beginning to the Present Time.* 2 vols. New York: Lippincott, 1919.

Howard, John Tasker. *Stephen Foster, America's Troubadour.* New York: Crowell, 1934.

Hughes, Glenn. *A History of the American Theatre (1700–1950).* New York: Samuel French, 1951.

Hutton, Laurence. *Curiosities of the American Stage.* New York, 1891.

——. "Negro on the Stage," *Harper's Monthly,* LXXIX (1889), 131–45.

——. *Plays and Players.* New York, 1875.

Ireland, Joseph N. *Fifty Years of a Playgoer's Journal 1798–1848.* New York, 1860.

——. *Records of the New York Stage from 1750–1860.* New York, 1866–67.

Isham, Samuel. *History of American Painting.* New York: Macmillan, 1915.

James, Henry. "The American on the Stage," *Atlantic Monthly,* LXIII (1889), 846–48.

James, Reese Davis. *Old Drury of Philadelphia.* Philadelphia: Univ. of Pennsylvania Press, 1930.

Jefferson, Joseph. *Autobiography.* New York, 1889.

Jennings, John J. *Theatrical and Circus Life.* St. Louis, 1886.

Jones, George. *History of Ancient America.* New York, 1843.

Keeler, R. "Three Years as a Negro Minstrel," *Atlantic Monthly,* XXIV (1869), 71–85.

Keiser, Albert. *The Indian in American Literature.* London: Oxford Univ. Press, 1933.

Kendall, John S. *The Golden Age of the New Orleans Theater.* Baton Rouge: Louisiana State Univ. Press, 1952.

Kimmel, Stanley. *The Mad Booths of Maryland.* New York: Bobbs-Merrill, 1940.

Klitgaard, Kaj. *Through the American Landscape.* Chapel Hill: Univ. of North Carolina Press, 1941.

Langworthy, Helen. "The Theatre in the Lower Valley of Ohio, 1797–1860." Master's thesis, Univ. of Iowa, 1926.

Law, R. A. "Charleston Theatres, 1735–1766," *Nation,* XCIX (1914), 278–79.

Lawson, Hilda Josephine. "The Negro in American Drama." Doctoral dissertation, Univ. of Illinois, 1939.

Leverton, Garrett H., ed. *Plays for the College Theatre*. New York: Samuel French, 1933.

Logan, Olive. "Ancestry of Negro Minstrelsy," *Harper's Monthly*, LVIII (1879), 687–98.

Lovejoy, Arthur O. "On the Discrimination of Romanticism," *PMLA*, XXXIX (1924), 229–53.

Lucas, Frank L. *The Decline and Fall of the Romantic Ideal*. New York: Macmillan, 1936.

Ludlow, Noah. *Dramatic Life as I Found It*. St. Louis, 1880.

McGlinchee, Claire. *The First Decade of the Boston Museum*. Boston: Humphries, 1940.

Mackaye, Percy. *Epoch—Life of Steele Mackaye*. 2 vols. New York: Boni and Liveright, 1927.

Macminn, G. R. *Theatre of the Golden Era in California*. Caldwell, Idaho: Caxton Printers, 1941.

Matthews, Brander. "The American on the Stage," *Scribner's Monthly*, XVIII (1879), 321–33.

———, ed. *Bunker Hill*, by John Burk. New York, 1891.

———. "Drama in the 18th Century," *Sewanee Review*, XI (1903), 1.

———. "Rise and Fall of Negro Minstrelsy," *Scribner's Magazine*, LVII (1915), 754–59.

Mayorga, Margaret G. *A Short History of the American Drama*. New York: Dodd, Mead, 1934.

Minnigerode, Meade. *The Fabulous Forties*. New York: Putnam, 1924.

Moody, Richard. "Negro Minstrelsy," *Quarterly Journal of Speech*, XXX (1944), 321–28.

———, and A. M. Drummond. "The Hit of the Century: Uncle Tom's Cabin," *Educational Theatre Journal*, IV (1952), 315–22.

———, and A. M. Drummond. "Indian Treaties: The First American Dramas," *Quarterly Journal of Speech*, XXXIX (1953), 15–24.

Moses, Montrose J. *The American Dramatist*. Boston: Little, Brown, 1911.

———. "American Plays of Our Forefathers," *North American Review*, CCVI (1922), 790–804.

———. *The Fabulous Forrest*. Boston: Little, Brown, 1929.

———. *Representative Plays by American Dramatists*. 3 vols. New York: Dutton, 1921.

———, and J. M. Brown. *American Theatre as Seen by Its Critics*. New York: Norton, 1934.

Mowatt, Anna Cora Ogden. *Autobiography of an Actress*. Boston, 1854.

———. *Mimic Life*. Boston, 1856.

Muir, Edwin. "The Meaning of Romanticism," *Freeman,* VIII (1923–1924), 368–70, 416–18, 443–44.

Nelligen, Murray H. "American Nationalism on the Stage: The Plays of George Washington Custis (1781–1857)," *Virginia Magazine of History and Biography,* LVIII (1950), 299–324.

Nevin, R. P. "Negro Minstrelsy and S. C. Foster," *Atlantic Monthly,* XX (1867), 608–16.

Odell, George C. D. *Annals of the New York Stage.* 15 vols. New York: Columbia Univ. Press, 1927–49.

Orians, G. Harrison. *A Short History of American Literature.* New York: F. S. Crofts, 1940.

Parrington, Vernon Louis. *Main Currents in American Thought.* 3 vols. New York: Harcourt, 1927–30.

Paskman, Dailey, and Sigmund Spaeth. *Gentlemen, Be Seated!* Garden City, New York: Doubleday, Doran, 1928.

Phelps, Henry P. *Addenda to Players of a Century.* Albany, 1889.

———. *Players of a Century.* Albany, 1880.

Pierce, A. "Early Intolerance Toward the Theatre in America," *The Drama,* XVIII (1928), 146.

Pollock, Thomas Clark. *The Philadelphia Theatre in the Eighteenth Century.* Philadelphia: Univ. of Pennsylvania Press, 1933.

Quinn, Arthur Hobson. *American Fiction.* New York: Appleton-Century, 1936.

———. "Early Drama 1756–1860," *Cambridge History of American Literature,* Vol. I. New York: Putnam, 1921.

———. *History of American Drama from the Beginning to the Civil War.* New York: Harper, 1923; Appleton-Century-Crofts, 1943.

———. *History of the American Drama from the Civil War to the Present Day.* 2 vols. New York: Harper, 1927; Appleton-Century Crofts, 1943.

———, ed. *The Literature of the American People.* New York: Appleton-Century-Crofts, 1951.

———, ed. *Representative American Plays.* New York: Appleton-Century, 1917.

———. *The Soul of America.* Philadelphia: Univ. of Pennsylvania Press, 1932.

Reed, Perley Isaac. *Realistic Presentation of American Characters in Native American Plays Prior to 1870.* Columbus: Ohio State Univ., 1918.

Rice, Edward. *Monarchs of Minstrelsy from "Daddy" Rice to Date.* New York: Kenny Publishing Co., 1911.

Robertson, John G. *Studies in the Genesis of Romantic Theory in the Eighteenth Century.* Cambridge: Cambridge Univ. Press, 1933.

Roden, R. F. *Later American Plays, 1831–1900.* New York: Dunlap Society Publications, n.s. No. 12, 1900.

Rourke, Constance. *The Roots of American Culture.* New York: Harcourt, 1942.

———. *Troupers of the Gold Coast.* New York: Harcourt, 1928.

Rusk, Ralph Leslie. *Literature of the Middle Western Frontier.* 2 vols. New York: Columbia Univ. Press, 1926.

Saint-Gaudens, Homer. *The American Artist and His Times.* New York: Dodd, Mead, 1941.

Schick, Joseph S. *Early Theatre in Eastern Iowa.* Chicago: Univ. of Chicago Press, 1939.

Schlesinger, A. M., and D. R. Fox, eds. *A History of American Life.* 12 vols. New York: Macmillan, 1927–44.

Schoolcraft, Henry Rowe. *Algic Researches, Comprising Inquiries Respecting the Mental Characteristics of the North American Indians.* New York, 1839.

Seilhamer, G. O. *History of the American Theatre.* 3 vols. Philadelphia, 1888.

Seldes, Gilbert. *The Stammering Century.* New York: John Day, 1928.

Sherlock, Charles Reginald. "From Breakdown to Ragtime," *Cosmopolitan,* XXXI (1901), 631.

Smith, Henry Nash. "The Frontier Hypothesis and the Myth of the West," *American Quarterly,* II (1950), 3–11.

Smith, Solomon F. *The Theatrical Journey.* Philadelphia, 1854.

———. *Theatrical Management in the South and West.* New York, 1868.

Smither, Nelle. *A History of the English Theatre at New Orleans, 1806–1842.* Philadelphia: Univ. of Pennsylvania Press, 1944.

Sonneck, Oscar George Theodore. *Early Opera in America.* New York: G. Schirmer, 1915.

———. *Report on "The Star Spangled Banner," "Hail Columbia," "America," "Yankee Doodle."* Washington: Government Printing Office, 1909.

Spiller, Robert E. *Fenimore Cooper—Critic of His Times.* New York: Minton, Balch, 1931.

Spitzer, Marian. "Lay of the Last Minstrels," *Saturday Evening Post,* CXCVII (1926), 197.

Swanson, Wesley. "Wings and Backdrops; Story of American Stage Scenery from the Beginnings to 1875," *The Drama,* XVIII (1927), 41–42, 78–80, 107–10.

Tenkate, H. F. C. "Indian in Literature," *Smithsonian Report* (1921), 507–28.

"The Theatre," *Tracts for Cities*. Vol. IV. New York, 1849.

Tompkins, E., and Q. Kilby. *History of the Boston Theatre*. New York: Houghton Mifflin, 1908.

Troesch, Helen de Rusha. "The Negro in English Dramatic Literature and on the Stage." Doctoral dissertation, Western Reserve Univ., 1940.

Trux, J. J. "Negro Minstrelsy," *Putnam's Monthly*, V (1855), 72–79.

Tyler, Moss Coit. *Literary History of the American Revolution, 1763–1783*. New York, 1897.

Wecter, Dixon. *The Hero in America*. New York: Scribner, 1941.

——. *The Saga of American Society*. New York: Scribner, 1937.

Wegelin, Oscar. *Early American Plays, 1714–1830*. New York: Literary Collector Press, 1905.

Wemyss, Francis Courtney. *Twenty-Six Years of the Life of an Actor and Manager*. New York, 1847.

——. *Chronology of the American Stage from 1752–1852*. New York, 1852.

Wilburn, Elizabeth. "American Theatre Buildings in the Eighteenth Century." Master's thesis, Cornell Univ., 1940.

Willard, George. *History of the Providence Stage, 1762–1891*. Providence, 1891.

Willis, Eola. *The Charleston Stage of the XVIII Century*. Columbia, S. C.: The State Co., 1924.

Willis, N. P. *American Scenery*. London, 1840.

Willson, Clair E. *Mimes and Miners*. Tucson: Univ. of Arizona, 1935.

Wilson, Arthur H. *History of the Philadelphia Theatre, 1835–1855*. Philadelphia: Univ. of Pennsylvania Press, 1935.

Wilson, Garff. "American Styles and Theories of Acting from Edwin Forrest to David Belasco." Doctoral dissertation, Cornell Univ., 1940.

Winter, M. A. "American Theatrical Dancing from 1750–1800," *Musical Quarterly*, XXIV (1938), 58–73.

Winter, William. *The Wallet of Time*. 2 vols. New York: Moffat Yard and Co., 1913.

Wittke, Carl. *Tambo and Bones—A History of the American Minstrel Stage*. Durham, N. C.: Duke Univ. Press, 1930.

Woodruff, Jack. "America's Oldest Living Theatre—The Howard Athenaeum," *Theatre Annual*, VIII (1950), 71–81.

Wyatt, Edward Avery. *John Daly Burk*. Charlottesville, Va.: Historical Publishing Company, 1936.

SELECTED PLAY LIST

The place and date of publication are given first in each entry; the place and date of performance, second. In a few instances the facts of publication and performance were incomplete or not available.

The type or principal theme of each play listed is given in parentheses immediately after each play title.

Adler, George J.
Iphigenie in Tauris (Conventional Romantic), New York, 1855
Aiken, George L.
Uncle Tom's Cabin; or, Life Among the Lowly (Negro, Yankee), 1852
Troy Museum, Troy, N. Y., Sept. 27, 1852
Aldrich, Thomas Bailey
Judith of Bethulia (Conventional Romantic), Boston, 1904
Tremont Theatre, Boston, Oct. 13, 1904

Mercedes (Conventional Romantic), Boston, 1894
Palmer's Theatre, New York, May 1, 1893
Aldridge, Ira
The Black Doctor (Negro), London, 1841
Alexander, James B.
King Solomon (Conventional Romantic), Minneapolis, 1899
Anonymous
Alfred the Great (Conventional Romantic), New York, 1822

American Tars in Tripoli (Conventional Romantic, Wars with Barbary States), Philadelphia, 1804–5

Americana; or, A New Tale of the Genii (Revolutionary War), Baltimore, 1802
City Theatre, Charleston, S. C., Feb. 9, 1798

Bad Breath, the Crane of Chowder (Negro Minstrel Burlesque)

Barber of Seville (Negro Minstrel Burlesque)

265

Anonymous

The Battle of Brooklyn (Revolutionary War), New York, 1776

_____

Battle of Buena Vista (Mexican War)
Barnum's Museum, New York, April 17, 1858

_____

Battle of Lake Erie (War of 1812), 1842
Tremont Theatre, Boston, Nov. 2, 1842

_____

Battle of Mexico; or, Halls of Montezuma (Mexican War)
Bowery Theatre, New York, Jan. 17, 1848

_____

The Battle of Stillwater; or, The Maniac (Revolutionary War), 1840
National Theatre, Boston, March 16, 1840

_____

Benjamin Franklin; or, Days of '76 (Revolutionary War)
Chestnut Street Theatre, Philadelphia, Oct. 24, 1849

_____

The Better Sort; or, A Girl of Spirit (Yankee), Boston, 1789

_____

The Black Rangers; or, The Night Hawks (Revolutionary War),
Philadelphia, 1853

_____

Boston Boys in '76 (Revolutionary War), 1835

_____

The Boston Tea Party of 1774 (Revolutionary War)
Olympic Theatre, Philadelphia, Nov. 25, 1843

_____

Captain Barrington (Revolutionary War)

_____

Capture of Major André (Revolutionary War), Baltimore

_____

Catherine Brown, The Converted Cherokee (Indian), New Haven,
1819

_____

Cerro Gordo (Mexican War)
Arch Street Theatre, Philadelphia, June 5, 1847

_____

Charles the Twelfth (Conventional Romantic), New York, 1817

_____

Cinderella; or, The Little Glass Slipper (Conventional Romantic),
New York, 1807
Philadelphia Theatre, Philadelphia

Anonymous

Clameel; or, the Feet of a Go-Getter (Negro Minstrel Burlesque)

_____

Columbia and Britannia (Revolutionary War), 1787

_____

Daniel Boone (Frontier), 1889

_____

The Danites; or, The Heart of Sara (Negro Minstrel Burlesque)

_____

Deserted; or, The Last Days of Brigham Young (Frontier)
Wallack's Theatre, New York, May, 1858

_____

The Domini's Daughter (Revolutionary War)

_____

Down East; or, The Militia Training (Yankee), 1830
Park Theatre, New York, April 7, 1830

_____

The Eagle Eye (Indian), 1849
Bowery Theatre, New York, Mar. 12, 1849

_____

Ethan Allen (Revolutionary War), 1847
Bowery Theatre, New York, 1846–47

_____

The Federal Spy; or, Pauline of the Potomac (Civil War)
Bowery Theatre, New York

_____

The French Revolution (Conventional Romantic), New Bedford,
Mass., 1793
Dartmouth College, Hanover, N. H., 1790

_____

General George Washington; or, The Traitor Foiled (Revolutionary
War), Philadelphia, 1850

_____

The Great Mutton Trail (Negro Minstrel Burlesque)

_____

Green Mountain Boys (Revolutionary War)
Park Theatre, New York, Feb. 22, 1822

_____

Hamlet (Negro Minstrel Burlesque)

_____

Hannah the Mother of Samuel the Prophet and Judge of Israel (Conventional Romantic), Boston, 1839

Anonymous

Harlequin Panatahah; or, The Genii of the Algonquins (Indian),
New York, 1809
   Park Theatre, New York, Jan. 4, 1809

The Hero of Two Wars (War of 1812). Published in *Truth's Advocate and Monthly Anti-Jackson Expositor*, Cincinnati, March–Oct.,
1828

Ill—True—Bad—Doer (Negro Minstrel Burlesque)

The Indian Wife (Indian)
   Park Theatre, New York, June 4, 1830

The Inquisitive Yankee (Yankee)
   Park Theatre, New York, Dec. 4, 1832

Irish Assurance and Yankee Modesty (Yankee), New York
   Chestnut Street Theatre, Philadelphia, Aug. 4, 1853

The Last of the Serpent Tribe (Indian)
   French Street Theatre, New Orleans

A Live Woman in the Mines; or, Pike County Ahead (Frontier), New
York, 1857

Lucrezia Borgia (Negro Minstrel Burlesque)

Macbeth (Negro Minstrel Burlesque)

The Manhattoes (Indian)
   Park Theatre, New York, July 4, 1829

Mary of Scotland; or, the Heir of Avenel (Conventional Romantic),
New York, 1821
   Anthony Street Theatre, New York, May, 1821

Mazeppa, an Equestrian Burlesque (Negro Minstrel Burlesque)

Merry Wives of Windsor (Negro Minstrel Burlesque)

Miantonimoh (Indian)
   Camp Street Theatre, New Orleans, Feb. 5, 1831

Anonymous

Miantonimoh and Narrahmattah (Indian)
Park Theatre, New York, Jan. 15, 1840

Mioutoumah (Indian)

Narramattah (Indian), 1830
Park Theatre, New York, Jan. 15, 1830

The National Guard (Civil War), 1862
Niblo's Garden, New York, June 30, 1862

New York Patriots; or, The Battle of Saratoga (Revolutionary War)
Barnum's Museum, New York, June 2, 1856

Old Fellow; or, the Boor of Vengeance (Negro Minstrel Burlesque)

The Old Guard (Conventional Romantic), New York

Onoleetah (Indian), 1846
Arch Street Theatre, Philadelphia, Feb. 23, 1846

Ontiata; or, The Indian Heroine (Indian)

Oroloosa (Indian)

Oroonoka (Indian)

Osric and Lencastro (Conventional Romantic), New York, 1826

Our Flag Is Nailed to the Mast (Mexican War)
Arch Street Theatre, Philadelphia, April 17, 1847

Our Union Saved; or, Marion's Dream (Civil War)
French Theatre, New York, Jan. 16, 1861

Outallassie (Indian), 1834
Park Theatre, New York, Sept. 29, 1834

The Patriots of '76; or, The Jersey Blues (Revolutionary War), 1851
Arch Street Theatre, Philadelphia, Nov. 27, 1851

The Paxton Boys (Indian), Philadelphia, 1764

Anonymous

Philip; or, the Aborigines (Conventional Romantic), New York, 1822

The Pioneers (Indian), 1833
  Park Theatre, New York, April 21, 1833

Robinson Crusoe and Harlequin Friday (Negro)

Roman Nose and Suet (Negro Minstrel Burlesque)

The Russian Banquet (Conventional Romantic), Boston, 1813

Sarah—Heart—Burn (Negro Minstrel Burlesque)

Sassacus; or, The Indian Wife (Indian)

Saul (Conventional Romantic). Published in the *American Monthly Magazine*, June, 1829

The Scouts of the Prairies (Frontier)

The Secret; or, The Hole in the Wall (Conventional Romantic), New York
  Chestnut Street Theatre, Philadelphia, Jan. 10, 1835

1777; or, The Times that Tried Us Americans (Revolutionary War)
  April 5, 1844

The Seventy Sixer (Revolutionary War)

Sharratah; or, The Last of the Yemasseeshe (Indian), 1842
  Walnut Street Theatre, Philadelphia, Nov. 18, 1842

Shepherdess of the Alps (Conventional Romantic), New York, 1815

Sidney; or, The Self Murderer Reclaimed (Conventional Romantic), New York, 1801

Siege of Mexico (Mexican War)

Smerdis and Merea (Conventional Romantic), Boston, 1826

The Spirit of '76 (Revolutionary War), 1835
  Walnut Street Theatre, Philadelphia, Sept. 23, 1835

Anonymous

The Star of the West (Indian), 1852
   Arch Street Theatre, Philadelphia, Dec. 10, 1852

___

The Swamp Fox (Revolutionary War)
   Arch Street Theatre, Philadelphia, April 2, 1846

___

Sylla (Conventional Romantic), New York, 1827
   Chatham Theatre, New York, Jan. 15, 1827

___

Tan-Go-Ru-A (Indian), Philadelphia, 1856

___

Three Eras of Washington's Life (Revolutionary War), 1849
   Walnut Street Theatre, Philadelphia, Jan. 1, 1849

___

The Times; or, Life in New York (Yankee), 1829
   Park Theatre, New York, Dec. 10, 1829

___

Tippecanoe (Indian), 1840
   Bowery Theatre, New York, May 8, 1840

___

The Traitor; or, The Battle of Yorktown (Revolutionary War)
   Bowery Theatre, New York, 1845–6

___

A Trip to the California Gold Mines (Frontier)
   Arch Street Theatre, Philadelphia, Jan. 10, 1849

___

Tuscatomba (Indian)

___

Tutoona (Indian)

___

Two Pages of Frederick the Great (Conventional Romantic), New York, 1826

___

Two Tragedies: Immola and the Three Milanese (Conventional Romantic), New York, 1835

___

The Tyrant's Victims (Conventional Romantic), Charleston, S. C., 1818

___

Ulysses; or, The Return of U. S. Grant (Civil War)
   Union Square Theatre, New York, Sept. 11, 1871

___

The Unionist's Daughter; or, Life in the Border States (Civil War)
   Bowery Theatre, New York, Jan. 1864

Anonymous
  The Vermonter (Yankee)

  Victory upon Victory; or, Triumphs on Land and Sea (Mexican War)
    The Circus Theatre, Philadelphia, April 24, 1847

  Wacousta (Indian)

  Washington; or, The Retaliation (Revolutionary War)
    Walnut Street Theatre, Philadelphia, Jan. 9, 1832

  Washington, the Savior of His Country (Revolutionary War)
    Arch Street Theatre, Philadelphia, May 22, 1831

  The Wigwam; or, Templeton Manor (Indian)
    Park Theatre, New York, July 3, 1830

  Wilhemina (Conventional Romantic), Boston, 1826

  Wissahickon; or, The Heroes of 1776 (Indian, Revolutionary War)
    National Theatre, New York, Jan. 17, 1857

  Xerxes the Great; or, The Battle of Thermopylae (Conventional Romantic), Philadelphia, 1815

  Yankee in China (Yankee)
    Broadway Theatre, New York, 1853

  Yankee in France (Yankee)
    Broadway Theatre, New York, 1853

  The Yankee in Time (Yankee)
    Bowery Theatre, New York, April 7, 1840

  The Young Carolinians; or Americans in Algiers (Wars with Barbary States), Charleston, S. C., 1818

  Zampa; or, The Marble Bridge (Conventional Romantic), Philadelphia, 1841

  Zula (Conventional Romantic), Philadelphia, 1839
Anthon, Charles Edward
  The Son of the Wilderness (Conventional Romantic), New York, 1848

Austin, Mary
    The Arrow Maker (Indian), 1911
        New Theatre, New York, Feb. 27, 1911

Bacon, Delia Salter
    The Bride of Fort Edward (Revolutionary War), New York, 1839
Bailey, John J.
    Waldimar (Conventional Romantic), New York, 1834
        Park Theatre, New York, Nov. 1, 1831
Ballou, M. M.
    Miraldi; or, the Justice of Tacon (Yankee), Boston, 1859
        Howard Athenaeum, Boston, 1858
Bamburgh, William Cushing
    Giacomo (Conventional Romantic), New York, 1892
Bannister, Nathaniel H.
    Gaulantus (Conventional Romantic), Cincinnati, 1836
        Walnut Street Theatre, Philadelphia, Aug. 31, 1837

———

    The Gentleman of Lyons; or, The Marriage Contract (Conventional
    Romantic), New York, 1838
        Camp Street Theatre, New Orleans, 1837; Walnut Street Theatre,
        Philadelphia, Aug. 16, 1838

———

    Marmion; or, The Battle of Flodden Field (Conventional Romantic),
    New York, 1812
        Park Theatre, New York, April 13, 1812

———

    The Old Waggoner of New Jersey and Virginia (Revolutionary War)
        Arch Street Theatre, Philadelphia, Feb. 4, 1832

———

    Oua Cousta; or, the Lion of the Forest (Indian), 1850
        Arch Street Theatre, Philadelphia, Nov. 8, 1850

———

    Putnam, The Iron Son of '76 (Indian, Yankee, Revolutionary War),
    Boston, 1859
        Bowery Theatre, New York, Aug. 5, 1844

———

    Richmond Hill (Revolutionary War)
        Greenwich Theatre, New York, May 11, 1846

———

    Superstition (Conventional Romantic), Philadelphia, 1826
        Chestnut Street Theatre, Philadelphia, March 12, 1824

Barker, James N.
   The Indian Princess; or, La Belle Sauvage (Indian), Philadelphia, 1808
      Chestnut Street Theatre, Philadelphia, April 6, 1808

___

   Tears and Smiles (Yankee), Philadelphia, 1807
      Chestnut Street Theatre, Philadelphia, March 4, 1807
Barnes, Mrs. Charlotte M. S.
   The Forest Princess; or, Two Centuries Ago (Indian), 1848
      Arch Street Theatre, Philadelphia, Feb. 16, 1848
Barnett, Morris
   Sarah, the Creole (Negro)

___

   Yankee Peddler; or, Old Times in Virginia (Yankee), St. Louis, 1841
      Tremont Theatre, Boston, 1839–40
Barrymore, William
   The Dream of Christopher Columbus (Revolutionary War)
      Walnut Street Theatre, Philadelphia, Feb. 22, 1832

___

   The Snow Storm; or, Lowina of Toboloskow (Conventional Romantic), Baltimore, 1818

___

   The Soldier of the Revolution (Revolutionary War)
      Walnut Street Theatre, Philadelphia, Feb. 4, 1832
Bateman, Mrs. Sidney
   Self (Negro), New York, 1856
      Burton's Theatre, New York, Oct. 27, 1856
Beach, L.
   Jonathan Postfree; or, the Honest Yankee (Yankee), New York, 1807
Behn, Aphra
   The Widow Ranter; Bacon in Virginia (Negro, Indian), 1690
Belasco, David, and Franklyn Fyles
   The Girl I Left Behind Me (Civil War, Indian), 1893
      Empire Theatre, New York, Jan. 25, 1893
Belasco, David
   The Heart of Maryland (Civil War), 1895
      Grand Opera House, Washington, D.C., Oct. 9, 1895

___

   May Blossom (Negro, Civil War), New York, 1883
      Madison Square Theatre, New York, April 12, 1884

___

   Paul Arniff; or, The Love of a Serf (Conventional Romantic)
      Baldwin Theatre, San Francisco, July 19, 1880

Bernard, Boyle
The Kentuckian's Trip to New York in 1815 (Frontier)
Covent Garden, London, April 1, 1833
Bickerstaffe, Isaac
The Padlock (Negro), London, 1769
Bird, Robert Montgomery
The Broker of Bogota (Conventional Romantic), 1834
Bowery Theatre, New York, Feb. 12, 1834

―――

The Gladiator (Conventional Romantic), Philadelphia, 1837
Park Theatre, New York, Sept. 26, 1831

―――

Oralloosa, Son of the Incas (Conventional Romantic, Indian), 1832
Arch Street Theatre, Philadelphia, Oct. 10, 1832

―――

Pelopidas; or, The Fall of the Polemarchs (Conventional Romantic),
1830
Boker, George Henry
Ann Boleyn (Conventional Romantic), Philadelphia, 1850

―――

The Betrothal (Conventional Romantic), Boston, 1857
Walnut Street Theatre, Philadelphia, Sept. 25, 1850

―――

Calaynos (Conventional Romantic), Philadelphia, 1848
Walnut Street Theatre, Philadelphia, Jan. 20, 1851

―――

Francesca da Rimini (Conventional Romantic), 1853
Broadway Theatre, New York, Sept. 26, 1855

―――

Glaucus (Conventional Romantic), MS dated 1886

―――

Konigsmark (Conventional Romantic), Philadelphia, 1869

―――

Leonor de Guzman (Conventional Romantic), Boston, 1856
Walnut Street Theatre, Philadelphia, Oct. 3, 1853

―――

Nydia (Conventional Romantic), MS dated 1885

―――

Widow's Marriage (Conventional Romantic), Boston, 1856
Booth, Junius Brutus
Ugolino (Conventional Romantic), New York
Chestnut Street Theatre, Philadelphia, April 20, 1825

Boucicault, Dion
   Belle Lamar (Civil War, Negro), 1874
      Booth's Theatre, New York, Aug. 10, 1874
   _____

   Jessie Brown; or, The Relief of Lucknow (Indian), 1858
      Wallack's Theatre, New York, Feb. 22, 1858
   _____

   The Octoroon (Negro, Yankee), New York, 1859
      Winter Garden Theatre, New York, Dec. 5, 1859
   _____

   The Pope of Rome (Conventional Romantic), New York, 1858
      Niblo's Garden, New York, Oct. 27, 1858
   Rip Van Winkle (Folk), New York, 1895
      Adelphi Theatre, London, Sept. 4, 1865
Brackenridge, Hugh H.
   The Battle of Bunkers Hill (Revolutionary War), Philadelphia, 1776
   _____

   The Death of General Montgomery (Revolutionary War), Norwich,
   1777
      Brackenridge's Academy, Maryland
Breck, Charles
   The Trust (Yankee), New York, 1808
Breck, Joseph
   West Point; or, A Tale of Treason (Revolutionary War), Baltimore,
   1840
Brougham, John
   Benjamin Franklin (Revolutionary War), 1846
   _____

   The Declaration of Independence (Revolutionary War),
      Mobile Theatre, Mobile, Ala., Feb. 27, 1844
   _____

   The Demon Lover; or, My Cousin German (Conventional Romantic),
   New York, 1856
      Wallack's Theatre, New York, Sept., 21, 1824
   _____

   Dred; or, The Dismal Swamp (Negro), New York, 1856
      Bowery Theatre, New York, Aug. 18, 1855
   _____

   The Duke's Motto (Conventional Romantic), Princeton, 1941
   _____

   The Great Tragic Revival (Conventional Romantic), New York,
   1858
      Burton's Theatre, New York, March 17, 1858

Brougham, John
The Irish Yankee; or, The Birthday of Freedom (Yankee, Revolutionary War), New York, 1856
St. Charles Theatre, New Orleans, 1840

Life in New York (Negro), New York, 1856
Bowery Theatre, New York, ca. 1856

Love and Murder (Conventional Romantic), New York, 1856
Wallack's Theatre, New York, Jan. 27, 1854

Metamora; or, the Last of the Pollywogs (Indian), 1847
Adelphi Theatre, Boston, Dec. 1847

The Miller of New Jersey; or, The Prison Hulk (Revolutionary War), New York, 1858
Bowery Theatre, New York, 1856

Neptune's Defeat; or, The Seizure of the Seas (Conventional Romantic), New York, 1858
Wallack's Theatre, New York, Oct. 5, 1858

Pocahontas; or, the Gentle Savage (Indian), 1856
Wallack's Theatre, New York, Dec. 24, 1855
Brown, David Paul
The Prophet of Saint Paul's (Conventional Romantic), Philadelphia, 1836
Walnut Street Theatre, Philadelphia, March 20, 1837

Sertorius; or, The Roman Patriot (Conventional Romantic), Philadelphia, 1830
Chestnut Street Theatre, Philadelphia, Dec. 14, 1830
Brown, William
West Point Preserved (Revolutionary War)
Haymarket Theatre, Boston, April 17, 1797
Brown, William Wells
The Escape; or, A Leap for Freedom (Conventional Romantic, Negro), Boston, 1858

Miralda; or, The Beautiful Quadroon (Conventional Romantic, Negro), Boston, 1855
Buckstone, John Baldwin
Jack Sheppard (Conventional Romantic), New York, 1854
Bowery Theatre, New York, Nov., 1853

Bunce, Oliver B.

Love in '76 (Revolutionary War), New York, 1857
Laura Keene's Theatre, New York, Feb. 28, 1857

Burgoyne, General

The Blockade of Boston (Revolutionary War), 1776

Burk, John Daly

Bethlem Gabor, Lord of Transylvania; or, The Man Hating Palatine
(Conventional Romantic), Petersburg, Va.; 1807
Richmond, Va., 1803

———

Bunker-Hill; or, The Death of General Warren (Revolutionary War),
New York, 1797
Haymarket Theatre, Boston, Feb. 17, 1797

———

The Death of General Montgomery (Revolutionary War), 1797

———

Death of Joan D'Arc; or, Female Patriotism (Conventional Romantic), New York, 1798
Park Theatre, New York, April, 1798

Burke, Charles

The Revolution (Revolutionary War)
Bowery Theatre, New York, Nov. 15, 1847

———

Rip Van Winkle (Folk), New York
National Theatre, New York, Jan. 7, 1850

Burnett, J. G.

Blanche of Brandy Wine (Negro, Revolutionary War, Yankee), New
York, 1858
Laura Keene's Theatre, New York, April 21, 1858

Byers, S. H. M.

Pocahontas, a Melodrama (Indian)

Calhoun, Colonel Alfred R.

The Color Guard (Civil War), Pittsburgh, 1870
California Theatre, San Francisco, Sept. 22, 1879

Calvert, George Henry

Arnold and André (Revolutionary War), 1864

———

Brangonar (Conventional Romantic), Boston, 1883

———

Count Julian (Conventional Romantic), Baltimore, 1840

———

The Maid of Orleans (Conventional Romantic), New York, 1874

Calvert, George Henry
  Mirabeau (Conventional Romantic), Boston, 1883
Campbell, Bartley
  My Partner (Frontier), Princeton, 1941
    Union Square Theatre, New York, Sept. 16, 1879

_____

  Olio (Conventional Romantic), 1878
    McVicker's Theatre, Chicago, 1878

_____

  Siberia (Conventional Romantic), 1882
    California Theatre, San Francisco, Nov. 26, 1882

_____

  The Vigilantes; or, The Heart of the Sierras (Frontier)
    Arch Street Theatre, Philadelphia, May 21, 1877

_____

  The White Slave (Negro), Princeton, 1941
    Haverley's Theatre, New York, April 3, 1882
Cannon, Charles James
  The Compact (Conventional Romantic), New York, 1851

_____

  Dolores (Conventional Romantic), New York, 1857

_____

  The Oath of Office (Conventional Romantic), New York, 1854
    Bowery Theatre, New York, March 18, 1850

_____

  Rizzio (Conventional Romantic), New York, 1851

_____

  The Sculptor's Daughter (Conventional Romantic), New York, 1857
Carleton, Henry Guy
  Memnon (Conventional Romantic), Chicago, 1881

_____

  Victor Durand (Conventional Romantic), 1884
    Wallack's Theatre, New York, Dec. 18, 1884
Chase, L. B.
  Young Man About Town (Yankee), New York, 1854
Chivers, Thomas H.
  The Sons of Usna (Conventional Romantic), Philadelphia, 1858
Clarke, Mrs. Mary Carr
  The Fair Americans (War of 1812), Philadelphia, 1815
Clarke, N. B.
  Battle of Brandywine; or, The Green-Riders of Santee (Revolutionary War), 1856
    National Theatre, New York, July 2, 1856

Clinch, Charles P.
The Spy; A Tale of the Neutral Ground (Negro, Revolutionary War),
1822, Princeton, 1941
Park Theatre, New York, March 1, 1822
Cobb, James
Paul and Virginia (Negro)
Codman, Henry
The Roman Martyrs (Conventional Romantic), Providence, 1879
Cody, Isaac
A Tragedy Founded on the History of Joseph and His Brethren (Conventional Romantic), Schenectady, New York, 1808
Comfort, Richard
Nero (Conventional Romantic), Philadelphia, 1880
Conrad, Robert T.
Aylmere; or, The Bondman of Kent (Conventional Romantic), Philadelphia, 1852

———

Jack Cade, the Captain of the Commons (Conventional Romantic),
London, 1868
Walnut Street Theatre, Philadelphia, Dec. 9, 1835
Conway, H. J.
Hiram Hireout; or, Followed by Fortune (Yankee), New York, 1852
Chicago Theatre, Chicago, 1851

———

Our Jeminy; or, Connecticut Courtship (Yankee)
Broadway Theatre, New York, July 15, 1853
Crawford, Francis Marion
Dr. Claudius (Conventional Romantic), 1897
Fifth Avenue Theatre, New York, Feb. 1, 1897

———

Francesca da Rimini (Conventional Romantic), London, 1902

———

In the Palace of the King (Conventional Romantic), 1900
Republic Theatre, New York, Dec. 31, 1901
Cromwell, Oliver (of South Carolina)
Kosciusko; or, The Fall of Warsaw (Conventional Romantic), Charleston, S. C., 1828
Custis, George Washington Parke
The Indian Prophecy (Indian), Georgetown, 1827
Chestnut Street Theatre, Philadelphia, July 4, 1827

———

The Pawnee Chief (Indian), 1830

Custis, George Washington Parke
  Pocahontas; or, The Settlers of Virginia (Indian), Philadelphia, 1830
    Walnut Street Theatre, Philadelphia, Jan. 16, 1830

Daly, Augustin
  Horizon (Frontier), 1885
    Olympic Theatre, New York, March 21, 1871

———

  A Legend of Norwood; or, Village Life in New England (Civil War, Negro, Yankee), 1867
    New York Theatre, New York, Nov. 11, 1867

———

  Pique (Frontier), 1884
    New Fifth Avenue Theatre, New York, Dec. 14, 1875

———

  Under the Gaslight (Negro), 1867
    New York Theatre, New York, Aug. 12, 1867
Dana, Elizabeth A.
  Iona (Indian), 1864
Dance, Charles
  Horse Shoe Robinson (Revolutionary War)
    National Theatre, New York, Nov. 23, 1836
Da Ponte (Ponte), Lorenzo L.
  Almachilde; or, the Lombards (Conventional Romantic), New York, 1830
    Park Theatre, New York, Aug. 11, 1829
Davidson, E. M.
  The New Englanders (Revolutionary War), 1882
Dawes, Rufus
  Athenia of Damascus (Conventional Romantic), New York, 1839
Dazey, Charles T.
  For a Brother's Life (Civil War), New York

———

  In Old Kentucky (Frontier), 1894
    St. Paul, Minn., June, 1893
Deering, Nathaniel
  Bozzaris (Conventional Romantic), Portland, Maine, 1851.

———

  Carabasset; or, the Last of the Norridgewicks (Indian), Portland, Maine, 1830
    Portland Theatre, Portland, Feb. 22, 1831
Deffebach, Lewis
  Oolaita; or, the Indian Heroine (Indian), Philadelphia, 1821

Delchamps, J. J.
  Love's Ambuscade; or, The Sergeant's Stratagem (Civil War),
  1863
Dement, R. S.
  Napoleon and Josephine (Conventional Romantic), Chicago, 1876
De Mille, William C.
  The Warrens of Virginia (Civil War), 1907
    Lyric Theatre, Philadelphia, Nov. 18, 1907
Densmore, G. S. and Mark Twain
  The Gilded Age (Frontier)
    California Theatre, San Francisco, April 23, 1874
De Walden, T. B.
  British Neutrality (Civil War)
    Olympic Theatre, New York, July 1, 1869

———

  Kit the Arkansas Traveler (Frontier), 1870
    Boston Theatre, Boston, Feb. 14, 1870
Dibdin, Thomas
  The Banks of the Hudson; or, The Congress Trooper (Negro), London
    Coburg Theatre, London, Dec. 26, 1829
Dockstader, Lew
  Black Faust (Negro Minstrel Burlesque)
Doddridge, Joseph
  *Logan, The Last of the Race of the Shikellemus, Chief of the Cayuga
  Nation* (Indian), 1821
Dodge, Mrs. H. M.
  Hese[i]lrigge; or, The Death of Lady Wallace (Conventional Romantic), Utica, 1827
Duffee, F. H.
  Onylda; or, the Pequot Maid (Indian)
Dunlap, William
  André (Revolutionary War), 1798
    Park Theatre, New York, March 30, 1798

———

  The Father; or, American Shandy-ism (Yankee), New York, 1789
    John Street Theatre, New York, Sept. 7, 1789

———

  Fontainville Abbey (Conventional Romantic), Philadelphia, 1806
    John Street Theatre, New York, Feb. 16, 1795

———

  The Glory of Columbia—Her Yeomanry (Revolutionary War), New
  York, 1817
    Park Theatre, New York, July 4, 1802

Dunlap, William

The Knight's Adventure (Conventional Romantic), New York, 1807
    John Street Theatre, New York, June 7, 1797

Leicester (Conventional Romantic), Philadelphia, 1806
    John Street Theatre, New York, March 11, 1799

The Modest Soldier; or, Love in New York (Yankee), 1787

Peter the Great; or, The Russian Mother (Conventional Romantic),
New York, 1814
    Park Theatre, New York, Nov. 15, 1802

Pizarro in Peru; or, The Death of Rolla (Conventional Romantic),
New York, 1800
    Park Theatre, New York, March 26, 1800

Ribbemont; or, the Feudal Baron (Conventional Romantic), New
York, 1803
    John Street Theatre, New York, Oct. 31, 1796

Rinaldo Rinaldini; or, The Great Banditti (Conventional Romantic), New York, 1810
    Park Theatre, New York, 1810

The Soldier of '76 (Revolutionary War)
    Park Theatre, New York, Feb. 23, 1801

The Temple of Independence (Revolutionary War)
    Park Theatre, New York, Feb. 22, 1799

A Trip to Niagara; or, Travellers in America (Negro, Yankee), New
York, 1830
    Bowery Theatre, New York, Nov. 28, 1828

Yankee Chronology; or, Huzza for the Constitution (Yankee, War of
1812), New York, 1812
    Park Theatre, New York, Sept. 7, 1812
Durivage, O. E.
    The Stage Struck Yankee (Yankee)
        Eagle Theatre, Boston, 1845

Eaton, Nathaniel W.
    Alberto and Matilda; or, the Unfortunate Lovers (Conventional Ro-
    mantic), Boston, 1809

Ellet, Mrs. Elizabeth Fries
  Euphemia of Messina (Conventional Romantic), New York, 1835

  Teresa Contarini (Conventional Romantic), Philadelphia, 1835
    Park Theatre, New York, March 19, 1835
Ellison, James
  The American Captive; or, Siege of Tripoli (Wars with Barbary States), Boston, 1812
Emmons, Richard
  Tecumseh; or, The Battle of the Thames (Indian, Frontier), Philadelphia, 1836
    Walnut Street Theatre, Philadelphia, Oct. 3, 1836
English, Thomas Dunn
  The Mormons; or, Life at Salt Lake City (Indian, Frontier), New York, 1858
    Burton's Theatre, New York, March 16, 1858
Eustafiev, Alexei Grigorevich
  Alexis, The Czarevitch (Conventional Romantic), Boston, 1812
    Boston Theatre, Boston, March, 1814
Everett, David
  Daranzel; or, The Persian Patriot (Conventional Romantic), Boston, 1800
    Haymarket Theatre, Boston, April 16, 1798

  Slaves in Barbary (Wars with Barbary States), Troy, New York, 1897. Published in *The Columbian Orator,* 1810

Faugères, Margaretta Bleecker
  Belisarius (Conventional Romantic), New York, 1795
Featherstonhaugh, George William
  The Death of Ugolino (Conventional Romantic), Philadelphia, 1830
Field, J. M.
  Family Ties; or, The Will of Uncle Josh (Yankee)
    Park Theatre, New York, June 19, 1846

  Job and His Children (Conventional Romantic), Princeton, 1941
Finn, H. J.
  Montgomery; or, The Falls of Montmorency (Yankee, Revolutionary War), Boston, 1825
    Boston Theatre, Boston, Feb. 21, 1825
Fitch, Clyde
  Barbara Frietchie (Negro, Civil War), 1900
    Broad Street Theatre, Philadelphia, Oct. 10, 1899

Nathan Hale (Revolutionary War), 1898
  Hooley's Theatre, Chicago, Jan. 31, 1898
Foster, J.
  Siege of Monterey (War with Mexico)
    Arch Street Theatre, Philadelphia, Oct. 31, 1846
Fry, J. R.
  Leonora (Conventional Romantic), Philadelphia, 1845
    Chestnut Street Theatre, Philadelphia, June 4, 1845
Furman, A. A.
  Philip of Pokanoket (Indian), 1894

Garden, Alexander
  Kosciusko; or, The Fall of Warsaw (Conventional Romantic), Charleston, S. C., 1828
Gayler, Charles
  Bull Run (Civil War)
Gillette, William
  Held by the Enemy (Civil War, Negro), 1898
    Criterion Theatre, Brooklyn, Feb. 22, 1886
  _____

  Secret Service (Civil War), 1895
    Broad Street Theatre, Philadelphia, May 13, 1895
Glover, Captain Stephen E.
  The Cradle of Liberty; or, Boston in 1775 (Yankee, Revolutionary War), New York, 1832
    Tremont Theatre, Boston, 1832
  _____

  The Last of the Mohicans (Indian), 1831
    Camp Street Theatre, New Orleans, March 19, 1831
  _____

  Rake Hellies (Revolutionary War)
    Camp Street Theatre, New Orleans, March 24, 1831
Godfrey, Thomas
  The Prince of Parthia (Conventional Romantic), Philadelphia, 1765
    Southwark Theatre, Philadelphia, April 24, 1767
Godwin, William
  Antonio (Conventional Romantic), New York, 1806
Graves, Mrs. Adelia Cleopatra
  Jepthah's Daughter (Conventional Romantic), Memphis, Tenn., 1867
Grice, C. E.
  The Battle of New Orleans (War of 1812), Baltimore, 1815
    Park Theatre, New York, July 4, 1816
Grismer, J. R., and Clay Greene
  The New South (Negro), 1893

Hackett, J. H.
   Jonathan in England (Yankee), Boston, 1828
      Park Theatre, New York, Dec. 3, 1828
Hamilton, Alexander (grandson of the statesman)
   Cromwell (Conventional Romantic), New York, 1868

─────

   Thomas à Becket (Conventional Romantic), New York, 1863
Harby, Isaac
   Alberti (Conventional Romantic), Charleston, S. C., 1819
      Charleston Theatre, Charleston, S. C., June, 1819

─────

   Alexander Servius (Conventional Romantic), 1807
Hardy, G. W.
   Nick of the Woods; or, the Salt River Rover (Frontier)
      St. Louis Theatre, St. Louis, April 13, 1839
Harrigan, Edward
   The Blue and the Gray (Civil War), 1875
      Theatre Comique, New York, Aug. 7, 1876

─────

   Iascaire (Conventional Romantic)
      Theatre Comique, New York, Nov. 20, 1876

─────

   The Major (Indian)
      New Theatre Comique, New York, Aug. 29, 1881
Harte, Bret
   Two Men from Sandy Bar (Frontier), Boston, 1876
      Union Square Theatre, New York, Aug. 28, 1876
Harte, Bret, and Mark Twain
   Ah Sin (Frontier)
      National Theatre, Washington, D. C., May 7, 1877
Hatton, Anna Julia
   The Songs of Tammany; or, The Indian Chief (Indian), 1794
      John Street Theatre, New York, March 3, 1794
Hawkins, Micah
   The Saw Mill; or, A Yankee Trick (Yankee), New York, 1829
      Chatham Garden Theatre, New York, Nov. 29, 1824
Heath, James E.
   Whigs and Democrats; or, Love of No Politics (Negro, Yankee), Richmond, Va., 1839
      Arch Street Theatre, Philadelphia, Oct. 31, 1844
Hentz, Caroline Lee Whitney
   De Lara; or, The Moorish Bride (Conventional Romantic), Tuscaloosa, Ala., 1843

Hentz, Caroline Lee Whitney
> *Lamorah; or, The Western Wild* (Indian), 1833
> Caldwell Theatre, New Orleans, Jan. 1, 1833

Herne, James A.
> *Margaret Fleming* (Yankee)
> Lynn Theatre, Lynn, Mass., July 4, 1890

> *The Minute Men of 1774–75* (Indian, Revolutionary War), 1886
> Chestnut Street Theatre, Philadelphia, April 6, 1886

> *The Reverend Griffith Davenport* (Civil War), 1899
> Lafayette Square Theatre, Washington, D. C., Jan. 16, 1899

Hielge, George
> *Montezuma; or, The Conquest of Mexico* (Mexican War)
> Arch Street Theatre, Philadelphia, Dec. 24, 1846

> *Putnam* (Revolutionary War), 1844
> Burton's Theatre, Philadelphia, Sept., 1844

Hillhouse, James
> *Demetria* (Conventional Romantic), 1811

> *Hadad* (Conventional Romantic), New York, 1825

> *Percy's Masque* (Conventional Romantic), New York, 1820

Hitchcock, Edward
> *Emancipation of Europe; or, The Downfall of Buonaparte* (Conventional Romantic), Greenfield, Mass., 1815

Hodgkinson, John
> *The Man of Fortitude; or, The Knight's Adventure* (Conventional Romantic), New York, 1806
> John Street Theatre, New York, June 7, 1797

> *Robin Hood; or, Sherwood Forest* (Conventional Romantic), New York, 1808

Holland, Elihu G.
> *The Highland Treason* (Revolutionary War), Boston, 1852

Home, Rev. Dr.
> *Douglas* (Conventional Romantic)

Hooper, Henry
> *Morca, The Blind Page* (Conventional Romantic), Cincinnati, 1855

Hosmer, William
> *The Fall of Tecumseh* (Indian), 1830

Howard, Bronson
> *Shenandoah* (Civil War), 1887. Privately printed
> Boston Museum, Boston, Nov. 19, 1888

Howe, J. Burdett
    The Golden Eagle; or, The Privateer of '76 (Revolutionary War),
    New York, 1857
        Brougham's Bowery Theatre, New York, April 6, 1857
Howe, Julia Ward
    Hippolytus (Conventional Romantic), New York, 1858
        Tremont Theatre, Boston, March 24, 1911

    Leonore (Conventional Romantic), Boston, 1857
        Wallack's Theatre, New York, March 16, 1857
Hubbell, Horatio
    Arnold; or, The Treason of West Point (Revolutionary War), Phila-
    delphia, 1847
Humphreys, David
    The Widow of Malabar; or, The Tyranny of Custom (Conventional
    Romantic), Philadelphia, 1790
        Southwark Theatre, Philadelphia, May 7, 1790

    The Yankey in England (Yankee), 1815
        Humphreysville, Conn., by amateurs, Jan., 1814
Hunter, Robert
    Androboros (Conventional Romantic), Moronopolis (fictitious im-
    print), 1714
        First American play printed. Only copy in this country in Henry
    E. Huntington Library, San Marino, Calif. Photostatic copy in Cornell
    University Library.
Huntington, Gurdon
    The Guests of Brazil; or, The Martyrdom of Frederick (Conventional
    Romantic), New York, 1844
Hutton, Joseph
    Fashionable Follies (Yankee), Philadelphia, 1815

    The Orphan of Prague (Conventional Romantic), Philadelphia, 1808

    The School for Prodigals (Conventional Romantic), Philadelphia,
    1809
        Chestnut Street Theatre, Philadelphia, 1808

    The Wounded Hussar; or, The Rightful Heir (Conventional Ro-
    mantic), New York, 1809
        New Theatre, Philadelphia, 1809

Ingersoll, Charles Jared
  Edwy and Elgiva (Conventional Romantic), Philadelphia, 1801
    Chestnut Street Theatre, Philadelphia, April 2, 1801
Ioor, W.
  *The Battle of Eutaw Springs and Evacuation of Charleston; or the
  Glorious 14th of December, 1782* (Revolutionary War), Charleston,
  1807
    Southwark Theatre, Philadelphia, June 9, 1813

Jefferson, Joseph
  Rip Van Winkle (Folk), New York, 1895
    Olympic Theatre, New York, Sept. 3, 1866
Johnson, S. D.
  The Shaker Lovers (Yankee), 1849
    National Theatre, Boston, 1849
Jones, George
  Tecumseh and the Prophet of the West (Indian), 1844
Jones, Joseph Stevens
  Captain Kyd; or, The Wizard of the Sea (Conventional Romantic,
  Yankee), New York, 1839
    National Theatre, Boston, 1830

———

  Carpenter of Rouen; or, The Massacre of St. Bartholomew (Conventional Romantic), New York
    Chatham Theatre, New York, Nov. 16, 1840

———

  The Green Mountain Boys (Yankee, Revolutionary War), New York,
  1860
    Chestnut Street Theatre, Philadelphia, Feb. 25, 1833

———

  The Liberty Tree; or, Boston Boys in '76 (Indian, Yankee, Revolutionary War)
    Warren Theatre, Boston, June 17, 1832

———

  The People's Lawyer (Yankee), Boston, 1856
    National Theatre, Boston, 1839

———

  Richelieu (Conventional Romantic), New York, 1826

———

  The Siege of Boston; or, The Spirit of 1776 (Revolutionary War)
    Tremont Theatre, Boston, Feb. 22, 1841

Jones, Joseph Stevens
    The Silver Spoon (Yankee), Boston, 1911
        Boston Museum, Boston, Feb. 16, 1852

    The Usurper; or, Americans in Tripoli (Wars with Barbary States).
    MS, Boston, 1842
        Park Theatre, New York, Nov. 27, 1835
Judah, Samuel B. H.
    A Tale of Lexington (Revolutionary War), New York, 1823
        Park Theatre, New York, July 4, 1822

Kelly, Thomas J. F.
    Henry IV of Germany (Conventional Romantic), New York, 1855
Kennicott, James H.
    Irma; or, The Prediction (Conventional Romantic), New York, 1830
        American Theatre, New Orleans
Kerr, John
    Rip Van Winkle; or, The Demons of the Catskill Mountains (Folk),
    1830–35
        Walnut Street Theatre, Philadelphia, Oct. 30, 1829

    Rip Van Winkle, A Legend of Sleepy Hollow (Folk), revised by T. H.
    Lacy, London

    The Wandering Boys; or, The Castle of Olival (Conventional Ro-
    mantic), Boston, 1821
        Charleston, S. C., 1812; as *Paul and Alexis* at the Park Theatre,
        New York, March 16, 1820
Keteltas, Caroline M.
    The Last of the Plantagenets (Conventional Romantic), New York,
    1844
Kinney, Mrs. Elizabeth Clementine
    Bianca Capello (Conventional Romantic), New York, 1873

Lacy, Ernest
    The Bard of Mary Redcliffe (Conventional Romantic), Philadelphia,
    1916

    Chatterton (Conventional Romantic), Philadelphia, 1900
        Hollis Street Theatre, Boston, 1893

    Rinaldo, The Doctor of Florence (Conventional Romantic), Phila-
    delphia, 1900
        Castle Square Theatre, Boston, Feb. 25, 1895

Lathrop, George Parsons
    Elaine (Conventional Romantic)
Lawson, James
    Giordano (Conventional Romantic), New York, 1832
        Park Theatre, New York, Nov. 13, 1828

    Liddesdale; or, the Border Chief (Indian), 1861
Lazarus, Emma
    The Dance of Death (Conventional Romantic), New York, 1882
Leacock, John
    The Fall of British Tyranny; or, American Liberty Triumphant
    (Negro, Revolutionary War), Philadelphia, 1776
Leavitt, A. J., and H. W. Eagan
    The Academy of Stars (Negro Minstrel Burlesque), New York
Leland, Aaron Whitney
    The Fatal Error (Conventional Romantic), Pittsfield, Mass., 1807
        Williams College, Williamstown, Mass., March 25, 1807
Leman, Walter
    The Battle of Germantown (Revolutionary War), 1846
        Walnut Street Theatre, Philadelphia, Jan. 9, 1846
Lester, C. E.
    Kate Woodhull (Revolutionary War), 1849
        Broadway Theatre, New York, Feb. 21, 1849
Levick, Milnes
    The Union Prisoner (Civil War), 1867
Lewis, Mrs. Estelle Anna Blanche
    Helemah; or, The Fall of Montezuma (Mexican War), New York,
    1864

    The King's Stratagem; or, The Port of Polan (Conventional Romantic), 1813

    Sappho (Conventional Romantic), London, 1868
Lillibridge, Gardner R.
    Tancred; or, The Rightful Heir to Rochdale Castle (Conventional
    Romantic), Providence, Rhode Island, 1824
Lindsley, A. B.
    Love and Friendship; or, Yankee Notions (Negro, Yankee), New York,
    1809
        Park Theatre, New York, 1807
Linn, John Blair
    Bourville Castle; or, The Gallic Orphan (Conventional Romantic),
    John Street Theatre, New York, Jan. 16, 1797

Little, Sophia
  The Branded Hand (Negro), Pawtucket, R. I., 1845
Lockwood, Ingersoll
  Washington (Revolutionary War), 1875
Logan, Cornelius A.
  The Vermont Wool Dealer (Yankee), 1840
      Bowery Theatre, New York, April 11, 1840

  Yankee Land (Yankee), 1834
      Bowery Theatre, New York, Nov. 19, 1842
Longfellow, Henry W.
  Giles Corey of the Salem Farms (Indian), Boston, 1868

  The Golden Legend (Conventional Romantic), Boston, 1851

  The Mask of Pandora (Conventional Romantic), Boston, 1875

  Montgomery (Indian), 1825

  The Spanish Student (Conventional Romantic), Cambridge, 1843
Lord, William Wilberforce
  André (Revolutionary War), New York, 1856
Low, Samuel
  The Politician Outwitted (Yankee), New York, 1788

McCabe, James D., Jr.
  The Guerillas (Negro, Civil War), Richmond, Va., 1863
      Richmond Varieties, Richmond, Va., Dec. 22, 1862
McCloskey, J. J.
  Across the Continent (Negro, Frontier), Princeton, 1941
      Park Theatre, New York, Nov. 8, 1870
McCord, Mrs. Louisa Susannah
  Caius Gracchus (Conventional Romantic), New York, 1851
McHenry, James
  The Maid of Wyoming (Indian), 1830

  The Usurper (Conventional Romantic), Philadelphia, 1829
      Chestnut Street Theatre, Philadelphia, Dec. 26, 1827
Mackaye, Steele
  Dakolar (Conventional Romantic)
      Lyceum Theatre, New York, April 6, 1885

  Rienzi (Conventional Romantic), 1886
      Albaugh's Opera House, Washington, D.C., Dec. 13, 1886

McLellan, R. C.
  The Foundling; or, Yankee Fidelity (Yankee), Philadelphia, 1839
    Chestnut Street Theatre, Philadelphia, 1839
Macomb, Alexander
  Pontiac; or, The Siege of Detroit (Indian), Boston, 1835
    National Theatre, Washington, D.C., 1838
Magnu[e]s, Maurice
  Eldyle (Conventional Romantic), New York, 1898
Mansfield, Richard
  Don Juan (Conventional Romantic), Boston, 1891
    Garden Theatre, New York, May 18, 1891

  Monsieur (Conventional Romantic), 1887
    Madison Square Theatre, New York, July 11, 1887
Mapes, Victor
  Captain Barrington (Conventional Romantic)
Markoe, Peter
  The Patriot Chief (Conventional Romantic), Philadelphia, 1784
Marriott, Mrs.
  Death of Major André; or, The Land We Live In (Revolutionary War)
Mattison, H. B.
  The Witch; or, A Legend of the Catskills (Revolutionary War)
    Chatham Street Theatre, New York, May 24, 1847
Maturin, Rev. Charles
  Bertram (Conventional Romantic), 1816
Medina, Louisa H.
  The Last Days of Pompeii (Conventional Romantic), New York
    Bowery Theatre, New York, Feb. 9, 1835

  Nick of the Woods (Frontier), New York
    Bowery Theatre, New York, Feb. 5, 1838

  Kairrissah (Indian), 1834
    Bowery Theatre, New York, Sept. 11, 1834

  Wacousta (Indian), 1833
    Bowery Theatre, New York, Dec. 30, 1833
Merry, Robert
  The Abbey of St. Augustine (Conventional Romantic), Philadelphia, 1797
    New Theatre, Philadelphia, March 20, 1797

Miles, George Henry
DeSoto; or, The Hero of the Mississippi (Conventional Romantic), 1853
    Chestnut Street Theatre, Philadelphia, April 19, 1852

———

Mohammed, The Arabian Prophet (Conventional Romantic), Boston, 1850
    Lyceum Theatre, New York, Oct. 27, 1851

———

Senor Valiente (Conventional Romantic), Baltimore, 1859
    Holliday Street Theatre, Baltimore, 1859
Miller, Chester Gore
Chihuahua (Conventional Romantic), Chicago, 1891
Miller, Joaquin
The Danites in the Sierras (Frontier), San Francisco, 1882
    Broadway Theatre, New York, Aug. 22, 1877

———

Forty-Nine (Negro, Frontier), San Francisco, 1882
    Haverley's Theatre, New York, Oct. 1, 1881

———

An Oregon Idyll (Indian, Frontier), San Francisco, 1910

———

Tally Ho! (Frontier), San Francisco, 1910
Milman, Rev. H. H.
Fazio; or, The Italian Wife (Conventional Romantic)
    Chatham Garden Theatre, New York, Feb. 1, 1825
Minshull, John
Rural Felicity (Yankee), New York, 1801
Moore, Horatio Newton
Orlando; or, A Woman's Virtue (Conventional Romantic), Philadelphia, 1835

———

The Regicide (Conventional Romantic)
Moore, J. Owen and Kilpatrick, Gen. Judson
Allatoona (Civil War)
Moos, H. M.
Mortara; or, The Pope and His Inquisitors (Conventional Romantic), Cincinnati, 1860
Morris, George P.
Briar Cliff; or, A Tale of the Revolution (Revolutionary War), 1825
    Chatham Garden Theatre, New York, June 15, 1826

———

The Maid of Saxony (Conventional Romantic), New York, 1842

Mowatt, Anna Cora Ogden (Ritchie)
Armand; or, The Peer and the Peasant (Conventional Romantic),
New York, 1849
    Park Theatre, New York, Sept. 27, 1847

Fashion (Negro, Yankee), New York, 1845
    Park Theatre, New York, March 24, 1845

    Gulzara, The Persian Slave (Conventional Romantic), 1840
      Flatbush, Long Island
Munford, Robert
The Candidates; or, The Humours of a Virginia Election (Negro),
Petersburg, Va., 1798

    The Patriots (Revolutionary War), Philadelphia, 1776
Munford, William
Almoran and Hamet (Conventional Romantic), Richmond, Va., 1798
Murdoch, Frank H.
Davy Crockett (Folk, Frontier), Princeton, 1941
    Rochester, New York, Sept. 23, 1872
Murdock, J.
The Politicians; or, A State of Things (Negro), Philadelphia, 1798

    The Triumph of Love; or, Happy Reconciliation (Negro), Phila-
delphia, 1795
      Chestnut Street Theatre, Philadelphia, May 22, 1795
Murray, Judith
The Traveller Returned (Yankee), 1796
    Federal Street Theatre, Boston, March 9, 1796

Nack, James
The Immortal (Conventional Romantic), New York, 1850
Neal, John
Otho (Conventional Romantic), Boston, 1819
Noah, Mordecai Manuel
The Fortress of Sorrento (Conventional Romantic), New York, 1808

    The Grecian Captive; or, The Fall of Athens (Conventional Ro-
mantic), New York, 1822
      Park Theatre, New York, June 17, 1822

    Marion; or, The Hero of Lake George (Revolutionary War), New
York, 1822
      Park Theatre, New York, Nov. 25, 1821

Noah, Mordecai Manuel
   Natalie; or, The Frontier Maid (Revolutionary War), 1840
      Tremont Theatre, Boston, May 1, 1840

   She Would Be a Soldier; or, The Plains of Chippewa (War of 1812),
   New York, 1819
      Park Theatre, New York, June 21, 1819

   Siege of Tripoli (Wars with Barbary States)
      Park Theatre, New York, May 15, 1820

   The Siege of Yorktown (Revolutionary War)
Nunes, J. A.
   Fast Folks; or, Early Days of California (Frontier), New York, 1858
      American Theatre, San Francisco, July 1, 1858

O'Conway, Matthias James
   The Knights Templars (Conventional Romantic), Philadelphia, 1809
O'Neill, James
   Monte Cristo (Conventional Romantic), Princeton, 1941
      Booth's Theatre, New York, Feb. 12, 1883
      The play was sold to O'Neill by Charles Fechter in 1885 for
   $2,000, but O'Neill changed it so radically that he considered the play
   his own.
Osborn, Laughton
   Bianca Capello (Conventional Romantic), New York, 1868

   Calvary (Conventional Romantic), New York, 1867

   The Cid of Seville (Conventional Romantic), New York, 1869

   The Double Deceit (Conventional Romantic), New York, 1867

   The Heart's Sacrifice (Conventional Romantic), New York, 1870

   The Last Mandeville (Conventional Romantic), New York, 1870

   The Magnetiser (Conventional Romantic), New York, 1869

   Mariamne (Conventional Romantic), New York, 1873

   Matilda of Denmark (Conventional Romantic), New York, 1870

Osborn, Laughton
  Meleagros (Conventional Romantic), New York, 1871
  _____

  The Monk (Conventional Romantic), New York, 1870
  _____

  The Montanini (Conventional Romantic), New York, 1868
  _____

  The New Calvary (Conventional Romantic), New York, 1871
  _____

  The Prodigal (Conventional Romantic), New York, 1869
  _____

  The School for Critics (Conventional Romantic), New York, 1868
  _____

  Uberto (Conventional Romantic), New York, 1869
  _____

  Ugo Da Este (Conventional Romantic), New York, 1869
  _____

  Virginia (Conventional Romantic), New York, 1867
Owen, Robert Dale
  Pocahontas (Indian), New York, 1837
    Park Theatre, New York, Feb. 8, 1828

Palmer, John Williamson
  The Queen's Heart (Conventional Romantic), Boston, 1858
Pardy, Henry Oake
  Nature's Noblemen (Yankee), New York, 1854
    Burton's Theatre, New York, Oct. 7, 1851
Paulding, James Kirke
  Bucktails in England (Yankee), 1815
  _____

  The Lion of the West (Frontier)
    Park Theatre, New York, April 25, 1831
Payne, John Howard
  Brutus; or, The Fall of Tarquin (Conventional Romantic), London,
  1818
    Park Theatre, New York, March 15, 1819
  _____

  Charles II; or, The Merry Monarch (Conventional Romantic), New
  York, 1829
    Park Theatre, New York, Oct. 25, 1824
  _____

  Fall of Algiers (Wars with Barbary States), London, 1825
    Drury Lane, London, Jan. 19, 1825; Philadelphia, 1827

Payne, John Howard
  The Last Duel in Spain (Conventional Romantic), Princeton, 1941

———

  Mahomet (Conventional Romantic), New York, 1809
    Chestnut Street Theatre, Philadelphia, Dec. 11, 1811

———

  Mazeppa (Conventional Romantic), 1825, Princeton, 1941
    Bowery Theatre, New York, June 22, 1833

———

  Mount Savage (Conventional Romantic), Princeton, 1941
    May 27, 1822

———

  Richelieu (Conventional Romantic), New York, 1826
    Chestnut Street Theatre, Philadelphia, 1829

———

  Romulus The Shepherd King (Conventional Romantic), Princeton, 1941

———

  The Spanish Husband; or, First and Last Love (Conventional Romantic), Princeton, 1941
    Park Theatre, New York, Nov. 1, 1830
Percival, James Gates
  Zamor (Conventional Romantic), New Haven, Conn., 1821
    Yale Commencement, New Haven, Conn., 1815
Phillips, Jones B.
  Camillus; or, The Self-Exiled Patriot (Conventional Romantic), New York, 1833
    Arch Street Theatre, Philadelphia, Feb. 8, 1833

———

  Oronaska; or, the Chief of the Mohawks (Indian), 1834
    Bowery Theatre, New York, Jan. 1, 1834

———

  Zamira (Conventional Romantic), New York, 1835
Pilgrim, James
  Harry Burnham; or, The Young Continental (Revolutionary War), 1851
    National Theatre, New York, March 10, 1851

———

  Robert Emmet, The Martyr of Irish Liberty (Conventional Romantic), New York, 1857

———

  The Silver Knife; or, the Hunters of the Rocky Mountains (Indian), 1856
    National Theatre, New York, March 2, 1856

Ponte. *See* Da Ponte
Poole, John F.
Grant's Campaign; or, Incidents of the Rebellion (Civil War), 1865
New Bowery Theatre, New York, Dec. 1865

Ye Comedie of Errours; A Glorious Uproarious Burlesque (Negro Minstrel Burlesque), New York, 1856
Potter, Reuben M.
Phelles, King of Tyre; or, The Downfall of Tyranny (Conventional Romantic), New York, 1825
Park Theatre, New York, June 13, 1825
Power, Tyrone
Born to Good Luck; or, The Irishman's Fortune (Conventional Romantic), New York, 183–
Preston, William
Death of Louis XVI (Conventional Romantic), New York, 1794
Preuss, Henry Clay
Fashions and Follies of Washington Life (Negro), Washington, D.C., 1857
Price, T. B.
Kissing a Soldier (Civil War), 1863

Quincy, Josiah Phillips
Charicles (Conventional Romantic), Boston, 1855

Lyteria (Conventional Romantic), Boston, 1854

Reed, George H.
The Grecian Cross, and Rose of Falmouth (Civil War), 1872
Rees, James
Anthony Wayne (Revolutionary War), 1845
National Theatre, Philadelphia, Jan. 13, 1845

Washington; or, The Hero of Valley Forge (Revolutionary War)
Camp Street Theatre, New Orleans, 1832
Renauld, John B.
Our Heroes (Civil War), 1873
Ricord, Mrs. Elizabeth (Stryker)
Zampa; or, The Insurrection (Conventional Romantic), Cambridge, 1842
Robertson, John
Riego; or, The Spanish Martyr (Conventional Romantic), Richmond, Va., 1850

Robinson, J.
   The Yankee's Stratagem (Yankee), 1792

   The Yorker's Stratagem; or, Banana's Wedding (Negro), New York,
   1792
         John Street Theatre, New York, May 10, 1792
Rogers, Major Robert
   Ponteach; or, the Savages of America (Indian), 1766
Rowson, Mrs. S. H.
   American Tars (Wars with Barbary States), 1798
         Chestnut Street Theatre, Philadelphia, June 17, 1796

   Slaves in Algiers; or, A Struggle for Freedom (Wars with Barbary
   States), Philadelphia, 1794
         Chestnut Street Theatre, Philadelphia, Dec. 22, 1794

Sandburg, C. H.
   Telula; or, the Star of Hope (Indian), 1845
         Boston Museum, Boston, Feb. 7, 1845
Sargent, Epes
   The Bride of Genoa (Conventional Romantic), Boston, 1836
         Produced under the title *The Genoese,* Tremont Theatre, Bos-
         ton, Feb. 13, 1837

   The Priestess (Conventional Romantic), Boston, 1854

   Velasco (Conventional Romantic), Boston, 1837
         Tremont Theatre, Boston, Nov. 20, 1835
Savage, John
   Sibyl (Conventional Romantic), New York, 1865
         St. Louis Theatre, St. Louis, Sept. 6, 1858
Schonberg, James
   Oscar the Halfblood (Negro), New York, 1867
Seawell, J.
   Valentia (Conventional Romantic), Mobile, Ala., 1859
Sheil, Richard
   The Apostate (Conventional Romantic), New York
         Park Theatre, New York, Sept. 22, 1817

   Evadne; or, The Statue (Conventional Romantic)
         Park Theatre, New York, May 24, 1819
Sherbourne, John H.
   Osceola (Indian), 1843
         National Theatre, Philadelphia, Oct. 15, 1841

Shields, C. Woodruff
   The Reformer of Geneva (Conventional Romantic), New York, 1898
Simmons, James Wright
   Manfredi (Conventional Romantic), Philadelphia, 1821

   Valdemar; or, The Castle of the Cliff (Conventional Romantic),
   Philadelphia, 1822
Simms, William Gilmore
   Michael Bonham; or, The Fall of Bexar (Frontier), 1852
      Charleston Theatre, Charleston, S. C., March 26, 1855
Smith, John N.
   Romanzo, The Conscience Stricken Brigand (Conventional Roman-
   tic), New York, 1840
Smith, John W.
   The Quack Doctor (Negro Minstrel Burlesque), New York
      St. Louis Amphitheatre, St. Louis, March, 1851
Smith, Jonathan S.
   Siege of Algiers; or, The Downfall of Hadgi-Ali-Bashaw (Wars with
   Barbary States), Philadelphia, 1823
Smith, Richard Penn
   The Actress of Padua (Conventional Romantic), 1836
      Walnut Street Theatre, Philadelphia, June 13, 1836

   Caius Marius (Conventional Romantic), 183–
      Arch Street Theatre, Philadelphia, Jan. 12, 1831

   The Deformed; or, Woman's Trial (Conventional Romantic), Philadelphia, 1830
      Chestnut Street Theatre, Philadelphia, Feb. 4, 1830

   The Eighth of January (War of 1812), Philadelphia, 1829
      Chestnut Street Theatre, Philadelphia, Jan. 8, 1829

   Siege of Algiers (Wars with Barbary States), 1823

   The Triumph at Plattsburg (War of 1812)
      Chestnut Street Theatre, Philadelphia, Jan. 8, 1830

   William Penn; or, The Elm Tree (Indian), 1829
      Walnut Street Theatre, Philadelphia, Dec. 21, 1829
Steele, Silas S.
   Battle of Tippecanoe (Indian), 1840

Steele, Silas S.
   The Brazen Drum; or, The Yankee in Poland (Yankee), New York,
   1841
         Arch Street Theatre, Philadelphia, Jan. 27, 1841
Stevens, George Lionel
   The Patriot; or, Union and Freedom (Yankee, Revolutionary War),
   Boston, 1834
Stone, John Augustus
   The Knight of the Golden Fleece (Yankee)
         Park Theatre, New York, Sept. 10, 1834

   _____

   Metamora (Indian), 1829, Princeton, 1941
         Park Theatre, New York, Dec. 15, 1829

   _____

   Tancred, King of Sicily (Conventional Romantic), Princeton, 1941
         Park Theatre, New York, March 16, 1831

   _____

   Tancred; or, the Siege of Antioch (Conventional Romantic), Phila-
   delphia, 1827
Story, William Wetmore
   Nero (Conventional Romantic), 1875

   _____

   Stephania (Conventional Romantic), 1875
Strong, Henry King
   The Fall of Iturbide; or, Mexico Delivered (Conventional Roman-
   tic), 1823
         Pittsfield, Mass.
Swayze, Mrs. J. C.
   Ossawattomie Brown; or, The Insurrection at Harper's Ferry (Civil
   War), 1859
         Bowery Theatre, New York, Dec. 16, 1859

Talbot, Charles S.
   Captain Morgan; or, The Conspiracy Unveiled (Revolutionary War),
   Rochester, 1827
Talfourd, Thomas Noon
   Ion (Conventional Romantic)
         Park Theatre, New York, Feb. 2, 1837
Tayleure, Clifton W.
   Horseshoe Robinson; or, The Battle of King's Mountain (Revolu-
   tionary War), New York
         Holliday Street Theatre, Baltimore, April, 1856
Taylor, James Bayard
   The Masque of the Gods (Conventional Romantic), Boston, 1870-71

Taylor, James Bayard
Prince Deukalton (Conventional Romantic), Boston, 1878

The Prophet (Conventional Romantic), Boston, 1874

Taylor, Tom
The Fool's Revenge (Conventional Romantic), New York, 1878

The King's Rival; or, The Court and the Stage (Conventional Romantic), New York, 18–

Our American Cousin (Yankee)
Laura Keene's Theatre, New York, Oct. 18, 1858

Two Lovers and a Life (Conventional Romantic), Boston, 185–

Thaxter, A. Wallace
The Grotto Nymph (Conventional Romantic), Boston
Howard Athenaeum, Boston, 1858

Thomas, Augustus
Alabama (Frontier), 1898
Madison Square Theatre, New York, April 1, 1891

Arizona (Frontier), 1895
Hamlin's Grand Opera House, Chicago, June 12, 1899

Surrender (Civil War), 1892
Columbia Theatre, Boston, Nov. 21, 1892

Thomas, Lewis F.
Cortez, the Conqueror (Conventional Romantic), Washington, 1857

Thompson, Mrs. Amira
The Lyre of Tioga (Conventional Romantic), Geneva, New York, 1829

Thompson, Denman
The Old Homestead (Yankee)
Boston Museum, Boston, April 5, 1886

Tobin, John
The Honeymoon (Conventional Romantic)
Park Theatre, New York, 1846

Torrence, Frederic Ridgely
Abelard and Heloise (Conventional Romantic)

El Dorado (Conventional Romantic), 1903

Troubetzkoy, Mrs. Amelie
Athelwold (Conventional Romantic), New York, 1893

Troubetzkoy, Mrs. Amelie
  Herod and Mariamne (Conventional Romantic), New York, 1888
Trowbridge, J. T.
  Neighbor Jackwood (Negro, Yankee), Boston, 1857
    Boston Museum, Boston, March 16, 1857
Trumbull, David
  The Death of Nathan Hale (Revolutionary War), 1842
    Yale College, New Haven, Conn., 1842
Twain, Mark, and G. S. Densmore
  The Gilded Age (Frontier)
    California Theatre, San Francisco, April 23, 1874
Twain, Mark and Bret Harte
  Ah Sin (Frontier)
    National Theatre, Washington, D.C., May 7, 1877
Tyler, Royall
  The Contrast (Yankee), Philadelphia, 1790
    John Street Theatre, New York, April 16, 1787

———
  Joseph and His Brethren (Conventional Romantic), Princeton, 1941

———
  The Judgment of Solomon (Conventional Romantic), Princeton, 1941

———
  The Origin of the Feast of Purim; or, The Destinies of Haman and Mordecai (Conventional Romantic), Princeton, 1941

Villeneuve, Le Blanc de
  Le Père Indien (Indian), 1753

Wainwright, J. H.
  Rip Van Winkle (Folk), New York, 1855
    Niblo's Garden, New York, Sept. 27, 1855
Walcot, Charles
  Hiawatha; or, Ardent Spirits and Laughing Water (Indian), New York, 1856
    Wallack's Theatre, New York, Dec. 25, 1856
Walker, Alfred
  Giorgione (Conventional Romantic), Cambridge, 1869
Walker, C. E.
  Wallace (Conventional Romantic), Philadelphia, 1822
    Walnut Street Theatre, Philadelphia, Nov. 16, 1821
Walker, G. H.
  The Old Flag; or, The Spy of Newbern (Civil War), 1870

Wallack, Lester
  The Veteran; or, France and Algeria (Conventional Romantic), New
  York, 1859
      Wallack's Theatre, New York, Jan. 17, 1859
Wallack, W. H.
  Paul Jones; or, The Pilot of the German Ocean (Revolutionary War),
  New York, 1828
      Chatham Theatre, New York, March 21, 1827
Warden, E.
  Robert Make-Airs; or, The Two Fugitives (Negro Minstrel Bur-
  lesque), New York
      Minstrel Hall, New York
Warren, Mrs. Mercy Otis
  The Blockheads; or, The Affrighted Officers (Revolutionary War),
  Boston, 1776

────

  The Ladies of Castile (Conventional Romantic), Boston, 1790

────

  The Sack of Rome (Conventional Romantic), Boston, 1790
Welcker, Adair
  A Dream of Realms Beyond Us (Conventional Romantic), Sacra-
  mento, 1885

────

  Flavia (Conventional Romantic), Sacramento, 1885

────

  Romer, King of Norway (Conventional Romantic), Sacramento, 1885
Weston, J. M.
  Lucretia Borgia (Conventional Romantic), Boston, 1856
      St. Charles Theatre, New Orleans, 1844
Wheeler, Mrs. W.
  A Cup of Tea (Revolutionary War), 1875
White, Charles
  Coal Heaver's Revenge (Negro Minstrel Burlesque), New York, 1874
      Howard Athenaeum, Boston, Dec. 21, 1868

────

  Mazeppa (Negro Minstrel Burlesque), New York, 185–

────

  The Mystic Speel (Negro Minstrel Burlesque), New York
      Bowery Opera House, New York, Oct., 1855

────

  Oh! Hush! or, The Virginny Cupids (Negro Minstrel Burlesque),
  New York

White, Charles
   Old Dad's Cabin (Negro Minstrel Burlesque), New York, 185–

———

   A Slippery Day (Negro Minstrel Burlesque), New York, 1875
      Alhambra Theatre, San Francisco, Feb. 14, 1872

———

   Vilkens and Dinah (Negro Minstrel Burlesque), New York
White, Rev. James
   The King of the Commons (Conventional Romantic), New York, 184–
White, John Blake
   Foscari; or, The Venetian Exile (Conventional Romantic), Charleston, S. C., 1806
      Charleston, S. C., Jan. 8, 1806

———

   The Mysteries of the Castle; or, The Victim of Revenge (Conventional Romantic), Charleston, S. C., 1807
      Charleston Theatre, Charleston, S. C., Dec. 26, 1806

———

   Triumph of Liberty; or, Louisiana Preserved (War of 1812), Charleston, S. C., 1819
Wiley, Sarah King
   Cromwell (Conventional Romantic), New York, 1900
Willard, Edward
   Julius Caesar (Conventional Romantic), Philadelphia, 1890
Williamson, A. J.
   Preservation; or, The Hovel of the Rocks (Conventional Romantic), Charleston, S. C., 1800
      Federal Street Theatre, Boston, Feb. 27, 1797
Willis, Nathaniel Parker
   Bianca Visconti; or, The Heart Overtasked (Conventional Romantic), New York, 1839
      Park Theatre, New York, Aug. 25, 1837

———

   Tortesa the Usurer (Conventional Romantic), 1839
      National Theatre, New York, April 8, 1839
Wilmer, Lambert A.
   Gloriana; or, The Enchantress of Elba (Conventional Romantic), Philadelphia, 1828

———

   Merlin (Conventional Romantic), Philadelphia, 1823
Woodworth, Samuel
   The Deed of Gift (Yankee), New York, 1822
      Boston Theatre, Boston, March 25, 1822

Woodworth, Samuel
   The Forest Rose; or, American Farmers (Yankee), New York, 1825
      Chatham Garden Theatre, New York, Oct. 6, 1825

   King's Bridge Cottage (Revolutionary War), New York, 1826
      Richmond Hill Theatre, New York, Feb. 22, 1833

   Lafayette; or, The Castle of Olmutz (Conventional Romantic), New York, 1824
      Park Theatre, New York, Feb. 23, 1824
Woolf, Benjamin E.
   The Doctor of Alcantara (Conventional Romantic)
      Boston, 1870

   Off to the War (Civil War), Boston, 1861

Young, Edward
   The Revenge (Conventional Romantic), New York, 1806
Young, William
   Ganelon (Conventional Romantic), 1891
      Broadway Theatre, New York, Jan. 5, 1891

   Pendragon (Conventional Romantic), Chicago, 1881
      Chicago, Dec. 5, 1881

   The Rajah (Conventional Romantic), 1882
      Madison Square Theatre, New York, June 5, 1883

INDEX